A TRAIL TO THE FUTURE ...

Tom Sandcrane stared down at the Sacred Arrows.

"Gather the Arrows," Coby Starving Elk said. "And gather the People. You will be the Arrow Keeper."

Tom shook his head. The Arrows were not for him. He had glimpsed the future and wanted to be a part of it. He wanted to be more than a reservation Indian. These beliefs and rituals were echoes of the old ways and would only hold him back.

"I cannot."

Coby Starving Elk looked stunned. "What?"

Tom met the gaze of each of the elders, looking from one to the other as he repeated himself. "I cannot."

"But the All-Father has spoken . . ." Coby began.

"He has not spoken to me," Tom replied. He had to be careful and had no desire to offend anyone. "I must follow a different path." The faces in the crowd were a blur as he walked from the circle of light to where his father waited.

Tom held up his hands to show they were empty. "I'm sorry. But the Arrows should be kept by someone who will follow the old ways."

"But the Spirit Songs . . . I taught them to you."

"They are the echoes of the past," said Tom. "The days of the buffalo are gone. It is time to learn new ways." He placed his hand on his father's arm. "We must learn or we will die."

"I think you are already dead," said Seth in a voice thick with resentment.

ALSO BY KERRY NEWCOMB

Morning Star
Sacred Is the Wind
In the Season of the Sun
Scalpdancers

THE MEDAL SERIES
Guns of Liberty
Sword of Vengeance
Only the Gallant
Warriors of the Night
Ride the Panther
Jack Iron
Scorpion

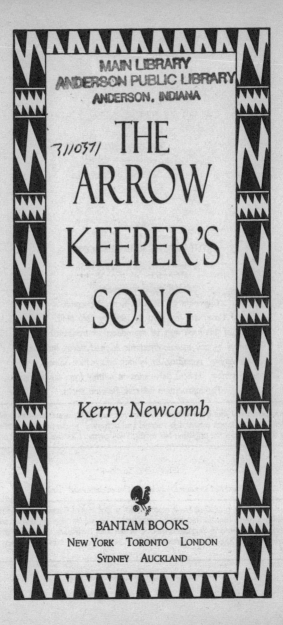

THE ARROW KEEPER'S SONG

Kerry Newcomb

BANTAM BOOKS
NEW YORK TORONTO LONDON
SYDNEY AUCKLAND

THE ARROW KEEPER'S SONG

A Bantam Book / May 1995

All rights reserved.
Copyright © 1995 by Kerry Newcomb.
Cover art copyright © 1995 by Tom Hall.
No part of this book may be reproduced or transmitted in any
form or by any means, electronic or mechanical, including
photocopying, recording, or by any information storage and
retrieval system, without permission in writing from the publisher.
For information address: Bantam Books.

ISBN 0-553-56955-4

Published simultaneously in the United States and Canada

Bantam Books are published by Bantam Books, a division of Bantam Doubleday Dell Publishing Group, Inc. Its trademark, consisting of the words "Bantam Books" and the portrayal of a rooster, is Registered in U.S. Patent and Trademark Office and in other countries. Marca Registrada. Bantam Books, 1540 Broadway, New York, New York 10036.

PRINTED IN THE UNITED STATES OF AMERICA

RAD   10   9   8   7   6   5   4   3   2   1

For Patty, Amy Rose, P.J., and Emily Anabel, with whom I walk the Great Circle.

ACKNOWLEDGMENTS

The Sacred Arrows, the Mahuts, are the Southern Cheyenne's most revered possessions. They are a direct gift from Maheo, the Supreme Deity, also called the All-Father, who presented the four arrows to Sweet Medicine inside a cave in Sacred Mountain, a place the *vehoe* (white men) call Bear Butte, near Sturgis, South Dakota. The Sacred Arrows are a direct link to the All-Father and thus are incredibly powerful objects that give the bearer supernatural dominance over the elements, the animals, and men. The presence of the Sacred Arrows among the Southern Cheyenne reinforces the union between the People and the All-Father and sets them apart from all other races. The Cheyenne devoutly believe that without the Sacred Arrows they would undergo great misfortune and cease to exist.

When presenting certain aspects of the ceremonies and prayers relating to the Sacred Arrows, I have purposefully altered my descriptions so as not to infringe on the customs and culture of the Cheyenne religion as it pertains to these holy relics. I do so out of affection and deep-rooted respect.

I have tried to make this work as authentic as possible and have drawn upon such acknowledged historians as George Bird Grinnell and Peter J. Powell, as well as my own personal experiences while living with the Cheyenne during the 1970's. I must also pay homage to my dear friend Ken Kania, a teacher of Native American culture and history at Dull Knife College and Labre Indian School on the Northern Cheyenne Reservation in Montana, for his invaluable assistance. Ken and his wife, Pam, continue to work tirelessly for the betterment of the Cheyenne People.

I wish to thank Aaron Priest, my agent and friend, who somehow keeps the lights lit when the night is darkest. Thanks also to the good folks at Bantam—especially Tom Beer, my editor, and Tom Dupree, for being accessible and true believers. No expression of gratitude is ever complete without the names of my parents, Ann and Paul Newcomb, and my brother, Jim, whose sustaining love helps me to keep the faith.

"Now you must select a good man; one who is good-natured and of good character in every way. He will be the man to take charge of the Arrows. He will be the man to take the pipe in his hands. In his prayers he must not forget to pray for the people, for their food, and for all the game, that the animals may be plentiful. All the animals living in the water must also be remembered in his prayers four times. No one will be in the tipi when he prays in the morning. That is strictly forbidden. And the Maiyun will be with him during the time he is alone."

—Baldwin Twins, Keeper of the Sacred Arrows, from a conversation with Peter J. Powell, in *Sweet Medicine*.

PROLOGUE

CHAPTER ONE

Oklahoma Territory, 1896

"Maheo. All-Father.
To the four winds I cast my prayers.
Upon the four winds my voice drifts like smoke.
I hold my People as I hold the Arrows in my hand.
What am I? What am I?
Fire in the blood of nako-he, the Bear;
The crack of ice on frozen rivers,
The call of the wild geese.
I ride upon hotama haa-ese, the North wind.
Call me Spirit Catcher, Sweet Medicine,
By many names men have called me.
I am the Arrow Keeper's Song.
I walk here."

THE HAND OF MAHEO, THE ALL-FATHER, APPEARED IN THE center of a circle of old men whose stern features were etched in stark relief by the brightness of the apparition. The heartbeat of Maheo filled the air and caused the earth to tremble. The Maiyun, the spirits of those who have gone before, leaped soundlessly one moment, gyrated madly the next, as if to distract the elders from their somber ritual.

Tom Sandcrane, blind to the hand of God, saw only the

leaping flames from a briskly burning fire. To his ears the heartbeat of the Creator was no more than the hypnotic tap-tap-tapping of the ceremonial drums. No spirits but the tribal elders' own shadows danced upon the buffalo-hide walls of the ceremonial lodge.

Tom stood with the other young men, apart from the ceremonial fire. His twenty-two years hardly qualified him for a place in the circle traditionally reserved for the elders of the Southern Cheyenne. Although Tom was held in high esteem throughout the reservation, here in the Sacred Lodge tradition and custom had to be obeyed, and he could join only if summoned by one of the elders.

Sandcrane shifted his stance and kicked a dirt clod with the scuffed toe of his right boot. He'd been gentling a horse for Allyn Benedict, the local Indian agent. Sandcrane's hard, wiry physique had taken a pounding, but the money had been good, and the experience had afforded him a chance to visit with Allyn's pretty daughter, Emmiline. That green-eyed beauty was worth a hard ride any day.

It was mid-December, the time of the big-hard-face-moon, the third Sunday of Advent, in the last days of 1896, and Tom Sandcrane wished he could have accepted Allyn Benedict's invitation to accompany the Indian agent and his family to church and, afterward, to the house for a late dinner. Emmiline had never looked prettier. But Tom Sandcrane had promised his father he'd attend this night's ceremony . . . so here he was. He'd spent the last hour standing in the shadows and awaiting his father's humiliation. It was difficult to be sympathetic. The horny bastard had brought this on himself.

Tom removed his faded gray Stetson and brushed back his close-cropped black hair with the palm of his hand, then settled the sweat-stained, broad-brimmed hat back on his head. It was warm here in the lodge; he considered removing his wool-lined denim jacket and would have if there had been a place to set the coat aside. Tom sighed and shoved his hands into his pockets. His movements distracted Seth Sandcrane, who noticed his son standing outside the circle of light. Seth appeared curiously relieved to see that his son had made it to the council. The older man began to take heart. There was still hope that all wasn't lost.

Tom Sandcrane, cut from his father's image, stood a couple inches under six feet. Like his Cheyenne forebears, Tom's was the blood of warriors, the finest light cavalry in the world, which had once roamed the plains and followed the great herds of buffalo and answered to no one. Boarding school had done nothing to dull the young man's natural skills. There wasn't a horse he couldn't ride—no brag, just the plain fact. Tom was sharp as a whipcrack, leather tough, with his father's dark-brown eyes.

Once lean and wiry like his son, Seth Sandcrane now carried an extra twenty pounds and was beginning to show a paunch. His features were creased, not smooth like Tom's, and a white crescent-shaped scar marked his right cheek just below his eye. Still, the forty-five-year-old man could sit a horse as well as any young buck. Seth was dressed in the traditional garb of fringed buckskin shirt and leggings, and his long, streaked, silver hair was braided and decorated with an eagle feather with three notches for each time he had counted coup in battle. Usually a good-natured, easygoing soul, Seth Sandcrane wore a grave expression this wintry night. By force of will alone, he shielded his feelings as the elders began to speak. He would not give them the satisfaction of seeing his pain. Seth lowered his eyes to the buckskin Medicine Bundle on the ground before him. The bundle was tied with rawhide and decorated with the sign of the hawk, the buffalo, and horse. Whorled designs of finely stitched beadwork ran along one side from the tied top to fringed bottom. No one needed to view the contents to know what the bundle contained. These were the Mahuts, the Sacred Arrows brought long ago to the Cheyenne by Sweet Medicine, the prophet, as a gift from the All-Father. The Arrows were the most powerful and sacred objects the tribe possessed. They nurtured and guarded the People and were as crucial to the survival of the Southern Cheyenne as the very air they breathed or food they ate. Seth Sandcrane had been the Arrow Keeper for almost a decade, but that honor was about to come to an end.

The majority of the tribe had learned of Seth's indiscretion through rumor and hearsay, but Tom had heard the story firsthand from his father's own lips. Seth had become enamored of Kanee-estse, Red Cherries, who was the wife of Jordan Weasel Bear, one of the elders of the tribe. Jordan, after learning of his wife's infidelity, went into a fit of drunken rage and savagely beat his wife, then fled on horseback into the black night. A couple of days later the rancher's body was found alongside the carcass of his gelding. It seemed the animal had stepped in a prairie-dog mound and broken a leg, crushing Jordan as it fell. The tragedy had tarnished Seth's reputation and jeopardized his position as Keeper of the Sacred Arrows, a man who must be above reproach.

Tom shifted his stance and surveyed the circle of elders. He recognized Luthor White Bear, a crease-faced man with steely gray hair in braids that hung to his shoulders. Approximately the same age as Seth, he had made no effort to conceal the fact that he coveted the role of Arrow Keeper.

To begin the council, Luthor removed the Medicine Pipe from a buckskin bundle in his possession, brushed the red clay bowl with dried sage and brittle stalks of sweetgrass, and then lit the contents of the bowl, a mixture of tobacco and cherry bark.

Luthor's features were marked by a single white band painted across his eyes like a narrow mask. The elder, seated at the southeast point of the circle, represented the originator of life and light.

"I am morning, I bring new life to the People. The sun is my servant," intoned Luthor White Bear. He smoked the pipe and then passed it to Henry Running Shadow, seated at the southwest point. The latter's traditional buckskin shirt and leggings were baggy and seemed almost comical upon his frail torso. He looked as if he were trying to shrink out of his clothes. His elderly features were concealed behind a mask of red paint.

"Thunder lives in me," continued Henry Running Shadow in a gravelly voice. "I journey from the south, bringing rain and warm weather. In me the grass grows and the earth becomes green again." He was fifty-seven years old, and his hands had a slight tremble from the onset of palsy that would one day kill him. He smoked the pipe and handed it to the Cheyenne seated at the northwest. At fifty years of age, Abe Spotted Horse had lived long enough to grow restless for the old days. Chasing buffalo and raiding the white man's villages and towns had provided plenty of opportunity for a warrior to count coup and prove his bravery. Peace had left him brooding and restless. His color was yellow, the color of the sunset.

"I am the place where the sun sleeps. I am that which is without blemish, the ripeness and beauty of the world." He smoked, and again a cloud of prayer smoke billowed up above the heads of those gathered in the lodge. Abe Spotted Horse stretched out his hand, and the pipe was taken by the last of the painted elders.

The face of Coby Starving Elk was smeared with a band of black paint. He too was in his midforties. A stocky man with a belly that overhung his beaded belt, Coby was unflaggingly honest and could be counted on to hold a wise council.

"I will smoke this pipe," said Coby. "For I am the killing storm, the blanketing snow and the crippling cold. I am your death. I am always seated at your fire. But as you honor me, I will stay my hand." He puffed on the pipe three times and paused, allowing his words to ride the prayer smoke to heaven. He pointedly refrained from offering the pipe to Seth, who remained sitting on his haunches close to the fire. When Coby had returned the Medicine Pipe to Luthor White Bear, Seth leaned forward and untied the bundle of brushed deer hide and mallard skin and unwrapped its contents.

The Sacred Arrows were about six inches longer than a normal hunting arrow. Each shaft was ringed with varying bands of color corresponding to the painted elders: a white arrow, a black, a yellow, and a red. The Mahuts were tipped with glassy black obsidian arrowheads. Each shaft was trimmed with eagle feathers, although the arrows would never know the touch of a bowstring. Their power was mystical in nature.

Tom had seen the relics before, in his father's house, the first time as a lad of thirteen when he had furtively peeked inside the Medicine Bundle. He had been frightened, then, of invoking the wrath of a host of evil spirits. Now the Arrows meant no more to him than the tradition they represented. He had accompanied Allyn Benedict to the nation's capital and had seen the cities of the East, the power of commerce and invention that had fueled the white man's conquest of the frontier. Tom had glimpsed the future, that unstoppable juggernaut, progress, which the Southern Cheyenne could either climb aboard or be ground beneath. What were a bunch of wooden sticks compared to the raw power of industry? The sooner his people left the old ways behind, the better.

Seth Sandcrane looked down at the Arrows, his features remaining impassive. He'd been a fool to become involved with Red Cherries and should have kept his pants zipped. But Red Cherries was the kind of woman who could make a boy feel like a man, and an old man like a boy again. Seth sighed and, looking up, met Luthor White Bear's icy stare. There was no love lost between the two elders. Luthor had coveted Seth's role from the moment the bundle had been placed in Sandcrane's hands. Luthor made no attempt to hide the disdain he felt for his rival.

Coby Starving Elk cleared his throat and, with a wave of his hand, gestured for the drummers to cease. The three braves immediately complied, and a silence, broken only by the crackling fire, filled the lodge.

"Long ago, in the time of those who have gone before, Maheo, the All-Father, sent the Sacred Arrows to us. Sweet Medicine was the first Keeper. And after his death came men like White Thunder and Rides Horse. Once there came a time when the Pawnee stole the arrows and many Cheyenne rode the warpath to recover that which was taken. Great was the suffering. Five of those brave young warriors were killed before the Arrows were returned." Coby looked from Luthor to Henry Running Shadow and Abe Spotted Horse and then settled his gaze on his old friend Seth Sandcrane. Regret was plainly evident in Coby's expression. But sympathy could not undo what had been done. Yet the two men had agreed on one way the Arrows might remain beneath Sandcrane's roof.

Coby was willing to give his old friend one last chance, in a matter of speaking. "Our five grandfathers were killed recovering the Sacred Arrows," he continued, "and so it was decided that the Arrow Keeper should come from one of our families. You have been the Arrow Keeper, Seth Sandcrane, as was *your* father, before Maheo called him by name. You have renewed the Mahuts with your prayers and sacrifice and guarded them well."

"Until now," Luthor White Bear spoke up.

"I have done what I have done," said Seth Sandcrane. "I have brought the Mahuts and unwrapped them so that one and all can see they have been well cared for."

"But they are heavy with your shame," Luthor replied. "It is time for another Arrow Keeper to be chosen, or surely all our people will suffer for the actions of this one."

"Luthor's words are straight," Abe Spotted Horse interjected. He had often hunted with Seth, and the two had shared many campfires together. He took no pleasure in bringing Seth before the council, but the welfare of the Southern Cheyenne came first. The Sacred Arrows must be placed in proper hands.

"I have brought the Mahuts. I place them upon the earth before you. My hands can no longer reach them. Let another come forward and gather them," Seth proclaimed in a voice thick with emotion.

That was all Luthor White Bear needed to hear. He rose from his place and started forward with a look of triumph in his eyes. "As Pipe Bearer, I must care for the Mahuts until the next renewal ceremony."

"Wait, my brother," Coby called out, blocking Luthor's path. The Pipe Bearer was caught completely unawares. Coby turned to face Seth and winked before explaining his actions. "Ten winters ago Maheo revealed to us that the Sacred Arrows should be kept in the lodge of Seth Sandcrane. Who are we to go against the will of All-Father?"

"But they cannot remain beneath his roof," Luthor protested. "This one has dishonored the Sacred Arrows!"

"His son has not," Coby said.

Seth knew what was coming and had to struggle to refrain

from flashing a look of triumph at the Pipe Bearer. Thank the
Great Spirit Tom had made it to the council on time. Seth
watched with relish as Coby ordered the young men ringing
the elders to stand back and form a path through their midst.

Tom blinked and came alert. My God, what was happening? Everyone was standing aside, and suddenly there was
nothing but empty space between him and the ceremonial
fire. A hand nudged his shoulder, and he glanced back to find
Willem Tangle Hair, a freckle-faced, sandy-haired twenty-
four-year-old half-breed grinning and urging him on. Willem,
member of the tribal police, had worked his way around the
perimeter of the lodge to stand alongside his childhood
friend. It was said of Tom and Willem that they were two arrows from the same quiver. They had played together as children. And in the rough-and-tumble days of their childhood,
one was always sticking up for the other.

"Looks like they want you up front, Tom," said the blue-
eyed breed.

"Damn," Tom muttered beneath his breath. What had his
father gotten him into now?

"Tom Sandcrane," Coby Starving Elk called out. Beads of
sweat had begun to glisten on the elder's thick features. Trails
of moisture streaked the rolls of flesh beneath his chin. But
his black, beady eyes glinted with crafty intelligence as he invited the son of Seth Sandcrane to join him in the center of
the lodge.

All eyes were on Tom as he advanced toward the fire and
gingerly approached the man who had called him by name. "I
am here," Tom said. His movements were cautious, his right
leg threatening to cramp. The leaping flames highlighted the
uncertainty in his eyes.

Seth stood up as his son entered the circle. The Arrow
Keeper's last official act was to surrender that which he trea-
sured most. Seth placed a hand on Tom's shoulder and gave
the younger man a reassuring pat, then turned and walked
away from the Sacred Arrows lying upon the bundle. He held
himself ramrod straight, head unbowed, clinging to the last

remnants of his dignity as he walked with measured steps from the circle. It soothed his battered pride to think he'd denied Luthor White Bear yet again the role of Arrow Keeper. He retraced Tom's path through the crowd of Cheyenne, walking past the leaders of the various warrior societies who were waiting for the matter to be resolved. He reached the entrance to the lodge, pulled back the flap, and disappeared into the darkness outside.

The cold, clear moonlit air greeted Seth like a slap in the face after the stifling interior of the ceremonial lodge. He breathed deeply and exhaled slowly, managing to stifle the scream of anguish that welled up from his wounded spirit. He clenched his fists and walked to his horse, and there he waited on the edge of the wooded slope overlooking the deserted, wheel-rutted streets of Cross Timbers, the Cheyenne settlement nestled between two hills near the Washita River. An amber glow filled the windows above the mercantile, but the other four buildings that constituted the center of town were dark. Father Kenneth's mission church on the east end of town was ablaze with light. No doubt the choir of St. Joachim's was practicing for midnight mass. Lantern light also gleamed in the windows of several of the houses surrounding the settlement. He glowered at one in particular, the gray-washed walls of Allyn Benedict's home, there on the north hillside. Seth had no use for the Indian agent and resented the man's influence on Tom, who wasn't alone in abandoning the Old Ways.

Too many of the young men of the tribe shared Tom's sentiments. One by one the traditions and beliefs were dying. Yet there was still magic . . . still mystery . . . still power. The Sacred Arrows remained. And late last night, in the depths of the Arrow Keeper's despair, they had called his son by name.

Tom Sandcrane stared down at the Sacred Arrows while the room seemed to fill with an almost palpable silence. He still didn't understand what was expected of him.

"Gather the Arrows. And gather the People. You will be the Arrow Keeper."

"No!" Luthor White Bear blurted out. "He is too young. It is not for him to claim the Mahuts."

"It is not for you to defy the will of Maheo," said Coby. The circle of Cheyenne crowding the lodge tightened around the elders as the curious struggled to hear what was being said. Henry Running Shadow stood with the assistance of a member of the Bowstring Society who lent the chief a steady arm. Henry pointed at Abe Spotted Horse.

"We have walked in a dream," he said. Then, gesturing to Coby, the old man repeated himself. "Him too. We walked in a dream and the Maiyun guided us."

Abe nodded. "Henry's words are straight. The last night of our sweat, the Spirits of Those Who Have Gone Before came to us and showed to us the will of the All-Father."

"Each of us saw what we saw," Coby added, fixing an accusatory stare on Luthor, for the latter had seen the same visions as his companions. Luthor grew less adamant and ceased his protests. Coby, satisfied, returned his attention to Tom Sandcrane. "Pick up the bundle."

Coby's voice sounded far away, as if he were speaking from the distant end of a tunnel. His command reverberated in Tom's mind. The faces of the crowd became a blur. The longer he stood over the Sacred Arrows, the harder it became to focus on anything else around him. He could no longer feel the warmth of the fire or hear the crackle of the logs. A loud, rasping noise filled his head, and he strained to identify the sound, concentrating intently until it came to him. He was listening to his own breathing, each and every breath made resonant, yet for his ears alone. No sight, no sound, save for his hammering heart that seemed to increase in volume. Didn't they hear? Why couldn't they hear?

Tom shook his head and wiped a hand across his face to clear his vision. The Arrows were not for him. He had glimpsed the future and wanted to be a part of it. He wanted to be more than a reservation Indian. These beliefs and rituals were echoes of the old ways and would only hold him back.

He tried to speak but his mouth had gone dry. He swallowed and tried again, this time managing a hoarse reply.

"I cannot."

Coby looked stunned and retreated a step. "What?"

Tom met the gaze of each of the elders, looking from one to the other as he repeated himself. "I cannot."

"But the All-Father has spoken . . . ," Coby began.

"He has not spoken to me," Tom replied. He had to be careful now, for he had no desire to offend anyone. "I must follow a different path." The faces in the crowd were a blur as he walked from the circle of light and followed in the footsteps of his father into the night air.

Tom paused to allow his vision to adjust and, breathing a sigh of relief, started toward his dun gelding. He spied Seth Sandcrane waiting for him by the tethered horses and dreaded what was to come.

Made a widower while Tom was still a toddler, Seth had raised the boy to manhood, unaided and alone. Tom knew he owed this man more than he could ever repay. Hurting his father was the last thing in the world Tom Sandcrane wished to do, but there seemed no way to avoid it. As he drew closer to the dishonored Arrow Keeper, Tom held up his hands to show they were empty. Seth's elation dimmed when he realized his son did not cradle the bundle in the crook of his arm. He frowned and his expression became puzzled.

"Tom . . . ?"

"Now I know why you insisted I attend this . . . this ceremony. You are a wily old fox, Seth, but it didn't work. I'm sorry."

A horned owl whooshed across the night sky. It glided from the tangle of live oaks and dropped onto a small rodent attempting to cross the clearing. With the bird's prey screeching in its cruel black talons, the owl lifted from the earth on great gray wings and rose to the safety of the treetops, where it nested in the cleft of a towering white oak and proceeded to feed.

"Coby said he would offer the Arrows to my son."

"He spoke straight, father," Tom said. "But I could not take them."

"What?" Seth staggered back as if struck. "No!"

"I'm sorry. But the Arrows should be kept by someone who will follow the old ways . . . and the prayers and songs."

"But the spirit songs . . . I taught them to you."

"They are the echoes of the past," said Tom. "The days of the buffalo are gone. It is time to learn new ways." He placed his hand on his father's arm. "We must learn or we will die."

"I think you are already dead," said Seth, his voice heavy with resentment. Now the Sacred Arrows were indeed lost to him. He would never have the power again, never sing the songs of renewal or summon the Maiyun with a single prayer. *As my son has failed me, so I have failed all who have gone before,* he bitterly reflected. Cut to the quick by Tom's betrayal, Seth Sandcrane pulled away from his son. His gaze hardened until it became an impenetrable mask without a trace of paternal familiarity. He slowly turned on his heels and, with shoulders bowed by the weight of his despair, walked off through the darkness, following a trail that skirted the hill and the ceremonial lodge.

"Father . . . *ne-ho!*" Tom called out, his breath clouding the air. But the stand of timber had already swallowed Seth Sandcrane, draping the wounded man with its shadowed shrouds and hiding his hurt from prying eyes. Tom slowly exhaled, shook his head, and briefly considered following the older man. What was the use? Seth was beyond listening to what Tom had to say.

Despite the guilt Tom felt, he knew he had spoken the truth. There was no returning to the past, not even if he wanted to. Perhaps it was easier for a young Cheyenne like himself to understand this, while men like Seth were still too close to what had been, to the time when the Cheyenne had been lords of the plains.

The days ahead held challenge and change. Tom Sandcrane was ready. He doubted his father ever would be.

The dun gelding behind him nickered and stamped the ground. The animal was anxious to return to town and the comfort of a warm stall. Tom gathered the reins and swung into the saddle. Just as he pointed the animal toward town, a cold north wind sprang up and snatched the hat from his head. He made a futile attempt to catch it. The Stetson tumbled end over end and came to rest in the underbrush surrounding a pair of live oaks, its tall crown skewered by a forked twig. The dun fought Tom's steadying hand as the wind continued to whirl about them, moaning as it rattled the dry branches, and stung them with brittle leaves and grains of sand. The hair on the back of Tom's neck rose when he noticed that the other horses were wholly unaffected by the wind, while Tom had to struggle to keep his mount from bolting as the gusts buffeted him with unnatural force.

Suddenly the animal reared and pawed the air, and for a fleeting instant Tom spied a pair of warriors on horseback watching him from the grove where he'd lost his hat. The two warriors wore only breechclouts and leggings. Their naked torsos were swirled with red war paint, their faces obscured by garish red designs. They carried ten-foot-long spears tipped with stone blades that appeared to have been dipped in blood, and brandished war shields painted crimson like the powerful stallions they sat astride. Each wore a buffalo-horn headdress, the tip of which glistened a gory crimson in the moonlight.

The dun came down hard and almost dislodged its rider. A lesser horseman would have been sent tumbling. Tom held on for dear life, one hand on the reins and the other tangled in the gelding's mane. Tom's breathing became labored, and he felt consciousness slipping away. Then the wind ceased.

Tom gasped in a lungful of air, sat upright in the saddle, and brought the gelding under control. He glanced toward the grove of oaks to challenge the two warriors to identify themselves, but they had vanished without a trace.

"He-tohe!" Tom exclaimed, inadvertently returning to his native tongue. "What the . . . ?" He was alone outside the ceremonial lodge. He cautiously walked the dun over to the underbrush and, leaning down from the saddle, retrieved the Stetson. He took note that the two warriors, whoever they were, had managed to vanish without so much as breaking a twig or leaving a single track in the underbrush.

"Glo—ria in excelsis Deo. Glo—ria in excelsis De-o."

The faint strains of the advent choir drifted up the slope

from the gaily lit church where Father Kenneth rehearsed his songs of praise for the Christian God. The "Gloria" spoke to Tom and called him back from what he had just experienced. A gust of wind, he told himself. And his own mind playing tricks on him. He dismissed the experience and studied the church at the east end of Main Street. Father Kenneth would be there. And Allyn Benedict with his family. And there were others in the congregation, both Cheyenne and white, who had come to Cross Timbers.

The tribal drummers resumed their steady beat, two light strokes, then one heavy, emanated from the ceremonial lodge, announcing that a new Arrow Keeper had been chosen. Such matters no longer concerned Tom Sandcrane. Latin verses mingled uncomfortably with the wailing voice of the tribal elders. Tom did not linger to appreciate the discord, but started down the road toward the settlement, a young man with his eyes on tomorrow, following the strains of an Advent chorus, and guided by the brightness of his dreams.

CHAPTER TWO

New Orleans

HEAVENLY FATHER, WE ASK YOUR BLESSING ON THIS FOOD AND those gathered here who have come to partake of your great bounty. Lord, may you continue to bless the work of my hands. I thank you for bringing our family together. May you keep us joined in love and obedience to your divine will . . ."

Joanna Cooper noted how her father, Robert Bernard Cooper III, had worked the word "obedience" into the blessing. She immediately suspected their recent argument over her decision to leave New Orleans was now to be the topic of discussion here at the family table. Suddenly she regretted delaying her departure. Not that she didn't love her parents. That wasn't the issue. But her father had spent most of the afternoon voicing his displeasure with her plans and hoping to talk some "sense" into her. Joanna, though, had proven as stubborn as her father. Still, she did not want to be the cause of any more pain.

I should have never come home. A letter would have been kinder. Father will never understand. Maybe my plans are just one big mistake. But it is my life, isn't it? I must follow the path I believe is right for me. How can I do less? She looked around the handsomely appointed dining room with its elegant satin-backed chairs and mahogany china cabinet crowded with fine crystal and porcelain plates. That she was about to turn her back on a life of luxury made her a fool in her father's eyes. Could she blame him? To Robert Cooper there was nothing more important than power and prestige. Joanna studied her reflection in a window that looked out upon a spacious, carefully kept lawn and a brick walkway leading down to the shores of Lake Pontchartrain. The slender woman she saw in the window had finely etched aquiline features, with high cheekbones. Long auburn tresses were carelessly pinned back from pale, creamy-white features that would burn easily beneath the Caribbean sun. Hands that could tend a wound or set a broken limb were inexperienced at the dressing table. She thought of herself as plain—at least compared to Eleanor, her winsome sister, whom the men had always favored.

As a child Joanna liked to climb trees and run races with the boys. She could handle a dare or a fishing pole as well as any lad. Her childhood had been one of privilege, and she had never wanted for anything. But the nuns of the Ursuline Academy on Chartres Street had awakened in the impressionable girl a thirst for knowledge. Joanna voraciously devoured the books in the academy while dutifully keeping up with her studies. As she matured, colorful literature the likes of *Robinson Crusoe, The Count of Monte Cristo,* and *Treasure Island* instilled in her a desire to confront life on its own ofttimes harsh terms. The good Sisters gave her not only an education but a sense of responsibility for others less fortunate than herself.

Shortly after leaving the academy, Joanne entered medical school at Tulane, a move that sorely tested her father's patience. Yet he indulged her because he doubted any young woman would endure the rigors of higher education for much longer than a week. But Joanna proved tenacious and succeeded despite her father's disparaging views and the open animosity displayed by many of her male peers, who viewed this "doctor in skirts" as some kind of threat.

Now she was a physician, a healer, afire with the determination to help others. She had come home because she wanted to see her parents one last time. After all, there was no telling when she'd see home again. By the end of the month Doctor Joanna Cooper intended to be in Cuba and embarking on her own grand adventure.

"In remembrance of Your good works, O Heavenly Father, we will be certain to give Thee all thanks and praise. Amen."

Robert Cooper, a diminutive, pugnacious little man with a hawkish face and close-set eyes, looked up from his folded hands and studied the faces of his two daughters. Joanna had always been the rebellious one, whereas Eleanor was pliant, like her mother. His iron gaze settled on Roxanne, his wife, a flaxen-haired belle, sweet as a mint julep, pampered and playful. She made no apologies, Robert thought to himself, for enjoying to the hilt the creature comforts that his inheritance and successful import-and-export business had afforded them. He cleared his throat, breaking the uncomfortable silence that had filled the void left by the dinner blessing.

"Amen, my dear, and very nicely put," said Roxanne, reaching for a fork. "I always love the way you offer a prayer over dinner. You really missed your calling. Why, I should think you could have been a minister of the Church, I do indeed." Roxanne speared a chunk of cooked carrot and lifted it, dripping, from a pool of sugary brown glaze, plopping the tidbit into her mouth.

"And would you have been content to eke out your days in some humble priory while I brought the word of God to the less fortunate?" the merchant asked.

"Heavens no," Roxanne chuckled.

"*Heaven*, I daresay," Robert added, surveying the amply laden table with pride. Tureens of candied carrots, yams, slices of ham, snap peas swimming in butter and dusted with slivered almonds, plump pigeons roasted to a fare-thee-well, loaves of hot crusty bread, fresh churned butter, and, in keeping with the advent season, spiced mulled wine. Michel Raux, a servant of African and Indian descent, appeared at the table bearing a ladle and a soup tureen of shrimp gumbo. He paused alongside Joanna, who declined his offer to fill her bowl.

"Charlotte made the gumbo especially for you," Robert said.

"I'm not hungry, really," Joanna said.

"I should have thought breaking your parents' hearts would have worked up quite an appetite," the merchant matter-of-factly replied, and helped himself to a roasted pigeon, whose golden skin glistened with juices.

Her father's statement set the tone for the meal. Joanna had no stomach for the upcoming confrontation. She slid her chair back, rose and excused herself, and left the dining room. Her footsteps rang on the curved stairway that led to the upper reaches of the house.

"Husband . . . ," Roxanne chided.

"I only spoke the truth."

"At times it can be a most annoying habit."

"Then you are happy that your daughter intends to throw her life away, crawling around some filthy Cuban hovel."

"No. But I do not want to drive her from our lives forever. Eleanor, be a dear and go speak with your sister. She'll listen to you."

Their remaining daughter sighed and then smiled. "As you wish, Mama. But Joanna has *never* listened to me or anyone else. She's as stubborn as Papa." Robert Cooper raised his eyebrows; he obviously took umbrage. Eleanor, paying him no mind, lifted the hem of her day dress and followed after her sister, the thick Persian carpet muffling her slippered feet as she departed the room.

The scent of holly and the aroma of freshly baked pastries followed Eleanor up the stairs. She ascended quietly past a collection of oil paintings depicting the battle of New Orleans. Muskets and cannons spat flame and powder smoke, English marines bravely contested with a ragtag line of American defenders made up primarily of woodsmen and pirates. Eleanor paused and thought of her husband, the artist who had presented the paintings to her father. John Roddy was a lawyer by trade, but painting was his first love. He was in Washington now, where he hoped to secure a political appointment once the recently elected William McKinley was inaugurated. Eleanor and the twins intended to follow in the spring. My God, she missed him. It was too bad Joanna had never found a man.

Eleanor climbed to the top of the stairs and hurried down the lamplit hallway, past end tables displaying a collection of vases purchased in Macao. She entered her sister's bedroom without knocking.

"Jo, you can't just leave," Eleanor said, glaring across at her older sister. The admonition came somewhat tardily, as a trunk containing the bulk of Joanna's clothes had already been sent on to the pier to be loaded aboard *The Pearl of the Antilles,* a sleek schooner anchored at the Jackson Street docks. She intended to spend the night aboard ship, as they'd be sailing at first light.

In the front room Joanna, wearing a simple day dress of gray wool trimmed with a modicum of lace at the throat, donned a deep-blue cape. Her black button shoes clattered on the hardwood floor as she made her way around the bedroom, packing the last of her keepsakes in a cloth bag and closing it tight.

Eleanor would not have been caught dead in such drab attire. Her dress was cut from scarlet and gold damask and hemmed with swirls of gold thread as were the voluminous leg-of-mutton sleeves, which were all the rage now in New Orleans's social circles. The satin bolero jacket she chose made no attempt to contain her ample bosom.

"Please . . . not like this," Eleanor repeated. "I simply must insist. Dear Lord, I'll never hear the end of it. Father will do nothing but rant and rave for days on end and make everything dreadful."

"There's a carriage coming for me in a couple of hours, but we have time to stroll down to the lake." Despite her sister's coiffured hair and elegant fashion, Joanna could not help but see past the superficial trappings of wealth and find the smudge-cheeked baby sister she had played with on the shores of Lake Pontchartrain. Joanna smiled—she would miss her little sister. "And where are my nephews? I shall not leave until I give each one a hug and a kiss."

Eleanor, married three years ago at eighteen, had already given her parents a pair of darling grandchildren to spoil. Her twin boys had the run of the estate and were constantly tiring out a steady stream of servants hired to keep up with them.

Joanna, now in her midtwenties was the spinster of the family.

"I sent them off with Faith Louise. They're in the kitchen baking Christmas cookies," said Eleanor. Faith Louise, a youthful serving girl of cheerful demeanor and abundant energy, had been assigned the formidable task of keeping the three-year-old twins from underfoot.

"Well, then, let's go for a walk. I shall no doubt find myself longing for dry land the moment we weigh anchor." Joanna started toward the bedroom door.

"But, Jo, why leave at all? I mean, if you must . . . tend . . . sick people, there are plenty in New Orleans." Eleanor had tried to understand, but the whole idea seemed frightfully depressing.

"And remain under father's thumb? No. I cannot stay. And besides, Cuba sounds terribly exotic. There are four of us going in all. Just think of the adventure. The people of Cuba have been fighting against Spanish rule for nearly half a century. Read here. One rebellion after another. Martyr after martyr. I heard the most marvelous man speak at Tulane. A former teacher, now he is one of the leaders of the revolution. Antonio Celestial. The Spaniards have put a price on his head, yet he will return to the island."

"Why should he come to the United States in the first place?" Eleanor asked in a most skeptical tone of voice.

"To enlist donated funds and materials, to seek America's help in their struggle, which is so similar to our own revolution. President-elect McKinley has already sent stern warnings to the Spanish forces suggesting we might become officially involved. Celestial invited any of us to come to Cuba and put our skills to good use. And it ought to be very exciting, to actually be part of such a gallant struggle." Joanna's eyes lit up as she spoke.

"Excitement could get you killed," Eleanor soberly replied.

But her admonishment had no effect. Doctor Joanna Cooper held a firm belief in her own invulnerability. As far as she was concerned, her course was set. No turning back.

They descended the stairs together. Reaching the front room, Joanna left her leather bag by the door and walked out onto the veranda. White wooden chairs looked out on the circular drive. It was a damp, hazy night. The New Orleans Road beyond the cobblestone path was completely obscured by fog.

"I'm going back inside. It's too gloomy out here," Eleanor remarked.

"I'll join you in the dining room," said Joanna. "But if father starts in on me again, I shall have to await my carriage out here on the veranda."

"You two are something," Eleanor muttered with a wag of her head.

Joanna chuckled and stepped down onto the path that rounded the house and led down to the mist-shrouded lake. Great weeping willows and stalwart cypresses rose out of the mist as she drew closer to the shoreline. She stood there facing the silent gray expanse, lost in a world of her own thoughts. Images of her vanished childhood filled her mind, like characters in some play, each happy, innocent moment coming forward to take its bow, to say "good-bye."

The strains of "O How a Rose Ere Blooming" drifted through the mist. Joanna smiled. It was her favorite Christmas hymn, one that Roxanne always made a point of playing at this time of year. Catfish darted beneath the surface of the lake and sent wavelets lapping at the shore. Beyond the shrouded night, wild geese called across the black expanse.

Music and hearth and home touched the woman's heart. Steeling herself against her father's last-ditch effort to change her mind, Joanna turned and started back toward the house. But she'd gone only a step or two when a strange cold wind sent the mist churning around her like lost souls in a mad dance. It increased in intensity. The cape that had almost been too warm for the night became a boon. Joanna found herself clutching at the folds and wrapping herself in its woolen embrace. The strange wind howled, and for a moment she thought she heard keening voices and the deeper resonant cadence of beating drums. Joanna remained awestruck, unable to move while the eerie gust buffeted her and clawed at her with its icy talons.

What was that? That sound?

"Is someone there?" she called out.

The wind died as quickly as it sprang into being. The chill left her. The mist drifted apart like torn silk to reveal the stone path that stretched on to the house. Joanna brushed the debris from her dress, breathed deeply, and steadied her reeling senses.

"Well . . . ," she muttered, and continued on her way. "Well . . ." She searched the darkness. "I know what I heard." She paused and listened again. Nothing.

But for a moment, trapped in the center of the whirlwind, Joanna was certain she had heard neighing horses and pounding hooves as if the animals were being ridden at a gallop, close at hand. But she had seen no one. And the ground around her was devoid of tracks.

"I know what I heard," Joanna repeated, then wondered whom she was trying to convince. A ghost wind, the plaintive voices, spectral riders, drumbeats . . .

Up ahead Robert Cooper appeared at the corner of the veranda. He waited, hands tucked in the pockets of his frock coat, his features etched with concern.

"I thought I heard you call out," he explained as his daughter approached.

"It was nothing," she said, trying to convince herself with a lie. Suddenly she was grateful for the amber warmth spilling from the window, for the familiar sights and sounds she would soon be leaving behind.

"How can I make you listen to reason?" Robert said. The diminutive man was not about to accept defeat without one more last-ditch effort.

"Don't try, Father. Please." She climbed up the steps and slipped her arm in his.

"Bah. I might as well be talking to the wind," he remarked.

Joanna gave a start and glanced over her shoulder at the night. The icy kiss of that cold breeze seemed to clutch at her soul. But the drums . . . or had it been the beating of her own frightened heart? Spectral riders in the mist, their unearthly voices wailing . . .

Joanna shivered and hurried toward the light.

PART ONE

A PRAYER TO THE SUN

CHAPTER THREE

Oklahoma Territory, 1897

IN THE BEGINNING THERE WAS THE ALL-FATHER, MAHEO. AND
Maheo was lonely as He walked the Great Circle, so He
created a great sea and reaching down into the sea He
found little mounds of mud and these He shaped in the palm
of His hand and set them upon the water. And the little
mounds grew and grew until the sea was covered with land.
Then the All-Father took a rib from His right side and created
a man and took a rib from His left side and created a woman.
Maheo placed the man in the south and the woman in the
north. Man and woman walked toward one another, searching, always searching, for they too were lonely. And as they
journeyed, they saw all matter of animals and birds, and these
they named. Eventually man and woman found one another
and their lives became one. Maheo was pleased with them. To
their children He gave the sacred songs to bind the world,
songs of power so that the world would not end, songs of
healing and renewal and magic.

The Maiyun whispered these songs to Sweet Medicine
when the Cheyenne prophet received the Sacred Arrows. And
so the songs were passed from one generation to another,
down the long dark trails of time, from one Arrow Keeper
and his circle of elders to the next.

Seth Sandcrane knew the songs, and he had taught them to his son, preparing Tom for the day he would one day receive the Mahuts from Seth's own hands. Now it was all lost. Tom had abandoned the old ways. And though the songs still lived within Seth, he was no longer the Arrow Keeper and there was no point in singing them.

Seth emerged from the cabin he had built at the foot of a wooded knoll south of the settlement and glared at the newly risen sun as if he resented its arrival. Perhaps he did. Mornings were a hard go for a man without a purpose. He wiped his mouth on the tail of his whiskey-stained shirt and then tucked the shirt into his Levi's and pulled his faded brown suspenders over his shoulders. He scratched his back against the corner of the log cabin, working the blunt end of an out-thrust log between his shoulder blades. His gaze inadvertently drifted to the ceremonial lodge nestled between the oaks on the slope west of town. A ribbon of smoke unfurled like a banner above the treetops, and Seth could only imagine Luthor White Bear standing by the medicine fire atop the bluff overlooking the lodge. Seth began to sing softly to himself the creation song that the world might not end. But the words trailed off, his voice became a whisper, then grew still. Old responsibilities, like habits, died hard.

Seth studied the scattered buildings that made up the settlement and allowed his thoughts to slip back twenty-nine years. It was in the time of the hard-faced moon, November, and Chief Black Kettle's band of Southern Cheyenne were wintering on the banks of the Washita, about five miles upriver from Cross Timbers. Seth was sixteen years old. He had just gone down to the river when the bluecoats struck. Custer had chosen his time well, for many of the braves were on a hunt, and only a few remained to defend the old ones and the women and children.

Seth closed his eyes and sucked in his breath. He could still hear the pounding hooves of the cavalry, still smell the gunsmoke and hear the screams of the dying as the troopers fired into throngs of women and children. Seth waited for his chance and leaped astride a trooper's back, dragging a fresh-faced youth (who looked no older than his attacker) from the saddle and plunging his knife into the startled trooper's chest. He grabbed the dying man's Springfield carbine as a second bluecoat charged him with pistol blazing. Seth snapped the carbine to his shoulder and squeezed the trigger. The carbine roared. The trooper straightened in the saddle and fired into the air, then toppled backward and rolled across the rump of his horse and onto the ground.

The advantage was Custer's that day. The tribe, having lived in peace with the whites, had not expected trouble and was unprepared for such an attack. But when the shooting started and the Seventh Cavalry charged the camp, both men and women fought tenaciously as they struggled to escape. In the confusion of the melee, young Seth managed to lead several families to safety. Hidden among the wooded hillsides, they watched as Yellow Hair and the Seventh Cavalry burned the village and drove off the horses and assembled those stunned stragglers the troopers had taken prisoner.

Seth wrinkled his nostrils. Even now the stench of death assailed him from the crucible of his memories. He would never forget crouching in the shadow of the white oaks while the soldiers destroyed the lodges. His father, Strong Fox, crawled up beside his son and there in the emerald shadows removed the Sacred Arrows from the bundle. Seth remembered how his father had pointed the Arrows at the soldiers and begun to softly sing. His words could have been spoken by the wind, they came so softly. Words of vengeance and words of death. When Strong Fox had finished, Seth knew that Custer was doomed. Yellow Hair would pay for what had happened on the banks of the Washita, as would the troopers of the Seventh Cavalry. Eight years later he wasn't surprised to learn how the carrion birds feasted on the bones of the Seventh where they lay, butchered along with Custer in the valley of the Little Big Horn.

"Mr. Sandcrane?"

Seth turned and fixed Willem Tangle Hair in a steel-eyed stare. The tribal policeman looked fit for burying in his frock coat and black trousers, his red hair slicked down and blousy white shirt freshly washed. He nervously fumbled with his flat-crowned black hat as he sat astride a nimble-looking mare.

"I was looking for Tom," Willem explained.

Whenever Tom was in Cross Timbers and not working for Allyn Benedict and the Bureau of Indian Affairs, he stayed home with his father. A bedroom off either side of a main living room afforded both father and son their privacy.

Willem could feel the tension. For eight and a half months the former Arrow Keeper's disappointment and wounded pride had festered. Seth could be as hard and unforgiving as the land itself. "He's already gone on to church."

"Oh. We were going to ride over together," Willem replied. He suspected Tom and his father had started off the morning with a quarrel and his friend had left rather than continue the fight.

"Why don't you come along with me?" Willem suggested, hoping to bridge the gap between father and son. "You have friends over at St. Joachim's."

"The path of the white man is not my path. The white man's god does not call me by name," Seth retorted, then shrugged. "Anyway, I'm a mite dry." He walked up to the freckle-faced breed, the offspring of an Irish father and Cheyenne mother. Seth winked, patted Willem's horse, and continued on toward the split-rail corral beyond his house. Within the corral a piebald gelding thrust its muzzle through the rails to nibble at a few blades of grass growing at the base of one of the posts. The animal whinnied and pawed the ground as Seth approached.

Willem watched with obvious concern as Seth saddled the piebald. He understood what the older man had implied. Although whiskey was supposedly forbidden on the reservation, Jerel Tall Bull and his brother, Curtis, ran a tavern called Panther Hall in the hills north of the Washita. The roadhouse was frequented by many of the Cheyenne. With the impending dissolution of the reservation, the Tall Bulls operated their establishment with impunity. Allyn Benedict and the BIA had made no move against them.

"That's a rough lot out at the Tall Bulls'," Willem called out.

Seth waved in Willem's direction, brushing the half-breed's admonition aside.

The tribal policeman shrugged, took up the reins of his own brown mare, and turned the animal in the direction of the settlement. There was nothing more to be said there. But Tom might like to know how his father intended to spend this Sunday. Willem regretted being the bearer of such bad news. As he rode off toward the settlement, the hooves of his mount kicked up a whiskey bottle within a couple yards of Seth's front door.

By late morning the August sun rode high overhead, baking the earth until even the yellow grass seemed to bow beneath the weight of the sunlight. At this time of year Father Kenneth always kept his sermons brief and to the point, releasing his parishioners to seek their own respite from the heat. The settlement showed little activity. Women gossiped beneath the willows or laundered their clothes on the banks of the Washita. Men swapped lies on the shade side of their houses or wandered into town to gather in the mercantile and sample Luthor White Bear's cider while philosophizing over the cracker barrel. A handful of children chased one another across the meadow. Cattle clustered in a grove of oaks, now and then bestirring themselves to follow the shifting shade or meander down to the banks of the Washita for a drink.

At his desk in the Bureau of Indian Affairs office, Tom Sandcrane tried not to brood about his father and concentrated on the pleasant fact that he had nowhere to be right at the moment. He tilted back on the rear legs of his chair and balanced precipitously between the wall of the office and the edge of his desk, rolled a smoke for himself, struck a match on the underside of the chair, and touched it to the tip of the cigarette. Exhaling a cloud of smoke, he shifted the papers in his hand and began to reread the tabulation of votes that showed the tribe's overwhelming approval of the land reforms. Tom had been touting the benefits of the Public Land Act for the past six months, crisscrossing the reservation, stopping at every creek camp, farm, and hardscrabble ranch from the Canadian River south to the Washita. The reservation, almost a million acres, was bounded on the west by the Texas panhandle and on the east by the unassigned lands of Indian Territory. Tom was certain he'd ridden across every acre and figured he'd worn out the seats of at least five pairs of britches. But he'd got the job done. And here were the results of the recent ballot in Cross Timbers.

For over a week the Southern Cheyenne had been coming to the BIA office, casting their votes either to approve the termination of the reservation or to contest the matter in the courts. Some of the elders of the tribe had spoken out against the arrangement, but Tom had led a coalition of young and old alike who were eager to cease being wards of the state and secure full citizenship for one and all.

Under an agreement reached between the tribe and the U.S. government, each male head of family would receive 160 acres free and clear, plus 90 acres for each family member. Every Cheyenne man, woman, and child would also receive a cash settlement, the amount of which had yet to be determined. The funds could be used to purchase additional acreage from the government before the remaining reservation lands were open to the public. An industrious family could carve out an empire of fertile grasslands for itself along the Washita or choose to gamble on the oil deposits to the north. Some of the Cheyenne intended to sell off a portion of their land grants to the white settlers who were unable to locate a free claim during the rush. There would be towns and jobs, industry and prosperity. The Cheyenne would own a piece of the future instead of being tied to the past, subsisting on grain allotments and the often uncharitable whims of a capricious government. With the end of their reservation status the Southern Cheyenne would be masters of their own fate, with the protection and freedoms afforded every U.S. citizen.

Tom glanced up as a mud dauber circled heavily in the afternoon light, its tiny wings stirring a galaxy of dust motes as it drifted off across the room and vanished into Allyn Benedict's office. A warm breeze stirred the papers on Edith Stands in Timber's desk, one fluttering to the floor like a leaf. The BIA secretary ruled with a firm hand and assigned every missive its proper file, allowing not so much as a bookmark to remain out of place. She'd have a fit come Monday if Tom left a mess. A plaintive meow sounded from Allyn's office, and a black cat with a blaze of white fur on the tip of one ear trotted through the door and made its way toward Tom. He chuckled and reached down to scratch the creature's neck. The animal, a stray, had made the BIA office home, and managed to sneak into the building at every opportunity.

"Hey *pohkeso,* how did you get in here?" Tom softly said. The cat arched and purred deep in its throat. "Now, my father would say you are a spirit, a trickster come to work mischief on me. Well . . . do your worst, eh?" The cat looked up at the sound of Tom's voice, its dark eyes full of primal wisdom. "No pranks? Hmm. I think you are just *pohkeso,* a kitten, nothing more or less." The cat meowed and scampered off, giving chase to shadows or a breeze-stirred scrap of paper.

Tom closed his eyes and allowed the chair to tilt back against the wall, enjoying a moment of quiet bliss. The BIA office was closed, as it was every Sunday. No one was around to disturb his reverie. A man had to take his peace where he found it. His lazy fantasies carried him from an oil-rich field to a pretty stretch of grassland lying between two tree-crowded ridges and fronting on Coyote Creek, a meandering ribbon of water that emptied into the Washita. He'd described the place to his father and suggested they split their land grants, gambling for a fortune in "black gold" while laying claim to Coyote Creek so father and son could build a place together. But Seth had resisted his son's overtures of friendship. The loss of the Sacred Arrows weighing heavy on his heart, Tom's father had begun to seek solace in the bottom of a bottle.

Tom was determined to change his father's mind. He'd see things differently once the Public Land Act went into effect. It was only a matter of time now. The land rush would commence at seven A.M. on the first of September, just one week away, when the reservation would officially become public domain. Like the other men of the tribe, Tom intended to have his property already claimed and recorded when the rush of white settlers began. He intended to sign his name to

a stretch of oil-bearing land as well as the meadowland along
Coyote Creek, from its bubbling source down to the Washita.
Too bad Seth's dreams didn't reach further than the next
drink. . . .

Tom frowned and shifted his thoughts to another, much
more pleasant subject. And just as Emmiline Benedict took
shape in his mind, a hand reached out and snatched the
cigarette from his lips. Tom nearly fell over backward. Instead, he rocked forward and slammed his knees against the
desk. A green-eyed, black-haired nineteen-year-old woman
laughed, perched herself atop the secretary's desk, and took a
deep drag on the cigarette. She exhaled, then took another,
reducing the cigarette to no more than a stub, which she
crushed beneath her boot, leaving a smear of ashes on the office floor.

Emmiline was wearing a split pale-green riding skirt, with
a matching jacket over a white cotton blouse. She propped
her right foot on an open drawer and leaned forward on her
bent knee.

"Smoking isn't proper behavior for a lady," Tom ruefully
observed, rubbing his bruised kneecaps.

"I'm an Indian agent's daughter. Who said anything about
being a lady?" Emmiline pursed her lips a moment, then lowered her head until her long black hair spilled forward and
she looked out at Tom through the strands. "Do you think I'm
a lady, Tom? Is that why you've never kissed me? Or are you
afraid of the scandal, a Cheyenne man and a white woman?
What would the ladies in Tulsa say? But, of course, things are
different on the reservation. Who's to take offense, other than
my brother? Maybe you're afraid of him."

Tom gulped and shifted uncomfortably in his chair. The
collarless striped shirt he wore suddenly felt two sizes smaller
and damn near began to cut off his wind.

"You looked mighty handsome in church today, Tom,"
Emmiline continued, running a hand along a sleeve of the
frock coat he had draped across the secretary's desk. She lifted
the empty sleeve and draped it across her bosom. "But then
you have always looked handsome." The agent's daughter

could tell she was having an effect on the man. "You could put your arm in the sleeve of this coat if you wanted."

Tom hesitated, tongue-tied.

"Well?" she asked.

Tom took a deep breath and reined in his carnal instincts. "Maybe I'll wait until you're done playing with it first," he replied.

Emmiline realized he had broken free of her spell. "Oh, you . . ." She tossed the coat at him. Tom caught it in front of his face. Now it was his turn to laugh.

"You think you are so smart," Emmiline pouted. She stood as he rose from the desk to don his coat. "You've gotten awfully full of yourself since the passage of the reform."

"Where's your father?" Tom glanced at the front door he'd left open to permit the cross-breeze. That was how she had managed to enter so soundlessly. He spied a surrey waiting in the street.

"How do you know he isn't with me?" Emmiline asked.

"Because you behave yourself when he's around," Tom answered with a chuckle.

"And so do you, Mr. Tom Sandcrane. You're the perfect gentleman when father has his eyes on you. But just who was it asked me to go for a moonlit stroll after the church social last week?"

"Your father suggested I walk you home," Tom said, although the idea had delighted him. He played his feelings close to the vest, like a gambler his cards, and wasn't about to reveal just how smitten he had become with the Indian agent's daughter.

"Did I hear my name?" a voice called from outside. Allyn Benedict stepped through the doorway. He was a tall, spare man with sandy hair, graying at the temples, and friendly, boyish features that belied the fact he was almost fifty. Emmiline, with her back to her father, made a face at Tom to show the young man that he didn't know her as well as he liked to think. Benedict turned in the doorway and waved a hand as if to indicate everything was all right. Tom checked the window and spied Emmiline's brother, Clay Benedict, cradling a Winchester carbine in the crook of his arm as he

stood alongside the surrey. Clay, a slender, devilishly handsome man of twenty-one, had arrived in Cross Timbers from
Connecticut only a couple of months before. According to rumors supplied by Edith Stands in Timber, the dour, secretive
young man had been expelled from the Yale Law School for
some episode of misconduct regarding a test.

At his father's signal, Clay, with what seemed an air of re-
luctance, returned his carbine to the scabbard he kept under
the bench seat. He leaned against the surrey, hooked his
thumbs in the pockets of his woolen trousers, and studied the
front of the building, a band of shadow beneath the brim of
his black cap masking the upper part of his features. Allyn's
son had a deep and abiding mistrust of the Cheyenne. He saw
them as a conquered people and little more than savages. The
more Emmiline made herself available to Tom, the more belligerent Clay became. Yet despite Clay's animosity toward
him, Tom felt a peculiar sense of kinship for Emmiline's
brother, who, like the Cheyenne, was struggling to be the
kind of son his father expected.

"Have you come to arrest me, Mr. Benedict?" Tom asked.

Benedict appeared embarrassed. "I was visiting Luthor
White Bear over at the mercantile when Clay comes riding up
and tells me that he and Emmiline have noticed the BIA office
door is wide-open. Well, the first thing I think of is some
drunken sorehead is after the ballots. Then I find Emmiline
has taken it upon herself to investigate without waiting for
me, so I came on at a run, until I spied that nasty-tempered
roan of yours hitched around to the side. . . ." The agent's explanation trailed off, and he grinned sheepishly and shrugged.
"Oh, hell, there's been some angry talk around the reservation
this week. I'll keep expecting trouble until after September
first." He glanced toward his office. "Come to think of it, why
are you here, Tom? My God, I should think this is the last
place you'd want to come after all the work you put in."

"I don't know," Tom said, shrugging. "I left church and
wandered down the street and just sort of wound up here.
Force of habit, I guess." He walked over to the territorial map
hanging on the east wall. The Southern Cheyenne reservation
was outlined in black and apportioned by a pattern of red

lines, as if covered with a spiderweb. Tom Sandcrane had traveled every strand of the web for Allyn Benedict and the BIA, not for the money the bureau paid him, but because he believed it was the right thing to do.

"I knew you were the man for the job, Tom," Allyn said. His shadow fell across the map. "No one could have pulled this tribe together like you did. What happens next will be in no small part your own doing. You ought to be proud of yourself." Allyn patted the younger man on the shoulder.

"Ask me after the first of September," Tom said.

"I won't need to," Allyn replied. "Think of it. There'll be towns, schools, maybe a real doctor or two. The future will be right here. And one day this territory will be a state, mark my words. A state! Why, you might even be the first representative!" Allyn turned to his daughter. "Congressman Tom Sandcrane of Oklahoma—how does that sound, Emmiline?"

"Nice, Papa," the girl said. "Real nice."

Tom's cheeks reddened, and he looked out the window at the quiet, dusty expanse of Main Street. The agent's enthusiasm was contagious. A Cheyenne representative in Congress—now, there was a thought. He imagined the settlement bustling with life, the street just one of many, and all of them crowded. "That kind of thing is a long way off," he said.

"It's closer than you think," Allyn told him. "Say, why don't you two spend Sunday together? I promised the troopers over at El Reno I'd oversee the baseball game between A and D companies. Seems I'm the only one who knows the rules, and the men of both companies trust me to be impartial."

"I cannot for the life of me figure out what is so special about a bunch of grown men hitting and chasing a ball and one another around a hot, dusty field," Emmiline added. She walked over and put her arm in Tom's. "You are my escort for the day, sir. And I will not take 'no' for an answer." She led Tom to the door. "Come along. I'll pack us a picnic basket."

Emmiline literally propelled Tom through the doorway. She waved at her brother, who only scowled at the sight of them. Tom ignored Clay's open disapproval and headed around the building to the hitching rail where he'd left the roan. It was obvious Clay resented the attention his sister was paying this man of the Southern Cheyenne. For the sake of Emmiline and her father, Tom continued to give Clay Benedict a wide berth.

Clay watched his sister disappear around the building arm in arm with Tom Sandcrane, then dismounted and entered the BIA office. He found Allyn in his office. The agent was carefully examining the locked drawers of his desk to satisfy himself that none of them had been forced. He looked up at Clay standing in the doorway, a slightly bemused expression on his face.

"Lose something?"

"No. But I shall lock the door from now on." Allyn straightened.

"Emmiline's gone off with the Indian."

"Yes. It was my suggestion."

"I don't like it," Clay flatly stated.

"No one asked you to," Allyn said. "She is occupying his time right now. I need for that to continue a while longer. I do not underestimate young Sandcrane. He is smart and extremely perceptive. I won't relax until after the land rush."

"I just think . . ."

"Don't," said Allyn. "Don't think. I'll do that. You listen. And obey your father. And maybe I can salvage something of the wreck you've made of your life." He patted his son on the shoulder. It was the same conciliatory gesture he had used with Tom. "Now, let's get on to El Reno. I have a most important meeting."

A clock out in the front office began to toll high noon. El Reno lay an hour's ride to the southeast. Allyn Benedict figured he had plenty of time.

"What about the troopers?" Clay asked.

"Don't worry," Allyn said. "I hold all the rules." He grinned, his features jubilant. "This game isn't about to start without me."

CHAPTER FOUR

THE INDIAN AGENT FOR THE SOUTHERN CHEYENNE LIVED IN A single-story shotgun house on the north side of Cross Timbers. With its whitewashed board and batten exterior, Benedict's home stood apart from the log cabins and sod huts surrounding the settlement. Allyn's wife Margaret—a buxom, heavyset woman who had forsaken her influential New England family and followed her husband to the "Wild West"—was working in the flower garden she had coaxed out of the arid Oklahoma soil. The garden, a collection of wildflowers she had painstakingly transplanted from sojourns with her husband, had become overgrown with weeds during her recent illness, and many of the blooms were in danger of being smothered by less-desired growths. Her garden was much more than a passing interest. Allyn had grown distant of late. Margaret liked to blame the worries of administering the reservation, but deep within her heart of hearts she suspected the problem was far more serious. So she turned to the garden, to her little blossoms, and tried to convince herself that all this would pass and her husband would one day fall in love with her again.

There was a barn and small corral just east of the house, and when one of the horses whinnied and stamped its foot to announce the approaching couple from the settlement, Margaret straightened up and waved at her daughter and Tom as they entered the yard. Margaret's round cheeks were streaked with moisture beneath the shade afforded by her sweat-stained blue bonnet. A couple of wayward strands of silvery brown hair had escaped the bonnet and were sweat-plastered to her neck.

"Good morning, Tom. Have you rescued Emmiline from her father's clutches?"

"I reckon so," Tom smiled, removing his hat. He looped the reins of the roan through the gate in a faded white picket fence that ran along the front of the house. "Glad to see you up and about." The gate creaked open as he permitted Emmiline to enter in front of him.

"A chest cold in August is the worst thing. No strength to move about and too hot to stay in bed," Margaret replied. She cast a forlorn eye at a cluster of firewheels she had recently watered. They'd live, but she was worried about the daisies. "A good, soaking rain would do wonders," she said. "A little tending while I was sick wouldn't have hurt either." She glared accusingly at her daughter.

"Mother . . . I simply don't have your skill and talents," Emmiline replied. She glanced in Tom's direction. "Mother thinks that everyone should be able to . . ." She frowned, her voice trailing off. Tom wasn't even paying any attention to her. He wore a curious expression and was staring at a dust devil that had sprung up only a few yards away. The miniature whirlwind ruffled the weeds, caught at the hem of Margaret's dress and apron, and fanned their faces with its hot dusty breath.

The voices of the women grew distant to Tom and were obscured by the sound of his breathing as it rose and fell like ocean swells, and underneath it all the cadence of his beating heart, and from somewhere deep in his soul a lone keening chant and the tap-tap-tapping of a gourd rattle.

Stop.

Stop this!

He wiped a hand across his face as the whirlwind spent itself and dissipated. The sounds vanished. But in their wake they left a disturbing premonition. Seth . . .

"Tom Sandcrane!"

He gave a start and then looked at the girl. "I'm sorry," he mumbled, and started toward his horse.

"But where are you going? What about our picnic?" Emmiline called after him, completely taken aback by his actions.

"I have to go. It's my father," Tom said as he vaulted the picket fence and leaped into the saddle.

"Tom Sandcrane—have you taken leave of your senses?" the young woman called out. But her escort had already turned the roan and, with a swat of his hat across its flank, sent the animal galloping off in a shower of pebbles and a billowing coffee-colored cloud of dust.

"Indians are so terribly unpredictable," Margaret sighed. "Be a good girl and make your mother a cup of tea." She knelt and caught a cluster of dandelions in a stranglehold, ripped them from the earth, and tossed the undesirables atop an ever-growing pile of weeds. "Wait. Never mind," the woman remarked. "I just remembered, we're out of tea. Perhaps there will be a package for us at the fort." She sighed. "It's the little pleasures I have missed most. Well . . . maybe things will be different."

"If father's plans work out," Emmiline added.

"I for one shall not hold my breath," Margaret said, kneeling in the garden. Allyn had promised much and delivered so little. Still, there was always a first time. She paused to dab the perspiration from her face with the hem of her apron and could not help but note that Emmiline continued to stare after the retreating figure of Tom Sandcrane. He was already past the Catholic church and following a well-worn trail up the cleared slope, dotted with half-a-dozen log houses, chicken coops, and split-rail corrals. A couple of mongrel hounds nipped at the roan's heels until Tom rode clear of the settlement and vanished beneath a canopy of white oaks.

"Don't like him overly much, dear," Margaret added. "It will only make things harder."

Words to the wise, thought Emmiline, *but too late, alas—too late.*

CHAPTER FIVE

PANTHER HALL WAS A LONG, LOW-ROOFED ROADHOUSE NESTLED among a grove of post oaks. The building's rough-hewn log exterior blended in with its surroundings and attracted little attention to itself. A man riding the North Road would never notice the roadhouse unless he chose to follow the wheel-rutted path that veered from the main road and cut across a hundred yards of meadow, dappled with crimson firewheels, Indian paintbrush, and brilliant yellow sunflowers. To reach Panther Hall, a man had to be willing to leave the daylight behind and enter shadow.

The consumption of spirits was expressly forbidden on the reservation, but that hadn't stopped Jerel Tall Bull and his younger brother, Curtis, from setting up their notorious establishment. There was some speculation that the commanding officer at Fort Reno received a share of Panther Hall's profits in return for his not sending troops onto the reservation to burn out the establishment. The Southern Cheyenne, even those among the tribe who disapproved of the brothers, were loath to lodge any complaints concerning their actions. Indeed there was a certain amount of grudging respect for the Tall Bulls. As for the BIA, Allyn Benedict had specifically chosen to avoid any confrontation with Jerel and Curtis. The brothers were the offspring of warriors and had a following among the tribe.

Jerel Tall Bull had thrown his considerable support behind
Benedict's efforts to abolish the reservation. He was as anxious
as anyone to see it dissolved and the entire grant opened to
settlement. The Tall Bulls would be able to operate without
fear of being closed down. There were far more profits to be
made in a thriving township than could ever be realized in
their present rural surroundings catering to a bunch of poor
Cheyenne.

So against official government policy, the Tall Bulls continued to operate their roadhouse with impunity in these waning
days of the reservation system. They offered a variety of vices
and thirsts. For whiskey, women, or a game of chance, the
roadhouse was the place to go. The only place. And only a
fool went there unarmed.

"Hold it right there, Tom," a voice called out. A pair of riders galloped up out of a draw to the right of Sandcrane. Tom
halted about midway across the meadow and allowed the two
men to approach. Both young men wore checkered shirts and
Levi's tucked into scuffed boots. They carried double-barreled
shotguns loaded with buckshot. Extra cartridges rattled in
their vest pockets. He recognized them both. Pete Elk Head
was a brash, troublesome youth with a history of brawls and
petty thievery that frequently landed him in the tribal jail.
John Iron Hail, the one who had called out, might be wild as
a green-broke stallion, but he did not share Pete's criminal
reputation. They were both seventeen, and like all seventeen-
year-olds, they deemed themselves immortal.

John was the first to reach Tom Sandcrane. He flashed a
grin, straightened his hat, and crossed his hands on the pommel of his saddle.

"Sorry Tom. Panther Hall's closed."

"I can't believe that," Tom remarked. "The Tall Bulls
wouldn't lock their doors until the last drop of whiskey's been
licked from the barrel."

"What he means," said Pete Elk Head, "is that Panther Hall
is closed to *you*." Pete was a swarthy half-breed youth with
broad shoulders, pockmarked features, and a nose that had

been flattened by a cantankerous mule. His knuckles were hardened scar tissue. John Iron Hail, unlike his quarrelsome companion, was by nature easygoing, if a bit lazy. But he'd never been able to walk away from a dare, a trait that often landed him in trouble. John even seemed embarrassed by this confrontation, for Tom had been like a big brother to him in the past.

"Jerel's orders. They have something special going on, just for their friends," John explained. He couldn't bring himself to level his shotgun at Tom. He pointed the barrel at Sandcrane's horse.

"The pit again?" Tom asked. The Tall Bulls had dug a hole in the prairie out behind the roadhouse where the patrons wagered bets on half-starved animals driven by torture and abuse into fighting to the death. The Pit was fifteen feet in diameter and three feet deep and was ringed by a three-foot wall to protect the onlookers and keep the combatants from escaping. The two men blocking the wheel-rutted path didn't need to answer. The sound of distant snarls and growling trailed on the summer breeze.

"My father pass through here?" Tom sternly inquired, his eyes narrowing. The question was directed at John, who shifted uncomfortably in the saddle.

"The likes of that drunken old sot are always welcome at Panther Hall," Pete answered as he rode up alongside Tom and then jabbed Sandcrane in the ribs with the muzzle of his shotgun. "Now, you can just turn that roan and ride back the way you come, 'cause the day ain't dawned a tamed buck like yourself could ever get past me."

A striking rattlesnake was slow as molasses in winter compared to what happened next. Tom's left arm shot out. His hand caught the shotgun halfway down the barrel and jammed the stock into Pete's belly. Air exploded from the young man's lips. Tom tore the weapon from Pete's loosened grasp and struck him again, this time in the face, breaking the man's nose for the second time in his young life. Pete, still gasping for breath, toppled from the saddle and landed on his rump in the middle of a patch of sunflowers.

"Sumbith! My nothe! You bath-tard. You broke my nothe."

Pete bellowed as he cupped his hands to his face and glared at his attacker. "John, you gonna juth thtand there?" Blood filled his mouth from a split upper lip and gum.

"Yeah, John," Tom added, without even bothering to look at Pete's companion. His fingers curled around the twin triggers of the weapon he had just confiscated.

"Shit," John Iron Hail muttered, wiping the back of his hand across his dry mouth and square jaw.

Tom glanced in his direction and saw the seventeen-year-old return his shotgun to its saddle scabbard, ending the incident before someone else, namely John Iron Hail, got hurt.

"It isn't like you to wear Tall Bull's brand." Tom commented.

"Just helping out," John replied with a shrug. "Their money spends as good as anyone's. And I aim to have me a little extra cash when the land goes public. I figure to claim me a fair piece of grazing land and raise some horses out on the strip north of the Canadian." Glancing past Tom, John's eyes widened. That and the sound of a broken twig were all the warning Tom needed. Pete Elk Head had mistaken the brief interchange for an opportunity to get at Sandcrane while he was preoccupied. With scarcely a break in the conversation, Tom turned and delivered a well-timed kick to Pete's jaw as the youthful assailant attempted to drag Sandcrane from horseback. Pete's head snapped back, and his eyes glazed over as he crumpled alongside the roan.

"Best watch the company you keep," Tom cautioned. "This one's trouble." He indicated the unconscious young man lying almost underneath the roan's hooves. Tom Sandcrane tucked the shotgun under his arm and glanced in John's direction. "Na-ase. I am leaving." He continued on through the warm August afternoon, following the tracks in the buffalo grass to Panther Hall.

John Iron Hail watched Sandcrane for a few moments, then looked down at Pete's unconscious form. The fallen man stirred, tried to raise upon his elbows, grunted, and sank to earth. "Trouble? Not much," John Iron Hail said, bemused and shaking his head. He unslung his canteen and proceeded to trickle water across his companion's bruised and battered face.

Three flies upon the tabletop alighted and cautiously approached the crumbs of fry bread that had spilled from Seth's plate. Seth's hand darted out and closed like a snare. Then he slowly uncurled his fingers to make his count. A single fly crawled around his palm for a fleeting second and then took flight.

"There was a time you'd've caught all three," said the young, attractive woman Jerel Tall Bull had employed to serve his customers.

Seth looked up at Red Cherries, then glanced about the interior of the roadhouse. The rest of the tavern's patrons were outside, gathered at the fighting pit, where they railed at the hapless combatants and wagered money on their brutal sport. For the first time since the loss of the Mahuts, Seth and the widow of Jordan Weasel Bear were alone.

Red Cherries of the lilting laugh and teasing smile. Warm as summer to a lonely man's cold heart. Like her name, ripe and sweet and inviting . . . but forbidden fruit whose taste had cost him dearly.

She was achingly pretty and reminded Seth so much of his first wife, who had died shortly after Tom's sixth birthday. Red Cherries, a Northern Cheyenne, had been given to Jordan Weasel Bear, Seth's friend, for the sum of ten horses. Jordan, almost forty years the girl's senior, could at one moment be kind and caring, and the next, abusive. He'd lost all three of his sons in the Indian Wars that were the aftermath of the Custer debacle. Jordan dulled his sense of loss with the white man's whiskey. When the liquor fueled his jealous rages, Seth was always there to calm him down. Ironically, this act of friendship brought Seth and Red Cherries together. Over the months they also became friends, and then more than friends.

"There was a time when a Cheyenne woman would have lost the tip of her nose for taking another man to her husband's blanket," Seth replied.

"I've been punished," Red Cherries said. "I spent the last six months in Dallas."

"Doing what?"

Red Cherries chuckled and indicated the interior of the tavern with a sweep of her left hand. "This," she said. "And other things." She shrugged, keeping part of her story private. "I had to stay alive. And it wasn't like I had a man to care for me. No one exactly came forward after Jordan's death."

"It wasn't my place," Seth defensively replied. "Not after what we did."

"Seems like it was *your* place more than anyone else's." Red Cherries brushed a strand of hair back from her face and pretended she no longer cared. Perspiration beaded her lip, her brown eyes wide and luminous despite the building's shadowy interior. She wore a loose-fitting embroidered cotton blouse and a Mexican skirt, whose billowing folds concealed her slender legs. Her features had lost the bloom of innocence—but, then, she was twenty now, a widow, and she had been to Dallas.

Seth shook his head and sighed. He poured himself another drink and tossed it down, his throat numb from the half a bottle he had already finished off. He cast his eyes across the room. There was nothing fancy about Panther Hall. One wall was dominated by a bar and rows of glasses from behind which the Tall Bulls dispensed such curiously named libations as Old Bronc, Three Fingered Jack, and Thunder Water, along with the more traditional elixirs—rye whiskey, sour mash, beer, and hard cider. Seth had seen a cat go mad after lapping up a puddle of Thunder Water. But the whiskey was brought in from Fort Reno, and though it had a hard edge, the liquor had never made him froth at the mouth.

The rest of the interior consisted of tables and chairs and an enormous stone hearth that filled the far wall and resembled the yawning mouth of a cave. Oil lamps hung from the beams that crisscrossed the ceiling, and could be raised and lowered as needed. The Tall Bull brothers had built the roadhouse to withstand the often turbulent Oklahoma weather, and nothing short of a tornado's direct hit would rattle its walls.

"Why did you come back?" Seth asked, downing another drink in a single gulp. His cheeks were flushed from the effects of the liquor. He'd been lying to himself, pretending all along that a craving for drink had brought him out to Panther Hall. But the widow had been the real reason. The minute word had reached him of Red Cherries' return, Seth was lost. He had to see her again. Nothing could have kept him away.

"Despite the opinion of the good people who fill the pews at St. Joachim's, I am still Southern Cheyenne." The woman stiffened her spine as she spoke. She misjudged his scrutiny for a look of disapproval. "I have done what I have done. I seek no forgiveness, nor do I expect any." Realizing she had raised her voice, the widow glanced about in embarrassment, hoping the two of them were still alone. Relieved it was so, a melancholy smile transformed her expression, making her seem wise beyond her years. "No doubt the 'good Christian Cheyenne' would agree my place is here." Red Cherries studied the older man's bedraggled appearance. There was hardly a hint of the power and the mystery that had drawn her to him months ago. The loss of the Sacred Arrows had divided his spirit and left him a cripple.

Seth took note of her scrutiny and scowled. "What are you looking at?" She was judging him, like all the rest. "Keep your pity. Save it for yourself. Like you said, your place is here. Mine too."

"Yes. I work here. Jerel pays me. And he treats me no worse than the other men I have known. But I do this to live." Red Cherries placed a hand on his shoulder. "I think you come here to die . . . a little at a time."

Seth managed to stand, steadying himself with the back of his chair. He grabbed for her hand, but she pulled away. "You could come with me. I'll take care of you." He wiped a forearm across his bleary-eyed features. His breath stank of drink. His clothes had been slept in for three days running.

"No. I waited for you after they brought Jordan back. But you did not come. Even when I sent word that I was planning to leave, you never showed your face." The woman's eyes narrowed, grew distant, as the wound reopened and she relived the hurt. After Jordan's death, friends began to ostracize her, and the man she trusted and thought loved her kept his distance. He clung to his pride and his precious Sacred Arrows and allowed her to leave alone, without entreating her to stay or offering to stand at her side.

"Take care of me?" She chuckled. "You cannot even take care of yourself." She turned and strode across the room, stopping by one of the rear windows to look out at the men around the pit. Some poor animal was dying for their pleasure. The thought sickened her. Why were men so cruel? Of course, the two women who plied the oldest trade in the back rooms were among the audience enjoying the blood sport. Red Cherries sensed her former lover behind her, and his hands grasped her shoulders. She attempted to pull free.

Seth tightened his hold and spun her around, pressing her against the wall as he covered her lips with his own. She did not respond but stood motionless as a statue, devoid of emotion and feelings. He drew back and looked into her eyes, his whiskey breath hot on her face.

"I don't like a man to put his hands on me unless I wish it," she warned in a quiet voice. "And right now I don't wish it." Seth retreated a step and wiped a hand across his mouth.

"You cost me everything . . . the Sacred Arrows, my peace, my life, even my son. Everything."

"If you are broken, it's because you are brittle," Red Cherries retorted. Though life had been brutally difficult in Dallas, she had survived on her own, with no one to express sympathy for her plight.

Seth cursed and raised a hand as if to strike her. But he hesitated, then looked at his upraised arm as if questioning its purpose. He sighed and stumbled away from her. The crowd at the fighting pit caught his attention. A dangerous smile crawled across his features as the liquor he had consumed continued to burn in his belly. The dozen or so men ringing the fighting pit clamored for a kill. The stench of violent death drifted in through the open back door. An idea began to form in the foggy recesses of the man's mind, and he chuckled. The sound made the young widow's skin crawl.

Seth hurried across the tavern and darted around behind the bar, searched beneath the counter for a few moments until he found what he was looking for, then straightened up and headed for the back door, an ax handle held loosely in his right hand.

"See you," he muttered.

"Where are you going?"

"I never had any use for that damn pit."

"Stay clear of Jerel Tall Bull," Red Cherries said. For old time's sake? Or somewhere, buried deep in her heart, beneath all the layers of hurt, did she still care? Seth either didn't hear or chose to ignore her counsel. He vanished through the back door and started down the winding path that led to the pit, and to the ring of hardened souls come to wager on a game of life and death.

The Mississippi Blue Heeler had lost the battle but remained defiant. Weighing fifty-four pounds of muscle and bone beneath its blood-spattered brown-and-tan fur, the dog, General Sheridan, retreated toward the hard clay wall. Pound for pound there wasn't an animal on the reservation that could have taken him. But the Tall Bulls had pitted General Sheridan against a pair of red wolves brought over from Louisiana. Though smaller than the Blue Heeler, the wolves were pack animals and operated as a unit, attacking simultaneously from the front and rear. General Sheridan had held his own for several long minutes, and the bloody smears on the walls and floor of the pit attested to the savagery of the contest. One of the wolves was down and lying on its side, fluids pumping from the mortal throat wound the Blue Heeler had inflicted. But while General Sheridan had concentrated on one wolf, its companion had ripped the Blue Heeler's belly and crippled one of the dog's hind legs. To make matters worse, General Sheridan could no longer see out of one eye, and part of his right ear was missing. Muscle spasms caused the dog's powerful shoulders to tremble as it retreated, limping toward the gate through which it had entered the arena. Curtis Tall Bull, disgusted that the dog had not performed as expected, made no move toward the gate. He was not going to allow the animal to escape with its life.

"Curtis! Appears to me that mutt of yours has called it quits," said Mickey Pallins, a Cherokee half-breed from the southeastern part of the territory, over near the Red River. He had brought in the wolves and was going home several hundred dollars to the good.

"He ain't dead yet," Curtis snapped, his darkly handsome features flushed with anger.

"That's the spirit, Curtis," one of the men around the pit shouted out. "Twenty dollars says the wolf kills him on the next lunge." Though the remaining red wolf bled from a few superficial wounds, the smaller animal continued to stalk its opponent, knowing it had the advantage now. The Blue Heeler could no longer match the red wolf's quickness. The cunning predator began to close in, its head lowered and feral eyes gleaming with battle lust.

Jerel Tall Bull leaned into his younger brother. "Open the gate, Curtis. You've lost enough. Anyway, that's a fool's bet." Jerel was heavyset and powerfully built. At first glance his lumbering gait, close-set eyes and thick, homely features made him appear slow-witted. Nothing could have been further from the truth. His reputation among the Southern Cheyenne was in many ways the equal of Tom Sandcrane's. There was grudging admiration for the way he had played the BIA and the army off one another while running a profitable enterprise expressly forbidden under the jurisdiction of the government. No one cared if some of his money made its way into the coffers of white officials. What mattered was Jerel's air of defiance toward the authorities, twenty years after the last battles of the Indian Wars had been fought.

But Curtis shrugged off his brother's advice and took the bets that came his way. General Sheridan may have lost the fight, but he wouldn't go easy. The red wolf was still in for quite a tussle.

Suddenly, without warning, the crowd parted, and Seth Sandcrane hooked a leg over the wall and dropped down into the pit. The adrenaline coursing through him belied the effects of the alcohol he had consumed.

"What the hell?" Curtis blurted out.

Seth strode to the center of the pit. The red wolf lunged for him. Seth batted the animal aside with his ax handle. The wolf howled and retreated toward the opposite wall, where its owner rose up in anger.

"Who the devil is this old drunk? You leave my animals be!" shouted Mickey Pallins. He opened the gate for the wolf and allowed the creature to scamper through the passage and into its cage. Pallins slammed the escape route closed. "Is this a friend of yours, Curtis?"

"He comes here to drink. But after today, not anymore!" the younger of the Tall Bull brothers replied.

Seth ignored the interchange, impervious to the insulting remarks and protests hurled his way. He walked over to the dog. General Sheridan's legs trembled, but he stood defiant, his hackles raised.

"Oes-keso," Seth spoke. The single word, uttered in Cheyenne, had a profound effect on the frightened, pain-crazed animal. A calm seemed to settle over the Blue Heeler. "Sure, you recognize me," Seth continued. "Poor old boy." He knelt by the dog and outstretched his hand, palm down, fingers tucked in. General Sheridan extended his bloody muzzle and sniffed the man's knuckles. The animal's hackles slowly settled. It recognized this man. The Blue Heeler continued to whimper as its strength failed and it sank to the ground.

"Sandcrane," Curtis said. "Sheridan cost me over a hundred dollars. Now I got a chance to win some back. This is none of your concern."

"The dog is finished. It can fight no more." Seth made his statement in a flat, clear voice as he lifted the dog into his arms.

"Goddam it, Seth, who the hell do you think you are?" Jerel blurted out.

"I'm the one who is going to take this dog home," Seth said. "He's dying."

"Then let him die here," Curtis said. His voice began to rise in pitch. "Now, put him down."

Seth continued across the pit and walked to the gate. Cradling the dog in one arm, he shoved the gate open and then passed through. There were no walls lining the passage, and he was able to climb past the cage and up onto the ground.

"You can't do this," Curtis said angrily, blocking Seth's path. Young and headstrong and full of himself, he cocked a fist.

Seth jabbed him between the legs with the ax handle. Curtis doubled over, hands clutching his privates as he struggled to breathe.

"Sonuvabitch," Curtis groaned.

Seth pushed past him toward Panther Hall, where he'd left his horse ground-tethered in front of the tavern. From out of the corner of his eye he noticed one of the other gamblers, a crony of Curtis Tall Bull, start toward him, knife in hand. He closed in fast, hoping to catch Seth off guard, only to be felled by an ax handle to the side of the skull. The remaining gamblers cleared a path for man and dog, giving Seth the impression of being home free. Then a Smith & Wesson thirty-eight-caliber double-action revolver cracked twice in the heat of the afternoon, and twin geysers of dirt erupted a couple of feet in front Seth, halting him in his tracks.

He slowly turned and faced Jerel Tall Bull.

"I think you've about wore out your welcome, whiskey-gut," said Jerel. Smoke trailed from the Smith & Wesson's six-inch barrel. He had another three rounds in the chamber, more than enough for the man standing in front of him.

"Well, then, reckon I better leave," said Seth.

"While you still can," Jerel replied. "Put down the dog."

"He's dying. What does it matter?" Seth asked.

"Remember . . . I am a Crazy Dog. We are men of principle."

"Ah . . ." Blood was seeping through Seth's fingers. General Sheridan's breath was coming in ragged, shallow gasps. He might still be saved, but the odds were against it.

"The animal stays here. Leave him on the ground and walk away." Jerel's brows knotted above the black buttons of his eyes. Behind him, Curtis Tall Bull shifted his weight from one foot to the other, like a boxer waiting to enter a match. He made no attempt to hide his excitement. No doubt he was anxious for his older brother to avenge the mistreatment he had suffered at Seth's hands.

"Look, whiskey-gut, don't try my patience."

Seth shrugged, slowly turned, and continued on toward the

corner of the roadhouse. He felt a twinge of pain between his
shoulder blades and steeled himself for the inevitable.

"Sandcrane!" Jerel shouted. He raised the thirty-eight and
sighted on the older warrior. Without warning, as if in response to Tall Bull's outcry, Tom Sandcrane rounded the corner of the roadhouse and was soon abreast of his father,
placing himself in the center of the conflict.

"Somebody call me?" Tom asked. He met Jerel face on, his
expression as grave as the Dog Soldier's as he shielded Seth
with the roan.

Jerel took a couple of steps forward. Curtis followed him
while remaining in his older brother's shadow. Both men noticed the shotgun Tom held in a one-handed grip, pointing a
load of buckshot at them both.

"Where's John and Pete?" asked Jerel.

"Back yonder where I left them. They're still watching the
road. Pete Elk Head was nice enough to let me borrow his
shotgun, though," Tom said. He glanced over his shoulder at
his father, who was surprised as anyone by Tom's timely arrival.

"What the hell are you doing, boy?" Seth muttered.

"Saving your ungrateful ass," came Tom's reply. He returned
his attention to Jerel Tall Bull.

"Whiskey-gut ain't leaving with our dog," Curtis spoke up
as he peered past Jerel's broad shoulders.

So that's the reason for the standoff, Tom thought. *We're about
to kill each other over what's left of a camp dog.* Keeping the
shotgun trained on the brothers, he fished in his Levi's pockets and brought out a crumpled wad of bills. "This ought to
be about twenty-six dollars," he said, tossing the greenbacks
toward Jerel. They fluttered to earth like falling leaves. "I'm
buying the dog."

"Twenty-six dollars! He's worth four times that!" Curtis
blurted out.

"Not anymore," Tom said as he watched his father depart
with the limp-looking animal cradled in his arms.

"Hell," Jerel grumbled, and lowered his thirty-eight. He
knew for a fact that Tom had never been involved in anything
more than a fistfight. Still, there was something in young

Sandcrane's eyes, a funny kind of look, like that of a peaceable man oblivious to his own capacity for violence. If Jerel Tall Bull was going to be the one to take a walk on the danger side of Tom Sandcrane, it would have to be for something worth a lot more than a dog. He ambled forward, scooped the bills off the ground, and tucked them into his pocket. He was close enough for his words to carry to Tom alone.

"Do not get the wrong idea. You were the son of the Arrow Keeper, yet you turned your back on the songs and the power. Fool. I think you are only a shell of a man now. And when it suits me, I may destroy you." Jerel's black eyes held the younger man in their malevolent stare. "Should you ever stand between me and that which I truly desire, I will grind you into dust." Jerel turned and rejoined the gamblers who, as a whole, appeared relieved. Blood sport was one thing, but no one wanted to be an innocent bystander to gunplay.

"That's it? You're gonna let him ride out?" Curtis exclaimed.

"You want to catch a belly load of buckshot for some damn dog that'll be dead before they take him a mile? Go ahead," Jerel snapped, and thrust the Smith & Wesson into his younger brother's hands. Curtis recoiled as if the revolver were white-hot to the touch. "I didn't think so," Jerel added.

Tom turned the roan and retraced his steps to the front of the roadhouse. In a minute he was out of sight of the pit. Jerel Tall Bull's behavior confounded him. There was more to the man than greed. The owner of the roadhouse would bear watching. In front of Panther Hall, Seth had already caught up the reins to his horse and climbed into the saddle. General Sheridan was draped across the skirt just behind the cantle, looking like a pair of saddlebags and just as lifeless.

"Who do you think you are—Crazy Horse?" Seth exclaimed. "You should have minded your own business. I didn't need your help. Jerel Tall Bull has killed men before. He could have shot you dead at any time." Seth touched his heels to his mount's flanks and urged the animal to a gentle trot.

Tom, speechless, looked aside and thought he saw someone in the shadow of the tavern doorway, catching a glimpse of skirt as the figure darted out of sight. He was unable to identify the woman, but she had most assuredly been watching them. Checking his father's trail, he saw the dust swirl in a tight, swift spiral, then settle in the heat. A whirlwind had sent him; another was telling him to leave. It was all strange, more than he could explain.

"You're welcome," said Tom to Seth's slowly diminishing figure. He eased down the twin hammers on the shotgun, dropped the weapon into the nearest horse trough, and rode away from Panther Hall.

CHAPTER SIX

COMPANY A AND THEIR BITTER RIVALS, COMPANY D, PLAYED
to a four-to-four tie in the heavy heat of the afternoon. Then, in the bottom of the sixth inning, with
D Company at bat, the game fell apart. Corporal Johnson hit
a line drive over the center fielder's head and the go ahead
run on third, a lumbering cavalryman of Czech extraction
named Pastusek, charged home while A Company's catcher
screamed for someone to throw him the ball. It was obvious
that the throw from the outfield was never going to make it
in time unless the catcher slowed Pastusek down, which is
precisely what he did. As Pastusek bore down on home plate,
the catcher palmed a derringer and shot the runner in the leg.
Pastusek yelped and crumpled to the ground, clutching his
calf. The catcher caught the throw from center field, trotted
victoriously along the base path, and tagged the runner out.
Pastusek reached up, caught the catcher by the throat, and
proceeded to throttle him. The two men rolled in the dirt,
gouging and pommeling one another as their teammates
charged across the playing field. The teams came together at
the pitcher's mound and went about settling the issue with
fists and baseball bats. Allyn Benedict, as umpire, declared the
game a draw and quit the playing field.

Uniformed officers hurried toward the melee in a futile attempt to restore calm. But the rivalries ran deep and had been

allowed to fester throughout the long, boring months of duty. It was going to take something more than a few barked commands to bring the situation under control.

Allyn spied his son waving to him from the sidelines and angled over to the young man. Clay grinned and nodded toward the brawling troopers.

"The rules out here are different from back east," he chuckled.

"In more ways than one, and for a lot more than baseball," Allyn replied. "Has Mr. Lehrman arrived?"

Clay nodded and indicated the cluster of cabins and barracks that made up Fort Reno. An impressive array of settlers arriving in wagons, carriages, and on horseback had been assembling at the fort since the end of July. The meadow east of the fort was a sea of white canvas tents and smoky cook fires. The impending land rush had attracted would-be landowners from all over the country. With change in their pockets and a fistful of dreams, these settlers were anxious to carve a place for themselves out of the soon-to-be-opened reservation. Already folks had begun to grumble about how unfair it was that the Southern Cheyenne would receive land allotments before even taking part in the rush. His thoughts on the turbulent days to come, Allyn outpaced his son as he entered the parade grounds and proceeded with all due haste toward the land office in which he had set up shop in anticipation of September 1.

Grasshoppers whirred in ungainly arcs, escaping the Indian agent's crushing steps. Dust billowed in his wake. Allyn's face felt dry and blistered from the sun, and he entered his cramped office with a sigh of relief. It was a sparsely furnished space, two chairs and a desk, a cabinet for documents, and a territorial map on the rear wall. A rotund man sweating in a frock coat sipped whiskey from a flask as he sat by an open window and fanned himself with a copy of the Tulsa *Register*.

"Sorry I'm late, Mr. Benedict. I am Artemus Lehrman, vice president of Prairie Oil and Gas. The driver I hired promised we'd be here by midmorning." He tossed the newspaper onto the desk and patted it with the fleshy palm of his hand. One news article dominated the front page: the impending land rush, which was destined to change the face of the territory for all time.

It was a lesser piece of reporting, however, that had caught Artemus Lehrman's attention. He jabbed a finger at a narrow column whose banner simply read "Tragedy in Cuba."

"Intriguing situation there. Deplorable. Simply deplorable. The damn Spanish are brutally suppressing the people of the island. One of their leaders, a charismatic rascal by the name of Antonio Celestial, has appealed to Washington for help. The president grudgingly turned him down—at least that's the rumor I heard. Although there is some popular sentiment to involve us." Lehrman folded his hands across his ample belly. "Think of it. A fine little war could prove quite profitable."

"We are a long way from Cuba," Clay interjected, breaking Lehrman's long-winded reverie.

"On the contrary, my good lad. The island is practically at our doorstep. Why, dash it all, the entire world is but a stone's throw away, at least that's the way it seems. A good steamer can take you anywhere on the ocean. Rails span the Americas and Europe." Lehrman's voice rose in pitch as well as volume as he expounded the virtues of the modern world. It clearly made him excited just thinking about the endless possibilities for a shrewd businessman like himself. "You'd do well to keep your eye on Cuba, young man. Mark my words: Their rebellion might be the magnet that pulls us onto the center stage of world events."

"You think big, Mr. Lehrman," Allyn flatly observed.

"Precisely. And it has made me a remarkably wealthy man. I intend to do the same for you, Mr. Benedict." Lehrman stroked his double chin. "Now, what do you say to that?"

"That's why I am here," Allyn replied. There was no reason to hide his enthusiasm. This was a goal he had worked toward all his adult life. And now it was finally about to be realized. Now he would come out of the shadow and bask in the light. Artemus Lehrman lifted a leather satchel to the table, unbuckled the flap, and removed a set of documents.

"I think you will find everything in order. Congress is

pleased with the arrangement. Once the reservation is termi-
nated, ownership of the northern oil fields will be transferred
to Benedict Exploration and Development, a subsidiary of
Prairie Oil and Gas. My company agrees to underwrite the
payment of a lump sum to be distributed to the tribe for the
benefit of all parties concerned. Read the documents at your
leisure. However, I can assure you . . ."

"My son and I are in no hurry," Allyn replied as he took a
seat by the desk. Donning his reading spectacles, he began to
study the papers in earnest.

"Your father is a shrewd man," Lehrman said with a glance
in Clay's direction.

"Read this with me, son," said Allyn. "Better that you become acquainted with the business. After all, one day it will
be yours."

Clay left his position by the door and joined his father behind the desk. The interior of the office was positively stifling,
and Artemus Lehrman was sweating profusely. Clay was also
uncomfortable. A droplet of moisture fell from his forehead
and struck the first page, causing a stain to spread on the
edge of the paper, near a clause outlining the relationship between the formidable conglomerate, Prairie Oil and Gas, and
its newly created subsidiary company, Benedict Exploration
and Development.

Deep within Clay Benedict, layered beneath the demands of
being Allyn's son and his desire to win his father's respect, the
small, quiet voice of his conscience stirred as he read the text
of the contract his father held. By signing these pages Allyn
Benedict was placing his own interests above those of the
Southern Cheyenne, the very people he was sworn to represent. Not that Clay had any love for Tom Sandcrane's people.
What would a bunch of uneducated redskins do with the oil
fields? And besides, each member of the tribe would receive
a cash settlement, that was something. Of course it wasn't
anything near the profits that could be realized from the oil
revenue. Then again, men like Lehrman and his father were
taking the risk of developing the wells, drilling, and market-
ing the oil and ought to be compensated. In the end Clay's innate decency proved frail; he turned a deaf ear to his

conscience and concentrated on the document in his father's hands, though much of the legal language was lost on him.

"The test we ran up on the north tract of the reservation has every indication of being a bonanza," Artemus said. "Yessir, a year from now you'll be a regular King Midas sitting on a throne of black gold." He removed a silk kerchief from his coat pocket and wiped his pink, round features. "I hope there won't be any snags."

Allyn did not reply. He was focused on the contract, carefully scrutinizing every line of text, every correction. And when he at last put pen to paper and signed his name to each draft of the agreement, it was with a sense of elation and, in all honesty, relief.

"We are in the endgame now," Allyn softly said as he handed Lehrman the drafts belonging to Prairie Oil and Gas.

"You play chess? Ah, we must have a game sometime," said Lehrman. The corporate vice president returned the documents to his satchel. Then he leaned forward, the chair creaking beneath his weight, and placed a pudgy hand upon Benedict's copy of the agreement. "Remember: Endgames can be very tricky. They can wind up a draw. Then nobody wins."

"Not this time."

"Let us all hope you are not overconfident, Mr. Benedict."

Allyn chuckled aloud, then nodded to his son, who rose and headed for the door. The Indian agent followed, after tucking the contract into his inside coat pocket. He paused in the office doorway, leaned a forearm upon the doorsill, and turned back toward the businessman, who had resumed fanning himself by the window.

"On this board," Allyn replied, "I control all the pieces, down to the very last pawn." He patted his coat pocket and the papers that were the summation of his dreams, then vanished into the burning glare of the afternoon.

Out in front of the office, Clay untied his horse from the hitching rail. Allyn draped an arm across his son's shoulder and leaned forward to speak softly, allowing no one else to overhear.

"You ought to be able to reach Panther Hall by dusk. Tell Jerel Tall Bull it is time. Tell him he must be finished no later than the thirty-first of August. We must have the oil fields completely staked out, just in case some senator tries to make trouble for us down the road. This way the land will have been claimed by our company under the Land Rush Act. Do you understand?"

"The thirty-first," Clay repeated. He hurried over to his horse and vaulted into the saddle, showing remarkable skill for a Yale man, even one who had been expelled from school. He glanced in his father's direction. "Father . . ."

"What is it now?" Allyn sounded exasperated. "Look. Just do what I say when I say it. I'm going to make something of you, boy, never fear."

Clay stammered a moment, struggling to give voice to his thoughts. It had been Allyn's idea he attend Yale and become a lawyer. The task had been beyond him. Sure, he wanted to be wealthy, but there were other emotions warring within him, too. Yet today, beneath his father's withering stare, he could find no voice of his own. Clay touched the brim of his hat and, pointing his mount west, cut a straight line across the parade ground and onto the road to Cross Timbers. Allyn Benedict watched him depart, and in a few minutes the solitary rider was lost in the shimmering haze.

CHAPTER SEVEN

WRAITHLIKE CLOUDS DRIFTED ACROSS A NIGHT SKY AWASH with stars. Death had freed these windblown "souls" from earthly bondage and set them on a course to the All-Father: They paid no heed to the couple on the porch below but sped silently on their way, traversing the black velvet sky on a southeasterly course that eventually carried them beyond the hills.

Tom and Emmiline stood arm in arm, between two shafts of lamplight that filtered through the shuttered windows. Within the house Allyn Benedict was relaxing in the front room, his attention focused on a recently acquired geologic survey of the territory. Margaret Benedict was voraciously making her way through the correspondence that Allyn had brought from Fort Reno. Many of the letters had been misplaced by the local postal clerk and left to gather dust at the fort for the better part of August. Margaret Benedict wouldn't rest until she had personally replied to each and every missive from home.

"Do you envy them?" asked Emmiline Benedict, nestled in the crook of Tom's right arm.

"Do I envy who?" said Tom.

"The clouds. They go where they want. They see it all and move on. So peaceful. Never knowing hurt or sorrow . . ."

"Or joy," Tom said. "No. I'd rather be alive and take my chances. Besides, I go where I want. So can you."

"Do you think so? Father has his plans for my brother and me. Big plans and great expectations." She sighed and reflected a moment. "He named my brother right. Clay. Easy to shape into whatever Father wants him to be."

Tom couldn't help but notice a hint of bitterness in her voice. Allyn might be ambitious, but he seemed no more overbearing to Tom than most fathers with a daughter sweet as a plum hanging ripe and tender on the vine. "What plans?"

"By the way, you owe me an apology for this afternoon," Emmiline replied, smoothly changing the subject before she inadvertently discussed her father's business. One casual remark could endanger all her father's hard work. "You missed a wonderful picnic. I guarantee you would have enjoyed yourself."

"I do indeed apologize," said Tom, allowing himself to be steered away from the topic she herself had begun.

"What got into you, riding off like that? One would think you had seen a ghost."

"Maybe I did," Tom said, remembering the dust devil. He was still troubled by the experience. It was a wind, he told himself, nothing more, just the heat currents rising from the ground. And the voices ... merely the product of his imagination.

"Oh, dear. You wipe that expression off your face right now, Tom Sandcrane. You look as if you're about to bolt again. Am I as frightening as all that?" Emmiline pressed against his side, her curves against his ribs, an enticing pressure. Maybe not frightening, he thought, but she made him nervous as all hell.

On returning to Cross Timbers from Panther Hall, Tom had ridden straight for Allyn Benedict's house, where he had a standing invitation to Sunday dinner, leaving Seth to worry over the mauled hound draped over the rump of his horse. Margaret Benedict always cooked more than enough, and tonight Tom found the Indian agent's company preferable to Seth's. He was still chafing at his father's hostility. The next time, Tom swore he'd ignore those damn voices in the wind, and if Seth's fat was in the fire, then so be it—let him stew in his own juice.

A carriage rolled out of the dark and wound its way up the road from the settlement. The vehicle pulled to a halt before the porch, and Father Kenneth peered around the edge of the leather cover. Moonlight glinted off the silver hair of Luthor White Bear, who was seated beside the priest in the carriage.

Father Kenneth was a stocky, good-natured man in his early fifties. His close-cropped blond hair was in retreat from his wide forehead; the inevitable hair loss would leave him bald by the time he turned sixty. A bushy blond beard and mustache and thick, round wire-rim eyeglasses were the significant features of this kindly man's face. Belonging to the order of Capuchins, he wore a hooded brown robe over his shirt and Levi's. A rope belt, from which usually dangled an assortment of carpenter's tools and a rosary, circled his waist. The priest's skills with hammer and saw and his willingness to use them for the benefit of the local Cheyenne had endeared him to the tribe. Father Kenneth was a man who preached by doing, but Sunday was a day of rest for the priest, and the tools of his former trade were back at the rectory.

"Evening, Tom. Miss Emmiline."

"Evening, Father Kenneth," Tom said, doffing his hat. He nodded as his gaze slipped from the priest to Luthor White Bear, the Keeper of the Sacred Arrows.

Luthor was the sole proprietor of the Cross Timbers mercantile. He was an ambitious and successful merchant who anticipated making even greater profits once Cross Timbers became a thriving town and not a mere reservation settlement. The merchant dreaded that others should think of him as just another tame Cheyenne, lumping him together with the rest of the tribe. He considered himself a man of substance and was determined to remain that way when the lands were open to homesteaders and townsmen.

"We're looking for my daughter," Luthor explained. Charlotte, his fifteen-year-old, was a wild and willful young woman who enjoyed the effect she had on men. "My wife, Rebecca, found her bedroom empty and her window open. I think she is out with that half-breed, Willem. Since he is a friend of yours, I thought you might know where they've gone."

"Luthor here is quite concerned, as you can see," said Father Kenneth. "I've tagged along to calm him down." The priest climbed out of the carriage and worked a cramp out of one of his legs.

"I *am* calm," Luthor growled. "But I instructed that daughter of mine to remain home. After all, she spent most of the afternoon with the half-breed. If he has taken her out to Panther Hall . . . !"

"Willem would not do that. The tribal police have no use for the Tall Bulls or their roadhouse." Tom studied the hilltop west of the settlement, then returned his attention to the man in the carriage. Father Kenneth sauntered over to stand alongside him.

"What is it, Tom? What do you see?"

"Luthor, were you up by the Council House this morning?" Tom asked.

"No. I do not think it is necessary for the Sacred Fire to be lit and the songs sung every morning. See, the world has not ended," Luthor said with a chuckle. Intrigued by Tom's question, he craned his head around the side of the carriage.

"Then you did not leave a ceremonial fire burning?" Tom asked.

"Absolutely not," Luthor blurted out. "Why do you ask?" He glanced toward the hill and for the first time saw what had attracted Tom's attention. Sandcrane had noticed it while keeping Emmiline company on the porch: an orange-red tongue of fire flickering on the hilltop. Someone no doubt enjoying the view while warming before a friendly campfire. One couldn't ask for a more romantic spot than Council Hill.

"Damn!" Luthor kicked off the brake and slapped his whip across the rump of his horse. Tom and the priest were left in a cloud of dust as the carriage sped away from the agent's house. The commotion alerted Allyn Benedict, who emerged from the house to discover for himself what was going on.

"Is everything all right out here? Oh, Father Kenneth. Welcome." The agent glanced in the direction of the departing carriage.

"That was Luthor White Bear, Papa," Emmiline explained. "He seems in quite a hurry."

"No matter how fast he goes, he'll never catch up to Charlotte," Tom said.

"Perhaps," Father Kenneth said. "But mark my words, time has a way of slowing us down, even the restless ones like Luthor's daughter." He patted the dust from his robes. "Good evening, Allyn. You're looking fit. Sorry if we disturbed you. I ran into Luthor at the stable and tagged along thinking I might be able to help the man rein in his temper." Father Kenneth sighed. "Raising a child is like trying to hitch a wild mustang to a surrey. It's a thankless task. Well, if you'll excuse me, I'll just walk on back to the church."

"You're welcome to stay for coffee, Father," Allyn said.

"Thank you, but no," the priest replied.

"Emmiline, it's probably time you came inside."

Emmiline frowned at her father and stuck out her lower lip. "Oh, Papa, just because Luthor left here in a huff."

"It is getting late. I'll walk with Father Kenneth," Tom said, defusing an argument before it occurred. He touched the brim of his hat and bowed slightly in a gallant farewell to Emmiline. "Thanks again for dinner."

"You are always welcome here, Tom," said Allyn. "And don't forget, we're going to plan a sure-enough celebration marking the end of the reservation. The whole tribe will be invited to join in." He stood aside and held the door open for his daughter. Emmiline sighed and retraced her steps into the house. Her mother glanced up from her lap desk, smiled at her daughter, and then resumed writing.

"Uncle Maynard has invited you to visit their family in New Haven. How would you feel about that, dear?"

Emmiline didn't answer. The living room was an all-too-familiar sight. The space was crowded with furniture, the papered walls festooned with photographs of family, and chromolithographs depicting a variety of autumnal landscapes and picturesque New England towns, none of which held any appeal for Margaret's daughter.

Emmiline slumped dejectedly on a well-padded cane-backed couch and considered the invitation her mother had read. Uncle Maynard was a middle-aged professor of literature, a student of antiquities, a stuffy, humorless man with a dour-looking wife. New Haven? Never.

Allyn entered the room and closed the front door, then crossed to the nearest window and parted the curtains ever so slightly to watch Tom and the priest proceed down the path to the settlement. Tom was leading his horse. The priest had no mount.

"What is it, dear? You were nervous as a tick all through dinner," Margaret observed without looking up at her husband.

"Nothing. Things have begun." He looked at his daughter. "What did you and Tom talk about?"

"Nothing that concerns you," Emmiline replied. "We just talked."

"I hope you were careful," Allyn said. "Not that there is anything Tom could really do. It is out of his hands now."

"It doesn't seem right," Emmiline said. "I mean, Tom Sandcrane has been a special friend."

Allyn Benedict walked across the living room to a triangular table of burled walnut, upon which rested a decanter of pear brandy, another of Kentucky Bourbon, and four glasses. He poured a measure of brandy for himself and returned to his rocking chair.

"You act as if I wish him harm," the Indian agent replied. "On the contrary, Tom will have his place on Coyote Creek. I've put that in the map. He'll be well rewarded for all his efforts. Satisfied?"

Allyn Benedict took a sip of brandy and sighed as the warmth spread through him. He thought of Luthor White Bear. Now, there was a man with an entrepreneurial spirit. Yes, the merchant would do well as the town grew. Charlotte, though, was quite the little temptress. Once, she had visited the BIA office on an errand for her father and found Allyn alone in his office. The young girl's visit had certainly aroused a few illicit fantasies in the Indian agent's mind. Allyn sipped his brandy and sighed. Changing his line of speculation, he wondered what was keeping Clay, then decided his son must have remained at Panther Hall to have a drink. What the devil, why not celebrate? *Benedict Exploration and Development.* Oil. Black gold. Now, there indeed was the stuff of which dreams were made.

Tom Sandcrane sat quietly in the humble little church and watched Father Kenneth secure the windows and sweep away the caked mud someone had tracked in front of the alter. The crucifix upon the rear wall bore an image of suffering that seemed to return Tom's scrutiny with eyes of sympathy and shared heartache.

"I get the feeling you and Seth have locked horns again. Well, there's an extra bunk in the rectory," Father Kenneth said with a sigh. He always referred to the drafty cabin out back as the rectory; it seemed more official that way. The log walls might need chinking and the roof tended to leak during a rain, but there was nothing wrong with the place that couldn't be fixed. He anticipated a bigger church and a real house when the settlement became a thriving town.

"No, that would be too easy. That ungrateful old basta—uh . . . man isn't going to keep me out of my own bed. Anyway, he'll be too busy tending to General Sheridan to worry about me." During their stroll down Main Street, Tom had entertained the priest with a brief account of the afternoon's events. The retelling helped cool Tom's temper.

"I'm sorry for Seth," Father Kenneth remarked. "In a way, his decline is partly my doing. I was the one who insisted you go off to the Indian school at Fort Reno. Seth never understood." The priest sat on the front pew and dangled a thick forearm over the back of the bench seat.

"They used to punish me every time I spoke Cheyenne," Tom ruefully chuckled. The rules, though well meant, seemed harsh and unfair, and yet because of them he had learned to speak fluent English. Reading had also opened up a whole new world to him, shattering forever the narrow confines of the reservation.

"I am sorry," the priest said. "Sister Jean Marie can be a harsh taskmistress."

"Don't be. You just wanted me and the other children to have a chance. Maybe there are better ways, but at least I have an education." Tom slowly stood and started toward the door. He feigned a yawn.

"Was there something I could help you with?" said the priest as Tom paused in the doorway. Nothing fooled him. "After all, I could have found my way home without your help."

Tom shrugged. "I wanted to ask you a question. It seems silly now."

"Ask anyway."

"You have lived among us a long time," said Tom. "Have you ever heard the wind speak?"

The priest's eyes widened. He set aside his broom, stepped down from the altar, and sat upon the nearest bench. "Well, now. The wind . . . indeed." He folded his hands as if in prayer and chewed on his lower lip as he pondered his reply.

"Never mind." Tom said, embarrassed at asking such a foolish question. "Good night, Father Kenneth." He stepped through the doorway and vanished into the night.

The priest called him back, but to no avail. Alone in the stillness of the church, the man of God communed with the emptiness forever lurking on the fringe of his own devotion. Oh, how he envied a man who had heard the wind speak.

CHAPTER EIGHT

THE HORSEMAN BY MOONLIGHT KEPT TO THE TREES AND hugged the shadows, cautiously approaching the settlement. The ride from Panther Hall had been long and tedious, but necessity had forced John Iron Hail to check his backtrail every few minutes, pausing in the darkness to listen for any sound of pursuit. Apparently his absence had not been noticed. But the seventeen-year-old wasn't taking any chances. He skirted the settlement, to avoid the empty streets of Cross Timbers, and studied the cabins on the hillside south of Main Street until he found the one belonging to Seth Sandcrane. A lantern burning in the barn cast a pool of amber light through the open doorway. It was the only sign of life in all the sleeping settlement.

What time was it? John Iron Hail guessed it was somewhere between two and three in the morning. He wondered who was in the barn and hoped it was Tom. *Then I can say my piece and get on back before Pete Elk Head or one of the Tall Bulls misses me.*

He cut across the east end of the road leading into the settlement, then struck a course directly toward the Sandcrane cabin. He kept to a wheel-rutted path that decades of use had worn into the hillside, riding unnoticed among the silent houses whose occupants were deep in slumber and oblivious to his passing. He reined in his horse and dismounted in front of the corral, draping his reins over the top rail of fence. Again John hesitated; this time he was loath to enter the pool of light, fearing to make a target of himself. Minutes crawled past as he debated how best to approach the situation. Finally he edged along the corral, stepped around a horse trough, and, avoiding the lantern-lit doorway, stole along the side of the barn until he came to a window that was missing half a shutter. The barn wasn't much—four stalls and a tack room barely wide enough for a man to turn around in. Tilting his hat back on his forehead, John peered in through the window. The sound of snoring carried to him even as he spied Seth Sandcrane asleep in the straw. The former Keeper of the Sacred Arrows, a man once looked up to and held in high esteem, was stretched out on a bed of hay, a bottle of corn whiskey nestled in the crook of his arm. General Sheridan lay in another stall. The animal had apparently survived its injuries, for its bandaged sides rapidly rose and fell with every breath.

John cursed his luck and retreated a step, backing into the business end of a Winchester carbine. He gasped, his brief existence passing before his eyes. He held out his hands to show that he carried no weapon. The young intruder's voice trembled as he spoke.

"Don't kill me, Jerel. You got this all wrong."

"What have I got wrong, John?" said Tom Sandcrane in a voice barely above a whisper. "I heard the horse. And saw you dismount. Is it Tall Bull's mischief you're up to?"

John breathed a sigh of relief and lowered his hands as he turned. Tom, clad only in Levi's, gave him some room and brought down the Winchester, though he gripped it loosely in his right fist and could bring it to bear if needed. John continued around to the back of the barn in an effort to avoid even the window's feeble glare, and came to rest in the shadow of a buckboard whose left front axle was propped up on a thick log. A wheel without an iron rim lay on the ground in a patch of weeds. A spider had strung its web from the underside of the wagon box to the singletree.

Iron Hail's behavior piqued Tom's curiosity, and he followed him, barefoot, over to the buckboard.

"Did Jerel send you?" Tom asked.

John nervously chuckled. "That's who I thought *you* were. He'd carve out my liver and eat it if he knew I was here talking to you." The youth nervously surveyed his surroundings. "Listen to what I have to say. And I'll call you a black liar if you ever tell I was here."

Tom was still drowsy and trying to make some sense out of this clandestine visit. He leaned a naked arm against the wagon box. The roan whinnied and Tom gave a start, his gaze darting to the corral. John Iron Hail's anxiety was infectious.

"Clay Benedict showed up at Panther Hall late this afternoon. He met with the Tall Bulls and then stayed around for a poke. Jerel called in me and Pete Elk Head and laid out a plan for Curtis and Pete and me to begin staking claims on the north plains, out where them oil pools smell so bad that the cattle won't graze."

"Claims? For who?"

"Curtis was bragging how over a third of the reservation has already been bought up by some outfit called Prairie Oil and Gas. Bought clean out from under the tribe. Me and the others are supposed to set out the claim markers before the land rush next week. That way no one will even try to register on their claims." John wiped his mouth on his shirtsleeve, his lips dry as dust. Tired as he was, the seventeen-year-old was ready to head on back. "You've always played straight with me, Tom. I owe you. Since you helped bring the tribe into this game and sort of cut the deck, I figured maybe you'd want a closer look at the cards."

"No." Tom's voice was soft but emphatic. He scowled, and shot his hand out to catch John by the front of his shirt. "What are you trying to pull?"

"I swear my words are straight," John exclaimed. "It's what I saw. If you have a problem with it, maybe you better ask Clay Benedict or one of the Tall Bull brothers." He managed to wrest himself free, though he tore his shirt in the process.

"This is one of Jerel Tall Bull's tricks. He sent you!" Tom snapped.

"Have it your way," John angrily replied. "But I got work to do." He leaped over the fence, hurried over to his horse, and climbed into the saddle. He patted a canvas bag that hung from the saddle horn, reached inside, and removed a foot-long wooden stake banded with white cloth. He tossed the stake into Tom's outstretched hand. It was evident the youth had plenty to spare. John pointed his mount toward the silent hills and galloped off across the meadow, leaving Tom to stare at the length of wood in his hand. His eyes bored into the claim marker as the blood drained from his clenched fingers. The Southern Cheyenne were supposed to have first claim on reservation lands and designate their allocated acreages on the BIA map. No one, not even a big company like Prairie Oil and Gas, had any business on reservation land prior to the first of September.

Seth's face suddenly appeared in the window. "Who . . . ?" he started to ask. Straw clung to his hair; he wiped a forearm across his pouchy features and struggled to focus on the figure in the night. "Heard . . . something." At last he recognized his own son. "Oh. It's you." A coughing spasm forced him to brace himself on the windowsill. When his body ceased to shudder, he spat in the dust and sighed. "I must have been asleep."

"Me too," Tom said, lifting his gaze from the claim marker to the darkened offices of the Indian Agency office. "Me too."

CHAPTER NINE

THE LOCKED DESK DRAWER IN THE INDIAN AGENT'S OFFICE WAS an open invitation to Tom Sandcrane. He had just broken into the place through the back window and wasn't about to stop now. Using the iron poker from the wood-burning stove, Tom dug at the wood and pried the lock until the front of the drawer splintered and gave way with a startlingly loud crack. He skinned his knuckles on the edge of the desk, muttered an oath, then knelt to examine the drawer's contents—which Allyn had obviously intended to protect. Tom removed a portfolio crowded with papers and sat in Allyn's personal chair below a map of the reservation. Ironically, the first item of interest the Cheyenne encountered was a map, again depicting the reservation, but with one difference from the one on the wall: The land north of Cross Timbers up along the Canadian was already under file and deeded to Benedict Exploration and Development. *Prairie Oil and Gas* was written in parentheses below the name of the company bearing the Indian agent's name. John Iron Hail had indeed spoken the truth. All the oil-rich lands—more than a third of the reservation—were already under ownership and unavailable for claim.

Tom glanced away, heartsick, and found himself staring at the sky through the window he had pried open just moments before. It would be sunrise within the hour. He heard a sound drift in from outside and tensed, wondering if his presence had been discovered. It sounded like footsteps. Tom's fists clenched as he rose from the chair and eased toward the back window, hoping to surprise whoever waited on the other side of the wall. Six feet away, now four, sweat rolled down the side of his cheek, he reached for the windowsill with the idea of peering out at the alley. Silent as a night spirit, a dark shape suddenly bounded from the shadows. Tom's heart jumped to his throat, and he cursed beneath his breath as a black cat with a blaze of white fur behind one ear leaped past him, landed lightly on the floor, and scampered off behind Benedict's desk.

"*Pohkeso,*" Tom muttered. "Where did you come from? You damn near scared me out of my boots." The cat meowed, bounded to a nearby bookshelf, and proceeded to clean a paw. The pounding in Tom's chest gradually subsided, and he returned his attention to the papers he had left in the chair. He tucked the map inside his shirt and proceeded to work through the remaining contents of the portfolio, finding the preliminary correspondence between Allyn Benedict and Prairie Oil and Gas and the official agreement that set up the agent's company as a subsidiary of the larger corporation.

Still other papers outlined how a lump sum was to be paid to the tribe in cash on the first day of September, when the Southern Cheyenne reservation would officially cease to exist. The corporate payments amounted to three hundred dollars for every Cheyenne male head of household. No doubt the corporation considered this a generous compensation, but Tom knew it was a pittance compared to the profits to be made from the oil reserves. That the arrangement had been finalized without tribal approval made him all the more furious. A sense of betrayal welled up in his heart. Using Tom's influence to pave the way, Allyn Benedict had sold out the very people he was supposed to represent and put himself in line to make a fortune.

Jerel Tall Bull must have known. Tom wondered what odious agreement Allyn had made with the proprietor of Panther Hall. Even now the Tall Bulls and their hirelings were claiming tribal lands for Benedict. No wonder the brothers had been given free rein by the Indian agent to operate Panther Hall with impunity, despite the fact that the sale of alcohol was forbidden on the reservation. Allyn Benedict had been forced to turn a blind eye or risk losing his Cheyenne accomplices.

"He didn't need to buy *me* off," Tom muttered to the silence. "Allyn recognized me for a blind fool." He stood and savagely kicked the drawer shut with a loud bang, startling the cat on the bookshelf. The frightened animal sprang out of the shadows and landed on the desk, brushing against the oil lamp and sending it crashing to the floor. The glass reservoir shattered, spilling lamp oil that instantly ignited. Tom leaped aside too late. His trousers caught fire as the oil spattered his legs. Instinctively, he darted into the outer office, grabbed an oval throw rug from the floor, and slapped his legs with the heavy woven fabric. The effort was successful but proved to be a costly delay. By the time Tom had finished with his smoking trouser legs, the office was nearly engulfed. Nevertheless, he hurried back to fight the flames and reached the doorway in time to catch a glimpse of the cat as it disappeared through the office window, a patch of black against a blazing backdrop.

"My father was right about you all along!" Tom shouted at the feline. Indeed, Pohkeso the trickster had worked her mischief after all.

Using the rug to smother the flames, Tom tried to beat a path to the desk. For a moment the Cheyenne thought he might succeed. Then the fringes of the rug began to smolder, and seconds later it ignited. He fought valiantly, but in vain. Flames blistered his cheeks, smoke stung his eyes and filled his lungs, searing his throat as he gulped for air. He tossed the rug aside and stumbled back, choking as he went. Too late. Too late. He staggered from the room, patting out his singed shirtsleeves as he headed for the front door, remembered it was padlocked, and altered his course. He opened the window and swung a leg over the sill. The portfolio! He shot a glance over his shoulder. A wall of flames barred him from returning to the Indian agent's office. Tom patted the map inside his shirt with a soot-blackened hand. At least he had something, some proof. But how to use it? He could track a deer, but the mission school had never taught him to follow a trail through the courts. Outrage burned within him as fierce as the blaze he left behind, fueling him, blocking his need for sleep. Rest must come later, much later. Now it was time to confront Allyn Benedict.

It was a ritual as constant as the changing seasons. Allyn Benedict rose early, before sunup, dressed in his woolen trousers, collarless shirt, and square-toed black shoes, and made his way to the kitchen. He stoked the embers in the cast-iron stove, added a few chunks of wood to feed the flames, then began to grind the coffee while he checked to see if enough water remained from last night to fill the black iron coffeepot. He hand-ground the correct amount of coffee and added it to the pot, then took a seat, stretched out his long legs, and waited for the water to boil and the aroma to fill the house. The contract he had signed with Artemus Lehrman lay upon the table. In the gray light he unfolded the document and began once more to read its contents. Again a feeling of accomplishment swept over him. Benedict Exploration and Development, as a subsidiary of Prairie Oil and Gas, now owned the reservation oil fields. If he felt a twinge of guilt, he immediately corrected the matter with a thought. After all, the situation justified his recent actions. The tribe lacked the expertise and business sense to develop an oil field. Let them run their cattle and tend their farms along the Washita. If it hadn't been Allyn Benedict, someone else would most certainly have come along and done the same thing, securing the ownership of the reservation lands. At least the Southern Cheyenne would always have jobs with Allyn in charge of things.

The agent's son, Clay, opened his bleary eyes, coughed and scratched, and rolled off the couch in the front room, where he'd been sleeping. Spying his father, Clay sauntered into the kitchen, yawning as he walked. His rumpled trousers and shirt looked slept in. A crusted-over scratch marred his right cheek from midear to the corner of his mouth.

"When will the coffee be ready?" he asked in a thick voice.

"Apparently not soon enough," Allyn said. "I waited up for you as long as I could last night. Was there trouble at Panther Hall?"

"No problems," Clay said. "The Tall Bulls will handle their end of the deal. I just got kind of delayed on the way home."

"Dallying with some young lady, no doubt."

Clay shrugged and managed a smug little chuckle that gave his father the impression he had identified the reason for his son's late return. It certainly sounded better than the truth. In reality Clay Benedict had drunken himself into a stupor and fallen off his horse not once but twice. A daggerlike branch was responsible for his wounded features. It was only by the grace of God he hadn't broken his neck. He frowned at the coffeepot for not hurrying itself along, groaned and rubbed his throbbing temples, and decided perhaps a lungful of fresh morning air would ease the hammering in his skull.

Clay rounded the stove and continued unsteadily over to the kitchen door, worked the latch, and made his way outside. There was a patch of shade on the west end of the house, so he made his way around front only to be brought up sharply at an astonishing sight that sent him charging toward the front of the house. He nearly knocked the door off its iron hinges as he burst into the front room and shouted his news.

"Fire! My God, the agency's burning to the ground!" His cry of alarm galvanized his father into action and sent the rest of his family stumbling from their beds. Allyn dropped the contract onto the table and headed into the living room.

At the rear of the house Emmiline bolted awake, climbed out from beneath her bedcovers, and hurried across the room. She tore aside the curtains and shoved her head through the open window, looking toward town. Sure enough, the office of the Bureau of Indian Affairs was consumed in flames. Tongues of fire lapped greedily along the false front and traveled the length of the roof. Fortunately, the building stood apart from the other structures that made up the settlement: the mercantile, the corral and blacksmith shop, and St. Joachim's Church.

The sun was up, bathing the wooded hills in golden light, but the bright-blue summer sky bore a sooty trail of black smoke that poured from the rapidly disintegrating structure. Emmiline ducked her head inside and, grabbing a robe from the foot of her bed, darted into the hall, nearly colliding with her mother, who had also been roused by Allyn's outcry. They reached the front room as Allyn Benedict bolted out onto the porch.

"What the hell is this?" he blurted out. As the alarm spread from cabin to cabin, the inhabitants of the settlement flocked to the street; men, women, and children, both the old and the young, made their way down the hillsides. No one attempted to save the BIA office. It was useless to combat the flames. There was little anyone could do; the fire was too far along. Although no other building was in immediate danger, a bucket brigade was formed to wet down the sides of the government warehouse from which every two weeks rations of sugar, flour, and stringy beef were doled out to men who had once been the lords of the plains. For many of the Cheyenne, the early-morning blaze was an exciting event to be viewed with curiosity and speculation. Perhaps the children were most thrilled by all the commotion. They began to jump and dance and chase one another up and down Main Street.

Luthor White Bear and his comely daughter, Charlotte, appeared on the wooden walkway in front of the mercantile. Another group of Cheyenne led by Father Kenneth joined Coby Starving Elk in front of his corral. Dogs howled and barked and tried to call attention to the fire, only to be driven off by a few accurately tossed stones. Willem Tangle Hair and several other young men arrived on horseback, dismounted near the office, and began to form a second bucket brigade in front of the BIA only to be driven back by the flames.

"Damn. The whole building's finished," Clay said. "What about the contract you signed with Prairie Oil and Gas?"

"It's in the house," Allyn snapped. He stood with hands on hips and watched with morbid fascination as the flames continued to engulf the office. "How could this happen?" he asked aloud. Emmiline and her mother moved up alongside the agent, the family arranging themselves in a rough line across the front yard.

"Never mind, Mr. Benedict, it's no great loss," a voice called out from behind them. "Anyway, you'll need a big new office to handle your company's business."

Allyn whirled around at the sound of his name and saw Tom Sandcrane standing on the front porch. He had entered the house through the kitchen door as the Benedicts hurried outside, distracted by the blaze in town. Tom held up the contract Allyn had left on the kitchen table. The Cheyenne's trouser legs were singed black. His hands and face were streaked with soot.

"Benedict Exploration and Development . . . that has an impressive ring to it."

"What are you doing, Tom? Put that down." Color crept to the agent's cheeks. His eyes widened with understanding. The condition of Tom's clothes told him all he needed to know. "Dear Lord, the fire is your doing. Why?"

"Because he's a crazy drunk like his father," Clay said, and lumbered forward with his fists clenched, his own misgivings about his father's transactions momentarily forgotten in the excitement of the moment. His family was under attack; nothing else mattered. Tom suddenly brandished the claim stake like a dagger and fixed Clay in a stone-cold stare that brought the younger man to a halt. This Cheyenne was in no mood to trifle with the likes of the agent's headstrong son. With Clay in retreat, Tom held the contract up to the front door and skewered the pages, driving the claim stake through the document and into the door. Then he reached inside his shirt and produced the map he had removed from the Benedict's desk.

"I found this map in your desk, Allyn. Funny thing, it's entirely different from the one you kept on the wall. I also found letters and contracts. They were all very interesting. Unfortunately the fire's claimed them. But maybe, just maybe, I can find someone to stand against you."

"Look. I can explain this," Allyn said. "I wasn't just thinking of myself."

Tom stepped down from the porch and trembling with

barely suppressed rage, advancing on the Indian agent. Allyn Benedict was no coward. He stood his ground, strong in the conviction he had done nothing wrong.

"See here, Tom, I've taken care of you. That stretch of land along Coyote Creek you always fancied. Look on the map. It has your name on it. And as for the oil grants . . ."

There was no reasoning with the Cheyenne. The agent could see that his words weren't reaching past the cold fury in Tom's eyes. In that moment Allyn Benedict glimpsed the warrior's heart that the mission school had never fully tamed. Tom Sandcrane was past talk; he had come for revenge. But he hadn't counted on Emmiline Benedict. One moment she was standing off to the side, and the next she was between her father and Tom, blocking his attack.

"No. Stop this!" she said.

His fingers were blistered and burned. Black sweat streaked his features. His neck was seared where a fragment of burning rug had fallen on him and left a nasty wound. Yet the wounds were nothing compared to the pain of betrayal.

"When did you know?" Tom asked, his gaze boring into the woman.

"Dammit man," interjected Allyn. "Don't think to paint me a villain. This is business. The tribe will thank me one day. And you too, my lad. I won't forget your people."

"When did you know?" Tom repeated, ignoring her father's remarks.

"All along. From the onset." Emmiline refused to avert her eyes. She wasn't proud of her father's actions, but she was determined to stand by him. And after all, she shared his desire for wealth. What would the Cheyenne do with those oil fields, anyway?

Tom nodded and slowly exhaled. The fight left him on the wings of a sigh. He looked at Allyn. Margaret had already hurried to his side. Clay was lurking off to the side, curiously unable to meet Tom's gaze. Emmiline stood before him, saddened yet defiant. "Father only means . . ."

Tom reached up and placed a finger on her lips and shook his head. "No more lies." Then he walked past them and down the hill, down through the drifting smoke and the ashes of what might have been.

Toward evening, Pete Elk Head rode his lathered, winded mount up to the front of the roadhouse, dismounted, and looped the reins over the hitching rail in front. Hurrying inside, he found Jerel Tall Bull hunched over a table, studying his brother's drawing of a larger, more prosperous-looking gambling hall. Curtis, demonstrating some artistic talent, had rendered the drawing in keeping with his older brother's description.

"Yes, little brother. You've caught it. This is the place we shall build once the territory is opened up. The roustabouts are going to need someplace to let off steam and spend their money. We'll stock Panther Hall with plenty of whiskey and gambling tables, and Red Cherries there will run the whores and keep 'em in line. They'll beat a path to our doors."

Curtis's eyes lit up at the prospect. "Sounds right good to me." Before he could expound further, Pete Elk Head interrupted the conversation.

"Mr. Jerel, I got news."

Jerel turned and pursed his lips, fixing his young hireling in his dark and steady gaze. "Well . . . ?"

"Tom Sandcrane's gone plumb loco. He burned down the BIA office in Cross Timbers and attacked Mr. Benedict. Then he took off. There's talk of him being arrested if he stays on the reservation."

Jerel slid back from the table and stood. He seemed to be staring right through Pete, as if suddenly focused on a distant goal, something once unattainable that had now moved within his grasp. Even Curtis looked puzzled.

"What is it? What the hell do we care about Sandcrane?"

Jerel ignored him and strode briskly to the front door, flung it open, and faced the sunset, the red rays lighting a path that seemed to beckon him. And in his mind a silent, swift prayer formed.

My brother knows nothing of the past, Grandfather. Forgive him. *But I know your story as it was told to me. You who were once the Keeper, the Spirit Singer, I am here. Shall it begin?*

He waited, watched for a sign. The voice in his mind continued. *Tom Sandcrane has broken the Circle. He has turned his back on the power that was his to take. Now he will have to leave. Only Luthor White Bear remains. And I shall deal with him in good time. But I must know, Grandfather. You must speak.*

And, as if borne on the wind of his silent prayer, a hawk glided out of the sunset, its wings bathed in the glow of the setting sun, the bird transfixed and crimson, dipped in the dying light.

"Blood Hawk." Jerel whispered the name aloud, in awe. "Grandfather. You have spoken. Now . . . now it begins."

CHAPTER TEN

"WHERE WILL YOU GO?" ASKED SETH SANDCRANE FROM THE doorway while his son changed clothes, casting aside his blackened, singed garments for a faded work shirt and Levi's, socks and boots. Seth was sober now, though his eyes were red and puffy and his back stiff from sleeping in the barn. He hadn't been surprised to learn of Allyn Benedict's "business dealings," for he had never trusted the Indian agent. But seeing the pain etched in his son's features killed any feeling of vindication. Indeed, the entire episode seemed to refocus Seth from his own bitterness. His son had left before, but this departure was different. It was final.

Tom cupped water from a basin and scrubbed the soot from his face, then poured the contents of the pitcher over his head. He had no need of a towel; the sun would dry him after he was five minutes on the trail. He hesitated, pondering his father's inquiry about his destination.

"Maybe over to Guthrie, or across the Red River. Maybe the Texas ranches are hiring," Tom said, giving the matter only the most perfunctory consideration. "There is nothing for me here."

"In the days before your grandfather, the Maiyun brought us visions and taught us songs, also the coyote and deer, the wolves and bear, the owl and grasshopper. Great was their power. No man who held them in his heart could be killed in battle."

"Then why aren't these mystic warriors still among us?" Tom retorted, heading for a wooden trunk at the foot of his bed. Seth stood just inside the room.

"Men find many ways to die."

"What are you saying now? I grow weary of your empty stories."

"It is you who are empty. You turned your back on the Mahuts, the Sacred Arrows, and broke the Great Circle. Yet you are surprised and wounded when you can no longer walk it." Seth was angry now, and the hammering in his skull that always came the morning after a drunk only shortened his patience. "Turning your back on the Arrows and the songs is a death. Running from the People to follow the white man's road is a death."

"What has happened cannot be undone," Tom snapped. How could he make his father understand that courtrooms were far removed from war parties and horse raids? He had nothing to fight the oil companies with. *Benedict won with the Tall Bulls' help while I played the fool for the Indian agent's daughter.* It was time to face the truth. A day ago Tom had been all puffed up with pride over his role in bringing an end to the Cheyenne reservation. But the bright future he had glimpsed from a distance had proved to be nothing more than an illusion, a shimmering veil of empty promises with no more substance than a mirage.

As Tom shoved an extra shirt and trousers into his saddlebag, he gave brief thought to the worn leather-bound Bible he had used at the mission school. He'd first learned to read from the Psalms. But he left the keepsake where it lay, closed the trunk, and brushed past his father on his way to the living room. General Sheridan, having abandoned the barn, was curled upon the cold hearth, bandages circling his neck and belly. The hound raised his head as Tom entered the room and then settled back, oblivious to the man's departure. Standing in the bedroom doorway, Seth cursed himself for losing his temper again. He had to do better, to think beyond his own hurt, or he would lose his son forever.

Tom grabbed a sweat-stained hat from a post by the door and stepped outside. The curled brim shaded his eyes from the painfully bright sunlight and enabled him to see Willem Tangle Hair standing by the roan Tom had saddled and tethered to the corral fence. The half-breed looked glum, his brows knotted in a frown. His freckled cheeks were sunburned, his clothes soggy and smeared with ashes, the legacy of the bucket brigade. Down in the settlement, the last remaining wall of the BIA office collapsed in a shower of embers and cloud of black smoke.

"I need to talk to you," Willem called out.

Tom headed straight for his friend. He had no choice if he wanted to take the roan. But he sensed trouble. Willem hadn't come to pay a social call.

A bumblebee whirred past, its bloated black-and-yellow body defying gravity as the insect glided and dived on blurred wings. A horned toad, relic of an ancient past, scampered out of harm's way and missed by an inch being squashed beneath Tom's boot.

"Allyn Benedict's ordered your arrest, Tom. For burning down the BIA office. All the other tribal police have been dismissed except me, what with the last days of the reservation and all. So it's my job. And here I am." Willem took a step forward.

"What are you going to do," Tom asked, approaching his friend, "if I refuse to come with you?"

"Well I hadn't thought that far," Willem sheepishly replied, kicking at the dirt. "I kinda hoped I wouldn't find you."

"Turn your back and wait five minutes and you won't."

"What the hell is going on?" Willem anxiously asked. "Did you really set the fire?"

"No," Tom said. "But I don't regret the loss. We no longer need the agent's office. There will be no more rationing, no dry beef and mealy grain for us. We'll make our own way from now on. I've seen to that. And you know what? Nothing will change."

"I don't know what you are talking about," the tribal policeman said, scratching his head.

"You'll find out soon enough," Tom bitterly replied. He

placed his hands on the saddle horn. "Time to fish or cut bait. I'm leaving. What'll it be, Willem?"

"I can't handle any of this," the half-breed growled. "You and Mr. Benedict are friends. And just about everyone figured you and Miss Emmiline would . . ." The look on Tom's face at the mention of the Indian agent's daughter was enough to cut Willem short. Like when a train jumps its tracks, some situations demand a man simply get the hell out of the way. "I'll tell Mr. Benedict I got here too late. And you'd already left."

The half-breed stood aside, permitting Tom to untether the roan from the corral gate and climb into the saddle. As he maneuvered out of the way, Willem inadvertently glanced toward the cabin and realized Seth was cradling a Spencer carbine as old as the Indian Wars. Now that Willem had declared his intentions concerning Tom's arrest, the fifty-caliber carbine was no longer needed. Willem had narrowly avoided lead poisoning.

Seth leaned the carbine against a post and stepped out of the shade. His long braids swayed as he hurried over to his son. Tom checked his stirrups and then looked up as his father approached. Seth reached into a white buckskin pouch and removed a medicine pipe made of wood and red clay. Animals were carved in relief upon the bowl. An eagle feather dangled midway along the length of the pipe's wooden stem. Seth knelt before the horse and drew a line in the dirt with the base of the red clay bowl. And as the pipe cut the dark-brown sod, he who had once wielded the power of the Mahuts chanted in a soft voice.

> "All-Father, my son is leaving.
> See, he has readied his horse.
> His pouch holds food but his
> Heart is empty."

Seth drew a second line and continued.

> "Tomorrow there will be another day.
> Tomorrow there will be light.

Guide him, O Mother. O Father.
I cut the earth at his feet."

Seth drew a third line.

"Lord of mountains, Lord of valleys,
Lord of barren rock and creeping vine.
The Song burns in him
Though he cannot feel the heat."

Seth drew a fourth line in the dirt, then climbed to his feet. He placed the pipe inside the pouch of beaded white buckskin and held it out for his son to take.

"What are you giving me, Father?"

"Mystery. For a life without it is not worth living."

"But these things have no meaning for me," Tom gently explained.

Seth nodded but refused to be dissuaded by his son's rejection. He merely walked alongside the roan and tucked the pipe away in Tom's saddlebag.

"You are the Arrow Keeper. You cannot escape the song. No matter how far you run, it will bring you back."

"Father . . . good-bye." Tom shook his head and walked the roan past Seth, past Willem, and headed toward the southern hills. He intended to cut east once he was out of sight of the settlement.

White oaks and cedars beckoned him with the emerald quiet of their secret places. Time lost all meaning for him. The sting of betrayal, his own conceit, the rage and the regrets—he rode through a gauntlet of these emotions in stony silence. But the sun-washed land embraced him like a willing bride and presented him with one last vision before he left Cross Timbers behind. When he looked to the hills, for a fleeting second Tom spied a fierce Cheyenne warrior, draped in all his warlike glory, watching him from the ridge. The warrior dipped his war lance and pointed it at Tom as a gust of wind brushed its warm breath against his cheek.

"No," Tom whispered, denying the truth before his eyes.

The breeze died. The warrior dissolved, becoming a patch-work of underbrush and shifting shadows.

Seth stood by the corral and watched until his son had rid-den out of sight. When that last visual link was broken and Tom was lost among the trees, the elder turned, realizing Willem had also excused himself and headed back down to the settlement. Seth wiped a forearm across his features and started back to the cabin. His shoulders bowed, Seth Sandcrane regretted having fought so much with his son, though the loss of his honor had wounded him nearly to death.

Seth returned to the cabin and looked down at the carbine, chuckling ruefully. The weapon wasn't even loaded. He searched his memory and tried to recall what he had done with last night's bottle and, after a moment, grinned in satis-faction. He remembered leaving a half-full bottle of whiskey in a bucket below the windowsill. It was still there, the bot-tle's dark, rust-red contents awakening a burning thirst in the man. There was just enough to carry him through another day. He started over to the bottle, retrieved it, popped the cork, and started to take a swallow. Seth never knew why, but he hesitated. Perhaps it was the lingering effects of the Pipe Song he had chanted for his son that stopped him in his spi-ral descent into that private hell he had called home since the loss of the Sacred Arrows. He would never fully understand. But that too was part of the mystery. One moment the bottle was tilted to his lips, and the next, he sent it spinning into the yard to shatter against a stump.

Seth braced himself against the post and the wood groaned, echoing his sentiments exactly as he stared after his son and found, at last, only a faint trace of dust to mark Tom's pass-ing. The prayer was incomplete. He must finish the song.

"Watch my son. Guard him on every path.
These are my words, these are my thoughts.
I may have said too much, All-Father.
Or not enough."

INTERLUDE

CHAPTER ELEVEN

IN THE WINTER OF 1898 THE EYES OF THE NATION FOCUSED ON
Cuba. The temperament of the American populace, fanned
by sensationalistic reports of Spanish atrocities appearing
in the major newspapers, burned white-hot. The leaders of
the Cuban insurrection, men like Maximo Gomez and
Antonio Celestial, were viewed as young Washingtons willing
to sacrifice everything to lead their people in throwing off the
yoke of Spanish tyranny.

It had been over thirty years since Americans had died in
war, littering the battlefields of North and South with the
bones of gallant men. Here was an opportunity for the nation
to rise together as a whole, setting aside animosities and prejudices and the legacy of old grievances to aid the Cuban people in that most noble of causes: Liberty. So the nation
watched and waited, tensions mounting, the clamor to inter-
cede on behalf of the Cubans continuing to swell while the
few remaining moderates tried to stem the tide of interven-
tion, only too aware that the war hawks would need only a
spark to ignite the threat of total commitment. Fate was the
flint.

Cuba, February 15, 1898

At nine-forty in the evening the battleship U.S.S. *Maine* exploded in the harbor of Havana, Cuba, maiming and killing 252 American seamen. About six hundred miles from the scene of this tragic destruction, a smaller blast, but one no less important to the Cuban resistance, occurred in the town of Santiago on the southeast tip of the island. A warehouse on the waterfront, loaded with a precious supply of gunpowder destined to resupply the Spanish navy, exploded with a thunderous boom and shot a ball of fire into the air that lit the docks and woke the residents of the port.

The warehouse, located at the end of the long, wide pier, was instantly reduced to rubble. Jagged shards of timber were strewn across the placid surface of the bay along with the grisly remains of four Spanish guards, members of Captain Diego Zuloaga's own De León Brigade, who were killed outright. The men of the Lion Brigade considered themselves more than a match for any rebels. This was their boast. But Cuban insurrectionists led by Antonio Celestial proved the Spaniards wrong. They entered the city, avoided armed patrols, and destroyed the warehouse along with the startled sentries charged with securing the munitions. Several of the other buildings along the waterfront suffered damage. Windows were blown out, signs toppled, and several small fires were started by flaming debris.

Antonio Celestial vaulted into the saddle and waved for his men to follow him as he headed back through the heart of the settlement. Time was working against them now. The explosion would have alerted Captain Diego Zuloaga, and by now he'd be mobilizing his troops. The element of surprise may have brought the rebels this far, but only speed would carry them to safety. Celestial reminded his companions not to stop until they reached the edge of town. It was understood that any wounded man unable to ride was to be left behind to find sanctuary among the townspeople, most of whom were sympathetic to the rebel cause.

The rebel leader cut a dashing figure in his loose white shirt, tight brown canvas pants, and knee-high black boots. But Celestial's most striking feature was his shoulder-length white hair. It fluttered like a banner in the wind as he finished his harangue and pointed his charger inland. To a man, the rebels turned their backs on the bay and followed their enigmatic leader away from the leaping flames. Celestial chose the most direct route through town, retracing the relatively clear course they had followed into Santiago. But fickle fortune now turned her back on the guerrillas, who managed to cover only a couple of blocks before riding straight into the arms of the enemy.

Fourteen Spanish sailors, rival gun crews from the Spanish battleship *Reina Mercedes* lying at anchor in Santiago Bay, were returning from a night of revelry when the explosion rocked the waterfront and staggered the crewmen, even knocking a couple of the Spaniards off their feet. Dropped rum bottles shattered on the cobblestone pavement; loaves of crusty bread and sacks of melons destined for lockers aboard the Spanish battleship spilled onto the Alameda. Then the sound of approaching horsemen, the clatter of hooves on cobblestone, and a chorus of wild rebel cries filled the night. The gun crews struggled to reassemble their ranks. More than one seaman recognized the Cuban guerrillas and their fiery, white-haired leader on horseback, bearing down on them.

"It's him!" a burly gunner shouted. "A purse of gold for the head of Antonio Celestial!" He unslung his Mauser carbine and worked the bolt, feeding a round into the breech. Outlined against the leaping flames, the Cubans were a fearsome and unnerving sight as they charged the disoriented seamen. The gunner sensed the flagging courage of his shipmates and held his ground, bellowing defiance. His companions, as if feeding on his strength, gathered around him and brought their weapons to bear.

"Viva Celestial!" cried the rebels, and opened fire with their Colt revolvers. The Spanish sailors returned fire with their bolt-action carbines. One of the Cubans lost the top of his head and pitched from horseback, dead before he hit the street. A seven-millimeter slug fanned Celestial's cheek and caused him to wince. Off to his left he saw another rebel, young Felipé, his cousin, grab his side and sag forward over the neck of his mount. Felipe clutched at the mane whipping his neck and managed to remain in the saddle.

The Spaniards outnumbered the Cubans, but they'd been caught off guard. As a series of lesser explosions shook the night, the seamen struggled to contain the guerrillas and put up a proper defense, but their bolt-action carbines had a slower rate of fire than the double-action Colt revolvers Celestial had brought back with him from the United States. The rebels emptied their pistols at a murderous rate and cut a path through the ranks of the sailors. Celestial snapped off his shots with methodical precision. Muzzle blasts blossomed all around him. Suddenly the Spanish gunner leaped out of the throng and, swinging his carbine like a club, delivered a vicious blow to Celestial's lower back, nearly knocking the rebel leader from his mount.

"Now I have you!" the gunner roared as he tried to drag Celestial from horseback. It wasn't every day a common seaman had a chance at a purse of gold, and the Spaniard was bound and determined to keep this opportunity from slipping through his fingers. He tossed his carbine aside and drew a scaling knife from his belt.

Celestial dropped his reins and caught his attacker's knife hand as the gunner attempted to plunge the blade into the rebel's chest. The Cuban guerrilla winced as the blade gashed his flesh, opening a ragged wound. Celestial worked his revolver free, jabbed it into the gunner's throat, and pulled the trigger. The Spaniard was flung backward through an arc of his own blood. He hit the street only to be trampled beneath the hooves of the horses.

The melee lasted a minute and left four sailors dead and another three sprawled in agony, their life's fluids staining the cobblestones crimson. The remaining seamen dived for cover behind a pair of abandoned market stalls and cowered there until the last of the guerrillas galloped off toward the center of town. Then, as the dust settled, the survivors gathered their wounded comrades and invented a story that the crews had been set upon by no fewer than fifty Cuban rebels and, after a brutal battle, had driven them off.

On the outskirts of Santiago, Doctor Joanna Cooper paced back and forth, wearing a path among the peasant's huts, *bohíos,* clustered along a meandering little spring-fed creek that flowed from the side of a nearby hill. The owners of the palm-bark shacks were nowhere to be seen. Here was another enclave of the poor where men, women, and children had been driven off by Captain Zuloaga's soldiers and herded into concentration camps garrisoned by Spanish troops. One such camp lay inland about three miles, just beyond San Juan Hill. The place was unassailable by rebel forces, who had neither the numbers nor the equipment to mount a direct assault against a heavily entrenched army. Mass graves dotting the valleys offered mute testimony to the barbaric conditions under which suspected rebels and their sympathizers were forced to exist within those cruel confines.

Joanna Cooper had talked her way into the camps on more than one occasion, hoping to alleviate some of the suffering. The task had proved overwhelming. As relations with the United States soured, so her freedom of movement within the city became curtailed. Captain Zuloaga continually dispatched his underlings to spy on the woman. And yet, despite the captain's efforts, Joanna had spent the past few months tending not only the poor of Santiago, but many wounded rebels as well. Sometimes even Antonio Celestial himself had spirited the American physician out of the port and into the mountains to tend to his comrades and their families.

"My God, he's pulled it off." Bernard Marmillon, another idealistic doctor and fellow classmate of Joanna's, emerged from the shadows of the palms and stood at her side there on the hilltop. Behind them cooling winds flowed down from the rugged heights of the Sierra Maestra, a range of mountains that blocked the western horizon. The breezes, ripe with the scent of cedar and mahogany and the duskier aroma of lush vegetation, set the branches of the royal palms in motion, black fronds swaying against the stars.

Joanna mopped her brow with a bandanna and then used the cloth to tie back her auburn tresses. She focused on the glow lighting the sky above the waterfront. The daughter of Robert Cooper III was thinner now, and the lines of her face more severe than when she had sat down to Christmas dinner at her father's table in New Orleans almost a year and a half ago. That warm, safe, pampered existence seemed a lifetime away, so far removed from her that it might have been a dream.

"There . . . you've had your wish. We waited to see if Antonio succeeded," said the handsome young physician at her side. "And he has. Now, let's get the hell out of here before Zuloaga comes looking for us. He knows damn well where our sympathies lie." Bernard Marmillon started toward the carriage they had driven out of town to keep their vigil there among the silent hovels. Back at the docks a dutch merchant ship waited for the two doctors to come aboard. With Captain Zuloaga's growing resentment toward the Americans, it had become much too risky to remain on the island.

Marmillon was halfway to the carriage before he realized the woman hadn't budged. He hesitated, backtracked a few steps, then waited, undecided, watching the woman. He was a tall, broad-shouldered man, chronically indecisive, whose hair was beginning to thin on top while the pecan-colored beard covering the lower half of his face continued to flourish. He and Joanna were the last of the original five newly graduated physicians who had journeyed to Cuba to aid in the struggle for freedom by bringing much-needed medical services to the populace. Three of the doctors had not lasted the year, returning home within months of their arrival.

"Dammit, Joanna, are you listening to me? We cannot stay. You know Zuloaga is a man of his word. He told us to leave or suffer the consequences. I'm as brave as the next man, but I won't do anybody any good by dying."

Joanna turned to look at her companion. He was handsome and powerfully built, with sweet ways, and for a time Joanna had even fancied a relationship with him. But the seriousness of their work and the immensity of the suffering she had seen had hardened her emotions and left her no time for romantic notions.

"Now, don't you go looking at me like that, Joanna Cooper. We both agreed it was time to go home. We've done our share. And more, if you ask me." Marmillon kicked at the dirt and shoved his hands into his coat pockets. He began to walk in tight circles, as he always did before taking direct action. It was his way of building up momentum. "Joanna? Goddamn it!"

"Stop cursing, Bernard," the woman said. "We have plenty of time. I want to say good-bye to Antonio."

"Christ almighty! She wants to say good-bye." Marmillon tossed up his hands in despair. He threw his short-brimmed hat onto the ground and kicked it toward the carriage. "What if he doesn't come this way? What if he's dead?"

"He'll be along," Joanna confidently replied. She patted the dust from the hem of the coarsely woven cotton dress that one of her patients had presented to her as a way of thanking the woman for her dedication. The darkness muted the fabric's colorful bands of red, blue, purple, and white. A simple blouse and sandals completed her attire. On casual observation she could pass for one of Santiago's local inhabitants.

"You cannot know that for certain. And don't fool yourself into thinking the Dutchman will wait forever. There are some men who are immune to your charms, shocking as it must be to hear."

"If you are worried, then perhaps you should go on," the woman snapped.

"Oh, fine. And leave you. How should I explain that to your father?"

"He'll understand. You both are so much alike. Why, his middle name is even Bernard, so you'll already have much in common."

"That's not fair," Bernard protested, his cheeks reddening.

"I agree. But it's where we are. Cuba. And there is nothing fair about the things we have seen." The atrocities that occurred in this civil war were permanently etched in her memory.

The hilltop permitted a view of the pouch-shaped bay,

three miles across at its widest part and ringed with the foot-hills of the Sierra Maestra. Other than the Dutch freighter, the remaining ships in the harbor—a battleship, two destroyers, and a gunboat—flew the Spanish flag.

The town itself, a sprawling cluster of single and two-story red-tiled houses, bustled with activity, aroused from its evening lethargy by the explosion on the docks. Joanna glanced aside at Bernard. He had outlasted all the others, save herself.

"Tell me the truth. You never wanted to come here in the first place. Isn't that correct?"

Marmillon retrieved his hat, dusted it off, and smoothed out the brim, then settled it on his head, taking care to cock it at a rakish angle.

"Yes," he admitted.

"My God, then why?"

"I wanted to sleep with you," Bernard sighed, amazed at his own honesty. "After all, I had never met anyone quite like you. I doubt I ever will again. Your passionate convictions—your naïveté—made you all the more attractive."

"Well, then, was it worth all this?"

"Ask me again when we are safely aboard the Dutch freighter and looking over our shoulders at the harbor as we head out to sea."

Joanna nodded, respecting his candor. They had been intimate, but even that seemed in another life. Surrounded by fear and death, they had clung to one another for sanity's sake. Thinking back, Joanna had no regrets, but no desire to continue what had probably been a mistake.

Her thoughts were interrupted by the pounding of hooves and the ghostly arrival of the guerrillas out of the darkness. Joanna stepped into a patch of moonlight. The rebels would be on edge and apt to open fire at shadows. It took a couple of minutes for the horsemen to make their way up the hillside to the abandoned settlement. Joanna looked for and spied the telltale shock of white hair that identified Antonio Celestial. The rebel leader rode in the lead, as was his habit. Joanna could not help but feel a thrill of excitement. Their cause had become hers. Over the months she had earned the respect of men such as these by her acts of courage and selflessness.

Joanna Cooper could probe a bullet wound, set a fracture, and deliver a baby under the most primitive conditions.

She counted the riders as they hailed her and circled their horses in the clearing among the *bohíos*.

"Galagos . . . Montenez . . . ?" she asked.

Celestial shook his head. Then he leaned upon the pommel of his saddle. "You continually surprise me, *querida*. I thought you would be having tea with Captain Schrader by now." His voice was soft and tense, his lips drawn in a thin line. He grimaced as he straightened in the saddle and sat erect. A dark-haired, thirteen-year-old boy by the name of Mateo walked his mount forward. Twin bandoliers crisscrossed his wiry frame.

"*Jefe*, you are hurt. Miss Joanna, he has been wounded."

Joanna hurried forward and reached up to help Celestial down from his mount, but the former schoolmaster waved her aside.

"Be still. Enough of your chattering, Mateo. One of those damn Spaniards clubbed me with his rifle, struck me across the back."

"You need attention," Bernard Marmillon spoke up, arriving at Joanna's side. "There could be damage to the spine."

"Attention . . . ? Captain Zuloaga will be only too happy to oblige if he finds me here." Celestial winced, sucked in his breath, and readied himself for the ride that lay ahead. "You have been a help to us, the both of you. We owe you a debt we can never repay," he said in a gravelly voice.

A groan escaped Felipe as two of his companions dismounted, lashed him to the saddle, then leaped astride their own mounts. Joanna looked from the wounded man to Celestial, and then to Mateo, dear young Mateo, her favorite. A child with the face of an innocent and the hands of a killer. He had witnessed his parents' execution at the hands of the Lion Brigade and spent the last six months exacting a terrible vengeance upon every unwary Spanish trooper he could find.

"I can't do it," Joanna said.

"What are you talking about?" Bernard asked in a worried tone.

"Mateo, unhitch the horse from the carriage," Joanna ordered. "I am going with you."

"Sí. With pleasure," Mateo said with a grin. The youth rode across the hilltop to the carriage and immediately began to free the mare from the harness. When the buckles caught, he used a knife to cut the animal from its leather trappings.

"Wait. Have you completely taken leave of your senses? Joanna . . . !" Bernard stood aghast, arms extended, an expression of disbelief on his face. He looked up at Celestial. "Talk some sense into her. Forbid it."

"I don't think so. We need her," said Celestial, brushing his white mane back from his brown features.

Bernard Marmillon angrily scowled, then glared malevolently at this man who had become the leader of the Cuban resistance around Santiago, a teacher and poet who had been a thorn in the side of Captain Zuloaga for almost two years. "Then you go to hell," said the physician.

"Not until the last Spaniard is driven from my homeland," said Celestial. "After that, well, let the devil have his due."

Mateo returned to the circle, riding the mare bareback and leading his own mount. He had taken the liberty of removing Joanna's medical satchel and a carpetbag from the carriage and had hung them from the saddle.

"I think you will do better with my horse," the youth said.

Joanna nodded her thanks, then turned to Bernard and placed a hand on his arm. He pulled away.

"It's no more than an hour's walk to the waterfront. I'm sorry. Have a safe trip back to the States, and if you see my parents, tell them . . . tell them . . ."

"Riders coming!" one of the guerrillas said, hurrying to rejoin his companions. The man's announcement sent a ripple of tension flowing through the remaining rebels.

"What about this one?" Mateo asked, gesturing toward Bernard with the business end of his revolver. "He has been to our camp in the mountains."

"He has helped us in the past," Celestial firmly replied. "The American will not be harmed. Besides, to betray us would be to betray Joanna as well. I do not think he would wish her blood on his hands." The rebel leader clapped

Bernard on the shoulder and pointed toward one of the deserted huts. "I suggest you hide until the Spaniards have passed." He did not wait to see if the physician followed his advice but walked his mount past Bernard. The remaining horsemen followed him into the night. Only Joanna lingered, and for a moment Bernard entertained the notion she might be reconsidering her choice. Then the moonlight fell across her features and revealed the exhilaration that literally left her trembling.

"Once long ago, at Christmas, the last Christmas I was home, I stood on the shore of Lake Pontchartrain on a cold and misty evening and struggled with my thoughts, wondering if what I was about to do was really and truly . . . right. I was trying to find my way and feeling so terribly uncertain. Then I heard the strangest thing. Drums. Indian drums. And a distant keening wail, like someone singing. Or chanting." She chuckled softly. "I swear I heard them, so faintly, like the voices of spirits. What did tribal drums have to do with Cuba? Don't ask me. But the strangest thing . . . listening to them helped me decide. I knew, deep in my heart, that I had to do this. I had to come to Cuba." Her gaze became centered, and she looked at the man who had worked at her side throughout those dangerous days. "I cannot abandon these people any more than Celestial and Mateo and the others can cease struggling and dying for their cause." She settled herself in the saddle, her eyes shrouded in shadow. "I just wanted you to understand."

"I understand you are quite mad," he said.

"Then God help me," Joanna replied, looking west to the black mountains that had become the stronghold of the revolution. She was drawn to the danger and had never felt more alive in all her life. "For I love it so."

PART TWO

WAY OF A GHOST

CHAPTER TWELVE

Indian Territory, April 2, 1898

H E WAS A CHILD OF THE WIND FOLLOWING A FENCE LINE THAT hemmed in the boundary of an overgrazed pasture on the outskirts of Tulsa. He was a ghost riding through a combustion of electricity and thunder where the ground rumbled underfoot and lightning scored the gunmetal-gray sky and split the heavens with its savage glare. The pummeling rain that glistened on the surface of his slicker had come too late to save this hardscrabble farm he had found. The drought of the previous summer had driven off the homestead's former tenant; nothing remained but a weathered farmhouse, the fire-scarred skeleton of a barn, and a broken windmill that creaked with every sudden gust and pumped its black air, dry as dust, out of the bowels of the earth.

The horseman rode into the mudslick yard and "hello-ed" the farmhouse out of habit, then dismounted and started toward the water trough, though the roan balked and fought his lead. A flutter of starlings erupted from the porch and lost themselves in the downpour as the man took a moment to study the trough, which the spring storms were attempting to refill. He heard the distinctive warning familiar to any plains-man and retreated a step as a rattlesnake, disturbed from its rest by the approaching human, darted its head out from beneath the trough. The reptile, coiled and ready to strike, was a chilling sight. The line rider used his bandanna for a hobble, then left his skittish mount in the yard and walked around the trough to the porch. He tore up a length of one-by-four from the flooring and used this makeshift club to harass the snake until the rattler abandoned the sheltering trough. The rattlesnake left an undulating track in the mud as it headed off toward the barn. With the menacing reptile safely retired, the rider freed his mount's forelegs; the roan cautiously approached the trough, dipped its nose into the few inches of rainwater lining the bottom, and slaked its thirst.

Tom Sandcrane took a moment to survey the homestead through the miniature rivulet pouring from the creased brim of his hat. There wasn't much to see. Vandals and the cruel blast of a previous storm had knocked down whole sections of a weathered fence that haphazardly surrounded a fallow garden where even the armadillos no longer cared to root for food. Pools of muddy water dotted the pasture, and bunchgrass was already beginning to sprout out of the thirsty sod. The pasture would have a good growth this year, but not a single cow remained to lead into the meadow. The main house, framed by a pair of emaciated live oaks, stood stark and empty-looking among the weeds, the front door creaking in the wind, opening and closing, as if inviting him to enter. The windows were partly shuttered, but Tom didn't need to peer inside; he could imagine the interior. Something spare and bleak and desolate. A place of grit and spiderwebs where the wind moaned as it blew through the cracks in the walls and down the remains of a soot-choked chimney, the top of which leaned at a precarious angle and threatened to collapse.

However bleak, the farmhouse offered protection from the fury of the elements spawned by a midspring cold front. The cold swept out of the Staked Plains like a herd of the buffalo that had once roamed the prairie in the days before the *ve-ho-e,* the white men, did, crisscrossing the land with fences, these spider men who tangled the free range in webs of barbed steel.

Tulsa, only a couple of miles to the northeast, wasn't going anywhere. Why endure the punishing downpour? Tom briefly considered sheltering the horse in what was left of the barn's interior, a caved-in, charred structure overgrown with weeds. But then he'd have to deal with the rattler again, so instead he decided to leave the reptile in peace and tethered the roan to a porch rail. The gelding turned his rump to the wind as Tom untied the saddlebags and coffeepot, slid the Winchester from the saddle boot, and ventured inside.

Sandcrane's imagination hadn't been far wrong. The place was empty and cheerless, and mice had left their tracks in the dust and debris littering the floor, but surprisingly enough, some previous traveler had been so kind as to leave a pile of mesquite wood close to the hearth. Tom lost no time in stacking the wood in the fireplace, and before long he was standing with his backside to a cheerful blaze and drying the seat of his britches. He opened a burlap bag containing a blue enamel pot and a tin of Arbuckle's coffee. He filled the pot with water from his canteen, tossed in the last of his coffee, and set it near the flames. There were a couple of scraps of jerky gathering lint at the bottom of the bag and a few hard biscuits left over from breakfast. Hunger was his only seasoning, and he quickly made a meal of what he had. He might find more substantial fare in Tulsa. A stall full of hay and a bait of oats for the roan wouldn't hurt either.

Tom Sandcrane had been drifting aimlessly since the day he had ridden out of Cross Timbers. Allyn Benedict's schemes had taken all the purpose out of him. Tom was angry at the Indian agent and angrier at himself, knowing both pride and his own infatuation with Emmiline Benedict had caused him to betray his people, however inadvertently. The reservation's real wealth and power would go to Benedict and the oil companies. He should have seen it coming. Benedict's trickery had cost Tom his dignity and set him adrift from the tribe. He could never have faced the tribal elders or the other Cheyenne once they realized the oil-rich lands had already been claimed right out from under them. Without family, without a sense of belonging, apart from his own heritage, Tom Sandcrane had indeed become like a ghost, wandering from place to place, never a part of anything, never feeling he belonged.

For six months Tom had taken whatever jobs had come his way. He'd broken horses in Lubbock and ridden fenceline on a spread over by Dumas in the Texas panhandle. Quitting the Dumas job after a quarrel with the range boss, he chose an easterly trail, while keeping on the Texas side of the Red River. Prize money at a Christmas rodeo in Sherman had provided him pocket money for a spell, but eventually it too played out. The headline on a two-week-old copy of the Tulsa *Territorial Register* left on the bar of the Red River Belle Saloon in Sherman, Texas, had given the fiddle-footed young wanderer a direction.

Two days ago Tom had headed up the Texas Road, forded the Red River, and entered the Indian Territory, once the lands of the Choctaw, the Creek, and the Cherokee. Here, too, the reservations had been abolished and the territory opened to homesteaders.

There were rumors that Indian Territory and Oklahoma Territory would one day be combined to form a state. In the event of such a grand occurrence Tom had no doubt but that Allyn Benedict was standing in the wings, ready and willing to perform in the political arena. It could happen. But young Sandcrane no longer cared one way or the other. This ghost, harboring no allegiance to what had been or would be, was caught between the past and the future and condemned to haunt the present. The wind no longer called him by name. Spectral warriors astride painted chargers rode on the periphery of his vision but refused to reveal themselves no matter how quickly he looked, which made their presence all the more infuriating.

"Things will be different in Tulsa," Tom muttered aloud as he added a few extra branches to the fire.

There wasn't much to the farmhouse—four small rooms and a privy out back. An overturned crate served as a makeshift stool. The place, though meager at best, had been someone's dream. *A failed dream,* Tom thought. And that was a subject he knew all about.

He was enjoying his second cup of strong black coffee

when his eyes inadvertently lowered to his open saddlebags and the beaded buckskin pipe bundle Seth had given him. The bundle was ever with him, like his father's recriminations, the symbol of his failure.

What do you want from me? You're clay and wood and nothing else. Maybe a few feathers and some sweetgrass. Old things. Remnants of yesterdays. There is no place in me for you. I can read. I can write. I've seen . . . things, machines, factories. I am not the man you think I am. Certainly Tom Sandcrane's world had changed, indeed he had been the agent—or perhaps the dupe—of that change.

News of the land rush in western Oklahoma reached him shortly after his departure from Cross Timbers, how white settlers hungry for land had swarmed across the former borders of the reservation. An oil boom on the north section of the Cheyenne tract, as it was now called, had caused a lot of excitement along with the man behind the discovery, Allyn Benedict. It appeared the former Indian Agent was prospering. *Emmiline and her father. They clouded my vision with images of a future in which I had no part. They led me like a well-trained show horse.* Every time Tom thought of the agent and his daughter, it was like opening a wound; a dark mood would settle on him, and he would have to move on, rootless as a tumbleweed.

Tom reached into the saddlebag and lifted up the pipe bundle, holding it in front of him. The silence was broken by a flash of light, followed by a rumble of thunder, and an increase in the intensity of the downpour. For one fleeting instant he was tempted to hurl the pouch across the room, to shatter the red clay bowl of the pipe against the wall and be free of it forever. Instead he gingerly placed the pouch aside and dug the Tulsa *Territorial Register* out of his saddlebags, opening it to the front page, to read again the banner that had attracted his attention:

AMERICA MUST FIGHT!

Underneath the banner, the article continued its appeal:

"Notice is given to all young men.
The Spanish Army has thrown down
the gauntlet. Will America rise to
the challenge? Cuba is awash with the
blood of martyrs both American and Cuban.
The *Maine* must be avenged!
A call to arms rings out across the
territory.
Attention! Skilled horsemen, proficient
in the use of firearms and with a longing
for adventure. The First United
States Volunteer Cavalry under the
command of Captain Robert Huston is seeking
recruits. The command will be formed in Tulsa.
The best men of each local militia
as well as those hardy souls exhibiting
talent and expertise may apply to
Captain Huston for permission to join
the ranks. No man proficient with horse
and rifle will be turned away.
Remember the *Maine*!"

Here was the answer for the heaviness in his soul. Here, plain as print, in boldface whiskey-stained type was a promise of glory and adventure, a holy cause, a place far from the southwestern plains and the life that reminded Tom Sandcrane of his failures. He was tired of wandering, of working someone else's land or cattle, tired of breaking someone else's horses. Perhaps he wanted to join for all the wrong reasons; patriotic fervor was the furthest thing from his mind. No matter. Once he had read the jingoistic appeal, he couldn't get Cuba out of his mind. The whole thing seemed incredible and, in its own way, grand. And he was determined to be a part of it.

Tom folded the paper and stared at the flames, losing all sense of time passing. An hour crept by. Maybe a few minutes more. No matter; he was oblivious to everything but the strangely eerie sounds of distant drums and the vision dancing before him in the flickering firelight.

He saw his father there, in the dancing flames, standing among wraiths of smoke. Seth Sandcrane looked as he did in the olden days when he sang the Arrow Keeper's song, and there was a delicate balance of joy and sorrow in his eyes, which in itself is the face of wisdom.

Father, why is there loneliness?

Seth held up a gourd rattle and shook it. There was no sound to accompany the motion of his hand holding the empty gourd. Then Seth inserted a dried kernel of seed corn into the gourd and shook it again, and Tom listened and he knew what loneliness sounded like. Then Seth emptied a handful of seeds into the gourd and shook it back and forth, and the noise was full and jubilant. Only when the seeds were shaken together did the gourd have meaning and a purpose. But to know that, he had to hear the sound of a solitary kernel, the lonely song.

And then the image of his father vanished, leaving Tom alone, in the dusty floor of another dreamer's ruins. The young Cheyenne blinked and rubbed his eyes, yawned and glanced about at the empty room. The blaze in the fireplace needed a log or two. He shook his head, stood, and stretched the stiffness from his limbs, realizing he no longer heard the droning rain, only the precisely regular pattern of droplets plunging from the roofline and spattering the glassy surface of a puddle. He emptied the coffeepot onto the coals and sent a column of steam rising through the chimney.

Tom Sandcrane's thoughts were of departure now. He repacked his saddlebags, pausing once to stare down at the buckskin pouch containing the pipe. Tom reached down for the pouch, then hesitated. *No. I'll never be free. You will always be pulling me back. Let it end here.* He shifted his stance, ignored the pipe bundle, and gathered the rest of his belongings. Staring straight ahead, he walked swiftly across the room and emerged from the farmhouse. The roan whinnied and snorted as if to say it was about time Tom reappeared.

Outside, the fresh-washed air was cool and clean smelling, tinged with the scent of mesquite and buffalo grass. He gulped in great lungfuls like a man who has nearly drowned only to burst through the mud-slick surface of a pond and find his life. It mattered not that gray clouds continued to spring up like dark, angry thoughts. He was moving on, away from the past. A flash of distant lightning distracted him, and Tom noted a shower tracking across the prairie off to the south, but nothing loomed between him and his destination.

I ought to be able to reach Tulsa without a soaking, Tom figured as he tightened the cinch and readied himself for the last two miles of what he hoped would be an uneventful ride. Once again fate intervened: The slap of leather, the jingle of harness, and the moist sound of horse hooves sinking into the mud alerted the wanderer to the fact that he had company. Tom Sandcrane, ever wary of strangers, stepped to the edge of the porch to check his backtrail and spied a pair of men riding the bench seat of a buckboard behind a team of tired mules. The wagon lurched its way through mud holes, swaying its occupants from side to side as the mules plodded toward the farmhouse.

Tom studied the men as they approached. Indeed, he found their clothing of keen interest. Both men, who appeared to be in their late twenties, wore uniforms that consisted of dark-blue woolen shirts, light-blue trousers, brownish hats, gaiters, and dark-brown rounded-toe boots. Canvas cartridge belts circled their waists, loops jammed with thirty-caliber ammunition. Amazingly enough, the two soldiers' uniforms were for the most part dry. Tom figured they had taken shelter beneath the buckboard when the storm hit.

"Howdy," the soldier holding the reins called out as the buckboard rolled to a stop. "The name's Tully Crow. The big sack of guts riding beside me is Sergeant Philo Underhill, First Volunteers." He instantly appraised Tom's features. "Cheyenne, huh? We're mixed-blood Creek."

"Tom Sandcrane," Tom said by way of introduction.

"Lucky you reached old man Sanders's place before the sky opened up. Me and Philo had to wallow in the mud beneath the wagon over 'neath a stand of scrub oak just off the road." Tully Crow was thin as a post, his hair and eyes brown as a squirrel pelt, while a hopelessly large nose loomed from his narrow, clean-shaven features. Philo Underhill, like Tully, was of average height but heavyset, with muscled forearms and thick shoulders. His large, round, puffy-looking eyes gave him a rather sleepy look. Philo was the typical ranch hand, good-natured and capable, with a ready grin and a keen sense of mischief.

"Howdy." He stabbed a thumb in Tully's direction. "Tully here ain't got much use for rank. But I'll learn him different once we reach the encampment." The heavyset man winked.

"We rode clear to Buffalo Springs and couldn't find nobody willing to put on one of these fancy uniforms," Tully Crow explained. "I was certain we'd recruit a couple of the boys from the Slash M." He shook his head, then studied the Cheyenne. "Captain Huston is gonna be pissed with both of us. He's liable to suspect we just taken this wagon and spent our time drunk down by the creekbank, seeing as we got nobody to show for our efforts."

"You have now," Tom said, answering the man's unspoken inquiry.

Tully and Philo exchanged looks, then concentrated on the Cheyenne as if they were both unable to quite believe their good fortune. Tom had the nagging suspicion that these two soldiers had indeed used their tour of the surrounding ranches as an excuse for a drunk. Both men appeared jittery, and Tully's eyes were red from lack of sleep, his cheeks crisscrossed with veins.

"Now, see here ... uh ... Tom," Philo began. "We cannot take just anyone. A cavalryman needs to know his way around horses. Can you ride?"

"Better than either of you in your present condition," Tom replied.

"Hell's bells, Philo, just take a look at his mount. This roan is prime horseflesh. A man doesn't sit an animal like this unless he can ride," Tully spoke up. The smaller man was not about to lose the only recruit they had.

The sergeant grudgingly conceded the point. But if he was going to bring a man into camp, he wanted to be certain that man was a good prospect for the Volunteers.

"Can you shoot?"

"Try me."

Philo Underhill reached behind him and brought out one

of the bolt-action rifles from the wagon bed and passed it over to the man on the porch. "This is a Krag-Jorgensen rifle. It fires a thirty-forty center fire and holds five rounds. Tully, you point out this Southern Cheyenne a target, and we'll see if he can hit it. Two times out of five will do."

"Sure," Tully replied, and with a sweep of his hand snatched the sergeant's campaign hat from his head and tossed it into the air.

Tom snapped the rifle to his shoulder, sighted, fired, worked the bolt, chambered another round, and fired again. The first slug lifted the hat as it started to sink back to earth, the second slug followed the first, ripping through the crown. Three more rounds in quick succession kept the campaign hat dancing in air. However, as the sound of gunfire faded, the target fluttered down into its owner's outstretched hands. Philo stared at the shapeless lump of brown felt that had been his hat, then glared at Tully, who was straining to contain himself.

Tom dropped the rifle into the wagon bed. "The sights need adjustment, but it will do," he dryly observed.

"Yes . . . and so will you," Philo said with a sigh, and tossed the remains of the hat over his shoulder into the wagon bed. "Ride along with us, Tom Sandcrane. Welcome to the First Volunteer Cavalry."

"I'll drink to that," said Tully, producing a smoked-glass bottle from beneath the wagon seat. He popped the cork and took a long pull, then passed the home brew to Philo, who offered it to Tom. When the Cheyenne declined, the sergeant shrugged and helped himself to a drink, gasped and shook his head, muttered something about "the rattlesnake piss gives it body," and then returned the bottle to Tully, who finished the last of its fiery contents. The smaller man smacked his lips, stood in the wagon, and, loosing a war whoop, tossed the bottle out into the farmyard. He palmed a revolver kept tucked in his canvas belt. *Crack* went the twenty-two-caliber pistol, and the bottle shattered. The breed tucked the revolver into his waistband, picked up the reins, and took his seat. It was Tully's way of showing that the Southern Cheyenne wasn't the only man who knew how to handle a gun.

"You ready?" he asked.

Tom started toward the roan, then hesitated, his hand on the saddle pommel. He shuddered, closed his eyes, felt a tearing in his soul, heard the sound of drums deep in the recesses of his mind. It was simple: Swing a leg over the horse and light a shuck out of there and don't look back. But the past wouldn't let him go. Invisible talons tore at his soul. The bleak, empty windows seemed to fix him in an accusatory stare. *You can't,* a voice seemed to whisper in his mind. *The pipe is from your father.* Whatever else had come between them, the gift had been Seth's way of saying he loved his son.

Tom realized the soldiers were waiting for him to climb into the saddle and accompany them east to Tulsa. They needed to leave if they wanted to outrace the cloudbursts. "No . . . just a minute." He turned on his heels and entered the farmhouse.

Sergeant Philo Underhill and Tully Crow, their expressions full of curiosity, stared at the empty doorway, unsure of what to expect. They heard the clatter of the Cheyenne's boot heels on the wood floor within the farmhouse and wondered what the man was about. Then Tom reappeared, a beaded pouch of brushed buckskin clutched in his right fist.

"What's that?" Philo asked.

"Something I thought I could leave behind," Tom replied, tucking the pipe bundle into his saddlebags. "I was wrong."

"Well, then," Philo said, nodding to Tully, who flicked the reins and started the team of reluctant mules back toward the road. "Let's get on to Tulsa."

"The devil, you say," Tom Sandcrane quietly added, his eyes on the distant storms. Let them come and do their worst. "On to Cuba."

CHAPTER THIRTEEN

CUBA, THE PEARL OF THE ANTILLES, COVERED EIGHT HUN-
dred miles from east to west. In width the island varied from twenty to one hundred miles. Most of the
terrain was made up of rolling plains and fertile, rich valleys,
a chain broken by mountainous ridges and rough terrain that
could easily swallow an army in its winding passes and hidden arroyos. The southeastern part of the island was dominated by the Sierra Maestra range, which featured some of the
loftiest peaks in the West Indies.

The American expeditionary force could have sailed into
any of the numberless bays, lagoons, and coves offered by the
broken, irregular coastline. But the military minds recognized
Santiago, in the shadow of the Sierra Maestra range, as the
key to taking the island. Here the Spanish forces were at their
strongest, and yet the most vulnerable. If the harbor could be
blockaded and the fortifications stormed, the back of the
Spanish military would be broken. Victory was a laurel to
those who moved swift and sure. One bold sweep along the
base of the mountains might win the war. Young American officers, eager for excitement and glory, were worried the Spaniards might not even make a fight of it. . . .

Cuba, June 21, 1898

Captain Diego Zuloaga sat among the palms atop Widow's Hill and finished his noonday meal while watching what seemed an endless stream of men and equipment disembark from the American transports that clogged the southern shore. He ate quietly, spooning chunks of moray eel, cooked plantain, and pineapple from the bowl on the small wooden table that also held a recently uncorked bottle of rum, the crusty remains of a flat, round loaf of bread, and a silver carving knife bearing the crest of his family, a relic of his forefathers' faded glory.

Diego's elder brother, after inheriting the family estate on the outskirts of Barcelona, had squandered the family fortune and impoverished his wife and children. He came to a sorry end, hanging himself from the bough of an oak tree in a garden he no longer owned. It was a tragic waste whose cloud had cast a shadow over Diego Zuloaga all his days and left him with deep and abiding bitterness.

The captain of the Lion Brigade dabbed the juices from his carefully trimmed mustache and goatee. Throughout his thirty years, an innate sense of contempt for those around him had charted Zuloaga's destiny. He had learned, however, to disguise his true feelings of superiority with displays of affection toward those who professed their loyalty to him. And the men of the Lion Brigade were absolutely devoted to the officer. Under the captain's leadership, the brigade was the only Spanish-cavalry unit to have any kind of success against the Cuban rebels. But such victories were Pyrrhic at best, much to Zuloaga's chagrin; they had not stalled the growing resistance nor resulted in the capture of Antonio Celestial, the one thorn in the Spanish side whom Diego Zuloaga had personally sworn to extract. For more than a year Celestial's rebels had carried out their partisan campaign, a reign of terror among the Spanish troops. Patrols disappeared. Soldiers were found beheaded or disemboweled, killed in the most brutal ways to strike terror into the hearts of the Spanish recruits.

War had wrought its changes on Diego Zuloaga, turning a
vain but basically decent man into a merciless and implacable
foe who considered the Cuban insurgents as little more than
savage brutes.

"Captain Zuloaga, when do you think they will attack?"
asked the captain's aide, a headstrong young lieutenant named
Emilio Garza. It was obvious the junior officer was eager to
meet the Americans in battle and was confident of driving
them into the sea.

"Who can tell? I doubt their own officers know." Zuloaga
covered his eyes with binoculars and studied the silvery-white
beach and the collection of thatch and mud-walled huts that
made up the abandoned shore settlement. Daiquirí, and indeed, much of the shore, were becoming increasingly
crowded with cavalry, infantry, horses, mules, and wagons.
The harbor was already littered with the contents of overturned johnny boats used to ferry the troops and supplies to
shore. The entire affair was unfolding with a great amount of
confusion and loss of equipment.

"The Americans lack discipline," said Garza with an impu-
dent sniff. He removed his narrow-brimmed hat and
smoothed his sandy-blond hair. The trace of a lisp could be
heard in his speech, indicating his Castilian origins.

"Something we have in abundance," Zuloaga admitted. He
was solid and dark looking, his black mustache and goatee
flecked with silver, the hair beneath his cap graying at the
temples. The captain's complexion was that of rusted iron, his
features seamed and weathered by the Caribbean sun. "However, in everything else we are outnumbered many times over.
They have more men, more horses, mules, guns, heavier cannons, more ammunition."

"Our victory will be all the greater," the aide proclaimed,
shifting his stance. He overturned a rock with the toe of his
boot, and a five-inch centipede scuttled out from underneath,
only to perish beneath the lieutenant's heel, reduced to a
brown smear. The analogy wasn't lost on Zuloaga. But the
American army, however disorganized, was hardly an insect to
be ground beneath boots of Spanish leather. Zuloaga might be
disdainful of the invaders, but he was no fool. He chuckled,

poured another measure of rum into his cup, and handed the drink to Garza.

"Here, my young friend, drink this. Perhaps it will clear your senses. Cuba is lost to us. Our discipline will only make the inevitable more costly in American lives. But be assured, Emilio, our generals will most certainly meet defeat with honor." Zuloaga carefully dusting his uniform, walked out of the shade of the palms and stood with his hands clasped behind his back. He was ever the figure of unperturbed authority. It was this cool resolve in the face of adversity that had won him the respect of his command.

Garza motioned for Alfonso Ramirez, a portly trooper who served as cook, to come clear the table. Farther back in the shade of the palm grove, thirty Spanish cavalrymen dressed in tan coats and trousers with bandoliers slung across their chests lounged around their cook fires, enjoying the afternoon's inaction and finding respite from the heat of the noonday sun. At the center of the brigade sat a ragged Cuban youth, one of a pair of rebels the brigade had intercepted on his way toward the coast, no doubt, the captain assumed, to join the Americans. The youth's companion had managed to escape the clutches of the Spanish under cover of night.

Zuloaga and his lieutenant wore much the same uniforms as the men of the brigade, though the officers' tunics boasted epaulets and extra brass buttons down the chest. Captain Zuloaga fancied a pale-yellow silk scarf knotted at the throat and tucked inside his shirt. His stern, arrogantly handsome features appeared etched in granite beneath the cap's leather brim as he surveyed the chaotic onslaught of American forces onto Cuban shores. He stood there for several minutes, unmoving, as if he had taken root in the rocky slope. Then, without warning, he spun on his heels and started back along the trail toward the palm grove. Lieutenant Garza hurried to join the captain on the path. And behind the two officers Ramirez followed, his belly jiggling as he trotted along with the captain's table folded flat beneath his arm.

"Captain Zuloaga, will you lead us against the Americans?" Garza asked, still anxious for a fight.

"Do not worry, my young friend," Zuloaga replied. "You'll

have your fill of fighting. But the Americans can wait. Before we are driven from this island, there is one thing I must have. And time is running out." The Spanish cavalrymen saw him coming and began to empty their coffeepots onto their cook fires and rise from their bedrolls. Zuloaga continued through the ranks of his men until he stood at the center of his command. He waited for them to quiet down, and when he spoke, they hung on his every word. "The Americans are below, on the shores of Daiquirí Cove. But we have other prey, my lions. And we will not be denied. From now on we hunt only the ghost of the Sierra Maestra. The deaths of our comrades at arms weighs heavy on my heart. Before I leave these mountains, I will have the head of Antonio Celestial!" The men around him cheered, and several fired their Mausers into the air as they hurried off toward their startled horses.

"But, Captain, is this the wisest course?" Lieutenant Garza complained, risking Zuloaga's displeasure. Celestial was a will-o'-the-wisp, while the Americans at Daiquirí were within striking distance. All he wanted was one brief foray to put fear in their hearts, a single sudden attack, quick as lightning, for the honor of Spain. "We have searched the mountains before and never even found a trace of the rebels."

"You make an excellent point, Lieutenant. But you see, we never had a guide before." Zuloaga squatted down by the prisoner, a dark-haired thirteen-year-old boy with a sullen, yet defiant, expression. "What is your name?"

The young rebel refused to answer.

Zuloaga motioned for Ramirez the cook to bring him the silver carving knife that was the captain's link to a vanished social station. He held up the blade to the youth's left eye and softly repeated the question as the lad recoiled in horror. "You know that raid in Santiago when you and your amigos blew up the warehouse? Some of my men were inside. I sent them there for supplies. Some were killed. I found one man, not much older than yourself, blinded by the blast, eh? His face all bloody. Well, enough of those painful memories. What is your name?" Zuloaga passed the knife back and forth, the blade drawing closer to the youth's left eye.

The young Cuban's choice was obvious—cooperation or

blindness. To the thirteen-year-old the latter was unbearable, despite his hatred of the Spanish.

He muttered a name.

"What? I did not hear." said Zuloaga.

The young rebel cleared his throat and spoke again. "Mateo. My name is Mateo."

"And what was the name of the lad who escaped, eh?"

"Enrico."

"Hmm, I think you lie."

"No, Captain, I swear it, on my mother's life."

"Ha. I do not think you had a mother unless she ran loose in the jungle and kept to the pack." The troopers within earshot laughed, their hearts hard as stone toward the prisoner.

"And you can take us to Antonio Celestial?" Zuloaga asked.

Again silence, as Mateo struggled with his own conscience and loyalty—but this time his hesitation bore a price. A flick of the wrist, the silver knife jabbed forward, and blood spattered the orchids, while parakeets with iridescent plumage rose from the treetops, riding a horrid, high-pitched scream of pure and utter agony into the cobalt sky.

CHAPTER FOURTEEN

For Sergeant Tom Sandcrane, the beauty and wonder of being at sea had worn off after the second day of internment in the foul-smelling bowels of the *Baltimore*. Fortunately, the entire First Volunteer Cavalry had managed to secure a release from quarters, and they spent the remainder of the voyage on the decks of the cruiser until the mountainous coastline of Cuba appeared like some wonderful reward, the promise of paradise floating on an aquamarine sea.

The *Baltimore* was one of the first cruisers to disembark, on the twentieth of June, permitting Tom and the First Volunteer Cavalry to discover for themselves the dark underside of the paradise they had glimpsed from afar. A day later, and Cuba had yet to offer the men from Indian Territory anything but mud, mosquitoes, and misery. Throughout the morning and afternoon of the twenty-first, johnny boats foundered or capsized, and equipment, men, and animals were lost in the bay. The air was still and laden with moisture, humidity that sapped a man's strength and made even the simplest task drudgery. The volunteers from the arid plains of the Southwest and Indian Territory especially suffered. They were accustomed to the prairie, where the dry wind stirred the buffalo grass and leached the perspiration from the air.

Headquarters for the expeditionary force was established at an abandoned sugar plantation whose hacienda was the only stone structure near the village. Topping a knoll overlooking the settlement, the once ostentatious household had been plundered by either rebels or Spanish troops in its owner's absence. But several pieces of furniture remained, and the American officers were grateful just to have a solid red-tile roof over their heads. Thatch huts and canvas tents would have to do for the common soldiers.

Daiquirí's once sparkling stretch of white beach had been churned into a quagmire from all the traffic. As the afternoon waned and the sun seemed to melt into the western horizon, swarms of tiny gnats and mosquitoes descended on the soldiers, biting and stinging and leaving tempers so frayed that fistfights erupted at the slightest provocation. It was not bravery but desperation that led Tom to volunteer for a forward position on the densely wooded hillside overlooking Daiquirí. Whatever danger the foothills of the Sierra Maestra might hold, they could present no greater threat than the miserable life to be found on the shore.

Although horsemanship and skill with a rifle won Tom a uniform and a place in the Volunteer Cavalry, it was his education, the ability to read and write, that brought him the rank of sergeant. Soon after Tom's enlistment Philo Underhill had lost his stripes for starting a drunken brawl in a Tulsa whorehouse and been reduced to private, the humble equal of Tully Crow, who delighted in needling his friend over his misfortune. Neither of the men appeared to resent Tom's advancement, however, and during the tedious weeks of training, the two Creeks had come to be his loyal if somewhat irascible friends.

So when Sergeant Sandcrane asked for volunteers, Philo and Tully were only too happy to follow Tom up the forested slope and away from the ordeal of unloading boats, dragging frightened mules out of the surf, and slogging through the deserted village in search of a dry place to store clothing and ammunition and guns.

Palm fronds formed a canopy above as the three comrades relaxed upon their bedrolls in a clearing ringed with palm and plantain, ebony and silk-cotton trees, whose trunks were wrapped with thick strands of *jagüey* vine and dotted with wild orchids in a variety of subtle cream-colored hues. The hill seemed to catch a breeze, and even the insects allowed the men some breathing room. The horses were ground-tethered and grazing contentedly. Yes, things were looking up.

Tom shuddered at the morass of men and equipment he had left a quarter of a mile away and thanked the All-Father that the Spanish army had not launched an attack and turned the nightmarish landing into a complete debacle.

"Never seen the like of it," Philo observed as he stacked wood to make a campfire. "You seen them crabs eating on that dead mule down yonder?" The heavyset man shuddered. "Gave me the willies." He searched in his pack and found a watertight packet of matches and a tin for brewing coffee.

"This is a cold camp," Tom reminded his sleepy-eyed friend. "We don't want to attract attention to ourselves, the three of us out here alone."

Philo coughed and spat. "Now, you ain't worried some of your friends might have trailed us from Daiquirí?" The Third Volunteer Cavalry from Oklahoma Territory had landed before noon. Seventy-five desperately seasick cavalrymen, some of whom were Cheyenne and hailed from Cross Timbers, had hit the beach and beat a straight path to the medical tents set up to serve the wounded. For reasons neither Philo nor Tully could fathom, Tom Sandcrane avoided contact with his tribe, a task made simpler once the First and Third cavalries had been assigned different transports and put out to sea.

"We've been posted to keep an eye out for Spanish scouts," Tom growled. He felt no desire to explain his actions to the Creek half-breed. He knew his kinsmen were among the ranks of the Third Volunteer Cavalry but saw no need to seek them out. Fate and a careful bit of maneuvering had thus far kept their paths from crossing.

"Scouts? Chances are we plumb scared them off," Underhill replied. He sighed and glanced at Tully, who was keeping watch at the edge of the clearing. The man was nervous as a cat in a pack of dogs. "Tully's got a bad feeling about this place. He's like a grocer fellow I once knew—he weighed everything." Philo flashed Tom a wide grin. "Weighed me out a cigar once 'cause I was a penny short. Trimmed the damn thing rather than let me get something a little extra. Anyway, that's the way Tully is. But somebody's gotta be his friend. Might as well be you and me, huh?"

"Philo . . . you're a philosopher," Tom said, chuckling.

"Sheeeit. I'm Creek and you know it." Philo studied the surrounding greenery, wholly unconcerned by the strangeness of the place. "Why, there ain't a Spaniard for miles around."

"Tell that to the rider I just seen coming straight on," Tully called in a hoarse whisper, hurrying over from the edge of the clearing. He waved for them to join him, and when Tom and Philo had scrambled to his side, the man stabbed a finger in the direction of the trees to the north.

Tom quickly ordered Philo to lead the horses out of the clearing and hide them in the shadows along the backtrail. The former sergeant grudgingly scattered his firewood with a few well-placed kicks and headed for the mounts. Tom ignored Underhill's grumbles and complaints, for both came as natural to the man as breathing. More important, Philo was as dangerous as a Texas twister when it came to a scrap and could be counted on to stand his ground no matter what the odds.

Tom hurried over to Tully's side. The wiry little man pointed at the tangle of trees and vines where brightly colored birds flitted through fading shafts of sunlight as emerald shadows stalked the hills.

"We're in for it now," Tully said nervously, handing Tom a spyglass. After several seconds Tom was able to pick up a narrow winding trail that led along the hillside. A flash of movement caught his attention, and he stiffened. There it was again. A solitary horseman momentarily filled the eyepiece before vanishing behind a thicket of banana trees and broadleafed fronds.

"You see him?" Tully softly inquired. The horseman's features were hidden beneath a straw sombrero. The rider wore faded brown cotton trousers and a loose-fitting shirt with a cartridge belt flung over his shoulder. "He means trouble or I'm a goddamn elephant."

"Hard to tell," Tom muttered. "That rifle might be a Mauser."

"Spanish issue. And he'll probably use it if we let him."

Tom considered the possibilities. Was the Spaniard alone? Perhaps this was a Cuban rebel. Either way he could open up on them with his rifle and in the process warn any other troops that might be in the vicinity, prowling the hills. Stealth, not gunplay, was required here. "Join Philo with the horses. Wait for me."

"What are you going to do?"

"If you hear gunfire, get on back to Daiquirí." Tom passed his rifle to his companion. It was obvious he was moving out alone to take up a forward position.

"Now, see here . . . ," Tully started to protest, then realized he'd been left to argue with the dangling vines and a screen of broad, waxy-leafed fronds. He had grown to feel a fraternal affection for Tom Sandcrane and didn't like the idea of the young sergeant hurrying off into the damn jungle alone.

A kingfisher soared past, and in the lessening light its large head and stubby wings seemed to take on a macabre, almost human appearance, like some spirit wearing a mask for the dead. Tully recoiled in horror, courage and concern momentarily failing. He tripped and dropped his rifle, but his outstretched hands broke his fall. Then he made a dash for the opposite side of the clearing, where he eagerly joined his companion by the horses.

"What is it? Where's Tom?" Philo asked.

"Out yonder."

"You let him go off alone?"

"That was his orders. We're to wait, and if we hear gunfire, we're to light a shuck for the beach."

Philo tethered the horses to a nearby tangle of roots and then strode halfway across the clearing. It took a few moments for him to notice he was alone. He looked over his shoulder at his companion. "Well?"

"I'm staying put. Orders is orders."

"Where's your rifle?"

"Damn," Tully muttered. "I dropped it." Being unarmed was as worrisome as confronting the supernatural. He walked up alongside Philo and then cautiously approached the trees. "I saw a demon."

"What? If this is another one of your goddamn tricks," Philo growled. Tully was a prankster by nature and viewed his companion's role to be the eternal butt of his jokes.

"I swear. It came this close to tearing my head off." Tully held up a finger and thumb about half an inch apart.

"More's the pity," Philo said. But just to be on the safe side, he unslung his Krag rifle and held it at the ready.

Perhaps not all the old ways were dead, Tom thought as he crouched half-naked among the sweet cedar and sandalwood along the faintly visible trail that wound through the forest. He had discarded his blue shirt, fearing the color, in contrast to the flora surrounding him, would reveal his presence. His dark, coppery skin blended with the greens and browns of the thicket in which he had chosen to hide, a stand of underbrush sprouting from a shelf of earth that protruded from the hillside and overlooked the faint trail he had glimpsed through the spyglass. As the sun, poised on the rim of the western ridges, prepared to surrender the foothills to the onset of evening, the Spaniard, astride a lathered, weary-looking mount, emerged from the forest and worked his way across a patch of cleared ground. The solitary rider, oblivious to the Cheyenne crouched like a panther waiting to pounce, rode unerringly toward Daiquirí. This might be the scout for a much larger force hidden in the hills and sent to spy on the American forces as they came to shore. Tom intended to take the Spaniard alive, if possible, and let him witness the fiasco on the shore from close-up, as a prisoner.

A butterfly sailed past, gracefully riding the currents of the late-afternoon breeze. A tree lizard scampered across Tom's boots, but he did not stir, and the reptile paid no notice to the man. Seth used to complain that books had never taught one to stalk a deer or to summon the Maiyun, the spirits of those who had gone before to give their counsel. Tom's father had always been fearful that education would ruin his son's natural skills. Tom was determined to prove his father wrong.

He remained motionless as the mosquitoes found him and began to feed. A boa constrictor, fully eight feet in length, worked its way down the trunk of a nearby mahogany tree. The Cheyenne's blood turned to ice. It was only with the utmost effort he held his ground and overcame the urge to run like hell. The horseman chose that moment to appear on the trail ahead. Tom mentally urged the Spaniard to quicken his pace, for the boa had evidently caught Tom's scent and was coming to investigate. Indeed, the horseman and the boa were having a race without even being aware of one another. Tom, on the other hand, continued to track the progress of both and silently urged the horseman along. He was about to throw caution to the wind and bolt from cover when fate intervened. A nest of newly born tree rats concealed in a nearby rotted log began to squeal and squeak and cry for food. The boa, distracted by the proximity of such an easy meal, altered its course and slithered out of the thicket, much to the Cheyenne's relief. He returned his attention to the Spaniard.

Twenty-five feet . . . twenty . . . fifteen . . . *Easy now. Come along. Easy. That's it.* Tom uncoiled like a spring, became a coppery brown blur of airborne muscle and bone hurling through the shadows toward the trail below. The rider sensed the attack and twisted in the saddle. Tom landed on the Spaniard's upper torso and knocked him from horseback, jarring the man's rifle loose in the process. The weapon went spinning off among the trees as its owner was sent sprawling onto the hillside trail. Tom rolled as he hit the earth, scrambled to his feet, and lunged toward the Spaniard, intending to take him prisoner as quickly as possible. The man's horse made a dash for the trail ahead. Tom refused the distraction and, drawing his bayonet, shouted *"Entrega!"* ordering the Spaniard to surrender even as he landed on his fallen opponent and pinned his shoulders to the ground. Tom raised his knife hand in a threatening gesture, hoping to convince the man . . .

Man?

Tom stared down at his victim's shirt, torn open during the fall, and the twin mounds of cream-colored flesh revealed beneath its ripped folds. He lifted his gaze to the sun-browned features, smooth and decidedly pretty, though weeks of worry and insufficient rest were visible there as well. Deep-brown eyes revealed strength of character. Startled by his attack, the woman had already begun to regain her composure. With her auburn hair tucked beneath the straw sombrero, and loose-fitting clothes to disguise her features, she had passed for a man.

"Well, what do we have here? If all the Spaniards are as pretty as you, I've no use for a gun." Tom grinned, amazed at his good fortune. "I'll just take prisoners." He made the mistake of relaxing his hold.

Joanna Cooper worked her right hand free from underneath Tom's knee and delivered a solid blow to his face. Her fist connected with a resounding smack that sent her good-natured attacker sprawling on his side. Tom howled and scrambled clear of the woman.

"Damn. On second thought I'll keep my gun," Tom said, cupping his right eye. He glanced up and discovered yet another indignity—the woman was standing over him, a revolver trained on his chest. He was now her prisoner. Tom mentally scolded himself for leaving his Krag with Tully Crow. "Hold it now, miss. I'd hate to see you do something we'll both one day regret."

"You're American." It was more an observation than a question. Joanna motioned for him to stand. His blue woolen trousers were obviously part of a uniform, but Joanna wasn't totally convinced, though he certainly didn't sound Cuban or Spanish. "There were rumors the Americans would land somewhere near Daiquirí. If it is true, I need to find whoever is in charge." Joanna paused, hesitant, appraising his dark, reddish-bronze appearance. "Where are you from?" Self-conscious of her bared bosom, Joanna managed to single-handedly close her shirt and tuck the hem into the gunbelt circling her waist. The double-action revolver in her right hand never wavered as she attended herself for modesty's sake.

"Indian Territory. I am Southern Cheyenne," Tom replied. He was beginning to tire of staring down the barrel of her thirty-eight-caliber Colt. "Sergeant Tom Sandcrane of the First

Volunteer Cavalry." He stooped over and retrieved his bayonet, heard the telltale click as Joanna cocked her revolver, then straightened and slowly slid the blade into its scabbard, uncertain which hurt worse, his eye or his pride. This wasn't the outcome he had intended.

"My name is Joanna Cooper. I'm an American, a doctor," the woman said, gingerly probing her rib cage. She winced at the bruised muscles she had suffered as a result of Tom Sandcrane's attack. Fortunately, a thicket of trumpet-shaped ferns had cushioned the impact of her fall from horseback. A quick assessment found no physical damage.

There had been a sawbones at Fort Reno, Tom remembered. A crotchety old bastard, as kind as salt in an open wound, who used to visit the mission school whenever he was sober enough to ride the mile from the fort. Tom and the other children dreaded his visits and preferred illness to an actual encounter with the man. Now here was a doctor cut from a different cloth, who might have had no shortage of patients.

"Never met a woman doctor before," Tom dryly commented, reserving his judgment.

"I need help," Joanna continued, deciding to trust the soldier. She eased the hammer down on the Colt and returned the weapon to the flapped holster at her side. "And there isn't much time." The woman didn't bother to add the obvious. Tom Sandcrane would learn soon enough. These days, everything was a matter of life and death.

CHAPTER FIFTEEN

TOM SANDCRANE FOUND A PLACE ON THE PORCH OF THE HACIenda, near the dining room's open window, through which he could overhear all that transpired between Joanna Cooper and the collection of officers commanding the American expeditionary forces. Much of what he heard, Doctor Cooper had already recounted to the Cheyenne and his two companions on their way down to shore.

Two and a half day's ride from Daiquirí, Antonio Celestial, one of the leaders of the Cuban resistance, lay injured and unable to travel, his hiding place an abandoned village in the Sierra Maestra range. The Spanish, intending to cripple the Cuban insurrection, were making a concerted effort to locate the former teacher and capture or kill him. It was common knowledge Captain Diego Zuloaga had sworn to apprehend Celestial at any cost. Such a triumph would certainly take the sting out of any American victory. Joanna Cooper was equally resolved to save the life of the Cuban. Unable to move him, Joanna and Mateo had come seeking the Americans in hopes of securing a detachment of troopers to follow her into the mountains and rescue Celestial. Separated from Mateo by a twist of fate, Joanna hoped the young rebel had escaped the clutches of Captain Zuloaga.

Tom Sandcrane had no opinion on the matter. He certainly did not know this Antonio Celestial, but he envied the man.

The woman doctor had been willing to risk her life for him. It spoke well for the Cuban. So Tom Sandcrane lingered on the porch and eavesdropped while the doctor made her plea. The woman intrigued him as much as the rebel she sought to protect. Her strength and resolve reminded him of the stories his father used to tell of the old days, during the Indian Wars, and the warrior women who rode and fought alongside the men. But no. He walked a different path now.

He shifted his thoughts and allowed his gaze to sweep across the crescent of shoreline ablaze with campfires and a mass of writhing shadow shapes. Soldiers milling across the white sand made him think of maggots on a rotting carcass. The brightly lit transports riding at anchor cast streamers of amber light upon the black waters of the bay. Now and then a signal rocket exploded in a red-orange starburst that disintegrated in an incandescent mist above the tides and momentarily outlined the cruiser or destroyer from which it came.

Tom leaned against the cool stone outer wall of the house and, hooking his thumbs in his cartridge belt, continued to listen as the woman's protests fell on deaf ears. His stomach growled. Tom appeased his empty belly with a banana, peeling the reddish skin back from the sweet, creamy meat. He hurriedly devoured the fruit, then dug another from his pocket. He had tasted his first banana shortly after wading ashore. So far the Cheyenne had sampled four different varieties and found three to be delightful. The fourth, he later learned, was a plantain and meant to be cooked like a potato. His back to the wall, he tossed the peels over the wooden railing and settled near the window.

Inside, Joanna Cooper shoved away the cup of coffee one of the officers had poured for her. Across the table sat Colonel Leonard Woods, a silver-haired officer with deep-set eyes and a careworn demeanor. Next to Wood another colonel, forty-year-old Theodore Roosevelt, formerly the undersecretary of the navy and at present the commander of five detachments of volunteer cavalry, listened intently to the woman's story. Joanna thought he resembled a bristling bulldog, anxious for a scrap. Captain Huston, well-bred and rugged, sat alongside the two colonels, sipping rum, his head nodding as he fought to keep awake. A trio of lieutenants whose names had already slipped from her memory were busily transforming the dining room into command headquarters, complete with campaign maps and dispatch books, and tables for the orderlies.

"My dear young woman," Wood began. He did not mean to be condescending—it simply came naturally to him, especially with this woman who reminded him of his own daughter back in Maryland. "I think I can speak for Colonel Roosevelt and the other officers when I say we applaud your remarkable exploits."

"Hear! Hear!" Roosevelt seconded. "Imagine. Hiding out with the guerrillas. You are a brave woman and your country is grateful. But war is better left to the men, don't you think?" The former undersecretary removed his wire-rimmed spectacles and cleaned them on a kerchief from the pocket of his khaki coat.

"In Cuba this war has been fought not only by men, but by old women, even children," Joanna snapped. "As for my country's gratitude, save it for later. Right now I need a troop of cavalry to help me save the life of Antonio Celestial!"

Tom, on the porch, had to smile. The woman certainly wasn't cowed by the military authorities who confronted her. He was so intent on listening to Joanna and the officers, he almost missed seeing another visitor materialize out of the night and hurry along a direct course toward the hacienda. Tom immediately left the window and began to pace the perimeter of the porch, pretending to stand guard. The new arrival, a tall, broad-shouldered officer with thinning hair, hurried across the trampled yard and climbed the steps two at a time. The newcomer wore a white medical officer's coat that boasted captain's bars on his right shoulder.

"You there, Sergeant . . . are you by any chance the one who brought the woman doctor into camp?" the man asked, pausing to catch his breath. He appeared to have run all the way from the hospital tents on the opposite side of the village.

Tom nodded. "I am."

"Well-done!" the medical officer exclaimed. "There'll be a handsome reward in it for you. Miss Cooper's father is a wealthy man and has been worried sick about her for many months now." The officer nodded in the direction of the front door. "She inside?"

"With Colonels Woods and Roosevelt," Tom replied.

"Ahh. Perhaps I had better wait on the porch," the officer muttered aloud.

Tom scowled. He wouldn't be able to listen at the dining-room window. Officers, like diarrhea, had a habit of showing up at the worst possible time and were impossible to ignore. He was no longer able to catch the particulars, but when the front door opened at last, and Joanna stepped out into the lantern light, Tom could tell at a glance that her requests had fallen on deaf ears.

"Thank you, my dear," she said, mocking Woods and Roosevelt. "We will let you know our decision, my dear. Bully for you." She glanced up, surprised to find the Cheyenne on the porch. Her expression softened. "Pardon me, Sergeant. You were most helpful." Then her eyes widened as the medical officer rushed out of the shadows and swept her into his embrace.

"Joanna! Thank God you're alive!"

"Bernard!" Joanna retreated and quickly appraised his uniform. She turned her cheek as he kissed her. Marmillon's affections were not returned in kind, though she was delighted to be reunited with her old schoolmate. "How?"

"The Dutchman dropped me off in New Orleans. I enlisted in the medical corps and here I am."

"And I thought you'd had your fill of Cuba and the revolution," Joanna nervously laughed. "But you came back."

"Not for some damn war. I came for you." He glanced across the porch at Tom, who couldn't think of anything better to do than remain at his post. The Cheyenne leaned on his rifle while he studied the troop-laden transports that had yet to disgorge their human cargo. Of course, some damn boat was the last thing on his mind.

"Come along. I've whiskey in the hospital tent, and you look all done in. A drink and several hours of sleep is what you need. Doctor's orders." He took her by the arm and steered her toward the front steps. Joanna was too weary to protest, and besides, she had nowhere else to go.

Tom watched them leave in silence. The porch seemed infinitely emptier. The space, however, was soon filled by another remarkable presence. Tom sensed the smaller man standing at his side, turned, and managed a semblance of a salute, which Colonel Roosevelt returned.

"So you are the Cheyenne?"

"Yes, sir," Tom replied wondering just how much trouble he could possibly be in.

"The Plains Indians I have known were some of the finest trackers in the world. Sioux, Cheyenne, Arapaho . . . What about you?"

"I can hold my own."

"We'll see." Roosevelt stroked his stubbled chin. Behind his wire-rimmed glasses the colonel's eyes, though bloodshot and pouchy from lack of sleep, revealed his shrewd intellect. Indeed, he was a bit of a schemer. "The woman who just left . . . I want you to *track* her. Don't let her out of your sight. That is an order. Am I clear? And dash it all, see that no harm comes to her." He placed his hands behind his back and, with a wink in Tom's direction, quietly added, "I may need her father's votes someday."

CHAPTER SIXTEEN

JOANNA COOPER CURLED HER TOES IN THE MOIST SAND AND watched the footprints she had left behind fill with seawater. She walked along a moonlit stretch of beach a good fifty yards beyond the glare of the lantern-lit medical tents, where orderlies and nurses under Bernard Marmillon's command tended to the needs of their patients, cleared the remains of the evening meal, and prepared to catch what little sleep they could manage before the beginning of another traumatic day. By first light the rolling tides would be dotted with longboats ferrying still more of the blue-clad troops to shore. Seven white canvas wall tents, each of them twelve by fifteen feet, were already crowded with men who had injured themselves during transport or succumbed to heat exhaustion and fatigue. To make matters worse, a disturbing number of soldiers had presented themselves showing fever and chills and were immediately quarantined to a tent by themselves until Marmillon or one of the doctors under his command could diagnose their illnesses.

Joanna's first instinct was to try to help where she could, but then common sense took hold. Without rest she was no good to anyone. Bernard, of course, offered his quarters, and Joanna accepted with the stipulation that her friend would have to sleep elsewhere. Marmillon scowled and assumed, to no avail, his most wounded expression. Joanna Cooper wasn't in the mood for a tryst. She found a cot, crawled beneath a blanket, closed her eyes, and tried to sleep.

For an hour she lay awake, her mind racing, unable to sleep. Finally, she sat upright, swung her legs over the edge of the cot, and, thankful to be alone, slipped out of the tent while Bernard was berating an orderly for some mishap. Joanna passed unnoticed from the circle of medical tents and made her way out of camp. She had to devise a plan. Antonio Celestial was alone and helpless, his men scattered or rotting in Spanish prison camps after conducting two disastrous raids on their own. And what of Mateo? She feared the Spanish had captured him. No matter how resolute the youth was, no matter how much he hated the Spaniards who had killed his family, Mateo was only flesh and bones. Zuloaga had ways of making men talk.

Joanna faced the bay, its black waves capped with silvery foam rolling out of a starry horizon. Memories borne on the tides washed over her. She was standing on another distant shore overlooking Lake Pontchartrain; it was Christmas, and her life was about to change forever. As if conjured by her thoughts, drumbeats drifted to her, gently throbbing, creeping out of the dark, real as the past is real. But these drums borne on the evening breeze and these keening voices were not the product of some reverie. Drums like the heartbeat of earth itself and chants as old as time had spoken to her once as she dreamwalked, and did again, only now she could see that the campfires belonged to the Indians. The stuff of fantasy had become real. Goose bumps rippled along Joanna's arms. The back of her neck tingled as she realized for the first time that perhaps something more than her own wide-eyed idealism had led her to Cuba.

She was not alone! For a brief second Joanna thought one of Zuloaga's soldiers had crept out of the palm groves to attack her. She spun on her heels and instinctively dropped a hand to her waistband before remembering she'd left her revolver underneath the cot in Bernard's tent. When Tom Sandcrane materialized out of the night, Joanna managed to hide her relief and save face.

"I didn't mean to startle you," Tom said.

"Then you ought to announce yourself," Joanna retorted. This was the second time he had surprised her. At least he hadn't vaulted out of the stygian shadows and knocked her to the ground.

"I stepped in the water twice," Tom said.

"What are you doing here?"

"Watching you. Colonel Roosevelt's orders." A wry grin touched his lips. "I was tempted to do it on my own."

"Oh?" Joanna cocked an eyebrow, suspecting his intentions.

"Like I said. I never saw a woman doctor before. It is something of a spectacle."

A cloud released the moon from its shrouds. Suddenly the beach was bathed in its glow, revealing the flashing crescent of Sandcrane's smile. *Well,* Joanna thought, *I have been called plenty of things in my life but never a spectacle.*

"Too bad you are so hard of hearing," Tom added.

"I was listening to the drums," Joanna said in her own defense.

The sergeant glanced over his shoulder. He recognized the chant, having heard it many times as a child, for it was an old song, a warrior's song. The woman physician and the dark-skinned soldier from Oklahoma Territory listened together, two strangers oddly at peace in one another's company. Finally Joanna bridged the gulf between them with a question.

"Who are they?"

"Southern Cheyenne. Like me," he explained. "Only they came ashore today." Tom's hopes of passing unnoticed among his kinsmen were already doomed. An hour earlier he had managed to blunder into the very campsite he had hoped to avoid. Several of the blue-clad Cheyennes hailed from Cross Timbers. He recognized many of the warriors, firelight glimmering on their stern, unforgiving features that stared at him with open distrust and hostility but made no move to impede his progress.

"What are they singing?"

"Songs to give them courage. And to remind them of home." Tom closed his eyes and listened to the voices, thinking of the home he had left behind with his wounded pride, and the future that would never be. "Oklahoma Territory, where the Washita cuts through strands of buffalo grass and wooded hills. It is a place of good grass and water lying golden in the morning. It has been Cheyenne land for as long as the People can remember. Until now." He listened to the voices in the night and, in a quiet voice, repeated the chant in English for the woman's benefit.

"Father, we walk a far country.
Guide our steps. Place our feet
upon the path of bravery.
May the blood of the bear
be in us.
May the heart of the panther
be in us.
Our song rides upon
the smoke of our fires."

Joanna found herself staring at the sergeant, caught up in the beauty of the song he interpreted in such a wistful tone. She sensed his loneliness, though she had known him for scarcely more than an afternoon. She saw the solitude in his eyes that were as brown as earth where the soil has slumbered under a mantle of autumn leaves. His time-sculpted features, even by moonlight, wore a haunted, distrustful expression.

Joanna stumbled for a reply. "Why aren't you with your . . . uh . . . people?" she managed, with immediate regret for the way it sounded.

"I walk a different path . . . and there is no place for a ghost at their campfire." His voice turned cold as he spoke. It was clear he intended to say nothing more on the matter. Joanna was intrigued by his reply and brass enough to push the issue. What did he mean . . . ghost? But the intrusion of Bernard Marmillon put an end to the exchange and rescued Tom Sandcrane from the woman's curiosity.

"Joanna! Is that you? Ah yes . . ." As Bernard hurried along the beach, waves spread a carpet of foam at his feet, impeding his progress. He stumbled in the wet sand, tripped on driftwood, and nearly fell. Tom used the opportunity to retreat into the shadows.

"Wait. You don't need to leave," Joanna called out. She felt silly talking to the night air and the incoming tide. The doctor thought she spied movement inland at the base of a palm grove, but it might have been the night breeze bestirring the fronds.

"Who on earth are you talking to?" Bernard asked, glancing around at the empty stretch of shore.

"Ghosts," Joanna said with a shrug.

Bernard gave her a quizzical look. "I gave up figuring you out long ago, my dear." He offered her his arm, intending to lead her back to camp. It was an incongruous gesture, considering the circumstances. This was hardly some dressed ball or the gardens surrounding the Cooper estate. And Joanna hardly looked ladylike, wearing a khaki shirt and regulation-blue trousers borrowed from the quartermaster's store of spare equipment. "Come back to camp. Captain Huston is waiting to talk to you." Bernard glanced back toward the hospital tents. "There he is."

Joanna could see the darkened silhouette of a soldier against a backdrop of campfires and fell into step alongside the medical officer. From time to time she glanced over her shoulder at the coastline and the serene grove of palm trees, where she imagined her solitary Indian chaperon kept his vigil.

Captain Huston appeared tired and smelled of rum, although he was steady on his feet. He removed his hat as the two physicians approached, a gesture in deference to the fairer sex, depite the fact that she was dressed like a trooper. The captain had been suffering from a bout of diarrhea ever since disembarking. Fearful of the medical profession in general, and determined to avoid a visit to hospital tents if at all possible, Huston was treating his symptoms with copious amounts of rum, hoping the alcohol would serve to kill off whatever had infected his gut.

"Evening again, miss . . . uh . . . Doctor Cooper. You know it probably isn't such a wise idea to go wandering off by yourself. There might be Spanish scouts in the woods." He lowered his voice. "And you *are* a woman." The captain spoke as if this were some shocking revelation.

Joanna had become inured to condescension. She had grown to expect it in men once they learned of her calling. Now and then she encountered someone like Antonio Celestial, who accepted her without pretense. The experience was always refreshing. Come to think of it, Sergeant Tom Sandcrane had also reacted in much the same manner. She might be a "spectacle," but he apparently did not disapprove. On the other hand, she considered her Cheyenne guardian quite an enigma. Perhaps after she saw to Celestial's rescue, there might be time to become better acquainted with the sergeant and satisfy her own curiosity concerning him and his people. She was fascinated by the Indian brigade, with their rituals and chants.

"Well, Captain Huston, I assume you have come from the colonels."

"Yes, ma'am. Your request was placed in Roosevelt's hands." Huston winced and rubbed his belly. "After much deliberation Colonel Roosevelt has decided that as important as this rebel leader is, the colonel cannot in good faith risk your life in obtaining his rescue." Joanna started to protest, but Huston cut her short. "However . . . if you can arrange for some volunteers to go in your place and perhaps draw them a map to guide them, he will permit the attempt. But headquarters cannot spare more than three or four men. Our main objective is Santiago. Capture the heights, force the Spanish to surrender, and Cuba is ours. That's the best way to help these people."

"That settles it, then," Marmillon blurted out. "Joanna does not know anyone among these rough riders."

"Present Colonel Roosevelt with my regards. I'll find the men and dispatch them come morning," Joanna replied.

Captain Huston stared at her in open disbelief. Finally he shrugged, saluted Marmillon, and strode briskly off toward the plantation house.

Bernard Marmillon was beside himself. Joanna had obviously been immersed in this madness for far too long and had no grasp of reality. She meant nothing to these troops. "Joanna. Forgive me. The situation is hopeless. You're a stranger to these soldiers. Where are you going to find men foolish enough to wander off into the mountains and risk their lives to rescue someone they have never even met?"

Joanna studied the night-darkened palm groves, a faint smile on her face. "If angels tred where wise men fear to go, might not a *ghost*?" she said. "Something tells me the woods are full of them."

CHAPTER SEVENTEEN

*H*E SOARED ABOVE CROSS TIMBERS ON THE GRAY-WHITE WINGS *of his namesake. Even in his dream the rush of wind and the sense of flight was altogether real. There was the Council House, strangely empty and dark. Something was wrong here. . . . The old ones were grieving, what were the voices saying? No. Let them call someone else. Ride the wind, away from here, quickly away. The land below sped past, and soon he was gliding over Coyote Creek, skimming the treetops of oak and cedar and willow. Sunlight on the ribbon of water glittered like diamonds. But the land was being cleared. Someone had claimed this precious glade. But why should he despair? He had turned his back on it long ago. But the voices held him. There was more. Look to the sun, they whispered. See what we see. And Tom obeyed. What was there? Only the blinding brightness. He could not bear it. But before he could look away, he spied a minute sliver of shadow, diving out of the sun, growing larger and larger in his sight, becoming more defined. It was a hawk, with plumage the color of blood, and it was diving straight for him, cruel talons curved and lethal, ready to sink into his flesh. Turn away! Turn away! Too late. Awake the sleeper. No! No!*

"Tom!"

They rushed him from the darkness. Fortunately, someone

called out his name and alerted him to the danger at hand.
The voice that had called out the warning jogged Tom's memory, but he had no time to search his mind for the identifying
features; he'd slept this night in harm's way.

Despite the Southern Cheyenne's natural quickness, one of
his assailants got in a few good licks with the toe of his boot
as Tom scrambled to his feet. Sandcrane grunted and rolled
with the kicks and winced as pain shot along his side. Struggling amid a rain of punishing blows, he lashed out at his attackers, left and right, his fists striking home with every
thrust of his powerful arms.

He blocked a punch aimed for his mouth, caught the fist,
and twisted until its owner screamed, then pulled the man
forward and slammed a forearm into his assailant's unpro-
tected gut. The man dropped to his knees and gasped for air.
Tom kicked him in the neck and sent him reeling into the
arms of his companions, who carried their fallen comrade to
safety.

A pair of brawny arms momentarily pinned Tom and left
him open to punishment. In a matter of seconds Sandcrane's
lips were puffed and bloody, his left eyelid swollen from a
flurry of punches as he struggled to extricate himself. The
moon drifted out from behind a cloud bank and bathed the
beach in a silvery light that revealed the identities of his attackers. They were Cheyenne, soldiers like himself, several of
whom he recognized. And they weren't finished with him.

Tom doubled over and fought free, spun in his assailant's
grasp, and delivered a vicious headbutt that flattened the nose
of the man behind him. Blood spattered from crushed bone
and cartilage. In the ghostly glare Tom recognized the pain-
bunched features of Enos Stump Horn, a Southern Cheyenne
from Cross Timbers. Stump Horn howled and abandoned the
fight.

His sudden departure seemed to cool the tempers of a couple of other Cheyenne, who followed the big man as he lumbered down the beach. But those who remained intended to
mete out the retribution they figured Tom Sandcrane so richly
deserved.

They weren't prepared for the fury with which they in-

tended victim charged among them and fought his way into
the open. Kneeling, Tom scooped up a handful of sand and
hurled it into the face of the first Cheyenne who followed
him. Momentarily blinded, the fellow was an easy target for
a hard driven right to the gut and a knee to the groin. Tom
grabbed the man by the scruff of his neck and the seat of his
pants and propelled him headfirst into the oncoming waves.
The effort cost Tom his balance, and he slipped in the moist
sand and fell to his knees. Bodies ploughed into him. He was
knocked on his back and pinned by their weight. A thumb
came too near his jaws, and he clamped his teeth on the digit
and ground until one of the men atop him shrieked and
pulled away. Tom twisted and kicked and squirmed free, then
staggered to a fighting stance only to find himself crouched
alone in the mud with the moon-flecked sea swirling around
his ankles as it spilled onto the shore. The remaining Cheyenne had dissolved like shadows and returned to the darkness from which they had sprung.

"Just as well," Tom muttered as his legs gave way and he
kneeled in the surf to catch his breath, his sides heaving and
pink spittle spilling from his mouth. He splashed his face
with seawater; though the salt stung like the devil, it helped
to revive him.

Someone chuckled, and Tom looked up to see Willem Tangle Hair squatting in the sand a few yards from water's edge.
The warning, thought Tom. Seeing Willem resurrected a painful wealth of memories that rose as unstoppable as the sea
bathing his bruised features. Without uttering a single word
of greeting, Willem stood and started to leave.

"Why the warning?" Tom asked.

"For old time's sake."

"Tell your friends the Cheyenne have become like dogs in
the night, sneaking out of the dark to attack me."

"They saw no reason to announce themselves. Did you
warn your own people how the oil companies would take
their land? No. You convinced us all how much better it
would be to open the reservation. Now Allyn Benedict owns
the northern oil fields. Cross Timber grows, but the township
is no longer Cheyenne. Much of the choice range land was

traded or sold off to the white settlers for money squandered on whiskey and the gambling tables." Willem removed his campaign hat and wiped his forehead on his shirtsleeve. His red hair was matted with sweat. "But your friend the Indian agent has done well. The Tall Bulls are building a new Panther Hall. It is even bigger, with more of everything to part a man from his money. They have done well. And Seth . . ."

Tom glanced up at the mention of his father.

"The Sandcranes are ranching the choice pasture lands along Coyote Creek. I've heard it was a gift from Benedict, in gratitude for all your help." Willem took a step toward the kneeling man. "Now I know why you burned the agency building. You destroyed all the evidence, anything that might have proved Benedict acted on his own behalf over ours. Then you left. Why? Did you really think we would forget?"

"Go to hell," Tom growled. He had lived with his own guilt long enough. He wasn't about to have it shoved down his throat. Tom straightened and staggered out of the water. Seth on Coyote Creek! The former Arrow Keeper had surprised his son yet again.

Tom gingerly worked his hands, checking his scraped and bloodied knuckles, thankful he hadn't broken any bones. Maybe he had deserved the beating. It certainly hurt no worse than the internal pummeling Tom had given himself during all these long months.

"I didn't see you in Tulsa," Tom mentioned.

"You'd left for Florida by the time I joined," Willem said. "But I heard you'd been around. I knew our paths would cross once we got to Cuba."

"Have Stump Horn and the others had enough?" Tom shifted his gaze toward the fire-dotted coast. "Does it end here?"

"Perhaps."

"It had better," Tom warned. "Before someone gets killed. From now on I'll be carrying a gun." To have the death of one of his former friends on his hands was the last thing Tom wanted. But neither was he about to endure another attack.

"An empty threat, Tom Sandcrane. You've never killed anyone. Remember . . . I know you."

"Oh?" Tom replied. The lingering horror of the nightmarish vision he had experienced marked him far deeper than any bruise. "Do you?" He stepped close and put his face in Willem's. He could smell the rum on the half-breed's lips.

Willem blinked, tried to steady himself, then retreated a few steps. He had been as close a friend as a man could have: The two had hunted together, ridden the same hills together, fought the same battles side by side. But the tormented expression on Tom's face and the hardness in his eyes gave the half-breed cause to wonder. He stood aside as Tom brushed past him and started up the shore to the palm grove.

"I know you!" Willem repeated. But his shout was lost to the tides and the rustling palms and the starry vastness overhead.

CHAPTER EIGHTEEN

ANTONIO CELESTIAL AWOKE WITH A CRY AND, GRABBING THE Colt revolver he kept beside his cot, fired two rounds through the rag-covered window of the mud-brick casita in which he lay. He screamed as his lower back brutally reminded him of the error of his ways. His outburst became a moan. The gunshots ringing in his ears, he eased back on the worn, faded blankets covering the cot's woven rope frame. "Mother of God," he moaned. Supplications and curses spilled from his lips with indifference these days. One served as good as the other. Whenever he attempted to stand and move about, his injured vertebrae ground together against the inflamed nerve endings; the result was excruciating pain.

For two years he had played a deadly game of cat and mouse with the Spanish, harassing them at every turn. He struck without warning and rode through gauntlets of gunfire, always to emerge unscathed. "And now to be felled by some clumsy sailor with a club," he muttered through clenched teeth while reflecting on his predicament.

He was virtually helpless, too incapacitated by the pain to be able to defend himself worth a damn. Glaring at the bullet-riddled remains of the rag curtains, which the breeze had stirred, Celestial noticed the husklike remains of a beetle wrapped in the silken strands of a spider's web. The injured man felt an unsettling kinship with the lifeless insect, which must have struggled in vain while awaiting the inevitable.

The nightmare that had roused Celestial from his uneasy rest had seen him dancing a gallows jig before Captain Zuloaga and the whole Spanish army. To his rum-blurred vision it appeared as if some unseen hand were brushing aside the makeshift curtains. A well-honed instinct for self-preservation had caused the startled rebel to reach for his gun and blast away at the threat.

Gun smoke banded gray and gold as it writhed through fractured sunlight. The casita's roof was pockmarked with gaping holes where the beams had rotted. Brightly plumaged birds nested in the rafters while field mice and lizards took up tenancy in the casita's kitchen and other bedroom. A ten-inch-long iguana clung to the back of a ladder-back chair a few feet from the cot. The reptile stared at the injured human with primitive indifference.

The rest of the mud-brick casitas and cruder-built jacals that surrounded the plaza suffered from similar neglect. Not even Celestial knew the village's history. Defying the pain, the rebel leader forced his protesting body to sit upright. Sweat beaded his brow, and his hands trembled as he put the gun aside and reached for the bottle of rum Joanna had left him to help control the pain. Now, there was a woman who undersood the proper medicinal benefits of "jack iron." He uncorked the clay bottle and took several swallows before setting the jug aside. He wiped a forearm across his stubbled jaw and dry, cracked lips and stared at his shadow on the wall. He rested his elbows on his knees and returned his attention to the iguana, whose bedside manner left a lot to be desired.

"Many years ago I stumbled upon the canyon and the remains of the village quite by accident." He spoke as if he were addressing an old friend. The iguana continued to watch him without care. Celestial blinked and wiped a forearm across his eyes. The pain eased if he remained motionless.

He had been a simple teacher then, enjoying a solitary sojourn into the Sierra Maestra to study and collect the wide variety of insects to be found among the towering ridges and in the darkened pockets of its canyons and arroyos. "I found this place just like it is right now, abandoned and still as death. I named the village for my mother, Rosarita. Now it has become my sanctuary. I, a madman conversing with lizards and mice."

Celestial ruefully chuckled and set the jug aside, then slowly, methodically reached for the revolver. He swung open the cylinder and ejected the spent shells onto the floor. At the clatter of the brass casings the iguana leaped from the chair and scampered across the floor, vanishing into the kitchen. Celestial managed to stand, again defying the pain, and walk to the doorway, where he leaned against the sill and surveyed the weathered remains of the village and the steep, forested ridges hemming in the sky. The former occupants of the valley had started a church on the outskirts of the village, about eighty yards from the plaza, a proper distance for a procession. The mud-bricked outer walls of the structure were all that existed, and these were pockmarked and worn like the faith of those Rosarita had sheltered.

The western entrance to the canyon was a trail through a dense stand of oak and mahogany with a sprinkling of pine that stretched from cliff to cliff. The woods began to thin and eventually played out within a stone's throw of the outermost jacal. East of the village a trail began in a grassy meadow about seventy yards wide and a quarter of a mile in length, then drastically narrowed to a defile cutting through a bluff that towered a thousand feet above the deserted village. The pass was a dogleg and almost invisible until glimpsed from close-up. On approach the bluff revealed itself as two separate ridges, which seemed to swing ajar like monumental gates, revealing an escape route from what appeared to be, at first glance, a box canyon.

Celestial watched his horse circle the confines of its corral, a hastily constructed fence between two casitas. The gelding was as much a prisoner as he. The rebel leader studied the patterns of the clouds drifting across the floor of the canyon. He looked longingly at the horse and for a moment even fooled himself into thinking he could sit astride the animal and escape Rosarita. But, in truth, it was an effort even to stand there propped in the doorway. He turned his back on the sunlight, staggered to his cot, and with a groan took his seat once more. He glanced at the rum, then looked away. No. Enough. No more jack iron. He must endure the pain, for Captain Zuloaga rode those mountains, searching, ever searching. Better to meet the devil cold sober and gun in hand.

Antonio Celestial stretched out on the cot and, with one arm behind his head, stared at the rafters and the patch of sky. He winced, the pain like a knife shoved clear through his spine. Perhaps the Americans hadn't landed at Daiquirí. Rumors had proved false before. Joanna might find nothing more than an empty beach. He forced the speculation from his mind. What was the point of worrying now? Today and tomorrow were in the hands of God. He stared down at the gun in his hand and became filled with grim resolve. The Spaniards might take him . . . but by heaven, they would not take him lightly.

CHAPTER NINETEEN

MY GOD, YOU LOOK TERRIBLE," JOANNA BLURTED OUT. TOM Sandcrane, bathing his battered torso in the aquamarine sea for the second time that morning, sloshed his way back to shore and stood, dripping, his trousers plastered to his limbs and salt water streaming from his naked chest and discolored features. Behind him, billowing clouds like some vast herd of white stallions swept up from the horizon of ships and sea and sky to trample the sapphire meadows of heaven. "What happened?"

Tom shrugged. "I had a difference of opinion with some friends. It was nothing."

"Then I'd hate to see *something*," Joanna retorted. "Come along with me this instant." She had no ranking, but the tone of her voice caused Tom to obey without thinking. He grabbed up his shirt, donned his hat, and fell in step alongside her. It struck him as odd that she should have wandered out of the medical compound and found him by accident. He had the feeling she had come seeking him. If that was indeed the case, then for what purpose? He was intrigued. Their boots dug into the sand as the sergeant and the woman doctor retraced the tracks she had left. Seagulls and terns filled the sky, attracted by the ships and men and opportunity for plunder among the debris left by such a mighty host. Long boats bobbed on the surface of the bay bearing a cargo of men and mules, and it was a toss-up between the two as to who exactly was the more nervous.

The aroma of coffee and flapjacks drifted from the central cook fire around which the medical personnel took their breakfast. The dining area was convenient to both the hospital tents and the private quarters of physicians and aides. A cheer had already gone up for Doctor Bernard Marmillon, who had substituted his own private stores of sugar-cured bacon for the foul-smelling tinned beef that was the staple foodstuff among the enlisted men.

With his name ringing in the air, Marmillon's look of pleasure at Joanna's return to the circle of hospital tents quickly changed to dismay when he recognized the soldier accompanying her. He did not like to think of himself as a prejudiced man, but Bernard was unable to free himself from the stirring of displeasure over the familiar way the Cheyenne sergeant had of addressing Joanna. After all, she came from an exceptional family who wielded a great deal of power in the lower Mississippi valley. The men of the Indian Brigade seemed to have very little regard for authority or for one's station in life. Still, he warmed to Joanna's return, and he hoped she might join him.

But the woman had other things on her mind than breakfast. She waved to Bernard and continued on to the nearest medical tent, an airy, three-sided canvas tent housing a couple of tables and an assortment of cabinets, trunks, and stools. The soldiers with superficial injuries often came no farther into the compound. Shirkers were immediately sent packing with a severe reprimand ringing in their ears. But Tom's bruises and cuts were genuine, though hardly fatal. Perched on the edge of a table, Tom played the part of the cooperative patient with a slightly bemused expression on his face, enduring what he considered to be the woman's unnecessary fuss.

"That laceration over your eye might need a few stitches," she mentioned.

"Is it bleeding?"

"Well, no, but it is pretty deep," Joanna said.

"It will be all right. I have a poultice of mud and spiderwebs and some herbs tucked in my saddlebags."

"An Indian remedy . . . you Cheyenne don't trust doctors?"

"We never had one on the reservation, except for a drunk old army physician. I wouldn't have trusted him with a stray dog." Tom winced as she probed his side. "In Oklahoma Territory most folks don't rightly give a damn whether the Southern Cheyenne live or die." In the distance horns blared from the ships in the harbor as more troops prepared to come ashore. *The sooner off this cursed shore, the better,* Tom thought. "Ow."

Her fingers had found a sore spot.

"Your ribs and diaphragm will be tender for a few days," Joanna dryly observed. She stepped back, searched a nearby tray, and came away with a vial of iodine and a cotton swab, with which she painted his cuts. She glanced once at his mouth. "Looks like you have a discrepancy on the distal intermediate cusp of one of your upper molars." Joanna noticed he was staring at her as if she were a madwoman uttering gibberish. "A chipped tooth," she explained. "Sorry. It's a way of being taken seriously. A woman doctor has to find ways to prove herself."

She put the antiseptic aside, washed her hands in a basin of water, looked around the tent for a towel, and then, as a last resort, dried them on her trousers.

"Now perhaps you'll tell me why you came looking for me," Tom said. The cut beneath his lip hurt like hell from the tincture she had applied. So did the one over his eye. The poultice tucked in his saddlebags would have felt cool and soothing and healed him just fine, but, as the woman said, she was the doctor. Joanna calmly appraised Sandcrane, renewed respect in her brown eyes for this sergeant from Oklahoma. She reached in her hip pocket and handed over the document authorizing her to secure volunteers to bring Antonio Celestial out of the mountains to safety. "I'd like you to take a ride."

Tom read the authorization as she explained Celestial's predicament. There were no surprises in the hastily scribbled note Joanna handed him nor in the woman's story itself, for he already knew much of her situation from having overheard her meeting with Colonel Roosevelt and the rest of the officers. No. For Tom Sandcrane the surprise came when he so readily agreed to go.

The 180 rough riders of the First Volunteers were spread along a fifty-yard stretch of palm grove on the northern perimeter of the encampment. That's where Tom had left his rifle and belongings, under the safeguard of the two mixed-blood Creek who had become his partners in uniform. Of course, he had ulterior motives, other than retrieving his rifle, for returning to the First Volunteers. Tom couldn't singlehandedly transport Celestial and fight off whatever Spanish patrols he might encounter. He needed men to back him, men who had eaten their fill of the dust of Daiquirí and would prefer the danger of the mountains to another day on these congested shores. He needed to look no farther than the woven thatch hut where he'd left his pack and bedroll under the watchful eyes of the two Creek who had been his saddlemates since Tulsa.

Tully Crow was seated in the shade of the *bohío,* smoke trailing from the campfire he had just coaxed from embers to a friendly blaze beneath a blue enameled coffeepot. Sweat beaded his angular features, and a bead of moisture hung precipitously from his large nose as he plucked a burning stick from the fire and lit the blackened stub of a cigar clamped between his teeth.

Philo Underhill, sitting cross-legged opposite his companion, was stirring the muddy-looking grounds at the bottom of the coffeepot with a long-bladed, double-edged knife whose elkhorn handle had been carved in the shape of a bear. Philo was softly singing to himself as he waited for the bacon to fry. A plate of blackened biscuits had already been set aside.

> "Gonna saddle me a big brown mare,
> and ride away from here,
> to where the wind blows free
> that's where a man oughta be
> on the lone prairie."

Too thirsty to wait any longer, he started to fill a cup with the black, bitter brew when Tom's shadow fell across the bedroll and Krag rifles neatly stacked against the hut. Joanna had already caused a flurry of curious looks as she entered the camp alongside Tom. The physician was certain such obvious interest was inspired by the fact that these men hadn't seen a woman in months, save for the few stern nurses who had accompanied Marmillon's medical unit ashore. The uniform, however loose fitting, revealed far more of her figure than a dress would have.

Joanna, aware she was rapidly becoming the center of attention, shifted uncomfortably beneath the openly lustful scrutiny of the soldiers. Celestial's men had treated her in much the same fashion for a while, but she had ultimately won their respect and admiration. The frequency of her clandestine forays into the countryside had bred a certain familiarity among the rebels, who had come to think of her first as a healer and a friend. Sex was of little consequence to a man with a shattered limb or a bullet in his gut.

Philo clambered to his feet and doffed his campaign hat. He offered his coffee to Joanna, who declined, and then to Tom, who gratefully accepted the cup and tilted it to his lips. "Appears you been busy, Sergeant Sandcrane," the Creek remarked, noting the bruises discoloring Tom's features.

"A few former friends paid me a call," he replied, draining the contents of the cup. The rum-laced brew burned the stiffness out of him.

"We'd have been pleased to make their acquaintance," Tully said, trying to take his eyes off Joanna. He flashed a toothsome grin, which, unfortunately, made him appear all the more homely.

"They didn't stay long," Tom added. He was struggling to shake off the image of that hawk with its crimson wings. It was a decidedly lethal specter he hoped never again to encounter.

"Hrumph! Lucky for you," Philo grunted, refilling the cup for himself. "Sure you won't have some, ma'am? Nobody makes better coffee than Philo Underhill. That's what my first wife used to say, God rest her soul." He glanced at Tully and then Tom, both of whom were accustomed to his many lies when confronted with a lady.

"No, thank you," Joanna said, wrinkling her nose as the aroma of burned bacon and biscuits assailed her nostrils. "I'm sorry about your wife."

"Don't be," Tom said, frowning at the soldier. "Philo's never been married. That's just a story he uses whenever he meets a pretty woman like yourself. He figures sympathy will get her all warmed up toward him." He ignored Philo's glowering features.

"I had assumed from the smell of breakfast that the poor lady died of poisoning," Joanna added with a wink.

"Haw haw haw." Tully doubled over, his hands on his knees. "She got you there, Philo."

The cook by the fire grumbled beneath his breath, but the woman before him had such a pretty smile, he couldn't hold a grudge.

"Listen up, fence riders. I'm going for a ride. It ought to take about a week," Tom said. "I thought maybe you boys would like to come along—unless you'd rather stay around here unloading boats and tending mules and drilling when Captain Huston decides you haven't sweated enough."

"A ride . . . where?" Philo asked, suspecting trouble, his sleepy gaze suddenly alert.

Joanna pointed to the rugged brown skyline through the palm trees. The mountains waited, silent and ominous, though bathed in sunlight. "Up there."

Philo Underhill and Tully Crow lifted their eyes to the Sierra Maestra. The whole blamed Spanish army was waiting beyond the horizon, hidden, poised to pounce like a wild cat.

"A man'd have to be plumb crazy to take a ride like that," Tully dryly observed.

"Sure as hell," Tom replied.

"How many are going?" Philo asked. Tom held up one finger. Philo looked at Tully, who nodded as if agreeing to an unspoken suggestion. They had always been lucky for one another, ever since Oklahoma; there was no sense in breaking up a good thing.

Philo held up three fingers. "When do we leave?"

"Today. As soon as I report to Captain Huston," Tom said. He tilted his hat back on his sun-darkened forehead, misgivings suddenly threatened to erode his confidence. Their horses were grazing in an overgrown garden that once served the needs of the village. "Philo, we'll need a wagon. A two-horse team. And cushion the wagon bed with as many blankets as you can find. Tully, draw food, ammunition, and a box of dynamite from supplies. Maybe an extra rifle or two. After all, we aren't going on a church picnic." Tom turned back to Joanna. "Now, ma'am, I think you said something about a map."

CHAPTER TWENTY

N EAR NOON ON THE TWENTY-SECOND OF JUNE, NINE DAYS BE-
fore San Juan Hill and the battle that would add to
his legend and eventually propel him to the White
House, Colonel Theodore Roosevelt waited in the company of
Captains Huston and Marmillon for the volunteers from the
Indian Brigade to file past the porch of the plantation house.
As the military amenities had been dispensed with, there was
no reason for the patrol to approach their commanding officers. A simple salute from a distance would suffice.

Roosevelt regarded with suspicion a cup of *panal*, a drink
made from the milk of green coconuts to which the medical
officer had added a portion of dark rum. The colonel risked
a sip of the thick, sweet beverage and grimaced.

"My God, Bob, you actually drink this stuff?"

Huston coughed and nervously cleared his throat. "It takes
a little getting used to, sir," he replied.

"So does castrating stallions," Roosevelt replied, harking
back to his days in the Dakota badlands. "Although necessary
at times, I never warmed to the undertaking." He pointedly
set the cup aside and patted the wrinkles from the carefully
tailored uniform he had purchased at Brooks Brothers prior to
the expedition. The once crisp blue and tan lines of his coat
and trousers were rumpled and sweat stained, despite the
shade on the porch.

Local beverages were the least of Colonel Roosevelt's troubles, thought Bernard Marmillon. It was plain to everyone that the dashing commander of the Rough Riders was eager to be off the beach and engaging the Spanish forces.

Marmillon's chief concern, on the other hand, was of a more intimate nature. With the rescue party dispatched into the mountains, Joanna would no doubt be happier. She had done all anyone could do, and now the matter was beyond her control. Bernard intended to give this attractive lady something else to think about. Already he had planned a shore dinner out beyond the army's sprawl of supplies and armaments. Bernard had in mind a campfire and perhaps a plate of panfried snapper and some oysters and, most important of all, the bottle of wine tucked away in the trunk beneath his cot. He intended to make this evening memorable. After all, Joanna had been attracted to him once. Bernard intended for that lightning to strike twice.

"My compliments on how well you've worked all this out, Colonel Roosevelt," the medical officer said, pointedly avoiding the clay cup of *panal* Huston had set aside for him. He was well aware of the concoction's potency. An entire afternoon of tending the ill and injured awaited him, and it wouldn't do to treat his patients while under the rum drink's heavy influence. However, Bernard didn't mind having one of the hard-boiled eggs Roosevelt's cook had left on a nearby table. Tapping the egg on the porch railing, he began to peel away the shell.

"How do you mean?" Roosevelt asked, ever mindful of a slight. The colonel's tone of voice gave Marmillon cause to worry that somehow he had offended the pugnacious commander of the Rough Riders, who was a proud and feisty individual determined to make a name for himself in this war. With a stroke of his bushy mustache Roosevelt turned to face the medical officer, and when he did, the lenses of his spectacles reflected the late-morning glare. It gave the illusion that sunlight was streaming from his eyes, as if he were generating the radiance like some human dynamo. The effect thoroughly cowed Bernard and left him stumbling for words.

"Well . . . uh . . . only . . . uh . . . that by sending out the

volunteers you've made Joanna happy. And . . . when her father learns you have found her alive and healthy, then I
should imagine his . . . uh . . . gratitude will be boundless."
Bernard bit into the egg as an excuse to gather his wits before
he talked himself into real trouble. He shifted his focus to the
flatbed wagon and horsemen threading their way through the
encampment. Tom Sandcrane was in the lead, astride a sorrel
gelding. A thin, leathery-looking man rode behind him, followed by a heavyset breed handling the pair of chestnut geldings pulling the wagon. Bernard continued to explain his
remarks without meeting the yellow fire of Roosevelt's stare.
"And when the locals learn of your attempt, whether it suc-
ceeds or fails, you will have won the gratitude of the Cuban
people."

"Do you think me insincere, Mr. Marmillon? Do you suspect my motives?"

"Why . . . uh . . . no. On the contrary. I assure you—"

"We shall attempt to rescue Antonio Celestial because it is
the just and decent and fair thing to do. And, by heaven, if
the United States stands for anything, it stands for justice and
decency and fair play. Spain is a bully, gentlemen. And I hate
bullies—always have and always will. Don't think for an instant I consider these men from the Indian Brigade expend-
able. If anyone can bring in Celestial, it is these volunteers.
The red man can pass unnoticed where a white man would
only call attention to himself. It has been my experience in
the wilds that a red man can outhunt, outfight, and outrun a
force three and four times his number. No—these three lads
will do fine. In fact, I've instructed them to rejoin us in Santiago. By then we will have either taken the city or be engaged in that endeavor."

"Five sir," Captain Huston corrected. He had finished his
drink and was standing off to the side, grateful that Bernard
Marmillon was receiving the brunt of Roosevelt's harangue.
The medical officer struck Huston as a little too big for his
britches, and it was enjoyable to see the colonel cut the man
down to size.

"What's that?"

"Five men, sir. Another couple of volunteers asked to join

Sandcrane just about an hour ago. I saw no reason to deny them. Five seemed like a good number to have if they run into trouble. See? There they are." Huston pointed to a pair of soldiers who had trotted their horses over to join the men leading the wagon up from the occupied village of Daiquirí.

Earlier that morning Huston had noticed Sandcrane's bruised features when Tom volunteered to rescue the Cuban leader. As the sergeant wasn't forthcoming about the cause of his injuries, Huston saw no reason to press the matter. Captain Huston's sole concern had been to find men willing to undertake Celestial's rescue. To the captain's delight Tom Sandcrane had not only volunteered, but he had arranged for another two men to accompany him on the patrol.

Joanna had expressed her obvious pleasure that the army was acting on the behalf of her Cuban friend. If Joanna Cooper was pleased, then Colonel Roosevelt was satisfied. And if Doctor Cooper's influential father back in New Orleans happened to received a cable describing how helpful Roosevelt had been toward his daughter, so much the better.

"Two more brave fellows, eh? Excellent, Bob," the colonel remarked. "I am certain the sergeant can handle the addition to his patrol."

"In fact, Sandcrane ought to be delighted to see them," Huston continued, pleased with the present turn of events and willing to take credit for any favorable outcome. "After all, they're Cheyenne, the same as he."

"Where's the doctor?" Tully asked, glancing aside at Tom.

"Yeah," Philo called out from the wagon. "The least she could have done was give us a proper send-off."

"What were you looking for—flags and a marching band?" Tom replied with a grin. He also found Joanna's absence strikingly curious but saw no point in making an issue of it.

"Not from her. I kinda figured a fare-thee-well kiss to be the least she could do, since we're so brave and all." Philo peeled a chaw from the plug of tobacco he kept in his shirt pocket and wadded the black leaves in his cheek. He glanced over his shoulder at the contents of the partly loaded freight wagon.

Save for some medical supplies and an extra box of ammunition for the Krag rifles, the only other items of note were a stretcher and a hardwood crate of dynamite along with a roll of fuse and a case of priming caps. "You loaded the damn explosives between my legs, Tully. If we run into any Spaniards, what happens if they shoot low?"

"Well, then you've precious little to lose," Tully said with a chuckle and a wink at Tom, who was suddenly oblivious to the good-natured banter of his friends. Tom's attention was directed toward the two men riding through the noisy encampment, headed straight for him.

Willem Tangle Hair, his features dark with freckles, and big Enos Stump Horn, his nose swollen and flat from its previous encounter with the back of Tom's head, rode up and placed themselves before Sandcrane's patrol. Both Cheyenne were armed as Tom and his men were, with Krag rifles and thirty-eight-caliber double-action Colt revolvers holstered on their hips. Cartridges for the Colt circled each man's waist. A bandolier of ammunition for the bolt-action Krags was slung across each man's shoulder. All soldiers carried knives, although big Enos favored an iron-bladed throwing 'hawk with a hand-forged iron head on an eighteen-inch hickory handle.

"Captain Huston said we could join you," Willem casually announced.

"He even told us to look after you," Enos said, his voice hoarse and distorted as it issued from his bruised throat.

Tom folded his hands on the pommel of his saddle. He could feel the attention of the nearby soldiers who watched with a mixture of sympathy and morbid fascination. The mountains of the Sierra Maestra loomed in the distance; those peaks, towering well over eight thousand feet, made a silent but ultimately forbidding panorama. Taking so few men into such an ominous landscape, even though Joanna promised a two-day ride, seemed the height of foolishness, bordering on suicide. There was a formidable Spanish force encamped around Santiago. No doubt there were patrols waiting in the shadow of the mountains eager to pounce and draw first blood against the American army.

"Suit yourself," Tom said. Tully and Philo were completely

taken aback that Sandcrane voiced no objection. "Fall in behind the wagon."

Willem muttered beneath his breath, his remarks for Enos alone. The broad-shouldered Cheyenne shrugged and followed Willem to the rear of the column. He made a point of staring belligerently at Tom as he rode past. Tully trotted his mount up alongside Sandcrane, and his worried expression spoke volumes.

"We can use the guns," Tom said, hoping to appease the man's objections.

Tully Crow wagged his head from side to side, making it clear he wasn't buying into Tom's logic. "Depends on who they're aimed at."

Hour after hot, interminable hour, Daiquirí baked beneath a dust-colored haze that stretched from the water's edge to half a mile inland. The military commanders had insisted the army complete its disembarkation by sunset. That meant every available soldier was involved in the effort. The trade winds stilled and the Caribbean sun beat down unmercifully, heating the well-trod sand and reflecting off the aquamarine waters of the bay with blinding effect. As a net result of so much forced activity, the medical tents were full of men injured through their own carelessness or by someone else's neglectful conduct.

Bernard Marmillon along with the other physicians, aides, and nurses was kept busy all afternoon, patching up the injured and sending them back into the fray. It wasn't until the sun dipped below the line of hills to the west and the horizon turned the color of an open wound that Bernard Marmillon staggered from the medical tent. There were still patients to see, but the other physicians could handle the load. Bernard had worked the entire afternoon without a break just so he could take a couple of hours for himself after sundown.

He'd given up on the idea of a shore dinner, but there was still a bottle of wine and a stretch of isolated beach where a couple might escape prying eyes and enjoy some small measure of respite from this troublesome war. Weary as he was,

Bernard's pace quickened as he approached his tent and knocked on the wooden frame to announce himself.

"Joanna?"

No answer. Bernard shoved aside the flap and entered the tent. His cot looked unslept in, which struck him as odd, because earlier in the day, just after supplying the patrol with a map indicating the quickest route to Celestial's hidden valley, Joanna had removed herself to Bernard's quarters, claiming all the symptoms of heat exhaustion. Bernard had been so busy in the medical tent, he had taken no notice of her coming and going. He shrugged and hurried over to his trunk. He unlocked and lifted the wooden lid and, digging beneath a spare uniform, an extra shirt, and underwear, found the bottle of wine he had so jealousy guarded since leaving Florida.

Tucking the bottle and a pair of glasses into the deep pockets of his white medical coat, he emerged from the tent and surveyed the perimeter of the medical compound, then walked out of the circle of firelight to study the crowded beach. A slight, minuscule fear began to nibble away at his confidence. Something was wrong. Joanna had no business among the troops, the majority of whom were already building the cook fires with which to prepare their evening meals of beans, tinned beef, biscuits, and coffee. In the fading light he spied a few longboats making their final run from transports to shore. The sturdy crafts bobbed in the water, oars dipped into the surface of the bay, propelling the boats inexorably to shore.

The successful completion of the landing was of little concern to the love-struck officer. He turned his back on the sea and retraced his steps to the center of the compound, to take a seat at the common table where the medical staff took their meals. A corporal by the name of Ramirez, who had been known to act as surgical assistant when his services as cook weren't required, approached Bernard with a pot of coffee and a blue enamel tin cup.

"Excuse me, sir," Ramirez said, filling the cup in front of Bernard. The Mexican-American was a dark-haired thirty-year-old man of pleasant disposition, a former trail cook whose culinary talents and a penchant for pleasing anyone of higher ranking had landed him a position with Bernard's command. Ramirez considered the hospital unit his own private domain. Here, duty meant keeping out of harm's way when the bullets began to fly. To insure against a transfer, the former trail cook pampered the physicians at every turn. There was always hot coffee and either biscuits or cinnamon cakes for the medical personnel to snack on. But cooking wasn't Ramirez's only talent, Bernard remembered, and as the man turned to leave with the coffeepot, he reached up and caught him by the wrist.

"Miss Cooper."

"Sir?"

"Have you seen Miss Cooper?" Bernard asked. "She became ill this afternoon and retired to my tent. I just went to check on her."

"She's gone."

"Yes, I found that out for myself," Bernard somewhat curtly replied. "Did you see her leave?"

Ramirez nodded. "Sí. Much hours ago. While you and the other good doctors were caring for the soldiers."

"But she was ill."

The cook could only shrug. "She did not ride like someone who was sick."

"Ride? Dammit man, what are you saying?" Bernard's features were red and angry as he rose to his feet and loomed over the corporal.

"Por favor, Captain Marmillon," the cook said, taken aback by the officer's reaction. He retreated until he backed into another table and almost lost his balance. "The lady doctor had a horse tethered back in the trees. I was gathering firewood when I saw her, but she did not see me. She rode a fine animal, a gelding with a white blaze and one white stocking foot."

Bernard knotted his brows, pain shooting through his skull, admonishing his own carelessness and cursing her duplicity. Damn her for being so incorrigible. "Did she ride toward the water or along the beach?" The captain had to ask, though he knew the answer.

"No," said the cook. "Up there." He pointed in the direction of the mountains, patched with shadows of deep purple and black velvet. But Bernard was no longer even looking at the cook. The physician settled back on the bench seat, slumped forward with his elbows resting on the table, his hands folded as if in prayer, his forehead pressed against his knuckles. He sat without moving for several long moments. Ramirez decided to leave the man to his thoughts and hurried back to the fire, where he was preparing a stew. Bernard ignored the cook's exit.

Colonel Roosevelt will be furious. There'll be hell to pay when he hears Joanna has taken off after Celestial. My heaven, how do I tell him? Our only hope is that Sergeant Sandcrane has the good sense to turn back. But, of course, these Indians are so blasted unpredictable. Joanna, you stubborn, willful, conniving, impossible . . .

Bernard sighed, reached into his coat, and tugged the dark-green wine bottle from his pocket. Using the blade of his pocket knife, he worked the cork into the bottle, and then, as the dry, slightly tart bouquet assailed his nostrils, raised the wine as if toasting an invisible party seated across the table from him. Actually, he looked to the mountains as they lost their definition against the darkening sky.

"*Salud,*" he said, and drank to the health and safety of Joanna Cooper, to this woman, bless her and damn her, who had more courage than sense.

Tom Sandcrane watched and waited beneath the blood-colored sky, allowing the shadows of night to creep like a panther across the low hills. Since leaving Daiquirí, his "war party" of Cheyenne and Creek soldiers had ridden over a rolling forested landscape and cut through meadows of wild grasses tall enough to tickle the bellies of the horses. They had exchanged the palm groves for stands of mahogany, sweet cedar, and logwood. Blooms of brilliant color dotted every meadow and vale to be rivaled only by the feathered creatures he had glimpsed darting across the sky.

And yet all the wonders of this land had not held his attention like the single campfire flickering beneath an outcropping of lichen-splashed limestone. Smoke trailed up from the humble little blaze and dissipated among the branches of the surrounding sandalwood that formed a natural canopy over the campsite.

Philo held the wagon about fifty yards farther back in the woods. Enos guarded their backtrail while Tully Crow and Willem Tangle Hair walked their mounts forward and reined them in to either side of Tom's sorrel. Tully slid the Krag rifle off his shoulder and cradled it in his arms, a finger on the trigger. Willem likewise armed himself.

"Spaniards?" Tully asked.

"Could be," Tom whispered. "But I don't think so." Seth, the Arrow Keeper, had often taken his son into the woods, to offset the book learning of the white man. Once in the wild, Tom's father had taught him to read the telltale rustle of a branch and the tracks around a spring, to watch patiently and really see what was happening around him.

Now Tom reached out with his senses, taking in the entire scene, listening for the telltale sound and noting when a mockingbird, preparing to alight among the sandalwood trees, suddenly altered its course and fluttered away. Without realizing it, he let a fragment of song drift from his lips, subduing his initial panic. Encountering the campsite so soon after leaving the comparative safety of the army at Daiquirí had startled Tom. But the song helped him to keep his fears as tightly reined as the sorrel. He unconsciously repeated the song:

"I am the hunter
invisible as a spirit.
Courage is with me.
And strength in my arm."

Tom became aware of his own singing and, shifting uncomfortably beneath the scrutiny of his curious companions, ended the chant. He walked the sorrel to the edge of the clearing, remaining just inside the shadows. Alone again, Tom studied the campfire, probing the setting in ways the Arrow Keeper's son thought he had forgotten.

This fire had been built to attract attention. And it was concealed from every direction but the one from which the patrol rode. He unfolded the map from his pocket and studied the site where the artist had suggested they make their first camp. Doctor Cooper had indicated a limestone hill with a spring at its base and good grazing for the horses. He lowered the map and saw a meadow of lush grass, a steep hill ringed by an outcropping of limestone. From the look of the fronds sprouting from the base of the ledge, there had to be water ahead. *If I was a betting man, I'd wager this fire was left by the one person who knew we'd be along,* Tom reasoned.

He holstered his revolver and touched his heels to the sorrel's flanks, urging the animal forward. The gelding needed no inducement, for the thirsty creature smelled water.

Tully tried to call the sergeant back, but Tom was a third of the way across the clearing before the Creek could act. And then it was too late.

"What sort of man is this?" Tully complained, fearing Tom was riding into a trap.

"That's what I'm beginning to wonder," Willem said, raising the rifle to his shoulder. The longer he was around Tom, the more he sensed the chaotic forces at work on the man who had once been his closest friend.

"Hey," Tully warned, training his own weapon on the redhead.

"I'm aiming at the grove of trees," Willem coolly remarked. "Something moved."

The Creek breed grudgingly shifted his aim, though he continued to watch Tangle Hair warily. "You'd better be telling the truth," he cautioned, "that Tom's backbone ain't in your sights."

"Don't worry," Willem said. "He's like a brother to me." He meant his remarks to sound sarcastic, but the words flowed out with more conviction then he had intended.

"Yeah." Tully was hardly convinced.

*   *   *

The altercation of the previous evening, and now this long afternoon on horseback, had taken their toll. Tom was ready to make camp for the night. This fire appeared inviting rather than cause for alarm. He dismounted and led the sorrel over to the spring. Lemon-yellow parakeets with olive-dappled wings scattered at his approach and grudgingly fluttered up to a shelf in the limestone wall, where they proceeded to chirp their complaints at Tom's intrusion.

"Doctor Cooper . . . you made good time," Tom said in a loud voice. "However, I think your map was not completely accurate. Perhaps there was a shorter route to this spring than what you drew." He turned his back to the pool of water and faced the grove of sandalwood trees as Joanna Cooper strolled out of concealment. She was dressed for the trail, in a loose-fitting shirt and army-issue trousers. A gunbelt circled her waist. Her hair was pulled back from her face and tied with a leather string. She clutched a wide-brimmed straw hat filled with custard apples whose rough, greenish-brown skin looked unappealing. She knelt and placed the hat by the campfire.

"A small but necessary omission. How did you know it was me?"

When his answer was not forthcoming, Joanna glanced up. The expression on the Cheyenne's face was one she would not forget. The man seemed painfully confused and terribly unnerved. What secrets were hidden behind the mask he presented to the world? What was the mystery behind his torment?

Tom waved a hand toward the patrol, and Tully started the men across the meadow, their horses following the path Sandcrane had left in the tall grass. But even his companions were just so many blurred images. His mind, his thoughts, were like a storm-tossed sea, and the fragments of the past—the songs, the old teachings—were floating to the surface, rising out of the black depths. Why now? The past was behind him, or so he had assumed, and yet the dreams and visions were returning. The song had come to his lips without any conscious effort. *No, it was just a trick of memory.* After all, he was no Arrow Keeper, just a ghost, without yesterday or tomorrow. That's how it had to be. He would forget the songs, forget his father's teachings.

"I'm going with you," Joanna firmly said. It was a statement of fact. She misread his silence for displeasure at her presence.

"Yes," he replied.

"Celestial is my friend. And besides— What? You aren't going to try to talk me out of coming along?" She'd had her arguments all prepared.

"No." The spell of his own troubled reverie was broken.

"Why?"

"It is your path." He squatted by the fire, took one of the strange, ugly fruits she had gathered, drew his knife, and peeled the skin away. He bit into the cool, creamy pulp and tilted his head to look at her. Joanna had the sensation he was peering into her naked soul and seeing her as she truly was. "And it is your right." Then he smiled, which for a moment startled her.

"What a strange man you are, Sergeant Tom Sandcrane." Then, lowering her defenses, the woman smiled back.

Across two ridges and nestled in a wooded ravine where a cold, clear creek provided water for horses, the Lion Brigade made its camp. Dinner consisted of bread, beans simmered with peppers and chunks of pork, and coffee. Twice during the afternoon the prisoner had fallen off his horse, poison spreading through his body from the bloodied empty socket where his eye had been. Poor Mateo, by his very presence, dampened the normally good-natured banter among the soldiers. The men pitched their bedrolls in silence and stretched out to sleep the night away.

Captain Diego Zuloaga prowled the clearing, restless as a caged beast. Moonlight filtered through the branches of the lignum vitae and cast a pattern resembling iron bars over the slumbering forms of his soldiers. One of the men, unable to rest, sat propped against the trunk of a tree, caressing a melody from the guitar cradled in his arms. The music failed to soothe the captain, and he continued to pace the perimeter of the campsite as he waited for Alfonso to finish with the prisoner and report on the youth's condition. The worldly cook was a repository for all kinds of knowledge and often acted as the brigade's physician as well.

Alfonso Ramirez could patch a wound and sew a man together with the same skill he used to pamper the culinary tastes of his commanding officer. Tonight he was especially thankful the captain liked his cooking. It might serve to temper Zuloaga's considerable wrath.

"Well?" the captain said, studying a constellation of fireflies swirling against a cosmos of black mountains and silent forest.

"The prisoner does not respond, *jefe*."

"The boy stalls us. He is protecting Celestial with this pretense," Zuloaga angrily replied.

"His fever is real."

"Then rid him of this fever! I command it."

"*Sí, jefe*, I will do everything I can," the cook meekly answered.

Zuloaga sighed. There was no point in taking out his frustration on the cook. "I know you will," the captain told him, gentling his tone of voice. Ramirez seemed relieved and dutifully hurried away. The commander continued to prowl the perimeter of camp, his jaws clenched, cursing Antonio Celestial, the man who had driven him to such behavior, torturing a boy for the knowledge he possessed. Zuloaga reminded himself that if their situation was reversed, the youth would have no qualms about killing and mutilating him.

Alfonso returned to the campfire, where he knelt by his young prisoner. The thirteen-year-old's features were sweat streaked beneath a crude bandage that covered the left side of his face.

"You don't lead us to Celestial, *el jefe* will have your other eye," Alfonso told the sleeping form.

Mateo stirred and moaned and called out for Miss Joanna. He lapsed into silence and then a few moments later began speaking as if to a loved one. Alfonso dipped a bandanna into the pan of cold spring water he had brought from the creek and placed the cloth on Mateo's forehead.

"What is he saying?" Handsome, blond-haired Lieutenant Emilio Garza knelt by the campfire. He tossed the gnawed remains of half a roasted quail into the fire and removing a kerchief from his coat pocket, wiping his hands clean with fastidious care.

"I think he speaks to his mother," said Alfonso.

"Captain Zuloaga grows impatient. We have wasted much time because of this one."

"There's nothing I can do," Alfonso hissed. "I'm not the one who stuck a knife in his eye. It's not my fault if infection sets in."

"Silence," Garza snapped. He glanced over his shoulder to see if Zuloaga had heard the cook's outburst. Fortunately, the captain was lost in his own ruminations. The Castilian returned his attention to Alfonso. "We cannot remain in these mountains much longer. Soon we must rejoin our forces protecting Santiago. If you value your neck, have this rebel bastard ready to sit a horse by tomorrow." The lieutenant left the glare of the campfire and made his way over to Zuloaga, fishing a flask of brandy from his coat pocket as he approached his volatile commander. Alfonso watched the younger man depart, taking note of the flask. He licked his lips. Life was never as hard for the officers.

"Now, you are in for it, eh?" one of the men nearest the cook remarked.

"No more than you," Alfonso growled. "Ybarra, fetch me another basin of water. This has grown tepid."

"Why me? I am tired. See, my eyelids grow weary."

"Do as I say, or perhaps the next time you eat my stew, you'll find a tasty scorpion in your bowl," snapped Alfonso.

Ybarra, a man in his midtwenties with thick, bushy eyebrows and a week-old growth of stubble on his chin, muttered a litany of complaints as he crawled out of his blanket. Alfonso chuckled and handed him the basin, and the man set off for the creek.

On the edge of camp Garza arrived at the side of the officer commanding the brigade. "Will you have some brandy with me, Captain?"

Zuloaga nodded and accepted the silver flask from the lieutenant's hand. He took a moment to admire the flask's design, for some silversmith had painstakingly etched a pastoral scene upon its shiny surface—three swans gliding amid water lilies on a tree-shrouded pond.

"My uncle's handiwork," Garza proudly explained. "There is no greater talent in all of Castile."

"Sí. You told me once before," Zuloaga said. "A month ago."

"Oh, yes. I beg your pardon."

"The taste of this fine brandy is enough payment for listening to you repeat yourself." Zuloaga raised the flask to his lips, swallowed twice, and returned it to the lieutenant. "Alas, my family's only talent was in squandering its resources. Had I been in charge of things . . . well. It is of no concern. What matters is the day to come. What matters is Antonio Celestial." Zuloaga hooked a thumb in his gunbelt. Shadows and gray light caught his attention again. A bristling speck of coppery-green light dropped from the heavens, cut its fleeting arc across the firmament, and then winked out. The soldiers awake around the campfire gasped and immediately blessed themselves, tracing the sign of the cross across forehead, lips, and chest.

"Celestial is out there, injured, alone," Zuloaga said. "That much our young friend has told us. I will have him before I turn my back on this cursed island. And if we are to die at the hands of the Americans, it will not be without satisfaction."

Garza frowned. Talk of dying and defeat was something he expected from the likes of Alfonso the cook, who lacked breeding. "Sir. You are a gentleman, a man of noble birth. Time and again you have proved your courage in battle. Your words do you disservice."

"I am also a realist," Zuloaga stated. "Another ten years and you too will see things as they are." He inhaled sharply, slowly released his breath. A great sense of exaltation coursed through him. "The hare is cornered at last." Zuloaga clapped Lieutenant Garza on the shoulder. "And the hound will have his day."

CHAPTER TWENTY-ONE

MORNING CAME EARLY FOR TOM SANDCRANE AND THE other soldiers. Weeks had passed since they had spent any time in the saddle, and it showed in their stiff, cramped muscles. Yet there was not a complaint to be heard, for at least they were off the beach and heading inland. The soreness was to be expected, but it wouldn't last—after all, the Southern Cheyenne had been masters of the plains in the days when a horse was merely an extension of the warrior astride its back. The Creek half-breeds broke camp without a grumble. Tully and Philo were top ranch hands and determined to prove themselves the equal of any Cheyenne.

The patrol hit the trail shortly after sunup, and by afternoon Tom had worked the tightness out of his muscles and, like the others, sat easy in the saddle, achieving a comfortable slouch that took pressure off the back and made the rider one with the movements of his mount. For her part, Joanna Cooper more than held her own. A year spent traveling the forested back trails of the Sierra Maestra had transformed the healer into an excellent horsewoman as well.

As they traveled farther inland, the hills grew steep and the horizon closed in, becoming a series of steep ridges and densely wooded slopes broken only by stretches of meadow that frequently opened onto shadowy arroyos, fragrant with wild orchids, where streamers of *jagüey* vine threatened to choke out the thickets of mahogany and sweet cedar. Many of the arroyos were large enough to conceal a Spanish patrol, and Tom did not relax until each pocket of emerald gloom was well behind them. He was keenly aware of the enemy's presence in these mountains. The night before, around the campfire, Joanna had spoken of her earlier encounter with Captain Zuloaga, how she and Mateo had separated in hopes that one would reach the Americans. She described the captain and his infamous Lion Brigade and briefly explained how Diego Zuloaga and the rebels led by Antonio Celestial had played cat and mouse for almost two years.

The Spaniards were unremitting in their quest. Even now, with the American army arrived to threaten the fortified city of Santiago, the Lion Brigade stalked the Sierra Maestra in search of Celestial. There was no way of telling how many men this Zuloaga had with him, but his brigade was bound to outnumber the American patrol. And if the Spaniards had caught Mateo and forced the youth to talk, then all of them could be riding into a deadly trap.

For the first few hours of the morning, Joanna, Tom, and the soldiers followed a wheel-rutted trail that wound through a series of valleys cutting deeper into the mountains. The trail was for the most part over level ground, and when Tom wasn't searching the canyons for enemy patrols, he was studying the map Joanna had drawn. She was hardly a gifted artist, but she assured Tom the layout of the deserted village of Rosarita was reasonably accurate. Tom noted the ravine that served as a rear entrance to the village. Here was a back door they might need to close in a hurry if trouble came their way. He congratulated himself for bringing along the dynamite.

At midmorning Joanna guided them onto an overgrown path that zigzagged up the side of a towering ridge. Tom questioned the wisdom of leaving the low road, but the woman explained her course would shorten the journey by nearly half a day and bring them into Rosarita through the same narrow gorge that had caught Tom's attention on the map. Tom acquiesced, conceding the doctor's experience in these mountains. Fortunately, the trail over the ridge followed, for the most part, a meandering creek, which flowed down through the trees, a sweet, sun-dappled ribbon of water.

Despite the proximity of a cooling drink, the steady climb took its toll on the wagon team, and by midafternoon Tom ordered the patrol to take a lengthy break before the push to the top. The other four soldiers were only too happy to obey. They dismounted and led their horses to the narrow rivulet of springwater that merrily gurgled down the wooded slope, spilling over mossy, water-smoothed stones and losing itself among the fern and bromeliads, whose pale cream flowers added an extra dash of color where sunlight streamed through breaks in the timber.

Tom checked his saddlebags for a leftover biscuit. His hand brushed against the beaded buckskin pouch containing the Medicine Pipe. He removed the pouch and held it up into the sunlight, running his hand along its soft white surface, feeling the weight of the clay bowl and the crackle of dried sage beneath his touch. He left his sorrel ground-tethered by the undulating brook and sauntered off alone through the lush twilight of the woods, where tree ferns towered thirty feet in height and birds with iridescent plumage chattered and scolded, decrying this latest intrusion of man.

Enos caught a glimpse of Tom as he vanished into the underbrush; the Cheyenne immediately began to plot his own escape. It wasn't long before Stump Horn found the opportunity to slip away from the patrol. Behind him Tully and Philo argued over the wisdom of taking the wagon any farther up the steep ridge, while Joanna strived to assure them that once at the summit, the irregular and treacherous path they were following would cut across a narrow trail running along the spine of the ridge and ultimately bring them down where a better passage awaited. Willem Tangle Hair, although intending to keep watch on Enos, had become preoccupied with dislodging a stone from the left front hoof of his mount. He'd have to work the tip of his knife beneath the iron shoe and loosen it before freeing the stone. No one by the creek no-

ticed Stump Horn ease behind a mahogany tree and creep off
into the shadows.

The forest thinned farther up the ridge, and a shelf of granite thrust out as wide as a man was tall to form an overlook.
Tom thought it the ideal place to check the patrol's backtrail,
for the gray outcropping made a suitable bench and had a relatively unobstructed view of the valley below. The decaying
remains of a *mangle blanc* tree had tumbled downhill and littered the shelf with branches and twigs. Tom climbed to the
ledge and gratefully took a seat after checking the stone's mottled surface for scorpions and centipedes. He unslung his rifle, set it aside, and sat with his legs dangling over the ledge,
his hands clasping the medicine pouch his father had given
him. As he studied the surrounding mountains and the pre-
cipitous path they had followed since noon, a gentle breeze
fanned his sweat-streaked features, providing a measure of
cooling relief. He continued, unconsciously, to rub the buckskin pouch with his thumbs.

He checked the distant skyline to north and east and south
for any sign of pursuit but found nothing to be alarmed
about; still, he continued to fix his steady gaze on the mountainous terrain and the valley they had traversed in the early-
morning hours. An eerie silence settled over the land as if all
the hills were waiting, watching. . . . Tom shuddered, half expecting to be revisited by the spirit warrior he had glimpsed
back in Oklahoma. In a way, he missed the apparition, while
at the same time dreading another encounter. Almost a year
had passed since his departure from Cross Timbers, and there
had been nothing to remind him of his heritage save the medicine pouch and the red clay pipe it contained. Now, in Cuba,
anything seemed possible. Had the Maiyun abandoned him
for a while, condemning him to their silence, to his empty
wandering, unconnected, like a ghost trapped between
worlds? Had an unseen hand guided his choices and set him
on this path for a purpose he was yet to discover? These constant deliberations were driving him mad.

Tom forced his thoughts to return to the present, to escape

once again the pain of the past. He imagined the American army was on the move by now, setting forth along the sea road on a course toward Santiago. Like some great shaggy buffalo plowing its way out of a wallow, head lowered, horns menacing, hooves pounding the earth as it gradually gathered momentum—so the American army would leave Daiquirí, the pace tortuously slow at first, but ever quickening until the troops became a juggernaut capable of overwhelming the Spanish fortifications. That would be something for even a ghost to see.

A twig cracked. Tom glanced around, one hand dropping to the rifle at his side. Enos Stump Horn stopped dead in his tracks, tomahawk in hand. He had climbed above the stone outcropping and slipped down on the other side of the shattered tree trunk to approach from Tom's blind side. But the debris left by the *mangle blanc* had tripped him up.

The big man's knuckles whitened as he gripped the shaft of the tomahawk, its forged-iron blade held down. No comfort there. Tom knew the man could throw underhanded and hit his mark with ease.

Enos, a large and formidable opponent with brawny arms and sloping shoulders, was made all the more intimidating by his ruined features. The man with the 'hawk had never been considered handsome, but after his previous altercation with Tom, poor Enos Stump Horn could have written the book on ugly. His nose was purple and swollen at the bridge, while the nostrils and tip were flattened and issued a slight whistling sound whenever he attempted to draw a breath through this bruised mass of cartilage and gristle.

The two men watched one another without speaking. Stump Horn's gaze lowered to the buckskin pouch and widened with recognition. He hadn't expected to find Tom praying, as it was common knowledge that the Arrow Keeper's son had refused the Mahuts when they had been offered to him. Yet here he sat with a pipe bundle in his hand. If he smoked the pipe, Enos would either have to depart in peace or confront Tom, disrupting the prayer and risking the wrath of the Maiyun.

Tom appraised the situation, seeking some way to avoid

bloodshed. If Enos had come to try to kill him, he thought, better to settle the matter here and now, once and for all. He could think of only one way out of the confrontation, although it was not without risk. Tom eased his hand away from the trigger and slowly turned his back to the would-be assassin. A tingling sensation shot the length of his spine, and the muscles tightened along his shoulders. It took every bit of self-control he possessed to keep from chancing a look over his shoulder. He'd seen Enos drive that tomahawk inches deep in a tree trunk. It was an image Tom wished he could forget. Using every ounce of willpower, the sergeant focused on the valley stretching to the east. Minutes seemed to crawl past.

To his relief there came no whisper of an iron blade cutting the air, no painful impact of steel, severing sinew and spine. Yet the bleak sound of Enos Stump Horn's voice, the man's sense of betrayal at the hands of a friend, wounded Tom more cruelly than any blade.

"We had cattle, horses . . . the land was ours. We got along all right. But you and Allyn Benedict said it could be better." Enos's voice grew thick with bitterness as he relived the unpleasant past. "You talked us into giving up the reservation and opening the land to the white man. We'd be citizens, you said. Well, we became citizens . . . with nothing." Enos paused. "My father and many others sold their homesteads to the white settlers, figuring to put the money with the cash allotments and buy a piece of the oil fields. Only the government had already sold the north tracts to Benedict and the oil speculators. Nothing was left for us but the scrub timber and the range along the Washita to the south." Enos took a step closer, his voice wavering. "Of course, you and Seth did all right. That's good range around Coyote Creek. But my father sold out for cash. When the government agents wouldn't let him buy into the oil fields, he went and gambled every dollar at Panther Hall. Father Kenneth found him the next morning, lying in front of the church. He'd put a bullet in his brain. I could have stayed around and worked in the oil fields, helped Allyn Benedict bring in his well. But this war seemed a better idea."

"I'm sorry about your father," Tom said. "But I didn't bring him to Panther Hall. He knew the way long before I ever spoke to him. But what the hell, Enos, blame me if it helps. Or if you must hate me, then make it for something I did. Hate me for being a fool. That's what Allyn Benedict played me for!"

Funny, Tom thought after his outburst. The hurt seemed less now. Even Emmiline's betrayal had begun to lose its sting. He wondered why. Was it Cuba or the company he was keeping? Still Tom could not blame Enos. Anger had a way of eating at a man and twisting him inside. But if blood was to flow, the man with the 'hawk would have to make the first move. And he'd have to make it soon. Tom shaded his eyes, checked the position of the sun, and announced, "Time to move out."

He stood, slung his rifle over his shoulder, and tucked the pipe bundle inside his shirt. He glanced in Stump Horn's direction. The big man seemed torn with indecision.

"I have waited here long enough," Tom said. He stepped from the ledge and proceeded toward the grove of trees beyond which the patrol waited.

Enos stared at the sergeant, taken aback by Sandcrane's seeming unconcern for his own safety. For months Enos had plotted Tom's demise, rehearsing Sandcrane's death scene should their paths ever cross. Now the moment had arrived to mete out justice—and Enos was questioning his own motives. Tom presented a willing target, and yet Enos suddenly lacked the will to take advantage of it. He wasn't even certain why.

A few yards below the ledge Tom paused and waved a hand toward the big man. "C'mon, Enos. We have a job to do," he quietly said.

Again, silence. Again their eyes locked, though it was not so much a contest of wills as two men searching for the truth in one another. At last Enos Stump Horn sighed, tucked the tomahawk into his belt, and with a shake of his head for dramatic effect, started downhill. Tom doubted their war was over, but for the time being he'd gladly settle for an uneasy truce.

CHAPTER TWENTY-TWO

THE NIGHT SKY WAS CLOUDLESS AND SCATTERED WITH STARS, bright as diamonds strewn upon a black velvet table-cloth whose centerpiece was the silver platter of the moon. If heaven was bedazzled, the earth below lay stark and broken. The summer wind sighed among the rattling branches of the trees, moaned as it crept from the valley floor through crevice and cave, and scoured the hilltops, rushing on to other summits.

After reaching skyline earlier in the afternoon, Tom Sandcrane's patrol spent the remaining daylight hours following a ridge that stretched before them like the spine of some enormous beast slumbering in the earth. The ridge created valleys, blocked canyons, and skirted taller mountains. It rose and fell, crooked left and right, sometimes wooded, at other times barren and bleak and studded with slabs of gray rock. There was no visible trail to follow, but the ridge itself provided a natural path that was a challenge both for the horsemen and for the driver of the freight wagon. Tom did not regret his decision to follow Joanna's lead, despite the hard going. Several times during the afternoon he noted how the patrol avoided an intricate maze of arroyos and canyons. Joanna assured him the low road added a day to the journey. At one point Tom was certain he had glimpsed a column of riders in the pass below, and calling a halt, he surveyed the densely wooded gorge for ten minutes. When the movement failed to repeat itself, Tom gave the order to press on toward the crimson horizon. With their hats pulled low to shade their eyes from the sun, the soldiers obeyed.

At last, when the going proved too risky to continue in the dying light, Tom ordered a cold camp for the night. There on the crest of the ridge a fire would be seen for miles, and the last thing he wanted to do was announce their presence. Dinner was tinned beef and crackers washed down with water from their canteens. Tully found a pool of rainwater large enough to provide the thirsty horses with a drink before being hobbled in a sparse grove of sweet cedar. The soldiers unrolled their blankets near the wagon, a stone's throw from their mounts.

Joanna declined the army's offer of tinned beef but helped herself to a few crackers and left the campsite, canteen in hand, to wander along the ridge. She found an overlook that appealed to her and sat facing the north, the direction they would have to head come morning, when she brought the soldiers down from the ridge. She could sense the men watching her with unabashed appreciation for the thrust of her breasts and the curve of her hips, yet in no way did she feel threatened by the soldiers' scrutiny. Theirs was an honest, good-natured appraisal of her as a woman. After hiding out in the mountains these past months, Joanna thought, it was reassuring to know she could still generate a little masculine interest.

"That, my friends, is a pretty woman," Philo muttered, peering at her over the tin in his hands. He shoveled a spoonful of congealed meat into his mouth and happily began to chew. The Creek breed had an iron constitution and was the only one among them who actually liked army rations.

"Pretty . . . hell. She's beautiful," Tully said.

"Same thing."

"The devil it is. 'Beautiful' is something a man like you or me can never have," Tully replied. "It's something fine. Too fine for down-at-heel ranch hands like us."

"She's kinda on the thin side," Enos spoke up. "A woman needs some heft, else there's nothing to hold on to in the night." He glanced in Willem Tangle Hair's direction. "Now, a woman like Charlotte White Bear . . ."

"Best you hold that wagging tongue of yours or see it split," Willem cautioned. His demeanor was cheerful but his words had an ominous ring. He set his tinned beef aside, stood, and made his way over to the horses, where he knelt by his own mount and checked its leg for any sign of swelling. He was relieved to find the animal still sound.

"You finished?" Philo called out, holding up the discarded tin.

"Take it," Willem replied.

Philo nodded, pleased, and helped himself to more of the stringy brown morsels of meat in the tin. The other three men grimaced at the enthusiasm with which he ate.

"Must be part goat," Enos muttered.

Philo was immune to insult. "You boys don't know what's good," he said with an indifferent shrug.

"Yeah, but we know what's food," Tully said, eliciting a laugh at his friend's expense.

Tom regretted putting an end to the levity, but there was work to be done. "Tully, once we reach the pass below, go ahead and prime the dynamite. And make the fuses short. There isn't any telling what we'll find when we reach Rosarita. Maybe nothing; then again, the place could be swarming with Spanish soldiers. The dynamite might give us the edge we need if they spring a trap and we have to fight our way out." He stood and worked the stiffness out of his legs, then walked off from the three soldiers. His shadow in the moon's cold glare passed over their features—grown suddenly sober now—and flitted across the cedars and the stark terrain as he made his way to Willem's side. The gelding whinnied and tugged at its lead rope as Tom approached, but he gentled the creature by speaking softly and stroking the animal's neck.

"Charlotte's still a sore spot with you," Tom said as the gelding shook its mane and then relaxed. A lengthy pause followed the statement he had casually dropped like a challenge. Willem stiffened at the name of Luthor White Bear's flirtatious daughter. "Why don't you marry her? Then you can take a stick to her if she ever looks at another man."

The tension eased between them, and for the moment they were the friends they had been in childhood. "I was going to," Willem said. "As soon as I staked claim on a tract of the oil land," he sourly added. "Luthor wouldn't let her marry just some ranch hand." The recent past had an ugly way of dampening a man's spirit.

"I never meant for things to turn out the way they did," Tom said, staring at the bone-colored ground aglow in the moonlight.

"Yeah . . . well," Willem said, "maybe it's just as well you did leave. Someone probably would have taken a shot at you by now. Hell, I figured Enos for taking the first crack." Willem straightened and looked across the rump of the horse at Tom. "What happened between you two the other day?" Willem scratched his thick mop of red hair. "When I realized you were both gone, I figured only one of you'd be coming back."

"We reached an understanding, at least for now."

"Beats me how you did it," Willem replied.

"Is that why you came along, to keep Enos out of trouble?"

"Something like that," Willem replied, reining in his feelings of friendship for the man. Finally he kicked at a rock and continued. "Aw, hell, Tom. You sure screwed things up. How did you let Allyn Benedict turn you around like that? You couldn't see what he was up to?"

"All I saw was Emmiline Benedict." Tom slapped the back of his neck as an insect tried to draw blood.

Willem nodded and sighed. "Seth managed to stake out the prettiest rangeland along Coyote Creek. That section you always talked about. Folks found it a mite queer how he managed to make out so good."

"They won't have to think on it for long. He'll have probably traded it to the Tall Bulls for an extra bottle of whiskey," Tom ruefully suggested.

"You never know. A man can change." Willem walked around the horse and started back toward the wagon, then paused and added, "You did." He reflected for a second. "And me. Funny thing. I never put much stock in all that talk of the Circle or the spirits and such. But lately . . . I don't know."

He ambled back the way he had come and rejoined the other men, who were already stretched out on their blankets. Conversation had died out as the day's effort took its toll. Up to now the patrol had been something of a lark. Suddenly, with their destination close at hand, the mood had become much more serious, as each man began to speculate on what tomorrow might bring.

Tom yawned and headed for his bedroll, then changed his mind and wandered off to the north overlook. Joanna heard him approach and greeted him with a tired but honest smile.

"You ought to be sleeping," Tom said. "Sounds like we'll have a hard day tomorrow."

"Spoken like a doctor."

"Just some friendly advice."

Joanna nodded. "You're right, of course. We'll have to push hard to reach Rosarita by nightfall." She glanced toward the army mounts. Her own gelding was mountain reared and accustomed to the terrain. It was a compactly built, muscular creature, an ugly and cantankerous horse that had never let her down. The army mounts had been culled from the local ranches throughout the Southwest. They were plains animals, prairie stock. "How are your horses holding up?" she asked. "Will they do?"

"I can make them go," Tom said with the air of an experienced ranch hand, "but I can't make them do." He knelt and peered past the overhang into the valley a couple of thousand feet below, a place of stygian recesses and clearings the color of bleached bone. Tom glanced aside at the woman next to him, marveling at how unlike Emmiline Benedict she was. What a fool he had been to allow himself to fall under Emmiline's spell. Time and distance had left him wiser. Not that she was all artifice and pretense or delicate as a rosebud—indeed the Indian agent's daughter had known what she wanted and just how to get it. That was the measure of her strength. Joanna Cooper might not be as hands-down pretty, but she had one quality that outshone all of Emmiline's put together: She had honor.

"What are you thinking?" Joanna asked.

Tom, embarrassed, realized he had been staring at her. He

coughed and cleared his throat. "I was thinking . . . how you remind me of a warrior woman. Among the Cheyenne there have been women who refused to remain in their lodges and wait for their husbands or lovers to return. They received visions calling them to ride into battle alongside the men. They are called warrior women."

"What sort of visions?"

Tom shrugged. "I'm only recounting what my father told me when I was a child."

"I'm intrigued. Have you ever had a vision?"

"No," Tom replied after a momentary pause that gave away his lie. He could feel Joanna's eyes boring into him, her features moonlit and disturbingly attractive.

"I have," she admitted. "I may not be an Indian, but it's true. Well, to be truthful, I didn't exactly see so much as hear it." She told him of the drums she had heard on the shore of Lake Pontchartrain, on the back lawn of her father's estate. Once begun, the words poured out of her as if the secret she had nursed for almost two years had suddenly burst through the dam of her self-imposed silence to come flooding forth. "I heard those same drums again in Daiquirí, that night you joined me on the beach and taught me the prayer song. I haven't forgotten." Joanna closed her eyes and recited. "May the heart of the panther be in us. Our song rides upon the smoke of our fire."

"You are a strange woman, Doctor Cooper."

"Stranger than a man who calls himself a ghost?"

Tom had no answer. He merely nodded and rubbed his jaw and tried to think of a way to change the subject. Of course, Joanna wouldn't let him off the hook that easily. She tied her hair back with the leather string and then scrambled to her feet and fell in step alongside Sandcrane, who had begun to amble along the length of the overhang.

"What are you doing here in Cuba, Mr. Sandcrane?"

"You can call me Tom," he said. "And I could ask the same thing of you."

"Fair enough," Joanna nodded. "Antonio Celestial managed to escape the island and come to the United States to buy guns and munitions and drum up support for the revolution.

He visited the university and the medical school I was attending and made an appeal for medical help. I was moved by what he had to say." Joanna's voice grew wistful as if remembering something pleasant, an innocent time before the ideals of a revolution had been replaced by the grim and bloody reality of the struggle she had witnessed. "Mother and father always expected me to quit school. They were certain I was just being headstrong and foolish. When I arrived for Christmas dinner as Doctor Joanna Cooper, my parents became more determined than ever to marry me off. They figured a husband would bring me to my senses." She glanced aside and met his dark-eyed stare. "I just couldn't remain in New Orleans, even if it meant breaking my father's heart. So I followed Antonio Celestial to Cuba. I came here because I wanted my life to count for something, I wanted it to matter . . . to me if no one else!" Joanna became aware she had raised her voice. The woman sheepishly glanced toward the grove of trees. Fortunately, her energetic remarks had gone unnoticed by the others. "And now that I've bored you with my story, I'll listen to yours."

Tom liked this woman. Indeed, who wouldn't find her attractive, bathed as she was in moonlight, a gentle breeze tugging at her auburn hair? But he had built a wall around his heart. Still, Joanna's story struck a familiar chord, for Tom also had rejected his father, turning his back on the Sacred Arrows and the traditions Seth Sandcrane embodied.

Joanna was waiting for a reply. Tom was stoic: "I'm here for the same reason as many of the others. It seemed like the thing to do at the time." Walking together, they continued along a winding path that fell and rose with the convolutions of the ridge.

"No," Joanna said, stopping in her tracks. The man inadvertently halted with her. "I think something brought you to Cuba. And not for some silly reason like you were just looking for a fight. I've looked into too many eyes this past year not to have learned something about the human spirit and the human heart."

"Don't make so much of my motives, Doctor."

"Don't make less of them, either." She looked over her

shoulder and discovered they had come quite some distance from the grove. She turned and found he was still watching her. A breeze stirred, and the branches of a nearby cedar trembled. The wind carried the scent of mahogany and cedar, of unwashed bodies and cooling horseflesh, and from the valley floor the faint, sweet aroma of flowering shrubs and ripened fruit. Between the man and woman the air was warm and still. Joanna could sense the change and, trying to swallow, found her throat dry as dust. "Maybe we had better start back," she said thickly.

Suddenly Tom reached out, encircling her waist with one arm, and pulled her to him. He acted on pure instinct, before his own sense of caution could intrude and bring him to his senses, letting the moment escape. His mouth covered hers. He was strong and demanding, the need in him both urgent and desperate. Joanna did not resist as his lips crushed against her own. Time paused, and the moon in its course, the stirring cedars, the twinkling stars, the gossamer wisps of clouds, all paused . . . and then resumed. The world spun on, the moon, the stars, the scudding clouds. Joanna backed away from Tom and caught her breath.

"Why did you do that?"

"Because I wanted to," he replied, his breath on her cheek. "Maybe because you wanted me to, you and your drums . . . and your visions." Overwhelmed by his own boldness, the Cheyenne turned to leave, stumbled and cursed his own clumsiness, then continued back to the camp at a brisk pace. Joanna called to him but he never broke stride. This was madness. He had no business being alone with this woman. He ought to have known better.

Joanna quickened her pace but could not catch up to him. Tom preceded her into camp by a couple of minutes. *My God,* she thought, *I think he's afraid of me. Why?*

The other four men were fast asleep. Even Philo Underhill's robust snoring failed to rouse the others from their rest, which was testimony to the day's efforts. Tom stretched out on his blankets, propped his head against his saddle, and attempted to clear his mind.

"*Savaa-he,*" Tom muttered in Cheyenne. *What was the use?*

He turned on his side, pulled his blanket up, and peered surreptitiously at the woman as she climbed into the wagon and lay down on her bedroll. Joanna's head appeared above the siding for a moment, her chin resting on her folded arms as she studied him for a moment or two before quietly sinking out of sight. Tom breathed a sigh of relief as he settled down for the night. Gradually, his limbs went limp, his muscles relaxed. But his mind, beset with questions for which he had no answers, continued to race. And when at last rest came, he dreamed of mountains and moonlight, of flame and Sacred Arrow, of prayer smoke and thunder, of a woman with blurred features and a warrior whose identity was hidden behind a garish mask of war paint.

Dreams and nothing more. Mere images, harmless, signifying nothing. Those were his thoughts when Tom woke the next morning. Disbelief was the security he clung to, the rationale for his troubled heart. It took a few moments to realize something was amiss. Glancing down, he found Seth's medicine pipe cradled in the palm of his hand, the buckskin pouch in his lap, his saddlebags open beside his bedroll. Startled, he checked the other slumbering forms as if searching out the culprit who had approached him while he slept.

No. This is my own doing.

He stared at the pipe and gingerly felt the bowl. It was still warm. Goose bumps formed on his arms and tingled the back of his neck. How? Had he walked in a dream? But that was madness. Surely such things could not be, such happenings were merely tales told by the elders, conjured for their own sake, to add to their stature and nothing more. He had tried to believe none of it.

Until now.

The Cheyenne tapped the bowl against his hand, and ashes spilled into his open palm. Tom Sandcrane shivered, despite the warm breeze, and his blood ran cold as the first faint blush of morning tinged the horizon and darkness receded from the mountains.

CHAPTER TWENTY-THREE

ALONG A SEEMINGLY ENDLESS LABYRINTH OF SUN-WASHED hills and broken ridges, a woman and five men came riding—watchful, alert, hemmed in by the unnatural stillness of the Sierra Maestra and sensing danger the further they progressed. A few hours earlier, while descending the ridge, they had nearly lost the wagon and its driver as the hillside path gave way beneath the iron-rimmed wheels. By noon the patrol had entered a series of narrow valleys strung together like emeralds on a lady's wrist. For several long hours they rode in the shade of trees whose trunks were banded with termite nests. Joanna recounted how the local farmers around Santiago used the chalky gray mounds for chicken feed, hacking a portion of the colony from the tree trunk and tossing it to the hens, who gathered at once to dine on the plump insects, scurrying about in a frenzy.

Where are the farms, where are the Cuban people? the men of the patrol wondered, unnerved by the solitude they had endured for most of the day. First the deserted shore village of Daiquirí, and now this. Joanna explained to her companions that only a relatively small number of Cubans had ever chosen these lonely hills for their home. Unlike the rich central farmlands west of Santiago, the rocky soil of this rugged range wasn't meant for the plow.

But even those few hardy souls drawn to the mountain

places had now fled to other parts of the island. They were unwilling to be mistaken for rebels. Joanna graphically related an incident she had personally witnessed. An innocent goatherd unable to adequately prove his innocence had been summarily hanged by a Spanish patrol who made a habit of considering everyone in these hills an enemy.

"Rebels, then, what of them?" asked Willem, mopping his forehead on the sleeve of his shirt as he studied the brilliant yellow orb dominating the western sky.

"Killed," Joanna said, "or gone to protect their families in Santiago or merely awaiting the arrival of the Americans. When the battle starts, the Cubans want to be in on the fighting. The Spanish army has much to answer for." She paused to gulp her fill of water from her canteen, and some trickled down the front of her shirt, plastering the material to her bosom. The men tried not to look too interested.

As the sun continued its golden flight, the temperature rose as the earth released its captured heat. Despite their fears of an ambush by Spanish patrols, Tom and the others were grateful to be off the ridge and into the forest, where the branches of mahogany and cedar and logwood formed a protective canopy, shielding the column from the sun's harsh glare. The trail they had followed for the past hour or so consisted for the most part of a dry creekbed—level going, but strewn with rocks. Tom and Joanna alternated the lead. At no time during the long hours of daylight had they been alone and out of earshot of the patrol. The glances they exchanged reflected nothing of the previous evening's encounter.

Tom's thoughts drifted to the column of men riding behind him. When the smoke had cleared and the issues were decided, the fate of this patrol would hardly matter. He doubted the historians would include the deeds of these five Indians from Oklahoma when it came time to tell the story of how Cuba was liberated from Spain. Maybe none of that mattered. The surrounding stillness was like a yoke that weighed on the emotions and caused the mind to dredge dire fantasies of death and destruction awaiting them all.

Sandcrane was grateful when Joanna raised her hand at the front of the column, but his heart sank when she waved them toward a darkened gorge seldom visited by daylight except around high noon. A reaction swept through the patrol, each man viewing the passage with a deep sense of foreboding. It was as if some machete-wielding giant had carved the path, slicing a wedge through a seemingly impenetrable mountain of solid stone.

They rode single file into the gorge: Tom, then Willem, Tully next, and the wagon driven by Philo, then Enos riding the drag. The walls closed round, and the enveloping gloom severed them from the afternoon. When Joanna passed the word along that Rosarita lay less than a couple hundred yards ahead, Tom ordered the patrol to halt while he and Joanna reconnoitered the passage. He saw no point in ordering the patrol to silence, as one of the freight wagon's rear wheels needed greasing, and the grinding hub issued a loud, incessant complaint that reverberated along the length of the passage.

Away from the others at last, Tom and Joanna walked their mounts past tumbled piles of boulders and slabs of debris that had come crashing down from cliffs a thousand feet in height. Tom cradled his Krag rifle and kept his finger curled round the trigger. His gaze swept the narrow defile, whose width he estimated at about forty or fifty feet across. If Zuloaga's men were waiting for them at the other end of this gorge, the rescue of Antonio Celestial would come to a violent end here and now.

Joanna was as watchful as her companion, but her thoughts were elsewhere, and when she broke the silence, she made it clear what was on her mind.

"For a 'ghost' you showed quite a lot of life last night," Joanna said. The kiss had surprised her. The experience was not unpleasant, however. Indeed, it had been a long while since she had felt anything akin to desire. There had been too much bloodshed and flight from the Spanish patrols. Every waking moment had been spent being a physician first and a woman second. Days and nights of caring for the wounded, only to watch them die or be healed to fight again, had taken all her passion. "Know I will not be laid hand on again, unless I ask it."

Tom absently nodded, being hard-pressed to remember anything past the moment he had awakened from his restless sleep and found the medicine pipe clutched in his hand. Joanna's words did indeed stir his memory, and the rest of the evening came flooding back. He had no explanation for his behavior. The kiss had seemed like a good idea at the time.

They reached the end of the pass and entered a grove of cedar, where they paused to survey the deserted village. Rosarita looked the same as when Joanna had left it a week ago. The sun-washed casitas looked as dilapidated as before. Celestial's gelding listlessly circled the corral, the animal's supply of dry grass nearly depleted. Ravens fluttered about the thatch rooftops. A pair of parrots with bright-green plumage sat atop the pockmarked walls of the church. Another formation of pale-blue and cream-colored parakeets alighted on the ground in front of the entrance to the church courtyard and began to feed on insects scratched from the dry earth. Tom estimated a couple of dozen mud-brick cabins were scattered around a central plaza. But all looked deserted save one of the casitas close to the corral, fronting the plaza. There, just beyond the doorway to the cabin, a man lay sprawled facedown in the shade of a thatch-roofed porch.

Before Tom could catch the reins of her horse and stop her, Joanna drove her boot heels into her mount.

"Joanna. No!" But she eluded his grasp. Her gelding lunged away, broke from concealment, and raced off toward the village at a headlong gallop. Tom, expecting the worse, cursed fate and bolted after her. If this was a trap, the Spaniards couldn't ask for more cooperative prey.

CHAPTER TWENTY-FOUR

THE WORST HADN'T HAPPENED YET, TOM THOUGHT, STANDING alongside the cot where Antonio Celestial lay unconscious and propped against a couple of blankets rolled to a proper thickness, which Joanna had placed beneath his mane of white hair. But there was still plenty of time.

The physician was seated on a three-legged stool on the opposite side of the rebel leader. She and Tom had carried Celestial inside and returned him to his humble bedding. The woman immediately began tending to the rebel leader. She filled a stoneware basin with water Tom brought her from a well in the plaza and, soaking a cloth, began to dab the man's brow.

Tom's nerves were still on edge from the wild ride into the village. He had expected to be greeted with a hail of gunfire, a Spanish rifle in every window. Thank heavens this had not been the case. And a few minutes later Willem Tangle Hair and the rest of the column had left the narrow gorge to join them in the plaza. While Willem and Tully made a perfunctory inspection of the village, Philo had driven the wagon up to the corral, unhitched the team, and led the weary animals through the gate, along with the mounts from the rest of the patrol. Enos Stump Horn, his belly growling, found his way to the kitchen at the rear of the casita.

Tom leaned over Joanna and scrutinized the man on the

cot. "I do not see a mark on him," he grumbled. Her recent disregard for their safety had left him in a bad mood.

"It's his back," Joanna explained, taking affront at the Cheyenne's attitude. "He took a blow across the spine several weeks ago. The injury has progressively worsened. It keeps him in constant pain."

Tom spied an empty bottle beneath the cot and picked it up. The last dregs of rum sloshed around the bottom of the glass jug. Tom knelt by the rebel leader and sniffed the man's breath.

"His back? Hell, he's dead drunk! There's nothing the matter with him that a dunk in the creek wouldn't cure. We've ridden all this way to rescue a sot."

Joanna's eyes flashed with anger now. "The rum makes it easier for him to bear the pain. Just get out of here. You have no idea what he's been through. Antonio Celestial is one of the most decent and courageous men I have ever known!"

"Well said, dear Joanna, but please. Not so loud." Celestial weakly interjected as he opened his gray eyes, winced, and then looked around the room until his gaze settled on Tom. "And you have indeed ridden all this way to rescue a drunkard." He sighed. "But for the ministering effects of jack iron, I'd spend the day screaming every time I sat up."

He took the cooling cloth from Joanna's hand and placed it on his forehead. "However, maybe I overdid the anesthetic. I was determined to leave, so I drank enough to deaden the act of saddling my horse and riding out. How far did I get?"

"Just outside the front door," Tom said, his sense of outrage easing. He was beginning to feel he had misjudged the rebel leader after all. But that didn't ease his misgivings. There was something about the village of Rosarita that disturbed him, although Tully Crow, Willem, and the other two men all seemed relieved at finding the village deserted and had begun to relax. Celestial and Joanna, however, did nothing to ease his fears.

"This is Sergeant Tom Sandcrane," she said. "He and another four soldiers volunteered to bring you out of the mountains."

"The Americans landed near Daiquirí, as we were told?" asked the Cuban.

Joanna nodded.

"And Mateo? Is he here with you?" Celestial continued. He glanced up, expectation in his eyes as Enos Stump Horn entered the room. The Cheyenne carried an enameled tin coffeepot and two cups. Celestial had obviously expected to see the orphaned young man who had once ridden at his side. His disappointment was obvious.

Enos noticed the wounded man was awake and realized he hadn't brought enough cups. He shrugged and handed one to Joanna and another to Tom, who passed it along to the man on the cot.

"I'll take some later," he told Enos.

Stump Horn nodded and filled the cups with the strong black coffee. He gave the Cuban a curious once-over, then returned to the rear of the house. Enos had pilfered the last of the bacon from Celestial's own meager supplies. The unmistakable aroma of frying pork wafted in from the kitchen.

After the man had departed, Joanna gave a quick account of her journey to the coast. Of Mateo's fate she could only guess. He might have been captured, but she couldn't be certain.

"Nevertheless, we must assume the poor lad is the reluctant guest of Captain Zuloaga. That vicious beast will force Mateo to lead the Lion Brigade right to the plaza."

"Mateo wouldn't betray you," Joanna replied, compelled to defend the youngster's honor. The boy had been devoted to Celestial and the cause of a free Cuba.

"He might find ways to stall and delay in order to buy me time. But in the end, if he was captured, Mateo will bring them here. Zuloaga never gives his captives much choice."

"Then we leave at daybreak," Tom said.

"Can you travel?" Joanna placed her hand on the Cuban's arm.

"But that is why you came back for me, my brave friend. Yet in truth, I don't know if I can sit a horse."

"There's a wagon," Tom replied. "We will make you as comfortable as possible."

"*Gracias*. And the Americans have brought a great army?" Celestial turned toward Joanna.

"They're probably marching on Santiago right this minute!" Joanna excitedly replied. She set the coffee aside and held the hand of her friend, hoping to impart her strength into his weakened frame. The constant pain had taken its toll. He seemed to have aged years over the past six months.

"And yet this one comes for me," Celestial said, with a glance in Tom's direction. "He risks his life for Antonio Celestial. A man he doesn't even know. Why?"

"She asked me to come," Tom said.

"As simple as that?"

"Just about."

"Yes. Joanna can be most persuasive," Celestial agreed. "And stubborn. Over and over again I tried to make her leave us. She could have stayed at the Dutch embassy with friends and been safe. But no. Right here in Rosarita, with the dirt and the death." The Cuban took a sip of coffee and sighed with satisfaction. "Now the Americans have come to drive the Spaniards from Santiago. I should like to see this. At last the hour has come." Celestial momentarily brightened, and his eyes flashed a fire of old. "After all these years." He fixed Tom in a riveting stare. "My people have paid the price for freedom, in blood. They deserve it. Can you understand, Sergeant?"

"More than you'll ever know," Tom replied, thinking of his own people's continuing struggle for freedom and a future. He looked away, inadvertently met Joanna's gaze and lingered a few seconds, then self-consciously turned aside to check the open window and the deepening purple sky. As daylight faded, the room gradually became a somber, dark place. A single candle would not dispel the gloom. Tom excused himself, touching the upturned brim of his hat as a gesture of farewell, and headed for the kitchen in search of a lamp or more candles.

Antonio Celestial finished his coffee, relishing every drop; then, when he and the woman were alone, the Cuban motioned for Joanna to draw closer. It was clear he was intrigued by Sandcrane and wanted to know more.

"An interesting young man. He's not like the gentlemen I met in New Orleans," Celestial softly said, "the politicians and the businessmen."

"He is a Southern Cheyenne," Joanna told him. "And they are a most peculiar people."

"Ah. You like him, then."

"What?" Joanna glanced about in alarm. She hadn't intended to raise her voice. "You *are* drunk."

"Yes. But not blind," the rebel wryly chuckled.

Tom followed his nose into the kitchen and helped himself to the coffee. Enos, with fork in hand, was poking at a black iron skillet, turning thick slices of bacon as the grease popped and spattered. He worked with his back to Sandcrane, oblivious to everything but the sizzling strips of meat. Tom announced himself with a cough. Enos glanced around at his visitor.

"Bacon's near done. The biscuits aren't half-bad. My sister taught me how to make 'em right." The man's rifle lay across the kitchen table. His Colt revolver was holstered on his right side, the shaft of his tomahawk tucked through his belt on his left. Tom doubted a more heavily armed cook had ever graced these humble walls.

As if impervious to the flames in the brick hearth that leaped and curled around the edges of the skillet, Tom gingerly used his pocketknife to spear a couple slices of bacon from the grease. He plopped them between two halves of a biscuit, then stepped through the side door, asking Enos to bring some candles into the front room for Joanna. Then he left the casita and stepped out into the dusk.

Philo was by the corral, hunched over one of the wagon wheels, greasing the hub. He glanced up as Tom approached and leaned upon the wagon siding.

"We'll need to push hard tomorrow," Tom said. "I want to put some distance between us and this village."

Philo straightened and wiped his hands on a rag he had draped across his shoulder. His right cheek was swollen with a plug of tobacco. "You worried? Things have been pretty quiet so far."

"I don't count on it to last."

"The way I see it, the Spanish have pulled back to Santiago. Hell, maybe by the time we get there, the battle will already be over. Maybe even the whole war."

"You're not looking for a fight?"

Philo shrugged and shook his head no. "Nor medals neither. Mind you, if fighting comes my way, I ain't about to step aside. No, sir. I've got as much sand as the next man."

"And twice the hot air," Tully Crow said, rounding the corner of the casita. The Creek had finished checking the village with Willem. "Philo's all mouth and gut wind."

"Go to hell, Tully," Philo growled. His friend's ribbing had struck a sore spot. And they were all tired and cantankerous, their nerves on edge.

"Yessir. I'm on my way," Crow replied, and started toward the kitchen in search of dinner. He stalled in the doorway and looked back at Tom. "Nothing out there but lizards and such. The town's empty 'cept for us. You reckon one of those fancy colonels will pin a medal on me, Tom? I mean when I come riding in with this here Celestial fellow?" Lamplight from the kitchen outlined the wiry man, his large nose and homely features accentuated in the sallow glare.

"I saw a soldier once all decked out in his Sunday best," Tully continued. "He had three shiny medals on his chest. Right proud he was of them, too. I'd sure like to have me one."

"Maybe," Tom said. He didn't believe his own words for a second, but if the notion made Tully happy, Sandcrane saw no harm in holding out the hope.

"There'll be nothing of the sort. Medals are for gentlemen. And you aren't nothing but a half-breed buck from Indian Territory," Philo scoffed, seeing the opportunity to repay Crow's earlier comments in kind.

"Philo Underhill, if they handed out medals for being a dumbass, you'd have a whole shirtful," Tully replied, and vanished through the door.

"Damn if he didn't get in the last word again. That

redstick's gonna open his mouth once too often. Mind you, we're partners, and I side with him. But blast it if I'll let him get away with calling me a coward."

"No one thinks you are, Philo. Easy, now." Tom clapped him on the shoulder. "You're the only man I know brave enough to haul a wagon loaded with dynamite down these ridges."

"You mean dumb enough," Philo corrected, and spat a stream of tobacco juice against a corral post. He wiped a forearm across his mouth and stepped around Tom. "Bacon smells good. That Enos can cook. Glad you didn't kill him the other day. Try not to—until we reach Santiago."

"I'll do my best, Philo," Tom replied. "Save me some coffee," he added as the stocky half-breed hungrily followed the aroma to its source.

Tom Sandcrane had no desire to reenter the mud-walled casita. He ambled along the corral until he reached the gate where his own mount waited to be released. The animals had been left saddled and ready in case Tom and the others needed to leave in a hurry. He reached into his saddlebags and removed the medicine pouch, then continued on to the plaza.

It promised to be another wondrously clear night, with the moon like a silver-plated disc suspended in a night sky already bedazzled with stars. The horizon changed from deep blue to obsidian as Tom reached the center of the plaza and a well that had one time no doubt served the entire community. A stone basin about seven feet in diameter and a pump on one side brought cold, clear water from a river belowground. Tom set the pouch aside, removed his hat, then worked the pump, cupping the water as it spilled forth. He splashed his face and the back of his neck, gasping at the bold, brisk contact. He stood there, bowed forward, his elbows on the edge of the well.

Tom circled around and sat with his back to the smoothed stone, facing the rugged hills that formed the north wall of the valley. He opened the pouch, removed the pipe, fit the stem into the red clay bowl. The ashes had fallen out, but the bowl still contained some of the brittle leaves of tobacco and cherry bark from the night before. The memory still chilled him. He could not remember even opening the pouch, yet there had been ashes in the pipe. At least now he was aware of his own actions—that was some comfort.

"Tom?" Willem approached from the casita where he had been standing on the porch as Sandcrane walked past like one entranced. He rounded the well as his startled friend struggled to his feet. Willem glanced down at the pipe, recognizing the workmanship. "What is this? So you have returned to the old ways?"

Tom shrugged and shoved the pipe back into the pouch. "I was just thinking. Nothing more."

Willem appeared doubtful. "I spoke to you from the porch."

"Oh. I didn't hear you."

"Obviously. What were you hearing?"

Tom started to fabricate another story but changed his mind and instead held up the pipe bundle. "This." He sighed and rubbed his weary eyes, then looked up, struggling to explain what was unexplainable.

Willem understood his dilemma and waved aside his friend's faltering attempts. "Your father would call it a mystery and leave it at that."

"I'm beginning to understand why," Tom replied.

"At least the Spaniards weren't here to welcome us," the red-haired breed said, checking his surroundings as he spoke. The humble casitas bathed in moonlight presented a tranquil scene. "I miss *o-kohome,* the coyote. The hills here are too damn quiet to suit me. Still, I prefer the silence to gunfire." He folded his arms and straightened. "I think we have done well. We have found the doctor's friend alive, and tomorrow we will bring him to safety. It is good."

"You talk as if the journey is over, Willem."

"And you sound like one of the old ones prepared to sing his dying chant." Willem chuckled and began to wail softly, singing a fragment he remembered from long ago:

"*Ho-aya. Ho-ka-aya.* Spirits, I am coming.
All you who have gone before,

I am coming.
All-Father, I am coming.
Do not hide your face."

Tom placed his hand over Willem's mouth and stifled the song. "No!"

Willem pulled free with a struggle, taken aback by Tom's behavior. They used to joke and laugh about the old ways together, how the warriors would sit and sing as death approached. Tom and Willem had made a pact to struggle to the end under such circumstances, or if all else failed, they resolved to run like hell rather than sit waiting to be killed.

"What's the matter with you, Tom?"

"Nothing. Just don't mock the song, especially not here in this place." Tom stepped back and slowly turned a complete circle, hills and mud huts crawling past until his gaze settled once more on his friend of long ago. "Do you remember when we were young, that time we fought Grover Weasel Bear and the other boys whose fathers were Dog Soldiers?"

"Yes. We were fishing downriver, near the mudflats," Willem said. "Suddenly you stood up and told me to grab a club. Then we stood back to back. And waited. Not for long. Grover and the rest came charging out of the rushes." Willem ruefully grinned. "We gave a good account of ourselves." He sauntered forward a few paces, then outstretched his arms and faced Tom. "But we're a long way from the Washita."

Tom Sandcrane clutched the pipe bundle in his hand. *What was happening? After weeks and months of silence, why now?* "We may be closer than you think." He started back toward the only house whose windows were aglow with life.

"Hey, Tom. Maybe you should have taken the Sacred Arrows after all," Willem Tangle Hair loudly called, unnerved by the exchange and seeking to make a jest of what had transpired, while an inner voice repeated Tom's warning. And from out of the night the echo of his voice, *after all . . . after all . . . after all,* hounded Tom as he crossed the plaza, quickening his pace, until at last he was running toward the light.

CHAPTER TWENTY-FIVE

ENOS STUMP HORN PLANTED THE TOE OF HIS BOOT BENEATH Tom Sandcrane's rib cage and nudged him awake with a quick, sharp thrust. Tom gave a start and kicked over a clay jug of water, then rolled out of his blankets and scrambled to his feet, his muscles protesting the sudden burst of action. The contents of the jug emptied onto the hard-packed earth in front of the casita. In the moonlight the water stain resembled a puddle of blood.

"You wanted the last watch," Enos remarked with a chuckle, and tossed his own bedroll down within spitting distance of the front door. "You're sure jumpy. There's nothing and nobody around, and that's a fact." There was still a note of antagonism in his voice, though he offered no immediate threat. As a gambler holds his cards close to the chest, secure from prying eyes, Enos kept his intentions to himself. It was clear he had not completely absolved Tom of blame for what had befallen the Southern Cheyenne after the reservation was opened to settlement. But what he planned to do about it was anyone's guess. The truth of the situation was like a thorn in the flesh; he had to let time take care of the problem or dig it out himself.

As far as Tom was concerned, Enos Stump Horn was the least of his problems. Without a reply Sandcrane took up his Krag rifle, walked out of the cabin's shadow, and stood in the moonlight, where he paused to locate the remainder of the patrol.

Philo was snoring in the back of the freight wagon and wouldn't wake until dawn. Joanna and Celestial were inside the room, Celestial in one cot, the doctor stretched upon another that Tom had placed against the opposite wall. He glanced upward and spied a pair of rifle barrels propped against the low wall concealing Willem and Tully, who had chosen to sleep on the roof of the casita. The barely audible rasp of snoring men asleep beneath the stars drifted down from above.

Tom yawned and rubbed his eyes, slung the rifle over his shoulder, and ambled toward the corral. A black shape scampered across his path and caused his heart to skip a beat before he recognized the shape of a tree rat, a foot-long rodent whose range had carried it a long way from timber. Tom threw a pebble in the rat's direction and watched it scamper beneath the fence, then race across the corral toward the jacals beyond.

One of the geldings whinnied and tossed its head as Tom climbed the fence, perched on the top rail, and cradled the rifle across his lap. From this vantage point he could watch both entrances to the moonlit valley. Overhead a rush of wings hammered the air, and a pair of shadowy silhouettes darted across the face of the moon. Then the world fell silent again, and only the trade winds dared whisper.

Again the gelding called attention to the man on the fence. And Tom, this time, was reminded of a prayer. The words floated up from the dim recesses of his memory, a place seldom visited, filled with ancient truths he struggled to deny.

> The horse neighs
> and daybreak appears,
> see how the moon,
> my mother, wanders
> beyond the hills.

"Father why must I learn the songs?" the boy asked.
Seth looked down at his young son, and his heart filled with

pride. "One day you will be the Keeper of the Sacred Arrows and you will sing the songs so that the world will not end and the people be forever lost."

Images of long ago drifted on the wind. Tom could see himself, no more than five or six years old, staring up into Seth's strong features, gentle now as he beheld his son. Young Tom stared at the bundle in awe, proud that one day the responsibility would pass to him. But mission school had changed everything.

Well-meaning teachers had forbade the children to speak *tsehese-nestsestotse,* the Cheyenne language. Put aside the old ways, they were told; the Maiyun were dead. There was only the white man's God, who did not speak in the wind and the shadows, the thunder and starlight, animals and stone. Mission school had shown him the world as it was and his conquered people for what they were. It had been a painful vision. Seth had been wrong. There was no magic. No mystery. For the Southern Cheyenne, the world had indeed ended while the elders had crowded the ceremonial lodge and the Arrow Keeper had sung his songs and chanted his prayers.

Vanquished, the night slipped away, in full retreat before the onslaught of morning. A last few stars clung to the western horizon like heavenly stragglers, while above the hidden eastern entrance to the meadow, the sky changed from velvet-black to slate-gray. Dawn's early glow found Tom no longer on the fence, but seated on the ground, his back against the wooden rails. The man had lost all sense of passing time. He had spent his watch in a realm of shadowy memories, assailed by images of childhood and stories his father had told him; he had walked in a land of dream and death and regret, of loss and gain, of duty and denial. Yet little of the journey remained. It was too fragile a thing to outlast the sunrise. Suddenly the veil of memories lifted, and he stared around, perplexed, then felt a rush of guilt and panic. He stood and checked his surroundings. It was a frightening realization—an entire army could have entered Rosarita, and Tom would have been completely oblivious.

He heard the scrape of wood as the side door of the casita opened and Joanna emerged from the little house, the first to rise. She held an enameled tin coffee cup in one hand and chose her steps carefully to avoid spilling the liquid on her fingers. She turned and eased the door shut behind her, then started toward the corral, a breeze tugging at her hair and the hem of the loose-fitting shirt she wore.

Tom neither moved toward her nor offered an acknowledging wave. He stood like a statue, his features somewhat haggard and sober. *What is happening to me?* His mind searched in vain for answers. He lowered his gaze to the gun in his hands. The Krag was an excellent rifle, accurate and trustworthy, and the thirty-eight-caliber double-action Colt riding high on his right hip was the finest handgun made. And though he had no desire to count coup in battle or grace his belt with some Spaniard's scalp, he knew how to use those weapons. Tom could hit anything he aimed at. Somehow none of these facts reassured him. After all, how could a man fight the past? The sooner he was gone from Rosarita, the better.

"Antonio is awake. I think he can handle the journey to Santiago," Joanna said. She handed Tom the cup. Coffee sloshed onto his knuckles, and he quickly took a sip, taking care not to scald his tongue in the process. Joanna had added a healthy dollop of rum to the coffeepot, and its effect was instantaneous. Tom immediately straightened up and gave her a sharp look.

"Something to get the blood going," she said, grinning.

Tom gasped as the jack iron went coursing down his gullet. "Yes, ma'am," he gasped. "The very thing to wake the others." For a moment he was at ease, and the images of yesterday laid to rest.

She relaxed against the corral gate and took a moment to enjoy the peace of the morning in Tom's company. The woman from New Orleans could not say she had been happy hiding there in Rosarita. There were too many memories of those who had ridden out never to return. But the mountains were lovely and deep, rugged bastions that had protected Celestial and his rebels for many a month. This was an old land, upthrust from the sea in aeons past, a place whose pockets of stillness were seldom intruded upon. She regretted none of the decisions she had made. And yet, standing there in the gray dawn, she began to sense a wind of change, that the path of her life was about to branch and take her elsewhere.

She glanced aside at her companion, a man she hardly knew, yet had come to respect and sympathize with. He seemed so lost. . . .

The humor drained from Tom's expression, and he straightened and tossed the contents of the cup aside, then strode purposely toward the plaza, his jaw set firm, his mouth a grim slash in a face filled with purpose. His whole body seemed poised, coiled tight, ready to explode. Joanna heard nothing but the silence, saw nothing but the same looming hills of the day before. Yet Tom appeared suddenly tense with expectation.

His flesh tingled, muscles tightened, and the sound of his own breath was a roar. He saw flashes of fire. He felt pain. He heard the sound of screaming men, and there was blood on the moon. And when he turned, his eyes blazed with intensity. He saw Joanna take a step back, unnerved by his behavior.

"We must leave. Now." He glanced at the casita and the men who had yet to awaken, as if the village itself had placed them under some sort of spell. "Now!" And his voice cracked like a rifle shot and shattered the peace.

Half an hour later the team of geldings had been harnessed to the single tree, and Philo, grumbling and rubbing the sleep from his eyes, drove the wagon around in front of the casita. The patrol had been awakened by Tom's outburst and galvanized into action by his relentless energy. Horses were saddled and cups of steaming black coffee gulped down with total disregard for the cost to mouths and throats. To their eyes Tom Sandcrane was a man possessed whom no one wanted to cross, though Enos Stump Horn came the closest. He did not take well to being ordered about, a quality that had already landed him in trouble since enlisting in the Indian Brigade.

As Tully Crow and Willem Tangle Hair proceeded to carry Celestial outside, Enos blocked their path.

"Sandcrane has lost his senses. I doubt there's another living soul between us and Santiago," Enos said, glowering. He held a bottle of run, which he tilted to his lips. He drained the contents, then tossed it aside, where it shattered against the wall of the casita.

"Liquor talk will get you into trouble, Enos. It always has. Now, stand aside."

Enos wagged his head no. Willem sighed and nodded to Tully, and the two men lowered the cot.

"In my opinion the sergeant's caution is justified. Perhaps we ought to heed his urgency," Celestial said from the doorway. He had insisted on walking to the wagon, as a matter of pride.

"This is none of your goddamn concern," Enos gruffly remarked, dismissing the Cuban outright.

"Ah, but you are in my country, friend. And everything here is my concern," Celestial said.

"The horses need rest. We all do. The valley has water and good grass . . . we're safe here." Enos once again addressed the men with the cot.

"Why don't you stay then, if this place appeals to you so?" Tully said. "Look. Maybe Tom's acting a mite peculiar. But he's wearing the stripes. Hell, I never met a young fella I'd sooner follow, so get out of the way."

Enos and Tully Crow seemed about to come to blows. Willem figured it was up to him to defuse the situation, as nothing would be gained by fighting each other.

"You heard him," Willem added.

"You siding with Sandcrane and these others?" Enos asked in disbelief. "I figured I could count on you, Tangle Hair."

Willem shook his head, then clapped his companion on the shoulder. "Let's just say I'm *not* siding with you. Tom Sandcrane isn't the man I remember. Maybe he's changed. Or maybe I'm just learning to see him better." The half-breed Cheyenne stooped over and picked up his side of the cot. Tully followed suit, and the two men brushed Enos aside, then continued over to the freight wagon while Stump Horn

grudgingly climbed astride his mount. The man perched unsteadily in the saddle and Willem, taking notice, only added
to the Cheyenne's embarrassment with an offhand remark.

"Bets you keep out of the rum, Enos. We've got some
thirsty miles ahead."

Celestial, following close behind his cot, tried to hoist himself up over the wagon side. Just as he was about to fall backward, Willem and Tully caught him by the arms. The Cuban's
features were drawn tight in a mask of pain as he was lifted
into the wagon bed, deposited in a corner, and propped
against a sack of provisions, his legs splayed out before him,
a line of perspiration forming at his hairline.

"Just rest easy. Prop your feet on the dynamite if you've a
mind to," Philo jovially called back to his passenger.
Underhill peered over his shoulder and grinned at Celestial's
alarmed expression.

Joanna appeared in the doorway, medical bag in hand. She
hurried to the wagon and stood alongside the rebel leader.
"Just a few days of this and we'll be in Santiago."

"In time to see the Spaniards driven into the sea, I hope,"
Celestial replied. He noted the woman seemed to be looking
past him and, turning in the direction of her stare, saw Tom
astride his gelding in the center of the plaza. What was he
watching for? What did he know that escaped the rest of
them?

"A most peculiar man," Celestial observed.

"The others are beginning to think him a trifle mad,"
Joanna said.

"And you?"

"Perhaps he is. Perhaps we all are."

"Sight beyond seeing . . ."

"What?" Joanna frowned, perplexed by his choice of words.
Years of violence had taken their toll. There was a time when
the gentleness in him had been difficult to find; once a man
of letters and an intellectual, revolution had transformed him
into a killer. But months of discomfort, incapacitated as he
was by his injured back, had allowed Celestial to become
more introspective and to recover some of the attributes of his
former life.

"I have seen it before among my own people. There are among us ones who have sight beyond seeing. Some call it a gift from God, a blessing—a curse, others might say."

"And you, Antonio?"

"Ah. What do I know of God . . . ?" The Cuban sighed, dismissing his own explanation with a shrug. But Joanna wasn't so easily fooled. She refused to believe the rebel had allowed his heart to become so hardened.

"Now what's gotten into Tom?" Philo muttered. Joanna looked up and saw the statuelike figure in the center of the village had come to life and left the plaza to ride off toward the valley's western entrance.

"I tell you, the man is *masanee!*" Enos growled, and with a savage tug on the reins of his gelding, rode off after Sandcrane. Joanna glanced at Willem for a translation, and the red-haired Cheyenne tapped his finger to his temple, a gesture the doctor immediately understood.

Tom halted about fifty yards from where the woods played out in a scattering of logwood trees that cast welcome patches of shade upon the tall grass and reeds. In the trees near the base of a humpbacked ridge, a meandering trickle of water bled into the meadow and softened the ground underfoot. He could smell the spring, the sodden, rotting blades of grass beneath the sorrel's hooves, tree bark drying in the sun, the oiled walnut rifle stock in his hand.

And he listened as a hunter listens, searching, straining to identify each and every sound borne on the breeze. The rustling leaves, the clatter of branches rubbing together, bird cry and whirring bee, something scurrying through the underbrush. And something more . . . horses?

"Sandcrane!" Enos bellowed from back down the trail. The name reverberated from the walls.

Much to Tom's chagrin, Stump Horn reined in his mount alongside the sorrel. Tom glared angrily at the man and motioned for him to be still. Behind them the sun topped the hills and poured its molten gold light across the valley floor. For a few moments, in the light of a new day, the deserted village called Rosarita positively glowed. The tableau was a thing of beauty, radiant and not the least bit threatening.

"We need to rest the horses, or they'll never last till Santiago. I'm not about to be stranded afoot in these damn mountains just because you panicked," Enos complained.

The distinct odor of rum assailed Tom's nostrils. Obviously, the man had downed more than one cup of Joanna's coffee. Perhaps he had gone straight to the source, Tom thought, and taken his spirits full-strength. The alcohol was already beginning to take effect, but then, Enos, for all his size, had never been one to hold his liquor.

"Shut up, you fool!" Tom hissed. He had heard . . . something . . . other than Stump Horn's gelding. A trick of the wind or loose rocks clattering down the nearby bluffs? Or horses?

But Enos was on the prod. Half an hour ago he had emptied the last of the rum down his gullet. That was plenty of time for the alcohol to take effect. And things were only going to get worse. On a drunk, Enos was a storm that had to play itself out, a gale full of bite and bluster looking for something to flatten. It might take a good hour or two for a man to sober up, Tom ruefully considered. However, this time fate itself lent a hand.

"Look, you!" Enos exclaimed in a booming voice. "The sun's barely topped the hills, and you've got us running from shadows and—"

A rifle cracked. Enos's head jerked back suddenly, and he dropped from horseback in a spray of blood as his gelding pawed and bucked, then broke toward town.

CHAPTER TWENTY-SIX

TOM SANDCRANE FOUGHT THE SORREL AND WITH A SAVAGE pull on the reins brought the animal under control as a second rifle shot rang out and something hot and deadly fanned the Cheyenne's cheek. He brought the Krag to bear on a solitary figure, a Spaniard dressed in a tan uniform with a black bandolier full of cartridges for the Mauser whose bolt action had momentarily jammed. The man looked up in alarm, his sunburned features a patch of brown in Tom's sights.

Squeeze the trigger, you damn fool, Tom inwardly cursed himself. And yet it is not an easy thing to take a life. There had been confrontations in the past when he had brandished a gun; he had bluffed Jerel Tall Bull in the shadow of Panther Hall, but the incident had been resolved peacefully. Suddenly Tom was confronted with the reality of this war he had so cavalierly joined. And in that moment of truth he hesitated, despite the risk to himself.

The Spaniard could not believe his good fortune and called over his shoulder for his unseen companions to join him. The man pried the errant shell from the chamber of his Mauser, slid the bolt home, and slapped the rifle to his shoulder. The Krag roared before the Spaniard could settle his sights, and a seven-millimeter round ripped through his chest. The slug's impact caused the Spaniard to fire wild. He twisted and slid out of the saddle but managed to land on his feet. Releasing his hold on the Mauser, he clawed at the reins with his numb fingers, then sank to his knees and bowed forward until his forehead touched the earth. He took his last breath in this attitude of supplication.

Tom chambered another shell and studied the woods, prepared to answer any other attempts on his life. His heart hammered in his chest, his breath coming in short, hurried gasps.

"C'mon, damn you," he muttered. "I'm ready for you."

Before long his request was answered. Five Spaniards, then seven, then a dozen and more came charging out of the woods, their rifles spewing flame and gun smoke. Dirt geysers erupted all around the Cheyenne.

"The hell with this!" Tom muttered, his defiance wilting before the Spaniard's onslaught. "I'm no Dog Soldier." He wheeled about on the sorrel and pointed the gelding toward Rosarita. In the distance Stump Horn's mount, galloping full out, had already reached the plaza. Tom leaped Enos's crumpled form and drove his heels into the gelding's sides, urging the animal to even greater speed. But he hadn't gone far when Tom heard his name ring out above the rifle fire.

"Sandcrane!"

Oh, damn. Tom glanced back and saw Enos stagger to his feet, blood pouring from a gash along the side of his head and staining the man's tunic crimson. Tom brought the sorrel about and galloped back to Enos as bullets continued to fill the air like so many angry wasps. Stump Horn seemed surprised that Tom should risk his life to aid him. But the big man didn't bother to question Tom's motives or voice his thanks. Enos leaped up behind Tom, who lost no time in turning the sorrel toward the deserted village. Sandcrane's gelding was a sturdy, long-legged animal with a fluid stride that, despite the extra burden of another rider, increased the distance between Tom and his pursuers. But it was an agonizingly slow process, for the Spaniards were much closer now, charging headlong, determined to apprehend their blue-coated prey or shoot him down. For all its speed, the gelding couldn't outrun a bullet.

Staring into the glare of the sun, Tom could barely make out the freight wagon and the rest of the patrol in the village as they pulled away from the casita. Galvanized into action by the gunfire at the western entrance, Joanna, Willem, and the Creek half-breeds raced across the meadow, following a weed-overgrown path toward the crumbling walls of the half-finished church on the edge of the village. The church was the only choice. The slow-moving freight wagon with the in-jured Cuban riding in the rear stood no chance of reaching the hidden gorge before the Spaniards overtook them. The church was their only chance. *The house of God will be our mighty fortress,* Tom thought, amused by his own cleverness. Now all he had to do was reach it alive.

"They're gaining on us!" Enos shouted in Tom's ear. The whole left side of his head was washed with crimson, but the man seemed totally in control of his faculties. For all the loss of blood, the wound was evidently superficial. "Can't you get this nag to run?"

"Maybe you ought to get off and push!" Tom replied through clenched teeth.

Enos tightened his grip on Tom's waist just in case Sandcrane had a change of heart. The wounded man returned fire as best he could with his revolver while Tom continued to rake the sorrel with his heels, coaxing every last ounce of speed from the horse. But the poor beast was carrying double and could not maintain its pace for long. All that saved them was the fact that the Spanish mounts had been ridden all night and were themselves exhausted. And the Spanish marksmen were firing into the sun.

Tom saw the wagon and riders disappear beneath the arched entrance to the church, and he took some comfort in knowing that Joanna and the others at least had a chance. The hard-packed earth of the plaza was underfoot now. The well flashed past, then the jacals and the casitas. Drumming hooves upon the trampled ground echoed through the narrow pathways of the village. Gunfire reverberated from every wall, volley after ragged volley, as the Spanish brigade tried to cut off their quarry from safety.

For a few brief moments it was touch and go, and Tom

thought all was lost. Then the church rose before him. Gunsmoke blossomed from the walls as Willem and Tully opened fire on Tom's pursuers. Twenty feet ... ten ... the sorrel lunged through the entrance and out of harm's way. The battlements varied in height from a low gap of six feet to about nine. Rubble, timber, and discarded crates provided the defendants a variety of perches from which to direct their gunfire.

Enos leaped from horseback and joined Philo at the freight wagon to help back it across the entrance. Then they un- hitched the horses and allowed them to join the other mounts in the center of the makeshift compound. Tom dismounted and made a quick survey, and, to his relief, everyone was ac- counted for. He saw Joanna rush forward to lead Enos off to the side. Ignoring his protests, she began patching his head wound. Celestial, carrying a lever-action Winchester '76, hob- bled over to the wagon and took up position behind one of the rear wheels, opening fire on the Spaniards charging the blocked entrance. Philo grabbed a rifle and joined Tully on the walls. Tom hurried toward the front of the church, hesi- tating by Joanna to see if she needed anything.

"He has a hard head," she said, looking up from her bloodied patient.

"That's a trait with us Cheyenne," Tom replied, and contin- ued toward the wall, struggling his way up a pile of crum- bling bricks until he could peer over the pockmarked wall. Willem Tangle Hair ducked down as bullets spattered the bat- tlement and showered him with fragments of hardened clay. He stood about seven feet away from Tom, balanced on bricks and a couple of hurriedly stacked logs.

"Well, at least we don't need to worry about running into a Spanish patrol," he shouted.

"I feel much better now," Tom said with a nod. Then both men rose up and rejoined the fray, their rifles blazing. Sight and squeeze off a round, work the bolt and chamber a fresh cartridge, fire again. No hesitation now for Tom Sandcrane. War made the choices simple—it was kill or die; remorse must come later, like spoils to the victor. The Krag's recoil shoved against Tom's shoulder, and in his sights the bullet dusted a cavalryman's tunic. The Spaniard tossed his arms wide, flung his rifle into the air, and rolled backward over his horse's rump. Tom shifted his aim, chose a new target, and fired again.

Had the Lion Brigade attacked en masse, they might have breached the walls, overwhelmed the American defenders, and carried the day. But due to the condition of their weary mounts, Zuloaga's patrol was spread out between the church and the village plaza. The headlong charge had taken its toll on the exhausted mounts, and many of the soldiers had fallen behind. Some of the Spaniards, including Captain Zuloaga himself, arrived on foot in time to watch in horror as no more than a dozen of his command, led by Lieutenant Emilio Garza, began an attack on the fortified church. Garza and the others surged forward across a clear field of fire.

The Spaniards were accustomed to fighting frightened farmers, merchants turned rebels, men poorly equipped and unaccustomed to firearms. They had never faced the likes of the American soldiers. The Spaniards rode straight for the wagon-blocked entrance, firing their Mausers and loosing cries of triumph. Suddenly men began pitching from horseback. Horses went down, tossing their riders onto the ground. The attack broke before the unremitting gunfire, men scattered to right and left. But that didn't stop the killing. Zuloaga hastily shouted orders to the men around him to open fire in hopes of pinning down the defenders on the walls. The attackers broke and fled back the way they had come, but the Americans continued to kill them. Five men lay sprawled in the morning sunlight, blasted from their saddles as they charged the walls. Another three pitched from horseback while fleeing for their lives. Only Lieutenant Garza and three other men survived the rout. Blond, handsome Emilio Garza, his eyes wide with fear and excitement, his confidence shaken. The aristocrat from Castile had lost his hat, and blood seeped from a crease along his right forearm as he slid his saber into his saddle scabbard and drew his revolver.

"More men—I need more men and I will breach the walls," he cried in a shrill voice.

"Idiot!" Diego Zuloaga exclaimed. "Will you destroy my entire command?" The captain grabbed Garza by the front of his tunic and dragged the brash young lieutenant from the saddle, shoving him against the side of the mud-brick shack. The casita, with its caved-in roof, stood on the periphery of the village about midway between the plaza and the church. Behind the two officers lay the comparative safety of Rosarita; before them, certain death to any man who made a target of himself by approaching the church. The Americans had already found the range of the building, and lead slugs began to spatter against the casita. The activity around the humble little dwelling had attracted the attention of the cornered marksmen in the church.

Zuloaga immediately began barking orders to the twenty troopers under his command. A couple of men remained behind in the shack while the rest of the brigade retreated farther into the village with orders to keep the Americans at bay until Zuloaga devised a plan to destroy them and the rebel leader he suspected was among their number.

Then, keeping a line of cover between himself and the American riflemen, Zuloaga strode briskly toward the center of the village where Alfonso Ramirez, the cook, had already begun to build a fire in the very same quarters that had recently housed Antonio Celestial. Once out of any accurate range of the Krag rifles, Diego Zuloaga strode to the well and splashed his dirt-grimed features with water. He straightened and glanced at Lieutenant Garza, who continued to tag along like a scolded pup, his shoulders hunched forward and his eyes downcast. The shame at being manhandled and scolded in front of the common soldiers was almost more than he could bear, and he longed for the opportunity to redeem himself. He was certain that if only Zuloaga would give him the entire command, another frontal assault would succeed. The aristocratic lieutenant was smart enough, however, not to make the suggestion.

A couple of stragglers entered the plaza, one of them a burly trooper named Chenez. At his side rode the thirteen-year-old prisoner who had brought them into the valley. Mateo sagged in the saddle, and when the soldier leading his mount halted near the captain, the lad slid from the saddle and stood dejectedly, his blinded eye covered with a strip of dirty cloth wrapped around his head. Mateo turned aside and stared balefully at the man who had recaptured him, a lantern-jawed trooper with bushy sideburns, who took him by his shackled wrists and brought him over to the officers.

"Where shall I put this one, Captain? He tried to escape, but I caught him before he reached the trees," Chenez cheerily reported.

"Ah. You no longer desire our company?" Zuloaga asked of the youth. "Perhaps you wish to join the doomed ones we have trapped in the church."

"Yes," Mateo replied, a note of hope in his voice. Better to die with his *compadres* than survive another moment as Zuloaga's prisoner.

"Do you think Celestial would have you with him when he learns how you betrayed him to us?"

Mateo's lips curled back in a defiant sneer. "You do not know him. I am already forgiven. Antonio understands what animals you Spaniards are." The thirteen-year-old spat on the ground in front of his captors; defiance was the only weapon left to him.

Garza's hand shot out and slapped the youth across the face with enough force to knock him to his knees. The lieutenant drew his leg back to deliver a brutal kick to Mateo's head, but Zuloaga once again halted the lieutenant.

"This insolent little fool is worth more to us alive," Zuloaga said as he shifted his stance to afford himself a clear view of the church. Judging by the way the American soldiers were keeping up a sporadic exchange of gunfire with the besieging force, ammunition was evidently not a problem for them. No matter. The captain estimated that his command outnumbered the defenders by more than three to one. And he had them trapped. But before he closed the jaws on his prey, he wanted to be sure Celestial was indeed within those walls. Without the Cuban leader all Zuloaga's efforts would be for naught.

"What if Celestial isn't even in there?" Garza asked as if reading the captain's mind. He was staring past his commander at the mission walls, his features unable to conceal his barely suppressed fury. Garza had been disgraced this morning, and as far as he was concerned, the men holed up in the mission were to blame.

"That is what we must find out."

"How?" the lieutenant asked.

"Simple," Zuloaga replied in a voice cold as a tombstone. "We ask."

The captain glanced at Mateo, who was still on his knees. The youth could feel the officer's scrutiny and looked up to search that face of cruelty for any semblance of mercy, a futile effort indeed, for Zuloaga was a man obsessed with only one thing now—the capture and execution of Antonio Celestial.

"I will do nothing else to help you," Mateo said, pink spittle oozing from his battered mouth.

Zuloaga smiled and lifted his gaze to the church once more. The sun washed his features in its golden light and made him seem radiant, almost angelic were it not for the cruel set to his mouth and the murder in his eyes. "We'll see."

CHAPTER TWENTY-SEVEN

I AM CORPORAL ENRICO MEDINA AND I WILL LIVE.

The Spaniard lay on his belly among the corpses of his *compadres*. Motionless, he passed for dead. Not once did Medina cry out, though the pain in his side was sharp and almost unbearable at first. His head had struck a rock as he fell, and an ugly lump had already formed on his forehead. Later an unnerving numbness settled over the injured man, but at least he was able to catch his breath without groaning. Medina was not a young man; he had been a soldier for almost twenty years. A wife, assorted mistresses, and children—at least six of whom he claimed—awaited his return to Madrid. In his thirty-one years the Corporal had drunk too much and sinned at every opportunity, yet he harbored no regrets save one—that here and now it might all be coming to an end. The shadow of a vulture passed across his fallen form like a portent of things to come.

Feed on the others, the Spaniard warned, repeating his warning. *I am Corporal Enrico Medina. And I will live.* The corporal was a hard, methodical soldier who felt confident he could handle a little loss of blood while he waited out the daylight hours. Clouds drifting across the face of the sun provided a measure of relief from the heat. *Wait for night,* Medina told himself. *Then you can crawl to safety.* He was tempted to reach for the Mauser lying just inches from his fingertips. But he resisted the urge. One of the American soldiers might notice the motion and put another bullet in him. The bastards could shoot . . . not like the damn rebel trash who ranged these mountains. Pig farmers, goatherds, it had been a demeaning task to fight them. *Of course, if they had been manning the walls of the church instead of the bluecoats,* Medina thought, *I would not be lying here now.* The wounded corporal closed his eyes and forced himself to relax, and in a few minutes he lost consciousness without realizing what had happened.

Tom remained on the wall throughout the morning. He kept watch while the other men climbed down into the church, reloaded their weapons, and raided the ammunition boxes. Joanna collected all the canteens to pool their supply of water and allowed each man half a cup of water. Despite the scudding clouds, the temperature continued to rise as noon approached. Tom unbuttoned his shirt and dabbed his brow on his shirtsleeve. There were no visions now, only the stark reality of death and the skimming shadows of the king vultures circling overhead. How had he sensed the approaching Spaniards? Seth would have attributed everything to the Maiyun and not given it a second thought. Tom had to struggle with such a notion. If he accepted the supernatural presence of the Ones Who Have Gone Before, then he must also accept that the power of the Sacred Arrows had touched his life. Perhaps they were even hounding him, propelling him headfirst from one unpleasant situation to the next as some kind of punishment for denying their power and refusing to become the Arrow Keeper and sing the Sacred Songs. He had tried not to listen, but the Maiyun were calling him by name.

A shot rang out, derailing his train of thought, and a bullet thudded against the side of the church about a yard below Tom's vantage point. He didn't bother to duck. He located the marksman in the casita farthest from the village and briefly considered a reply in kind, but the gruesome display of eight lifeless bodies sprawled before the church walls gave him a change of heart, and he took his finger off the trigger. The vultures had enough to feed on.

"*Voestaso* . . . come have a drink," Joanna called out, standing near the wall and holding out a tin cup and wooden canteen. The brightness of the sun forced her to squint as the Cheyenne rose against a backdrop of white-hot sky and leaped to the earthen floor. He landed soundless as a cat, leaned his rifle against a pile of weathered bricks, and gratefully accepted her offer of a drink.

"Aren't you going to ask me how I knew your name in the language of your people?" she asked.

"Enos Stump Horn told you while you were patching his head," Tom said. Joanna frowned, unhappy he had guessed so easily. "But I am puzzled why you asked him," he added.

Joanna shrugged. "I wanted to know everyone's name, seeing as I might have gotten the five of you killed." It was obvious to him she was quite serious.

Sandcrane tilted the cup to his lips and drank. The water was flat and tepid, but it eased the burning in his parched throat. Funny. His hands had been sweating even as his throat had become dry as dust during the dash to the church and throughout the attack. He wiped his palms on his trouser legs and took up his rifle.

"I had Enos move the dynamite out of the wagon," Joanna said. "It seemed like a good idea."

Tom nodded. "Yeah. I guess I forgot about that. And the water?"

Joanna sloshed the contents of the canteen. "Right here. There are a few swallows in a couple of the others. No one had time to visit the well, things happened so fast."

Tom pursed his lips and then sighed, blaming himself for their current predicament. "I should have seen that they were filled last night."

Joanna started to explain to the sergeant that none of this was his fault, but an all-too-familiar voice interrupted her impromptu lecture on guilt.

"Antonio Celestial!" It was the voice of Captain Diego Zuloaga, shouting from the protection of the casita nearest the church. "I would speak with you, my old friend."

"C'mon," Joanna said, hurrying over to the wagon to stand at the rebel leader's side. Tom followed along, curious to know what sort of enemy he had in the captain of the Lion Brigade.

"I have never been your friend!" Celestial replied. He walked around the side of the wagon and stood in the shadow of the entrance. Joanna's hand tightened on Tom's wrist as the Cuban came close to presenting a target to the Spanish Mausers.

"And the Americans . . . who speaks for them?"

Tom didn't need to issue an order—Willem, Philo, Tully, and even Enos had already scrambled up the piles of debris to assume their positions on the walls. The Cheyenne rounded the wagon and stood alongside Celestial.

"Say your piece, Captain," Tom called out. The hills threw his voice back at him.

Zuloaga materialized out of the shadows of the casita. He kept close to its protecting walls, however. The captain had courage but he wasn't a fool. "Send out the Cuban. I have come for him. Send him out and go with my blessing."

"He's a generous man," Tom muttered aside to Celestial.

"It is a chance to save yourselves," Celestial answered. "We are trapped here and you know it." His expression softened, the lines around his eyes smoothing as he made his case in a voice heavy with resignation. "Perhaps you should accept his terms and ride out. Take Joanna with you."

"It'd be safer to run naked through a cave full of angry bobcats than try to force that lady to do something she was dead set against doing," Tom said.

Joanna overheard their conversation and glared at both men, daring either of them to try to force her to leave. One look at her determined mien, and the rebel leader conceded.

"Ah, you have a point." Suddenly he noticed the color drain from Joanna's features, and he turned to see for himself what had caught her attention and left her shaken. "No," he whispered in a solemn voice. On the edge of town Diego Zuloaga had upped the ante in his deadly game and sent out poor Mateo.

"Antonio, I have brought a young friend to see you. He has been my loyal guide." Zuloaga's voice radiated confidence.

"Do you make war on children now?" Celestial exclaimed with sinking heart.

"Oh, my God," Joanna muttered beneath her breath. Mateo's face was partly obscured beneath a filthy, blood-soaked rag. His clothes hung in tatters and fluttered as he stumbled along the path to the church, the chains of his shackles rattling with every shuffled step. It was obvious he had endured torture at the hands of his captors.

Tom grimaced with distaste. "What sort of man is this?" he said.

"The worst," answered Celestial, and then called out, "Mateo!"

"Antonio. Forgive me!" Mateo weakly responded. He had begun to tremble and could not hold back his sobs. He cursed his faltering resolve.

"Surrender to me, and the boy shall live and go free. I will count to five. What happens after that will be your doing," Zuloaga carefully explained. He wanted to make absolutely certain his old enemy understood. Five seconds would give Celestial time enough to surrender but render him unable to formulate a plan of escape. Zuloaga reached out, and Lieutenant Garza, concealed along with five other men within the bullet-riddled walls of the casita that served as a lookout post, placed a Mauser rifle in the captain's hands. Zuloaga flattened against the side of the hut, shouldered the rifle, and drew a bead on his prisoner.

"Do not believe him, *jefe*. Stay where you are," Mateo pleaded, his strength returning.

"One!"

Celestial cursed and started to leave the crumbled ruins of the church. He had taken only a few steps toward the open field when Tom caught him by the arm and brought him up sharp.

"I didn't come all this way to watch you kill yourself," said the Cheyenne.

Celestial struggled to extricate himself from Tom's restraining grasp, but the rebel, hampered by his injured back, proved no match for Sandcrane.

"Two!"

"Damn you, let me go," the Cuban snapped. He tried to shove past, but Tom overpowered the man and pinned him against the side of the wagon. Celestial inhaled sharply as new waves of pain swept over him.

"Three!"

"Are you deaf? Release me, I say. I demand it," the Cuban exclaimed.

"Four!"

"Zuloaga will kill him. Don't you understand? He'll kill Mateo."

"Walking out there is the same as suicide," Tom flatly stated. There was simply no give in him. "From what Joanna's told me about this Zuloaga, his word isn't worth spit."

Antonio Celestial sagged against the soldier, the spirit draining from him. There was no denying the truth of Tom's words. He turned toward the thirteen-year-old who had become like a son to him. "Zuloaga . . . the revolution is over. The Americans have landed in Daiquirí. Soon they march on Santiago. Your war is over. Let there be a truce between us and no more blood spilled."

Mateo, hearing the voice of the Cuban resistance leader, raised a hand in salute with the last vestiges of strength flowing into his limbs. And in that moment his own agony left him and Mateo felt victorious.

"Viva Celestial! Viva Cuba!"

A gunshot rang out. Mateo staggered forward into the arc of his own blood as the slug passed completely through his slender frame. His eyes rolled up in his head, and he toppled forward and landed facedown in the dirt, his arm still outstretched and his right hand knotted in a fist.

"Five!" Zuloaga called aloud and chambered another shell.

The American soldiers on the church walls loosed a volley and peppered the walls of the casita, forcing Zuloaga to duck back out of sight. The gunfire echoed down the long hills and gradually faded, leaving only a looming stillness broken by the faint rush of wings as more of the carrion birds were invited to the feast.

"Remain here," Zuloaga ordered, focusing his smoldering gaze on the lieutenant and the five troopers. "The Americans may attempt to escape under cover of darkness. If that happens, stop or delay them until I bring up the others. The rest of the command will take quarters back in the village. We will wait until after midnight; then the Lion Brigade will storm the walls and put an end to our defiant friends."

"It will be as you say," Garza replied with a snappy salute and a click of his boot heels. He was anxious to regain the captain's good graces and kept up his assurances until Zuloaga had departed.

In the shadowy entranceway Celestial continued to stare at the lifeless body of the boy who had ridden with him into more skirmishes than he could count. Tom felt numbed by the display of brutality and the cavalier way the Spaniard had snuffed out the life of a mere boy.

"You will pay for this, Captain Diego Zuloaga. You've had your day of fire and blood, but there will be a reckoning, I swear it." Celestial's voice wavered and he could barely get the words out.

"The Spaniard cannot hear you," Tom gently said.

Celestial slowly focused on the Cheyenne. "No. But God can."

CHAPTER TWENTY-EIGHT

T OM WAITED OUT THE DAY, ALONE ON THE EAST WALL OF THE church, keeping apart from the other defenders, avoiding even the most casual conversation. Joanna and the soldiers accepted his behavior without trying to second-guess its cause. The woman, in her own way, understood. None of them felt much like talking. Sandcrane had been correct about the Spaniards' imminent threat; if he wanted to be off by himself, so be it.

Sometime during the afternoon Joanna found time to check on Celestial, who had been forced to seek the meager comfort of his cot. There was a little shade to be found within the ruins, and the rebel took advantage of it. He greeted her with a feeble wave of the hand as she approached. The woman doctor judged the pain in his heart to be far greater than that of his injured back.

"How are you doing, Antonio?" she asked, kneeling alongside the cot.

He laughed softly, without humor—a cold, frightening sound that caused her to shiver inwardly. "I am fine, Doctor Cooper." He reached down and patted the Winchester. "I have only one illness, a terrible ache that gnaws at me. But, you see, I already have the medicine. And when Diego Zuloaga lies dead at my feet, then I will be healed." His gaze grew distant as he added, "And my poor country will be healed."

"Yes," Joanna said, and placed her hand on his arm. She had not been able to cry. Maybe the tears would come later. She lifted her eyes and looked up at the solitary figure on the east wall.

"Is he still up there?" Celestial asked. He rose on his elbows and tried to look in Sandcrane's direction, but the effort set the nerves along his spine protesting.

"Yes. I wonder what he is doing." Joanna replied.

"Ah . . . only he can say. But mind you, when the sergeant comes down, be ready for anything," said the Cuban. He shook his head and sighed. "Poor Mateo."

"He was always proudest riding at your side."

"Yes. And the revolution was everything to him. The revolution . . . when it begins, it is a beautiful lady, grand and beautiful and full of promise, the kind of woman men gladly devote their lives to. But she does not remain a lady for long. Soon she is a whore, magnificent at times, yes, but a whore all the same. And she will take any man's life, or any boy's. She does not care. And her whore's heart feels nothing. I should have warned the boy. I should have warned Mateo about the whore." Celestial averted his face and placed a forearm across his eyes. And then he sighed, deeply. And Joanna left him with his dignity intact.

Tom Sandcrane tracked the course of the sun, the lengthening of shadows, the circling vultures held at bay by an occasional rifle shot from Antonio Celestial, who would not allow the carrion birds to alight among the bodies of the slain. The sky went from azure to burnished gold tinged with pink that deepened in hue until it became the color of blood. Tom stood atop the far wall out of sight of Spanish guns and faced the horizon, his mind searching for words, for the songs of long ago, but suddenly his father's teachings failed him, or so he thought. No songs, no prayers, only an empty yearning in his heart.

What had brought him here? Visions? Maiyun? And what

did it matter? The reasons were unimportant now. He lowered his eyes and took in his own appearance, found his torso bathed in gold and crimson, as if the left side of his body were dark with blood. A trick of shadows, he reasoned. "Sacrifice" . . . the word came from nowhere, yet arrived in the middle of his thoughts like a hurled spear. They could escape under cover of night. All he had to do was turn his back as he had done before in Cross Timbers and ride away. He owed these people nothing. Anyway, what happened here was meaningless compared to the clash of armies at Santiago. . . .

Tom watched the dying of the light and wondered who would live to see the dawn. Looking into the red sun, he was reminded of a most unsettling dream: the hawk with wings of blood, diving toward him, sinking its talons into his breast. The image suddenly filled his mind with such ferocity, he nearly toppled from the wall. It ended as quickly as it began.

He was emotionally drained, his spirit buffeted by the storm raging within, which refused him rest and in the end had changed him over the course of these days and nights.

"I have seen evil today," he said aloud. There was more to the darkness that stole across the valley than the setting of the sun. The image wasn't lost on him, that the line of shadow devouring the valley had its origin in Rosarita, where Captain Zuloaga and his cohorts waited and watched. It was time to act.

As the stars began to fill the sky, Tom rejoined his companions, motioning for even the two men keeping watch by the wagon to join him. The day's events had marked each person, and in the firelight it showed in their grave expressions and sober voices.

Tom leaned forward until his features were plainly visible to one and all. "Around midnight we need to be ready to ride. Have the wagon team hitched and your saddles cinched."

"Which way are we going?" Tully asked, arms folded across his chest.

"I want you to break for the gorge. Willem, you've worked with dynamite before. A few well-placed charges ought to close off the pass and keep them from pursuing the wagon. The doctor or Celestial here will have to find you another way into Santiago. Might be longer, but there's nothing to be done."

"What's to keep the Spaniards off our heels while we set the charges and blow the pass?" Willem asked.

"Zuloaga will be busy," Tom said.

"Doing what?" Philo asked, his sleepy-eyed stare boring into Tom.

"Chasing me," Tom replied.

"No," Joanna blurted out, then settled back in embarrassed silence. Tom looked in her direction, surprised at her reaction.

"I'll take half the dynamite. Give me a short fuse and a lit cigar, and I'll even the odds. 'Count to five,' the captain said. One, two, three, four, five. I might just teach Diego Zuloaga a thing or two about the price of arithmetic."

Enos Stump Horn scratched his cheek, then slapped at a mosquito that had begun to probe the back of his neck. The Cheyenne nodded in approval. "I will go with Sandcrane. Two men will keep the Spaniards busier than one."

"Three's a better number," Philo retorted.

"And I reckon someone's gotta come along to pull your fat ass out of trouble," Tully dejectedly remarked. "That makes it four."

"Now, look here," Tom began. "My orders . . ."

"Don't mean squat," Philo said, interrupting the sergeant.

"If you think I'm going to be left behind . . . ," Willem began to protest.

"Enough!" Tom snapped. "Someone needs to help Celestial and the doctor escape. You're elected."

"Suppose I refuse to leave," Joanna defiantly added.

"You'll ride out of here if I have to tie you to your horse," Tom replied.

"No. We must go together or not at all," Celestial spoke up. "You are all brave men. Do not throw your lives away. There will be another day for Diego Zuloaga."

"I have spoken," Tom said, ignoring the rebel leader's protest.

"Why should I be the one to leave? Philo's been driving the wagon," Willem continued to protest, but Tom had already started to leave. "Cross Timbers is a long way from here. Getting yourself killed isn't going to change things for our people. You don't have to prove anything to me."

Tom spun on his heels, stormed back into the circle of light, and hauled Willem to his feet by the front of his khaki-colored coat. He brought his face close to Willem's and spoke in a low, soft tone whose authority could not be denied.

"Hear me. You will drive the wagon. You will blow the pass. And then see you bring the Cuban and the doctor to safety." Was it the reflection of the nearby flames, or did his eyes blaze with supernatural fire? No matter. The voice must be obeyed.

"As you say, *nesene*, my friend," Willem evenly replied.

Tom glanced around at the other three men. It had not been in him to order anyone to stay behind, outnumbered and willing to carry the battle to Zuloaga—but in truth he would be glad for their company. As for Willem Tangle Hair, yes, he had an ulterior motive for ordering the man to leave with Joanna and Celestial. The red-haired breed was a link to the past, and if Tom was to die here, perhaps Willem would bring Seth Sandcrane word of what had happened and how the Arrow Keeper's son had met his fate.

Shadows danced in a circle about the campfire, mere reflections cast by the leaping flames to some; to others, though, these shadows were the Maiyun, the vision bringers, the secret ones who dwelled in the earth and in the trees and whispered in the wind. Tom no longer knew what he believed. But he knelt by the campfire and filled a tin cup with ashes, then added a trickle of water and a sprinkle of clay to form a paste.

The Cheyenne stripped off his coat and shirt and began to streak his forehead and daub his cheeks and torso with the mixture. Enos and the two Creek breeds realized what he was doing, and a murmur of excitement and pride swept through them. Zuloaga and his soldiers, the child killers, were about to get a nasty surprise.

As his father had done in the days of *esevone*, the buffalo, and his father's father when the Cheyenne were the undisputed masters of the plains, Tom Sandcrane was painting himself for war.

It took only a few minutes to prepare himself for battle. And when he had finished, Tom left the campfire, walked over to the crate of dynamite near the wagon, and began apportioning what he and the other men would need. Joanna joined him, seizing the opportunity to speak with him in private. She knelt by the wagon wheel as he began shoving sticks of explosives into his gunbelt. Behind the couple a moth drawn to the flames began to circle the campfire, risking its already brief existence to escape the gloomy clutches of night.

"You aren't going to say I'm sorry I got you into this," Tom said, casting a wry glance in the woman's direction.

"The furthest thing from my mind," Joanna replied. "You saddled your own horse and rode it here."

"That I did," Tom said.

"Zuloaga is no coward. Don't underestimate him. He is a formidable foe."

"*Nestama-xetsevatoe-shematse.*" The Cheyenne held up his fist, allowing a trickle of dirt to escape. "I will throw him down so hard, the dust will fly."

"Stay alive, Tom Sandcrane," the doctor said.

"*Savaa-he.* A ghost cannot be killed."

"I see a man of flesh and blood. A good man, I think." Joanna sensed his embarrassment and changed the subject after a quick appraisal of his war-painted visage. "I read my share of penny dreadfuls as a girl; I thought Indians were superstitious and afraid to fight at night."

"That's a little lie we told the white man so we could sneak up on him while he slept and lift his scalp and steal his horses," Tom answered. "I've been told it worked every time." He drew his revolver and checked the loads, then returned the Colt to its holster. It was almost time.

Philo Underhill and Tully Crow, each painted like Tom, began to hitch a pair of sturdy geldings to the wagon. Celestial shuffled forward and removed a couple of hand-wrapped cigars from his pocket. He broke each one in half and distributed them to Tom and the other three men. The cigars would burn slowly and keep the soldiers from having to strike a match each time they wanted to light a fuse. An hour crawled past and part of another. Tom suspected the Spaniards had pushed hard to reach the village, and wanted to allow them ample time to settle down for the night. Let weariness settle on them like a blanket. Give the sentries time to nod off, their eyes dry and burning from lack of sleep.

Near midnight Tom Sandcrane took up his rifle and turned to his companions. For a fleeting second he watched the campfire for some sign of the moth. Had it soared through the brightness unscathed, or sacrificed itself to the unattainable light?

"It is time."

CHAPTER TWENTY-NINE

W HEN CORPORAL ENRICO MEDINA REGAINED CONSCIOUS-
ness, he almost cried out for fear he had gone
blind. Craning his head around in this moment of
despair, he managed to look up as his vision cleared, allowing
a patch of stars to shimmer into focus through a break in a
cloud bank. *Of course, you idiot, it is night,* he scolded himself.
Relieved, the Spaniard forced himself to breathe slowly and
gather his strength for the task of returning to the village and
his *compadres.* Alfonso the cook would patch him up good as
new.

The pain had returned but was bearable now. The front of
his shirt was stuck to the ground where the blood had dried.
Medina shoved upward with his strong arms and drew up his
knees, working himself loose with a sickening sucking sound.
Something like a knife twisted in his lower abdomen, and he
bit his lower lip to keep from screaming.

In that moment of private agony, Medina heard footsteps
coming from the direction of the church. It sounded as if
someone stumbled, and he heard a muffled curse in English
and a second whispered admonition to be quiet. The Spaniard's hand darted out and, after a few seconds of frantic
pawing, came to rest on the Mauser. The weapon gave him
courage. The Americans were going to pay for crossing the
path of Enrico Medina. Had they somehow seen him move

and come to finish him off? Could they be attempting to escape or—worse—raid his unsuspecting *compadres* in the village?

He became a rock, a motionless patch of darkness. Medina even kept his face lowered and concealed in the crook of his arm. He risked one peek and counted four men, crouched low and walking abreast of one another as they passed within arm's reach of the wounded Spaniard. He caught a glimmer of light, the glowing red tips of four cigar stubs shielded in their cupped hands. Medina frowned, puzzled by the cigars, then dismissed their significance as he waited for the Americans to pass by, waited until he was well behind them. A coward would lie still and nurture his wounds. But there had never been a coward in the Lion Brigade, and Enrico Medina was not going to be the first. His finger sought and found the Mauser's trigger; then, summoning all his strength and steeling himself against the pain, he rose on his knees, leveled his rifle at one of the four soldiers, and fired.

Tom Sandcrane felt something slap him in the back. He twisted around and nearly fell as a nine-millimeter slug ripped through muscle and flesh on the underside of his arm and opened a gash along his side. Tully, Philo, and Enos all did an about-face and loosed a volley from their Krag rifles at the assailant to their rear.

Alerted by the gunshots, Lieutenant Emilio Garza, in the broken walled remains of the casita thirty yards ahead, roused the other five men under his immediate command and ordered them to repel the unseen attackers. In a matter of seconds the Spanish guns opened up and muzzle blasts lit the night. Enos and Philo flung themselves to the ground and returned fire.

Tom Sandcrane, reeling from the impact of Medina's bullet, glimpsed his assailant through a veil of white-hot pain and moonlight as the Spaniard squeezed off another round. Tom fired his rifle one-handed, forced to grip it like a pistol as his left arm hung useless. The hand refused to obey his commands as he tried to work the Krag's bolt action. Fortunately, the Cheyenne did not need a second round, for the Mauser slipped from Medina's grasp and the Spaniard rolled onto his side, clutching his chest and gasping his last breath.

"Tully!" Philo shouted, alerting the Cheyenne to some new danger.

Tom Sandcrane dropped his own rifle; the Krag was worthless to him now. He found his cigar stub on the ground where it had fallen from his now useless left hand. Retrieving the cigar, he clamped it between his teeth, then drew his revolver and turned back toward the village in time to see Tully Crow, dynamite in hand, charge through a hail of gunfire. The wiry breed seemed impervious to the Spanish rifles as he darted and dodged, howling mad, wild with the battle lust that had come upon him.

No . . . he stumbled . . . somehow kept his balance. Another bullet found its mark. He was staggering now, obviously hurt and yet refusing to fall.

"Tully!" Philo roared again. He emptied his rifle at the muzzle blasts of the Spanish troopers' guns and began to furiously reload.

A shower of sparks cut an arc through the air as Tully hurled a fistful of explosives over the walls of the roofless casita. The ragged volley from the Mauser rifles that flung him to earth like a discarded toy was followed by a roar and a lurid orange flash as the casita itself disappeared in a shower of mud and rocks and the human debris of its former defenders.

Tom willed himself forward, knowing his own time was running out. His wound was serious, he was losing a lot of blood, and the pain was terrible, but it propelled him onward. Philo and Enos rose, loosed their war cries, and dashed toward town, each man wanting to avenge their fallen companion. Tom struggled to keep pace but fell irrevocably behind. By the time he reached the remains of the casita, the other two men had entered the heart of the village and engaged the Lion Brigade. Tom paused by Tully's lifeless body and, kneeling, took the breed's revolver and tucked it into his belt. In the baleful illumination cast by the smoldering remains of the casita, Tully's shirt was black with blood and his eyes were open, unseeing, in death. Tom closed the man's eyelids. There was no time for words or grief. *Perhaps later,* Tom thought, *if any of us are alive.*

Zuloaga staggered from his bed, his coat unbuttoned, and struggled to pull on his boots. Alfonso Ramirez joined his commanding officer out near the plaza. Seeing *el jefe's* disarray, the portly cook immediately knelt before the man and helped him don his boots. Both men had heard the explosion, Diego Zuloaga dozing on the cot inside the humble dwelling that served as his headquarters when the distant blast in the direction of the church sent him reeling through the front door and out into the plaza. Ramirez had been preparing the captain's evening meal, beans and salt back and black coffee laced with brandy. By the time Zuloaga located the source of the explosion, and realized with dismay at first, and then cold fury, that Lieutenant Garza and his detachment of soldiers had been destroyed or driven off, a second and third blast occurred closer to home. The sound of gunfire rippled through the village as the men of the Lion Brigade spread out to stop this surprise attack in its tracks.

"Captain Zuloaga! What is happening?" Chenez shouted from the corral. The man who had been Mateo's captor and who had enjoyed bullying the thirteen-year-old was visibly shaken. It sounded as if they were under an artillery barrage by the American army.

"Stand with us," Zuloaga ordered. "All will be revealed." Ramirez ducked inside the casita and reappeared with the officer's gunbelt, which he promptly buckled around Zuloaga's waist. The captain checked the loads in his French-made revolver—a single-action Le Mat, a cap-and-ball weapon that had been converted to accept center-fire cartridges—then returned the weapon to its holster. Chenez and Ramirez armed themselves with their Mausers and, at the captain's command, began to fortify the casita. They moved quickly to secure the shutters on the windows. Zuloaga considered advancing into the village, but the officer was loath to stumble into an ambush. It was better to wait until word reached him of what was occurring; then he'd have some idea where to retaliate.

A war had broken out in the deserted streets of Rosarita. Gunfire filled the night air. Flames shot up from dynamited shacks. The screams of the wounded and the dying mingled with the furious exchange of gunfire while the horses in the corral began to circle and paw the earth, neighing loudly. Iron-shod hooves struck the gate and railings as the unnerved animals tested their confines; they were eager to bolt through the first opening they could find.

And for the first time Diego Zuloaga began to entertain doubts about his own judgment, his overconfidence and disregard for the enemy.

Perhaps the execution of Mateo had been . . . ill conceived.

Tom Sandcrane stumbled through a nightmare of burned and blasted bodies, his boot sinking inches deep in a pool of blood. He continued past a jacal as flames devoured the structure, turning it into a burial pyre. A terrible shriek sounded to his right, and a Spaniard bolted from another flame-swept hut. The man's clothes were afire as he howled in agony. The trooper glanced off one wall, waving his arms and batting at himself as the flames reached his face and burned out his eyes. Tom ended the man's agony with a bullet, then tried to get his bearings.

He had lost his companions and stood alone in the firelight, revolver in his right hand, his left arm dangling at his side. He was all too conscious of the blood seeping from his arm and side, soaking his trouser leg. He took a hesitant step, then another, drawn to the sound of gunshots and a series of explosions.

All sense of time was lost. He walked as if in a dream. Movement alerted him and he snapped off a couple of shots. Someone returned fire, then broke and ran, possibly wounded. The search continued, firing at shadows and cracking timbers. Tom didn't like the looks of the mud-walled shack before him. He tucked the Colt into his belt, took up a stick of dynamite, and touched the fuse to the glowing tip of his cigar, then tossed the explosive through the night-shrouded entrance. There was a flash of light followed by a muffled blast, which blew out the windows and destroyed part of a back wall. Satisfied, Tom left the hut behind and cautiously approached another pair of fire-gutted hovels and an alley littered with the dead and dying. Three Spaniards were sprawled in death. From the burning buildings came the sickening aroma of burning flesh. How many dead lay among the flames was any man's guess. Tom followed a trail of blood out of the alley. Someone had managed to crawl away from the pack. A couple of minutes later Tom discovered Enos Stump Horn propped against a chicken coop, revolver in one hand and tomahawk in the other. Enos's chest rose and fell in shallow gasps, and he looked up as Tom approached.

"*Nahaoone.* I'm thirsty," Enos said. He lowered his gaze to stare at the puckered bullet holes in his naked chest and belly. He couldn't remember where he had lost his rifle. Gun smoke curled from the barrel of his Colt. But he lifted his tomahawk and held up the iron blade. "My 'hawk has not been blooded." To him it was as important as counting coup.

"It will be," Tom said, and drawing close, he set aside the Colt revolver on a nearby post and took the tomahawk from the dying man's grasp. Enos nodded, satisfied. He stared at Tom, and the wounded man's features were suddenly full of wonderment. "Who are the others?" he asked.

Tom glanced to right and left and saw nothing but shadows, yet Enos seemed to be in a state of awe.

"They know you. They call you by name," the mortally wounded man said, coughing pink froth from his lips.

"I see no one," Tom whispered.

"You will," Enos managed to reply, his voice little more than a gasp. "I place my foot upon the path of the dead." He sighed and slowly exhaled, a sibilant sound; then his head bobbed forward, chin touching chest, arms lowered as his legs relaxed.

Tom slipped the shaft of the tomahawk through his belt at the small of his back. He heard footsteps directly behind him and, grabbing his Colt from the post, turned and drew deadly aim at Philo Underhill. The Creek held up his hands.

"It's me, Tom." He glanced past Sandcrane and spied Enos. "So now we are two." He wiped blood from his cheek.

Underhill's speech was somewhat muffled, and Tom had to struggle to understand him. A bullet had gashed his cheek and another had punctured his thigh, but he had stopped the loss of blood with a hastily fashioned tourniquet consisting of a bandanna tightened with a bayonet lifted from a dead Spaniard.

"We got them on the run, Tom. I blew my share to hell. But a bunch just took off for the corral, I think. I'm clean out of dynamite or I'd have—"

"Take mine," Tom interrupted. "I can't use it anyway."

"You hurt bad."

"Not bad enough," he said.

Philo grinned despite his ruined features and helped himself to the four sticks of dynamite left in Tom's belt while the Cheyenne clumsily reloaded the revolver he had taken off Tully. Tom had to grip the gun barrel with his knees and feed shells into the cylinder. At last he accomplished his task and straightened. Darkness appeared on the periphery of his vision, but Tom forced it to recede by the strength of his own indomitable will. *No. Not yet. It is not finished.*

Then both men quickly, quietly started out of the alley together. Smoke billowed around them, shrouding the men in its choking embrace as they made their way unchallenged among the flame-swept ruins of the village. Fire spread to the eastern meadow, the dry grass set ablaze by wind-borne embers, and threatened to reach the south wall of the valley. Against this backdrop Tom and Philo were hardly a threatening sight. Sweat streaked Tom's war paint, and each step seemed to thrust a dagger of fire into his side. But he rode the waves of pain and burned his own agony for fuel, one step after another, through a world that reeked of death.

Zuloaga overheard the commotion by the corral and Chenez on the roof called out to his companions to wait and leave the horses alone, and immediately the captain understood what was going on. He bolted out the side door, revolver in hand, and confronted the five troopers who had survived the explosions and the havoc in the village. The men

were convinced that an overwhelming force of American soldiers had launched an offensive against their sparsely fortified
positions. The captain was taken aback by their report and for
a moment considered the possibility that another detachment
of Americans had entered the valley through a passage unknown to him. By this time Chenez had climbed down from
the roof. Ramirez, who was less anxious for a fight than any
of them, worked his way into the corral and surreptitiously
began to saddle his horse.

Zuloaga considered ordering them to stand, when a leather
box of ammunition in one of the burning houses caught fire
and exploded with the fury of a Gatling gun. To the men by
the corral it sounded as if an entire detachment had opened
fire on them. The already panicked troopers hurried to their
horses, and this time Zuloaga was with them. It only made
sense to assess the situation from a distance, out of harm's
way. Two minutes later the horses were saddled and the Lion
Brigade trotted their mounts out into the plaza. Fate again
played its hand, as Zuloaga glanced toward the section of
town still ablaze from the attack and spied two men standing
in front of the well in the center of the plaza. The last of the
exploding rounds sounded in the distance. The captain
checked the perimeter of the marketplace for the rest of the
Americans and halted his brigade when he realized the men
by the well were alone.

Alone.

"Two! You run from two such as these!" Zuloaga twisted in
the saddle. The troopers behind him looked away, fearing to
unleash the harnessed fury in those eyes. "They have killed
your *compadres* and turned you into cowards. Ride them
down, I say. Kill them!"

Zuloaga drove his boot heels into the flanks of his gelding,
and the animal bolted forward in response to its rider's punishing blows. With a cry of rage the men of the Lion Brigade
regained their courage and urged their mounts into a gallop,
fanning out across the plaza in a headlong charge, Mausers
blazing, hunters to their prey.

*   *   *

Tom braced himself against the stone wall. His strength had taken him this far out of the choking clouds of smoke but no farther. It didn't matter; the Spaniards were coming to them.

"Poor bastards. They don't know we got them licked," Philo chuckled. He puffed on the cigar stub to keep the tip aglow. An inch of ash landed on the ground at his feet. "How do you want to take them, head-on?"

"Is there any other way?" Tom said as he thumbed the hammer back on his revolver. His features were a garish mask of streaked soot and clay where he had sweated through the war paint. Yet in a way it made his visage seem all the more fierce. In what he suspected were the final moments of his life, his senses seemed amplified. He could hear the hooves of the approaching horses, the gunfire before him, the crackle of flames in the fire-gutted ruins to his left. The air smelled smoky and rife with the stench of sweat and blood and charred bodies. Bullets kicked up geysers of dirt a few yards from the well. Others whined past, harmlessly at first, then closer as the Spaniards bore down on the men by the well.

Suddenly, from off to the side, bursting through a curtain of smoke, the freight wagon careened into the plaza and passed directly behind the battered remnants of the Lion Brigade. Joanna Cooper was at the reins, which accounted for the fact that the team of horses was not under complete control. Willem Tangle Hair and Antonio Celestial, the latter braced upright and levering shots from his Winchester, blasted away at the brigade. Zuloaga's men were caught completely by surprise and tried to alter their attack to meet this new threat.

Tom and Philo staggered out into the plaza, forcing their wounded bodies to make one last Herculean effort. Tom emptied the revolver in his hand as Philo tossed one stick of dynamite after the other among the bewildered Spaniards.

One—two—three—four explosions knocked horses to the ground and deafened the troopers. Caught in a vicious cross fire, their newfound determination proved brittle and shattered as saddles began to empty. Diego Zuloaga leaped from the saddle as the earth beneath him exploded in a shower of rocks and dirt. He rolled and staggered to his feet, blood streaming from a dozen cuts, his coat split down the back and his trouser legs in tatters. The heel of one boot had been blown away. Zuloaga looked about and called to his men. Chenez saw him and attempted to reach his side.

Tom Sandcrane tossed the empty revolver aside and drew his holstered Colt. Through blurred vision he managed to recognize Zuloaga and saw the trooper racing to the officer's rescue. Tom squeezed off a shot and missed, fired again, and then again, the Colt bucking in his fist with each report. The Spaniard on horseback doubled forward, clawing at a mortal wound to his vitals, and slid headfirst out of the saddle as Tom sank to his knees, his limbs trembling.

Zuloaga made a desperate grab for the animal's reins as Tom fired the last three rounds from his Colt in rapid succession, missing Zuloaga but twice wounding the startled gelding that Chenez had ridden. The animal tore loose from the officer's grasp and bolted toward freedom.

Zuloaga, seeing the remainder of his command break from the plaza and race toward the woods, cursed and shouted for his men to come to his aid. But all that remained of the Lion Brigade—Ramirez, the cook, and three other wounded soldiers—ignored the captain's orders. Only the cook looked over his shoulder in the direction of the plaza. But Alfonso Ramirez had made good his escape, and there was no going back.

"On to Santiago," he muttered, and followed his *compadres* into the sheltering embrace of the trees.

Zuloaga snarled in disgust, all his hatred focused now on the man who had denied his escape. He spied the Le Mat lying in the dirt where he had dropped it and lunged for the weapon, palming the gun and spinning around to put a bullet in Sandcrane. Philo snapped off a shot from his Colt and leaped in front of Tom as the Spaniard fired. The Creek breed shuddered and then sagged against his friend.

Antonio Celestial fired from the wagon bed as Joanna hauled back on the reins and applied the brakes. The slug from the Winchester knocked Zuloaga off his feet.

Tom tried to bear Philo's weight but could not keep him from slipping to the trampled earth. The wounded man gri-

maced. Blood spurted from a horrid wound in his neck. Tom
cradled the man and tried to stanch the flow, but there was
too much of it. Philo shook his head, as if to tell him not to
try. He knew his time was near. Something struck Philo as ri-
diculous, because he began to laugh, a horrible, choking
laugh, which only made matters worse. Then his brows furrowed as he tried to focus on the stars, but the haze from the
burning buildings was too thick and dark. He frowned and
shook his head. Another few seconds passed, and Philo
Underhill no longer cared about anything.

"*Madre*," Zuloaga groaned, and crawled to his knees, staring down in disbelief at the wound in his side.

Tom heard the officer and looked up from his dead friend
to Zuloaga struggling to stand. The officer still held his revolver. Tom couldn't have cared less. He was a ghost. No bullet could stop him. The Cheyenne rose from the valley floor
and reached behind his back to draw the iron-bladed tomahawk from his belt. The cry that spilled from his lips no
longer sounded human. He had seen too much, been pushed
too far; there was nothing in him but rage. He heard the
drums now, the war cries of his people down the corridors of
time when they had ridden into battle against their enemies.
Howling, war-painted wraiths surrounded him and carried
him forward as Zuloaga fired and missed. The captain tried
again, but his hand was quivering and he wasted the shot,
then tossed the gun aside in surrender. It was a useless gesture. He begged for his life and lifted his hands to ward off
the blow as Tom stood over him, tomahawk raised aloft. The
blade swept downward in a brutal slash that nearly severed
the Spaniard's arm. He screamed.

Tom struck him again, this time in the skull. The blade methodically rose and fell, with sickening effect. Zuloaga's
screams became cries of agony, then whimpers, then faded
until there was nothing but the 'hawk, the whisper of the
blade as it sliced the air, the crunch of flesh and bone.

Tom Sandcrane was red to the elbow before he finished his
butcher's work. And then the drums died, the warriors vanished in shadow and smoke. He staggered back, gasping for
breath, his sides heaving. The thing at his feet no longer re-

sembled a man, and he turned away; the tomahawk's shaft
now too slick to grasp, he let the weapon drop to earth. He
saw the freight wagon. He sensed Joanna watching him and
was grateful he could not see the expression on her face. He
tried to walk but his legs gave out. He tried to brace himself
but his left arm only feebly responded, and the hand had no
feeling at all, so he pitched over on his side.

Tom brought his right hand up to his face and wriggled his
fingers. "I'm still alive," he said, but the words were garbled
and faint. And the darkness Tom had held back for so long
at last swept forward in triumph to claim him.

CHAPTER THIRTY

ONE MOMENT DARKNESS, SILENCE, NOTHING. THEN CONsciousness. He was aware of a creaking axle reverberating beneath him, the crunch of iron-rimmed wheels over stone, a jostling motion, and pain. He moaned and opened his eyes to stare at a pair of dim faces whose features he struggled to identify through the haze of his blurred vision. A woman leaned over him, cradling his head, and tilted a canteen to his mouth. Cool water trickled between his parched lips. A man seated next to him spoke gently, his accent graceful and melodic.

"Do not die, my friend."

"Pull up a moment, Willem, one of the bandages has worked loose," the woman called out, and the motion gradually ceased. "Tom." She was unable to hide the concern in her voice. "Tom Sandcrane."

No! He didn't know anyone by that name, and closed his eyes.

Darkness . . . silence . . . nothing.

Red dreams.

He heard drums and chanting, the far-off voices of ancient ones who had gone before; prayers and whistles and the pad of primitive feet tracking buffalo across a sheen of frost. Images of fur-clad hunters faded, became a single warrior in a breechclout, leggings, and quill breastplate. His hair was braided, and he wore a buffalo hat adorned with eagle feathers, its horn tipped crimson. He sat astride a hammer-headed roan. This Cheyenne sentinel was familiar, but for whom did he watch, his fierce eyes brimming with wisdom and primal danger? For whom did he wait?

Me.

The image shimmered and drifted apart. And in the place of the warrior, a brilliant amber light almost too painful to face.

I hear laughter.

Two men approached out of the brightness. Mere specks at first, they increased in size as they closed in on the watcher. One of the men was Tully Crow, and alongside the wiry Creek breed stood Philo Underhill. They were speaking, their mouths moving, but no sound issued forth.

It is my fault. I carry your deaths upon my heart.

Tully grinned, or grimaced, and began to laugh. Or was it a scream?

Eano-vetano! Eano-vetano! Forgive me!

The brilliance faded and the world became a shadow place. The watcher stood with lantern in hand upon a broad, flat plain where a lonely wind sighed. A bloody hand ax lay at his feet upon a patch of earth dark with the moisture of a slowly spreading stain. On the perimeter of the firelight, barely visible in the flames' eerie glow, lay the grisly vessel of what had once been a man, bleeding from a dozen wounds, leaching his life's fluids into the thirsty soil.

Weariness and sorrow had followed the rage, and everywhere was pain, and he walked the land of the dead, like the ghost he had once claimed to be.

A voice whispered against his ear. "Tom Sandcrane."

Yes. I am.

Tom Sandcrane walked in a dream and saw an array of faces he recalled: Seth, kindly Father Kenneth from the reservation, green-eyed Emmiline, the Tall Bull brothers, Allyn

Benedict with his smug, satisfied smile, and Clay, his son. Suddenly he was standing among the tribal elders who had gathered around him in a circle, and firelight illuminated the ceremonial lodge so that the Maiyun danced like shadows on the wall. And in the corner of the lodge, seated apart from the circle, stood Tully and Philo, dead arms raised toward him, beckoning their friend to follow.

Tom opened his eyes and, lying still, took a moment to assess the situation before calling attention to himself. The wounded man had drifted in and out of the conscious state so often, reality and hallucination were thoroughly intermingled. He remembered the hardwood wagon bed and some of the jolting ride through the mountains. He thought he remembered lying by a campfire with Joanna, Willem, and Celestial nearby. Then Tom had awakened only to find himself in a canvas tent, surrounded by the plaintive cries of suffering souls whose identity he could only guess. An orderly approached him and began spooning broth into his mouth until he choked, and then the man mercifully left and Tom was alone again, too weak to move. Sweat trickled from his forehead and neck, soaking the blanket folded beneath his head. Then he had been grateful when the world shifted out of focus, and he again succumbed to the dark.

So Tom had good reason to doubt the reality of his surroundings when he found the tent gone, the din of sick and dying replaced by stillness, and the faint buzzing of a mosquito. Sun-washed curtains fluttered to the caress of a breeze through an open window. Tom wrinkled his nose and inhaled the saltwater scent of the sea. This wasn't Rosarita. And the mountains were far from the ocean. He lay in a brass bed in a mostly barren room with whitewashed stucco walls. To his right a water basin had been left upon a nearby cabinet along with a clay pitcher and a cup. He ran a tongue around the inside of his mouth and dry-swallowed; some water would sure go good. He looked to his left and found the room's only other article of furniture, a high-backed rocking chair on which a blanket and pillow had been casually tossed as if someone intended to pass the night there. Or several nights, he thought, and perhaps they already had.

He heard the sound of distant explosions and frowned, wondering how he had come there and if he was a prisoner and where the battle was raging. He seemed to remember fragments of a long journey. *Tosa-a!* Could he be in Santiago? His face felt hot, his eyes like coals, and his left shoulder throbbed like hell. He was feverish, sick with infection and poison and possibly dying. If that was the case, then he did not want his life to end in ignorance.

The view from the window might provide the answers to his questions. He tried to push himself up off the bed with both arms only to find his left arm crudely bandaged to his chest to keep it immobilized. His shoulder, upper arm, and side were tightly wrapped with gauze. He stared down at his left hand, clenched into a fist and pressed against his chest. He tried to wriggle the fingers, but he might as well have been trying to will the walls to speak for all the success he had. He noticed a khaki shirt, blue trousers, and coat neatly draped over the rail at the foot of the bed. Lifting the sheets with his trembling right hand, he found he was wearing a faded pair of long johns. He was looking past the foot of his bed at the dark oaken panels of the bedroom door when it swung open and a diminutive woman in a scarlet-and-orange-striped cotton dress and white blouse started into the room, saw that Tom was awake, did an about-face, and hurried back into what was apparently a hallway. He could hear her calling through the house. Tom searched the room for something he could use for a weapon, settled on the clay water pitcher, and struggled to swing his legs over the side of the bed. It seemed to take all his strength and willpower, but he persevered, though his head began to throb and the room reel like a river raft. His bandaged side hurt like the devil, but he worked through the pain and reached for the pitcher. The world careened wildly and he promptly lost his balance, grazed the clay jug with his fingertips, and curled forward onto the floor, landing with a loud and ominous thud. The pitcher shattered a few feet away.

Tom had no sense of how much time had elapsed—he thought only a few seconds—but when he came to again, Joanna Cooper and a Cuban woman were lifting him into bed. He watched Joanna through slitted eyelids as she leaned over him.

"You're on the outskirts of Santiago. This is the ancestral home of Antonio Celestial."

"Battle . . . ?" he weakly asked.

"It is the Fourth of July. The army and navy are celebrating their victory over the Spanish forces. It looks like we missed the war."

Missed the war, Tom thought. He'd gotten his friends killed, nearly himself too.

"I've asked Bernard Marmillon to come take a look at you when he's finished in the military hospital. Celestial gave a full account of your heroics. Colonel Roosevelt was pleased."

He was drifting off again. He could hear Joanna, though her voice seemed to echo in his head as if he were standing at the bottom of a deep well and her words were drifting down from above. Colonel Roosevelt was pleased. Tully and Philo and Enos were dead and the officers were pleased. Small comfort.

"You have to fight to live, Tom. Fight to live."

Why? he wondered. *For what purpose?* So that he could sell out his people again or maybe find some other friends and lead them to their deaths? While day turned to night, he listened to the beating of his heart as his pulse slowed and he sank into a comalike state.

Red dreams. Red visions.

Hea-vohe, the deathbringer, was hunting. He assumed the shape of a hawk with wings red as blood, swift against the dreadful gray sky, riding the wind in lazy spirals, transfixed against the gunmetal clouds, regal in his beauty. He glided aloft, poised to strike; cunning, swift, and merciless; certain as fate. Tom watched and waited, helpless, unable to run for fear of attracting the wraith. The hunted have nowhere to hide. Suddenly the demon hawk plunged earthward.

Hea-vohe attacked, in a blur of motion and flight, and the rush of its wings was a terrible thing to hear. The hunter loomed larger, larger; there was no escape as Tom raised his hands to ward off the inevitable. The wraith-hawk struck a crushing blow, talons tearing, skewering his chest and legs like so many lances. The noise of the impact sounded like ice cracking at first thaw.

"He's in pretty bad shape, Joanna. And you look exhausted. Of all the rash and foolish things you've ever . . . every time I think of you sneaking off like that . . ."

"Can we save him, Bernard?"

"I think that is up to Sandcrane. It depends on his will to live. Look at this wound. There is so much damage to the brachial plexus. He will have no use of his hand, I should imagine, and only marginal movement in his arm. Poor bastard. I doubt an Indian would wish to go through life a cripple."

"You don't know him."

"And you do?"

In dreamtime a minute, an hour, a day, were all indistinguishable; the vision unfolded at its own pace, like a blossom in sunlight, revealing its truth a petal at a time.

Deathbringer, in the shape of a hawk, carried Tom aloft, and he was helpless and dying in *hea-vohe's* grasp. Upward into the wind where loneliness reigns, then soaring beneath the lowering clouds, the wraith-hawk bore its struggling prey across familiar country—rolling hills, thickets of scrub oak and slash pine and cedar.

Now the sky darkened, turned from gray to charcoal, and thunder drowned out Tom's cries. The *hea-vohe* would be his killer, and there would be no one to help. As the storm unleashed its fury, the wraith-hawk swooped down and alighted upon the muddy bank of a rain-swollen river. Shattered trees and jagged clusters of roots rushed past, trapped by the fury of the flood. It was in this place of noise and elemental violence that *hea-vohe* chose to finish his prey. Beak and talons tore at Tom's flesh and he was powerless to resist. His blood mingled with the rain. The last thing he would see on earth was the onrushing river framed by a shattered tree trunk and reeds bowed beneath the downpour, and . . . what else? What was it? His gaze was drawn to the muddy debris left by the floor. Among the broken branches and mud and a patch of tattered buckskin, he found the heart of his vision. Four feathered shafts half-buried in the silt.

The Sacred Arrows! White, black, yellow, and red; their obsidian tips jutting from the muddy riverbank, they lay just inches from his fingertips. He stretched forth his hand, every muscle straining until he touched a wooden shaft. Using one Arrow, he maneuvered the others into his grasp, and when the Mahuts were his, he began the chant. The words sprang more from instinct than memory. He sang of the power of Mahuts and the way of Maheo, of sunsets and harvests, of a red dawn, and rebirth. There was no change in the outward appearance of the Arrows. And yet strength flowed into Tom and he was restored and the storm became his ally.

He sensed the fear in *hea-vohe* now as the wraith-hawk spread its wings and pummeled the air and battled the battering rain, seeking to escape its former prey by taking to the sky. But the chant had a power and a life all its own. A flash of lightning sprang from the Arrows and outlined the hawk in iridescent blue fire. *Hea-vohe,* the deathbringer, shrieked and plummeted into the raging waters and was instantly swept away, its protests lost in thunder. In that moment the downpour, its fury spent, became a fine, calm mist that settled on the Dream-Keeper of the Arrows and broke his fever and saved his life with the cooling kiss of peace.

INTERLUDE

CHAPTER THIRTY-ONE

Oklahoma Territory, February 1899

I N THE TIME OF THE LITTLE HOOP MOON, SOMETIMES CALLED THE
Little Hard-Faced Moon, a chill wintry wind frosted the
windows of Panther Hall and rattled an unfastened shutter like a prowler testing for a way to enter. An occasional
snowflake fluttered out of the night sky to settle on the brittle
remains of last summer's firewheels and paintbrush and sunflowers.

Time and prosperity had turned the roadhouse into an ostentatious three-storied structure, ablaze with lantern light
and reverberating to the din of its boisterous patrons. Panther
Hall offered gaiety, music, gambling, hard liquor, and ladies of
the evening in satin and feathers who were willing to con-
verse, dance, or satisfy the lusts of any man with money in
his pocket. A well-lit proscenium stage dominated the rear of
the hall. An orchestra pit just beyond the footlights often
housed a five-piece band capable of accompanying a visiting
chanteuse or the fandango dancers that often entertained to
the cheers of an appreciative crowd.

It was Jerel Tall Bull's intention to part each customer from
as much money as possible. To that end a roulette wheel and
monte table had been brought in all the way from Chicago to
offer Panther Hall's patrons—ranch hands, roughnecks,

townsfolk, and soldiers—a diversion from poker and black-jack. Two well-polished walnut-and-mahogany bars lined with brass rails faced one another from opposite sides of the poker tables and dance floor and served up an amazing array of potables from Kentucky whiskey and champagne, to hard cider, gin, bourbon, rye, beer, and a particularly nasty concoction simply referred to as "gutshot."

The second floor consisted of ten handsomely appointed boudoirs to serve the customer who was of a "sporting nature." Here a man could sample the vices of the flesh, indulging himself in carnal pleasures with as many women as he could pay for.

The third floor was the private domain of Jerel Tall Bull and his brother Curtis, with an office and two bedrooms and storage. A stairway at the end of the hall led down to the lower levels. Jerel's office could also be reached from a wrought-iron stairway connected outside to a balcony that fronted the third floor. The balcony, with its intricately fashioned ironwork railing, gave Panther Hall a decidedly New Orleans flair, incongruous with the open expanse of range-land surrounding it.

On this cold Friday evening Panther Hall was swarming with revelers who gambled and drank and danced to excess beneath the brass chandeliers. The noise seemed to travel up the walls and even managed to filter faintly through the floor of Jerel's office. The drillers and roughnecks employed by Benedict Exploration and Development were making up for lost time. Days of brutally hard labor in the oil fields had to be offset in a single night of unbridled revelry.

Jerel Tall Bull knew tonight's crowd was a volatile mix. Ranch hands had no use for roughnecks, and fights between the two groups were frequent. The Cheyenne who frequented the hall kept to themselves except when inebriated, and then would take on anyone and everyone; they made quarrelsome, angry drunks. Panther Hall was also entertaining its share of soldiers from Fort Reno and a few respectable citizens from Cross Timbers, drawn to the roadhouse under cover of night to partake of the establishment's rich menu of vices.

It came as no surprise to the elder of the two brothers

when Curtis blundered into the darkened office and broadly announced there was trouble downstairs and Jerel needed to make his presence known to keep things from turning nasty.

The Seth Thomas clock on the mantel above the fireplace struck a quarter to ten, a single note of punctuation to the younger brother's outburst. Curtis started across the room but struck his shin on a footstool, cursed, and decided to hold his ground, allowing his eyes to adjust to the gloom. He could barely make out the high-backed leather chair where Jerel was seated before a large picture window that overlooked the well-traveled road leading up to the front yard and the hitching posts. It was from this vantage point that Jerel often watched the sunsets when weather prevented him from venturing outside, a practice he had only recently begun and one that piqued his brother's curiosity.

Still night-blind, Curtis heard the rustle of clothes and glimpsed a blur of movement before the window as two forms untangled themselves. By the time his eyesight adjusted to the darkened interior, Red Cherries had emerged from the front of the office and brushed past the intruder without so much as a by-your-leave. There was surprising strength in Red Cherries' slender, dark-haired form; she was no one to cross. Surviving by her wits in this world of men had given her a heart that Curtis likened to blued steel. Once he had tried to force his attentions on her, but Red Cherries had called his bluff, much to Jerel's amusement, and sent the younger brother on his way, threatening to take a knife to his manhood should he ever be so bold again. From that moment on Curtis Tall Bull argued in vain to have Red Cherries dismissed, only to be overruled by his brother.

Jerel had taken a liking to Red Cherries. It was her job to keep Panther Hall's ladies in line and circulating among the patrons, encouraging each and every customer to part with his hard-earned wages. She was firm and efficient and easy to look at, and Jerel refused to dismiss her. There was another, more intimate reason, one that Curtis had now unwittingly blundered onto.

He watched Red Cherries hurry to the stairway, where she disappeared from sight, her ankle-high boots tapping on the wooden steps as she descended, her scarlet satin dress rustling with every step. He wrinkled his nose as the scent of musk and rose water assailed his nostrils. Then he continued into the office, where Jerel waited, his ruffled shirt untucked and open to midchest.

"Wipe the grin off your face, you clumsy bastard. I gave instructions not to be disturbed." If anything, time had only made the heavyset Cheyenne even more powerful looking, with great slabs of muscle bulging his sloping shoulders, his black hair cropped to just below his ears, his brutish exterior concealing a keen intellect.

"Except in an emergency," Curtis said. "You said to come get you then."

"Somebody go blind from gutshot again?"

"No. But there's trouble downstairs."

"Get Pete Elk Head and John Iron Hail to handle the roughnecks. That's what I pay those bar dogs for. What's a few broken heads? Nobody'll remember a thing come morning."

"This is worse. There's liable to be a killing. That soldier boy, Willem Tangle Hair, showed up a few minutes ago. Charlotte White Bear's downstairs, whiskey-hot and dancing and rubbing up just about anyone who'll buy her another drink."

Jerel sighed. He knew Willem considered Charlotte his own personal property. But after the red-haired breed took off for Cuba, Charlotte, never the most faithful of paramours, had found comfort elsewhere. On his return Willem had refused to accept that things had changed, and had begun to make a nuisance of himself. It was a volatile situation that could easily turn violent, best resolved as far from Panther Hall as possible. Not only would a killing make the gambling hall off-limits to the soldiers, but it would probably scare off some of the customers from Cross Timbers as well.

"Let's go," Jerel said, pulling on his frock coat and combing his hair back with his fingers. He lifted a gunbelt off a wall peg just next to the door, then returned the belt, tucking the Colt thirty-eight in his right pocket. He tried to blank out Red Cherries' visit and the taste of her on his lips, the firmness of her breasts beneath his hand. Damn. He finally had her hot and ready and Curtis had come blundering in to spoil the entire evening. Then again, the fault was Tangle Hair's, Jerel thought, scowling, anger quickening his descent, as his boots beat a brisk tattoo on the stairs. Curtis struggled to keep pace. In the sallow glow of the lamplit stairway, his slender form was all but obscured by his brother's shadow.

Willem had made the mistake of reaching for Charlotte and had torn the sleeve of her cotton blouse as she'd tried to pull away.

"You fool. You hot-tempered fool, look what you've done," Charlotte exclaimed. Her ample bosom strained the fabric and fueled the fantasies of the rugged-looking customers who had formed a circle around the quarreling couple.

"I know you've been running with someone else, and I know you're out here to meet him. Well? Who is it? Point him out!" Willem searched the surrounding faces, hoping to catch a glimmer of guilty recognition. He'd been drinking, and the alcohol was having its effect on him, despite the fact that he was steady on his feet. The khaki campaign coat he wore, a reminder of the Indian Brigade he had recently mustered out of, was dirt stained with patches of mud and grease, the residue of the oil fields. He had ridden straight from a drilling rig to Panther Hall in hopes of discovering the identity of the man who had replaced him in Charlotte's affections.

"He's someone who will take care of me, who will take me to the city and buy me pretty things. You'll see. And we won't ever come back." She swung about, long hair flowing, her body all sweet curves and sultry roundness, ripe and arousing. Her eyes were dark and lustrous and dared him to stop her.

"Hell, sweetheart," a man called out from the crowd. "I'll take you somewhere."

"Yeah, about as far as the barn," another voice replied, to a ripple of laughter.

"You're leaving with me," Willem said, his fingers digging into her arm.

"Let go. You're hurting me," she said, nostrils flared, irate and full of fight.

"Maybe *both* of you should leave," Jerel Tall Bull said as the crowd parted to allow him passage into the center of the circle.

"I'll leave when I am good and ready," Charlotte retorted. "My father—"

"Is a tired old man with a store to run and no time to rein in his daughter," Jerel said. He glanced over the crowd toward the orchestra pit where Curtis, standing alongside a pianist, two horn players, and a drummer, awaited his signal. The chandeliers were shrouded with tobacco smoke, but the stage lights burned bright. Jerel waved his hand in his brother's direction, and Curtis immediately barked orders to the musicians. The band struck up a fanfare, and the crowd gravitated toward the proscenium, jostling one another for the best position. Out rushed the fandango dancers in their gaily colored gowns and petticoats, and they began to kick up their heels to a merry tune, showing off their frilly underclothes. Willem and Charlotte were quickly forgotten in the roughnecks' haste to approach the stage, which had been Jerel's intent all along.

"Get out," he said to the quarrelsome couple when the crowd had disbanded.

"See here," Willem began. He didn't like being ordered around by a man he considered little better than a snake.

"No!" Jerel snapped, cutting him off. There was power in his voice. It surrounded him with an aura Willem had never noticed before. "That uniform doesn't cut you any slack as far as I'm concerned. Now, get going."

Words of protest and indignation died on Willem's lips. There was something about the man that forced him to retreat. He sensed Tall Bull's underlings standing off to the side. Lean, hungry Pete Elk Head brandished an ax handle while his partner, John Iron Hail, slapped a bung hammer against the palm of his hand. The customers were now oblivious to the confrontation. There were music and dancing beauties to hold the attention of the crowd.

A smug Charlotte White Bear watched Willem turn toward

the front door. But her expression soon changed when Jerel tapped her on the shoulder and said, "You too."

Her expression fell. "But I'm waiting for . . ."

"He won't be in tonight."

"But he promised."

"Go on home, woman," Jerel firmly instructed. "If he shows up later, I'll send him your way. Next time use the back entrance. Red Cherries will let you in." He took her by the arm and, retrieving her heavy woolen wrap from a nearby table, steered her toward the front door. Willem had lingered there, taking a moment to button his coat, stalling for time. He reached out to Luthor White Bear's errant daughter.

"Come with me, Charlotte. I don't care who you've been seeing, just come with me now and we'll start over."

Her hand lashed out and caught him across the face. "Don't touch me! Damn you, all of you!" There were tears in her eyes, her cheeks flushed from the rage she felt over her absent lover's betrayal.

Willem reacted on reflex, and his hand swept back to deliver a blow in kind. Charlotte's eyes widened and she retreated. Willem came to his senses and lowered his hand, glancing around to find a trio of gamblers watching him from a nearby table. There was considerable money on the table, and the card players had refused to abandon the pot for all the belles and bloomers in the Oklahoma Territory. Charlotte threw the door open with a crash, darted outside, and ran, sobbing, across the yard to the gelding she had ridden from Cross Timbers. Within seconds she had saddled up and galloped off, determined to shave ten minutes off the half hour's journey back to Cross Timbers.

Willem's cheeks reddened as the gamblers continued to stare at him, the bid momentarily forgotten. It was evident from the look on their faces that they disapproved of his behavior. Had he actually struck Charlotte, the men would have rushed to her defense out of a sense of honor, and appreciation for her full figure. As the gamblers returned to their game, the half-breed flashed Jerel an angry look, turned, and followed the woman out into the wintry night. The sound of music, its gaiety lost upon his troubled heart, followed him all the way to the hitching rail and drifted toward the scattered stars like prayer smoke.

The toe of his boot tipped a fist-sized rock. He retrieved it, then swung into the saddle, rode his mount up to the front of Panther Hall, and, with a well-aimed toss, sent the stone crashing through a window. He swung his mount about as a handful of the gambling hall's furious denizens, led by Jerel Tall Bull, came barreling through the front door. Elated at his own misconduct, Willem Tangle Hair left a chorus of curses and epithets shouted in his wake as he galloped off in pursuit of the woman he loved.

When Father Kenneth played chess, he lost all track of time. Here in Luthor White Bear's mercantile, assailed by a fragrant array of apples and leather goods, spilled flour and molasses, and the faint, rich aroma of smoked hams hanging from the rafters overhead, the Capuchin priest sat hunched over the chessboard opposite his friend and constant opponent, Luthor White Bear. The priest reached for a plate of corn-bread dressing that Rebecca White Bear, the merchant's quiet, unassuming wife, had left on the table for the chess players to finish off.

"The smoked venison was delicious," Father Kenneth began, "but this dressing . . ." It was late, nearly midnight, and he had no business eating; he would pay by tossing and turning through the wee hours of the morning. But these last few bites were impossible to resist. Besides, it had been all of five hours since dinner.

"They say gluttony is a sin," Luthor dourly observed. He was playing a desperate defense, having lost his queen and a knight only a few moves ago. Checkmate was a distinct possibility, and it soured his mood.

"And the road to hell is paved with corn-bread dressing and sweet rhubarb pie," Father Kenneth chuckled, and speared a giblet with his fork. Rebecca, who had long since retired for the evening, had begun her preparations early in the day. A couple pans of corn bread had to be baked, then a chicken boiled with onions and wild herbs for broth, and some of the meat set aside for another meal. She combined the corn bread with a leftover crumbled loaf of wheat bread, the stock, and chicken meat in a cast-iron skillet and baked the mixture until it assumed the proper thickness. Some of the stock she thickened for gravy and flavored with peppers and salt, spooning it over mounds of golden dressing. Father Kenneth knew the recipe by heart, but his attempts never turned out as delicious as hers, and he suspected she was deliberately concealing one or two ingredients just to keep him humble.

"I wish you'd never taught me this game, Father," Luthor scowled. "Looks like you've beat me for the third time tonight."

"No wonder, the way you've been playing," the priest replied. "You've seemed distracted for most of the night, indeed for several days now. What is it, my friend?" Father Kenneth eased back in his chair and stroked his bushy yellow beard as he waited for an explanation. He had gained the trust of his parishioners by being patient and confidential. And it was common knowledge where his sympathies lay, for he had been a vocal advocate for the rights of the tribe.

Since the land rush over a year ago, the Southern Cheyenne had become a minority in their own homeland. The change, much to the priest's dismay, had occurred literally overnight and brought more poverty than prosperity as many of the Cheyenne, deluded by the opportunity for a quick profit, sold off their own grants and invested their earnings in foolhardy schemes on the advice of dishonest speculators. The net result was that most of the tribe now subsisted on the charity of the church or worked for Allyn Benedict out in the oil fields. There were some tribal families who had kept their businesses in town and others whose ranches dotted the grazing range between the Canadian and the Washita, and they could boast of a modest financial success. Their accomplishments, however, paled to insignificance alongside the fortune that Benedict and his associates had begun to reap.

"Nothing is bothering me," the white-haired man answered too quickly. He rose from the game board and sauntered across the store to the window, to study with grave affection the town he barely recognized. Cross Timbers, after the land rush, had expanded its boundaries to the hillsides as the number of businesses increased and settlers built houses on land whose former owners had been Southern Cheyenne. Many of the tribal families had resettled a mile west of Cross Timbers in a cluster of cabins commonly referred to as Rabbit Town. Here many of the Cheyenne roughnecks lived with their families when they weren't out in the oil fields or squandering their hard-earned wages at Panther Hall. Luthor White Bear lived above his store, however, and had won the acceptance of the townspeople, who viewed him as just another businessman—albeit one with coppery skin.

A glass pane rattled as the wind pressed against the front of the building, kicked up the dust from the boardwalk, and stirred the leaves, setting them in motion like a column of charging cavalry that swept the street of an unseen enemy. Father Kenneth walked over to the merchant's side.

"Come summer there'll be folks in the street, even this late," the priest said with a sigh. "Winter is a lonely season— the wind moans, the fields are barren, the whole world just curls up and waits for spring." He clapped Luthor on the shoulder. "I won't press you, my friend. But if you should feel like talking, you know where I am." He lifted his coat from a wall peg near the door and pulled it on. "I'd best be going. Seth Sandcrane's putting up a barn, and I thought I'd help out for the next few days," said the priest. "Seeing as I'm the only decent carpenter in the territory," he added with a grin. Shrugging on his coat, he searched the pockets for a moment until he found a thick-woven knit hat. "Our new doctor gave this to me for Christmas." He was obviously quite pleased with the gift, which kept the top of his head and the tips of his ears toasty warm, even on gusty nights such as the one he was about to enter.

"Don't brood on me, Father," Luthor said. "The hour is late, and Charlotte has yet to return home. She defies me at every turn these days, and I am concerned for her."

"It is the way of parents and their children, ever pulling in opposite directions. You are not the only father to be tested by his daughter or son, and you will not be the last." Kenneth spoke with conviction, all the while suspecting there was more to the merchant's gloomy state than Charlotte's behavior.

Father Kenneth buttoned his coat and then opened the front door, allowing an icy draft to invade the interior of the store. It rustled the bonnets on their stands and caused the lamps to flutter. The pages of an open ledger flipped past several weeks all the way to the seventh of June, as if directed by an unseen hand. Luthor shuddered at the wintry evening's brisk intrusion and hurried back to the Franklin stove for warmth.

Out on the walk, Father Kenneth turned his back with some regret on the cozy familiarity of the mercantile and started up Main Street toward St. Joachim's. A wintry gust tugged at his beard with unseen fingers as he made his way past the darkened facades of the businesses that had come to town. The Lavender House Hotel and Lodging boasted thirty comfortable rooms that were frequently occupied by salesmen and oil-company officials come to meet with Allyn Benedict. Though the lobby appeared only dimly illuminated, the hotel saloon, whose doors opened onto a side alley, was doing a lively late-night business. Under Mayor Allyn Benedict's leadership, the town council had refused to permit any more than a couple of saloons to locate within the town limits. The Lavender House Saloon and a similar establishment connected to Yaquereno's restaurant across the street were the only places within town where a man could belly up to the bar and have a beer or whiskey. Gambling, other than perhaps a friendly game of poker, was not permitted in these saloons, nor were the "soiled doves" allowed to roost.

Mayor Benedict claimed his intentions were to keep the streets safe and the riffraff out of town, but Father Kenneth suspected there was more to this arrangement than civic-mindedness. The town ordinances certainly insured a steady flow of customers to Panther Hall. Every time the Capuchin organized a move to shut down the notorious establishment, his efforts were disregarded or surreptitiously defused by the mayor's office and the powers behind it. Once, another gambling hall had attempted to locate on the North Road within a couple hundred yards of Panther Hall, but the structure mysteriously burned to the ground before its doors even opened, and its owner mysteriously vanished, presumably to seek his fortune in a healthier clime.

Health. Now there was a subject worth concentrating on, Father Kenneth thought as he crossed the intersection of Main and Center, cutting across a scattering of windblown leaves. Overhead ephemeral clouds scudded through a sea of stars. He paused again and allowed his gaze to sweep across the burgeoning township, the hastily constructed businesses with their false fronts and the sprawl of houses on the north and south sides of town. He shifted his stance and looked past the church to the depot on the outskirts of Cross Timbers. A spur line of the Atchison, Topeka, and Santa Fe had reached town six months ago and continued on to the oil fields. The rails had speeded the town's transformation. The community was connected to the world now, and there was no turning back.

"Progress," Father Kenneth muttered. Well, it had brought a real doctor to Cross Timbers, and that was a good. The priest glanced back toward the clinic that had been built on the spot formerly occupied by the Bureau of Indian Affairs. Then, with a certain degree of displeasure, he noticed his competitor's place of worship. The Presbyterians had come to town and built a church on the north hill, among prospective parishioners. Holy King Triumphant Church was not only newer looking than its Catholic rival, but larger as well. Kenneth scrutinized the hilltop west of town. He pictured in his mind's eye the ceremonial lodge of the Southern Cheyenne. The place had seen little use of late. Spiders floated their webs across the doorways and windows. Field mice scampered with impunity across the blackened circle where the ceremonial fire had once blazed with life and summoned the tribal elders to bask in its sacred light; where once the Arrow Keeper sang his songs and dreamed his dreams and walked with the Mysterious One, Maheo. The slowly deteriorating medicine lodge seemed an apt metaphor for the condition of the Southern Cheyenne themselves, who with every passing day seemed to lose a little more of their identity and sense of worth. It was a downward slide, which Father Kenneth felt powerless to halt.

He lowered his head and continued up the street to St. Joachim's. The church was a humble structure, built along plain and simple lines, of yellow pine and native stone. A narrow vestibule opened onto a sanctuary capable of seating a hundred or so worshipers. The steeple jutting above the peaked roof contained a melodious brass bell that Father Kenneth had brought with him when he first came to live in the territory. The priest, with some help from the tribe, had not only constructed St. Joachim's but the humble, neatly kept cottage alongside that served as a rectory and sacristy. A covered walkway connected the cottage to the church, permitting the priest to don his vestments in his kitchen and then enter the house of worship through a rear door.

A whitewashed picket fence surrounded the church yard and provided a place for the parishioners to hitch their horses. In the spring the yard was often ablaze with Indian paint and firewheels and goldenrod as the earth in bloom offered its silent praise to the Lord. At least that was the image Father Kenneth perennially used in his homilies, every May.

"*Matse-omeese-he* is a long way off," the priest sighed, pulling up his collar and clutching his upper torso as the winter cold tried to worm its way past the woolen folds and through the button holes of his coat. A dark wind hounded him past St. Joachim's and followed him around to his cottage. It was then he heard the gelding neigh and, searching the darkness, spied the horse near the small corral and carriage shed the priest had built behind the rectory. At first he thought he had forgotten to latch the gate, permitting his own trusted mare to wander out, but on closer examination Father Kenneth discovered his own animal within the confines of the corral. This second horse belonged to Charlotte White Bear. The gelding stamped its foot and whinnied, recognizing the priest's voice. Father Kenneth looped the mount's rein over the top rail of the fence. A door crashed shut.

The priest jumped, startled, and glanced up as the door to the carriage house swung open to the unseen touch of the north wind and then closed again with a bang.

"I never left that open," the priest muttered beneath his breath. He entered the corral through the gate and hurried across the trampled earth to the carriage house, which was really nothing more than a small barn, large enough to house his carriage with an extra stall for the mare during inclement weather. He caught the door in midswing and held it open, standing framed in the doorway. Someone was in there, watching him; he could feel it. The hairs rose on the back of his neck.

"Who's there?" he called out. "Charlotte?"

The wind stirred the straw at his feet, a loose shingle rattled, an oil lamp creaked as it swung to and fro from a crossbeam overhead. The priest fumbled for a second, then found the lantern and lifted it down. One good shake and he heard oil slosh in its reservoir. He found a match in his coat pocket and, willing his hands not to tremble, lit the wick. Amber light immediately dispelled the gloom and revealed the identity and whereabouts of the intruder.

"Oh, my God . . ." Father Kenneth exclaimed, sucking in his breath. He nearly dropped the lamp.

Charlotte White Bear sat propped against the left rear wheel of the carriage. Her coat hung off her shoulders, and her blouse was ripped, revealing one breast, round and brown-tipped in the amber light. Legs splayed out before her, arms limp at her sides, the woman's head was tilted back at an extreme angle, and there were bruises on her throat and face. Her tongue looked swollen, and it parted her puffed, cracked lips. Charlotte's eyes, which had teased and invited but a few hours past, were wide and blank, staring through the priest and into the heart of a greater truth, into the mystery of her own brief life that someone had violently ended.

PART THREE

THE ARROW KEEPER'S SONG

CHAPTER THIRTY-TWO

April, 1899

THE LOCOMOTIVE, THIS GREAT BLACK IRON MONSTER, A HUFF-
ing beast with fire breath and its maw full of ruby coals
aglow like demons' eyes, loosed a piercing scream,
howling in the cold, still air, announcing the train's arrival to
the town of Cross Timbers. It slowed to a stop in front of a
single-room station, a boxlike twelve-by-twelve cabin fronted
by a wooden platform built on the edge of town. A telegraph
wire connected the station to a wood pole alongside the depot's platform. But there were no passenger cars today, only a
coal car and half-a-dozen flat cars carrying drill bits, timber,
spools of cable, and chain for the derricks under construction
to the north.

As the engineer and a flagman climbed out of the locomotive and prepared to take on water for the engine from a
nearby tower, a stowaway dislodged himself from among the
massive spools and dropped down to the rail bed.

Tom Sandcrane slung his saddlebags over his right shoulder and started down the wheel-rutted dirt road that led into
Cross Timbers. The presence of the depot was the first surprise Sandcrane encountered, but it was hardly the last. For
weeks he had rehearsed his return to Cross Timbers, pictur-
ing in his mind's eye how it would be, walking down Main

Street, the center of attention, Seth Sandcrane's errant son come home. He pictured the scores of familiar faces filing from their homes and businesses as he made his way through town, muttering to themselves, speculating as to the reason for his visit.

Just as Tom's imagination had concocted an elaborate drama, so reality came as quite a shock. Cross Timbers had grown. Businesses lined two streets that crisscrossed one another in the heart of town, Main and Center. Wagons and carriages, pedestrians and horsemen, crowded the streets and walkways in the midmorning light.

The sound of construction underscored the press of humanity as Tom Sandcrane stood alone, unrecognized, a stranger in what had once been his home. A pack of rosy-cheeked white children brushed past him, nearly knocking the solitary figure off his feet. They took no notice of the man but continued in their play, their lives full of the joyous abandonment of youth. South of the intersection and just off of Central, another half-dozen children laughed and dashed and darted in a never-ending game of tag on the playground of a bright new schoolhouse. A prim and pretty redhead leaned out of a window and gently instructed the children that school was dismissed for the day and their mothers were expecting them home. The teacher glanced up and spied the newcomer standing several yards away and instantly appraised him as another roughneck arrived in town and hoping for work out in the oil fields. Indeed, Tom looked the part. He was dressed in Levi's and a faded brown shirt with a fleece-lined denim jacket to blunt the bite of the north wind. His boots were worn and down-at-heel, his black hair hung to his shoulders, a battered military-issue hat shaded his features. A black glove covered his left hand, now clenched into a useless fist. The limited movement in his arm was a condition he had adapted to over the months since mustering out of the Indian Brigade.

Sandcrane touched the brim of his hat. The red-haired schoolmarm did not respond but tucked her head back inside the school, exercising caution in the place of cordiality, and slammed the window shut. Tom shrugged and swept the south side of town with a glance that only reinforced his own sense of displacement. Even the humble cabin he and Seth had shared was gone. The south side of town, like the north, had been taken over by the settlers who had moved in with the opening of the reservation.

An alley became a road that curved out of the town proper and led to a sheriff's office and jail, formerly the home of Willem Tangle Hair's tribal police force. The road extended another two hundred feet farther on before playing out among a collection of houses and gardens with nary a Cheyenne in sight.

Tom continued his trek up Main. The Lavender Hotel was new and Yaquereno's restaurant and other shops along Center Street, like the Paris Boutique, Winnow's Tonsorial, and Benedict Territorial Savings Bank, were foreign to him. It was a relief to find St. Joachim's at the corner of Main and Center. Sandcrane hoped Father Kenneth was still laboring "in the vineyard." Pressing on, Tom paused before the familiar entrance to Luthor White Bear's mercantile and noticed a black wreath on the door and a "Closed" sign in the window. He wondered who had died.

"Watch it, Injun!" a freight hauler shouted as his wagon rumbled past, churning a cloud of dust in its wake. Tom leaped to the wooden walkway to escape the congestion of the street. He studied the north side of town. Everything looked different—the houses, the businesses. A clinic appeared to have risen from the ashes of the BIA office. It probably offered the services of some hoary old white-haired bastard with a medicine bag in one hand and a whiskey bottle in the other. The sight of Allyn Benedict's old house brought back memories. Tom kept a tight rein on the heartache and disappointments of the past. He was not the same bitter man who had ridden from Cross Timbers on the eve of the land rush. Cuba had changed him, he thought, glancing down at his gloved left hand, a wry, wistful smile on his face.

He focused his attention on the Indian agent's house where he had finally learned the depths of Allyn Benedict's betrayal and the shallowness of Emmiline's affections. An entirely different family, from the looks of the children at play behind the picket fence, lived in the Benedicts' former home. Off to one side of the house a slender, boyish-figured woman in a gray dress and faded apron—obviously not the buxom, rotund Margaret Benedict—attempted to hang out her wash while keeping track of her boisterous young brood. A line of sheets and red flannel long johns, banners of domesticity, fluttered in the cold wind.

Where are my people? Tom thought. *Where are the Southern Cheyenne? This used to be their community.* He had expected some changes but nothing quite so drastic. Tom quickened his pace through town, making his way past men and women and children, all of whom were strangers to him. He wandered in and out of conversations, local gossip, ruminations about the weather, a heartfelt invitation to Bible school, chatter about the latest fashions at the boutique. Tom sensed a heightened tension in the air. More than once a heated discussion faded as he approached a cluster of townspeople whose weathered white features became veiled with suspicion once they recognized the coppery color of his skin.

An antebellum two-story house befitting some Southern plantation dominated the west end of town. It was an impressive structure built entirely of sandstone fronted by a broad, handsomely appointed porch with Mexican tile steps leading up to two stout mahogany doors. A pair of lions carved out of marble crouched upon pedestals at either corner of the porch in the shadow of two massive whitewashed columns that supported the roof overhead. Tom knew at a glance this could only be the home of Allyn Benedict. Stained-glass windows were set into the mahogany doors, adding yet another touch of stately grandeur to the house.

An office, located a discreet distance from the plantation house, boasted its own telegraph line, strung through town for the oilmen's convenience. "Benedict Exploration and Development" was painted in bold black letters on a sign above the office door. The building apparently housed a law office and a title company, whose signs were painted on the windows in gold leaf. A second, smaller building also constructed of sandstone proved to be the home of the town newspaper, the Cross Timbers *Clarion*, suspiciously in the shadows of Allyn's corporate headquarters.

Tom regarded the two-storied house with a mixture of awe and resentment; Benedict had done quite well for himself, profiteering off those whose interests should have superseded his own. The Indian Agent had arranged the sale of the oil-rich northern range for a fraction of its worth. *I should have stayed and fought him. Well, I'm back.*

A sudden tingling along his spine alerted the Cheyenne, and he lifted his gaze to an upstairs corner window over-looking the street, where he spied a silhouette concealed behind the sun's reflection on the pane of glass. Tom was being watched.

"Hello old *friend*," the Cheyenne muttered softly. "Just to make certain there were no doubts in your mind . . ." Tom removed his hat to reveal his features. The Cheyenne nodded toward the window, meeting the concealed man's stare for a few moments. He could have gone to the door and con-fronted the man and his family. Perhaps later, when he had accomplished the real purpose of his return to Cross Timbers.

Tom ended the game and, with his back to the Benedict house, headed across the street and through a wheel-rutted meadow to Coby Starving Elk's stable and blacksmith shop, nestled at the base of Council Hill.

This was familiar ground and Tom quickened his steps. However, the closer he came, the more he began to realize that something else had changed. The corral held a number of fine-looking horses, and the black smoke curling from the chimney above the smithy indicated the man inside was busy as usual. A flatbed freight wagon loaded with lumbered timber, tin sheeting, and a small wooden barrel marked "nales" blocked the entrance to the blacksmith shop. A pair of sturdy-looking geldings were harnessed to the wagon awaiting the driver.

Tom frowned as he read the sign above the stable doors, "Benedict Co." *Allyn Benedict casts a long shadow in this territory*, the Cheyenne thought, keeping to the sunlight, his worn boots leaving shallow tracks in the packed earth. Two men emerged from the darkened recesses of the stable as

Sandcrane approached. A miniature whirlwind cleared the ground of leaves before him, sweeping up the debris of the previous autumn in a spiraling dance, flashing yellow and brown in winter's rapturous embrace.

The chunky individual in his soot-covered apron, the sleeves of his faded blue workshirt rolled above his elbows, was Coby Starving Elk. And at his side, Father Kenneth, in Levi's, flannel shirt, and denim jacket, drew back as if he had just seen a ghost.

"Well, I'll be damned!" the priest blurted out, then blushed.

"I doubt that, Father." Tom grinned. "Unless Allyn Benedict has figured out a way to buy paradise and kick out the poor folks like yourself."

"Tom Sandcrane . . . I thought you were dead!" Coby exclaimed. He hesitated, debating whether or not the man in the yard was a ghost.

"Only a piece of me," Tom ruefully replied, raising his gloved hand. "Does that sign over your head mean I can't borrow a horse, Coby? I'd like to ride out to see my father."

Coby glanced over his shoulder and shrugged. "After the land rush white men showed up by the dozen. They wore fancy clothes and spoke with clever tongues and told of other oil lands. They promised to make us all rich, like Mr. Benedict. So we gave these men our government money to buy these leases in our name. But the white men were the only ones who got rich."

Coby leaned to one side and spit a stream of tobacco juice, then worked the chaw around in his mouth before continuing his story.

"They disappeared with our money and left us with nothing. So the Cheyenne went to work for Benedict. What else was there to do?" He turned to the priest. "That harness will hold now, Father. You don't need to worry." He shook Tom's hand as the younger man drew close. Coby, the blacksmith, was a plain and simple man with no talent for subterfuge and wholly unable to conceal his misgivings. He wanted to lend Tom a horse but was loath to risk Allyn Benedict's displeasure.

"Tom can ride with me," Father Kenneth happily interjected, relieved he could salvage the reluctant blacksmith's pride while assisting the son of Seth Sandcrane. "I'm helping your father build a barn. These supplies are his."

Tom nodded and climbed onto the wagon seat. He missed the look of concern Coby flashed at the priest. Indeed, Father Kenneth himself choose to ignore the blacksmith's unspoken warning. Benedict owned most of Cross Timbers but not the church, by heaven. The priest climbed up and joined Tom on the seat.

"What has happened here, Father?" Tom Sandcrane asked.

"Progress, my boy. Progress," the priest bitterly replied.

"And my people. Where are the Southern Cheyenne?"

Father Kenneth took the reins in hand. "I will show you."

Allyn Benedict patted smooth his graying temples and watched from his window as the priest left town with Tom Sandcrane at his side on the wagon seat. He heard footsteps clatter on the stairs, then become muffled by the carpet in the upstairs hall. Behind him Emmiline, her cheeks flushed, entered her father's bedroom without knocking, the satin-soft ringlets of her black hair flouncing with every step. The room's walls were covered with dark-blue fabric. The centerpiece was a massive four-poster canopy bed. A pastoral scene of buffalo grazing the short-stemmed grasses hung from one wall. A collection of Cheyenne war shields and lances adorned another.

"You will never guess who I saw," Emmiline said, her elegant features flustered from her recent discovery. "He rode right past the window downstairs. I was having morning tea with mother and looked up . . ." Her green eyes widened as she realized her father was now standing with his back to the window. "But you must have seen him. Tom Sandcrane has come home." She seemed to take a kind of special satisfaction in this announcement.

"Yes, I saw him," Benedict petulantly told his daughter, the fingers of his right hand drumming the walnut surface of his desk. The enthusiasm he detected in her voice troubled him greatly. "I thought he was dead," the former Indian agent wistfully added.

Last August, upon his own return to Cross Timbers, Willem Tangle Hair had entertained his companions with a colorful account of Tom Sandcrane's exploits in Cuba, ending his tale with Tom's disembarkation from Cuba. By the time the Indian Brigade had departed Caribbean shores and returned to Florida, Tom had already mustered out and disappeared for parts unknown. Tangle Hair's story had been repeated verbatim to Allyn Benedict.

"I wonder how long he intends to stay," Emmiline said, intrigued by this turn of events and enjoying her father's look of discomfort. She was not proud of the way she had toyed with Sandcrane's affections. One brief glimpse had dredged up old memories, nurtured dormant emotions she had never intended to feel, and had not forgotten.

Benedict removed a kerchief from the pocket of his tailored frock coat and dabbed moisture from his upper lip. Emmiline's attitude annoyed him. And he could still see Tom Sandcrane standing in that street, defiant, insolent, daring. Why had he come back? What was he after? "If he causes trouble, I can personally guarantee his visit will be cut short," Allyn added in a hushed, harsh tone.

From the president of Benedict Exploration and Development, this was more than an idle warning. Allyn Benedict meant business.

On the west side of Council Hill, a squalid collection of log cabins and mud-brick huts known locally as Rabbit Town sprawled along a dry creekbed and out onto the yellow plain. Perhaps thirty-five or forty Cheyenne families lived there, no more than a mile from Cross Timbers. Horses circled listlessly in split-rail corrals, their tails to the wind. Children oblivious to the wintry breezes and their own humble circumstances dashed among the cabins, running in packs like the scruffy mongrel pups nipping at their heels. Despite their jobs with Benedict's petroleum company, a pervasive air of poverty hung over the Cheyenne settlement, both of a monetary and spiritual nature. They seemed as dead as the plain of yellow grass upon which they dwelled.

Father Kenneth flicked the reins in his hands and drove the freight wagon through the middle of the settlement. The children recognized the wagon and the bespectacled priest and swarmed forward in a wave of squealing, laughing, excited voices. Hands outstretched to pat the priest's coat as he climbed down, reached beneath the seat, and produced a bag of peppermint candy, rationing out one to a child until each had received a treat. The delighted urchins, almost two dozen of them, scampered off.

Faces appeared in doorways, and shuttered windows momentarily cracked open as the inhabitants of Rabbit Town, the wives and mothers whose husbands were roughnecks in the oil fields, checked on their children.

Several dark-skinned women in shawls and woolen dresses emerged from their houses and came forward to greet the priest, exchanging, for the most part, lifeless pleasantries, all the while casting furtive glances in Tom's direction. By nightfall, Tom had no doubt, the news of his presence in the territory would have spread throughout most of the tribe. He sensed no animosity among the people, many of whom he recognized—nor any sense of welcome, not that he expected any.

Though his presence was the subject of some interest, not a word was addressed to him. Before long the chilling wind began to seep through the women's shawls and blankets, and one by one they drifted away from the two visitors. At last Father Kenneth bade the women farewell and climbed aboard the freight wagon, waved, then took up the reins.

"All of these families are pretty much tied to Allyn Benedict. Their husbands and fathers are roughnecks up north of here," the priest explained. "Those who didn't fall for the speculator's tricks and kept their land have farms here and about. Like your father's."

Tom studied the cluster of shacks and cabins and shook his head. So this was the future he had brought them to, hardscrabble farms and a bleak collection of cabins on the fringe of what had once been their own home. The malaise was palpable to him. He did not think they had ever seemed so defeated. "I'm surprised the women didn't try to stone me. I supported Allyn Benedict right down the line."

"When Willem came home to us, he gave a vivid account of finding you in Cuba and of your heroic deeds, that you rescued a Cuban leader from the clutches of the Spaniards and killed a Spanish general in hand-to-hand combat. It made your people proud." The priest sighed. "In this world you will find a hero can be forgiven much."

Heroic deeds? Images of the fire-gutted village of Rosarita and the freshly dug graves of the companions and friends he had left behind seeped into his mind like droplets of blood oozing through the crust of a reopened wound.

"Tom, are you all right?"

Sandcrane nodded, closed his eyes, and rubbed his forehead a moment, hearing the distant, muffled sound of gunfire that accompanied those images dissolve into the cadence of tribal drums, another auditory hallucination that plagued him with unceasing regularity.

"I shall . . . have to . . . thank Willem for preparing the way for my homecoming," Tom haltingly replied. "Where can I find him?"

"*Navaahe-nahtove?*" said the priest. "Who knows?"

"What do you mean?"

"He is in hiding." Father Kenneth stared down at his work-roughened hands that were more befitting a carpenter than priest.

The words were painful to speak. These were dark days for the Southern Cheyenne, and more especially for Tom Sandcrane's closest friend. The priest kept his gaze riveted on his scarred knuckles. "Willem Tangle Hair is wanted for the murder of Charlotte White Bear."

CHAPTER THIRTY-THREE

SETH SANDCRANE MADE A LUNGE FOR THE BLUE HEELER, BUT the brindle canine proved too quick for the Cheyenne and darted through the man's outstretched arms. Seth landed on his hands and knees in the dirt. General Sheridan halted just out of reach, spun around, and, with tail wagging, growled around the hammer gripped in his powerful jaws.

"I've eaten dog before, and so help me I will again if you don't bring me that damn hammer right now," Seth bellowed, plucking thorns from the palms of his hands. The dog remained defiant, eager for the game to continue. "I'll put a bullet in you and carve you for cutlets, you ungrateful bastard. Now, give me that hammer!"

General Sheridan scampered off through the skeletal beginnings of what would eventually be a barn. There were a couple of cross braces Seth wanted to nail into place before the priest arrived. It was a matter of pride. Seth Sandcrane, hoping to prove he was every bit the carpenter the priest claimed to be, crawled to his feet and dusted himself off, pausing to survey his surroundings.

He had built his cabin about a hundred feet from the banks of Coyote Creek in a small clearing flanked by live oaks and cedar. Willows and cottonwoods clung to the bank. Beyond the treeline a meandering string of meadows offered decent grazing for the dozen horses and hundred head of cattle he had purchased with the monetary allotment from the government. Prior to the land rush more than a year ago, a solitary sojourn by night—while avoiding federal patrols assigned to turn back "sooners"—had resulted in Seth's laying claim to the precise acreage his son had prized so highly.

The newly completed ranch house was a good deal larger than the cabin he had shared with Tom back in Cross Timbers, but it was nothing ostentatious, merely a comfortable, sturdy structure with a long, high ceiling in the front room, a kitchen off to the side, bedrooms at the rear, and a double outhouse a respectful distance from the back door. A low-roofed porch ran along the front of the house, where Seth preferred to sit and smoke his pipe and visit with the occasional friend who happened by.

His first barn had burned to the ground under mysterious circumstances. Seth suspected Curtis Tall Bull's hand in the calamity but lacked any proof. It was common knowledge Jerel's younger brother rode the wild side, nor was it any secret Curtis still harbored a resentment for the way Seth had humiliated him at the dogfighting pit more than a year ago. That General Sheridan had survived his wounds and followed Seth everywhere only served to aggravate the situation.

If Curtis was just plain mean for mean's sake, Jerel Tall Bull proved to be a driven man—ruthless, unwavering in his ambition. The few times Seth had crossed the Dog Soldier's path, Sandcrane had sensed an aura of danger surrounding Jerel, a darkness of the spirit more chilling than anything winter had to offer. It was as if Tall Bull's earlier dealings with the tribe and Allyn Benedict were only a prelude to something far more sinister.

Seth was sweating despite the biting cold. He slipped off his woolen work shirt, leaving only his flannel long johns to cover his muscular upper torso. He glanced down with pride, appreciating the fact he had worked off his paunch. His callused hands were steadier now, though there were moments when he thought he might have to hog-tie himself to a corral post to keep from taking a quick pull off a whiskey jug.

Each day was as hard as the one before, but he managed. More painful than his own unending struggle with alcoholism was the innate sense of loss he felt, watching his people's dissolution in the face of progress. He felt powerless to halt the gradual disintegration of the Southern Cheyenne. A kind of malaise held his people in an ever-tightening grip.

Luthor White Bear should have come forward, to call for a renewal and to rally the Cheyenne with the power of the Mahuts, the Sacred Arrows. But Luthor had not been forthcoming; indeed, his silence made the current situation all the more intolerable. Seth often wondered if the merchant was waiting for the Maiyun to whisper answers and was sick at heart with the certainty that when the Old Ones spoke, Luthor would not be able to hear them. Because no matter what had happened in the Council House more than a year and a half ago, despite the judgment of the elders, Luthor was not the Arrow Keeper. It was as simple as that. Men may have selected Luthor White Bear (poor bastard, grieving over the death of his murdered daughter), but the Sacred Arrows had chosen another, and the Maiyun would never let him go.

Seth Sandcrane sighed and surveyed his handiwork: house, chicken coop, smokehouse, corral, charred ground from which a new barn was rising phoenixlike, and a rectangular patch of ground plowed over, topsoil turned under, broken and waiting for spring.

Seth Sandcrane, the warrior, had become a farmer, a peacemaker, and in its own way, this was good. And it was good not to rage anymore, to war within himself. He had made many mistakes—too many—but like his shadow, they were behind him now. He thought of Kanee-estse, Red Cherries, and felt a tinge of remorse. And yet perhaps this too he would set right. Once she had called him brittle, back when he had been looking at the world from the bottom of a bottle. She had been right to say it. He intended to tell her that someday, maybe even bring her out to Coyote Creek.

A sandcrane, tall and gray with a wingspan as wide as a man was tall, rose from the creekbank, red plumage crowning its graceful head as the bird pummeled the air with its powerful wings. A grass snake wriggled in its long, pointed beak, helpless to avoid its fate. The bird glided above the farm and suddenly began to circle Seth where he stood. Seth watched the crane as it continued to circle him, and he heard the words whispered in his soul, with startling clarity.

The hairs rose on the back of his neck, his chest felt tight, and he walked out into the yard and faced east, positioning himself so that he could study the road to Cross Timbers through a break in the trees. The squirrels in the branches of the oaks fell silent; even the insects seemed to quit their flight, and the nearby creek, he swore, had ceased its gurgling song. The wagon in the distance announced itself with a tell-tale plume of dust rising in its wake. And as the shadow of the crane passed over him, the name rang in his heart and forced itself upon his lips.

"Tom?"

Yes, said the crane, *it is your son.*

"Ha-hey! Tsehee-haheto. The one who is my son!" shouted Seth in the language of his people. "Ene-ame-otse! He is coming!" His voice rang out in the stillness. Horses grazing in the meadow lifted their heads. The cattle began to bunch together at the sound of a familiar voice. Seth trotted back to the house, dashed inside, and retrieved his Winchester carbine from the mantel, then hurried out into the yard and called out in a strong voice.

"Ha-hey!" He fired the carbine into the air, levered another shell and fired again, and continued to do so as the wagon approached. *Crack-crack-crack* went the rifle in the cold air. The echoes had just about faded when Father Kenneth steered the team of horses into the yard and pulled up near the barn. Tom Sandcrane climbed down from the wagon and stood in front of his father. The changes in both men were obvious. Seth was older by more than a year, a bit grayer, but his eyes were clear now and his hands were steady and he had the lean, wiry look of his youth. Tom was scarred in body and soul, a fugitive whose eyes wore a wary, haunted cast, and Seth was reminded for a moment of Jerel Tall Bull. Tom had experienced some peculiar horror in the recent past, and the tendrils of that dark moment still clung to him. Seth noticed the black glove, his son's left arm awkwardly raised with the saddlebags draped over his wrist. Tom knelt as General Sheridan came loping up, barking with suspicion at first, then recognizing the intruder. The dog's tail began to wag and he dutifully approached, receiving a scratch behind his ears for his trouble. Tom straightened and faced Seth yet again.

"My father . . . I am here."

Without hesitation Seth Sandcrane ignored Tom's outstretched hand, stepped forward, and embraced his son. The older Cheyenne glanced up at the priest seated on the freight wagon. Father Kenneth winked and looked almighty proud of himself, having brought the "prodigal son" home.

They worked until sunset. When the sun sank below the line of trees, the three men left the barn and returned to the ranch house where Father Kenneth panfried a skilletful of tough chunks of beef and flavored them with onions, tossing in a couple of crushed chili peppers and several slices of potato. The hungry men sat around a hand-hewn table in the kitchen and finished off the food in short order, then washed down the meal with cups of strong black coffee. Throughout dinner Seth and the priest regaled Tom with all that had happened during his absence.

Members of the tribe, led by Father Kenneth, had taken Allyn Benedict to task for the sale of the oil lands on the north section of the reservation; however, the Indian agent explained that the government was forced to sell part of the acreage to make the monetary payments to the tribe. And after all, two thirds of the reservation was still open for settlement—none of which consisted of oil-bearing land.

Attempts were made to wildcat oil wells, but these individual efforts on the part of the Cheyenne had not panned out. The priest had petitioned Congress to open an inquiry, suggesting a conflict of interest on Allyn Benedict's part, but as of yet had received no reply. Father Kenneth was certain that if he pressed his case, some lawmaker would eventually see the impropriety in the Indian agent's dealings.

Of course, Allyn denied he had anything to do with the oil companies until after the land rush and the termination of the reservation. Tom knew different, but the proof had perished in the fire that had gutted the BIA office a year and a half ago.

Tom followed his father and the priest into the living room, a simple, spacious room boasting ladder-back rocking chairs and two couches Seth had built himself, covered with rawhide, and cushioned with bearskins and wolf pelts. The walls of the cabin were for the most part bare, although a war shield and feathered lance hung from one wall. A pair of buffalo hides covered the wooden floor. The log walls were thick and well chinked with clay and blocked the winter winds. A pair of Winchesters and a double-barreled shotgun, a Greener, hung from a rack to the left of the door. A buckskin shirt Seth was making for himself was stretched upon a willow rack in the corner. He was even doing the intricate beadwork across the chest, although Seth had never allowed anyone to see him at such woman's work.

A fire blazed in the fireplace, which Seth had built of natural stone with the help of the Capuchin. The chimney had an excellent draw, and very little smoke found its way into the living room. Tom sipped his coffee and studied the dancing flames.

"Allyn's family still lives here?" Tom at last said, fishing for news concerning the family to which he had once felt so close.

"Emmiline and her mother, yes," Father Kenneth replied. Clay's the sherriff." Tom looked up in amazement and dismay. "I know what you're thinking," the priest chuckled. "But he's actually done a credible job. Maybe it's being out from under his father's roof."

"And between the sheets of Miss Olivia Flannery, the schoolmarm," Seth added with a lascivious grin on his face that the priest made a point of ignoring.

"I don't have much use for Clay Benedict," Tom replied.

"People change," the priest said. "You two are evidence of that. Seth quit drinking the day you left, Tom. And you sure aren't the same man who rode away from here."

"That's the truth," Tom ruefully observed, rubbing his gloved hand. It was as useless as a leaden weight attached to his wrist.

"Where'd you go, boy? Willem said you returned from Cuba before him. What happened to you?" Seth asked.

"I jumped a train, rode the rails north to the white man's cities. Baltimore, Washington, New York. And this time I did not see them through the eyes of Allyn Benedict. This time I saw them with my own eyes. And I found there was nothing for me there. I thought the white man's vision spoke to me once and called me by name. But it was the agent filling my head with images that had no more substance than smoke." Tom glanced in the priest's direction. "There is much we can learn from your people, Father Kenneth. But I think there is also much your people could learn from us." He fixed his gaze on the dancing flames, writhing and leaping like spirits imprisoned in the hearth.

"And so you have returned," Seth said. "To stay?"

Tom did not reply. He crossed to the coffeepot and helped himself to a second cup of the strong black brew, then ambled over to the window and looked out at the night. He could not find the words for the turmoil in his heart, and yet he was confident this homecoming had been the right decision.

Seth accepted his son's silence and did not press the issue. He understood such moments and knew all questions were answered in time. "Lots of changes since you've been gone. They take some getting used to," he said from his ladder-back rocking chair near the fireplace. The flames warmed his backside and soothed his aching muscles. He didn't like to admit it, but he was getting old. Then again, it was a sight easier to build a tepee than a barn.

"Father Kenneth told me about Willem. I don't believe he would have ever hurt Charlotte," Tom said, studying the night shadows where the moon's frozen glare illuminated the front yard, delineating the line of trees bordering the creek, turning the tree limbs the color of bone, stark and spindly against the starry sky. He had arrived at a troubled time. Maybe that had been the plan all along.

"There's some think otherwise. Luthor White Bear's family, for a start," Seth replied. "They've already tried him in their hearts, found him guilty and sentenced him to hang. White folks are calling him a woman killer. Women are afraid to venture outside alone. Yessir, if Clay brings Willem in, I doubt anyone will wait for the judge."

Father Kenneth eased himself out of the chair and walked over to stand alongside Tom. "Still, some things have changed for the better, thanks to another friend of yours." His blond eyebrows rose as they always did when the priest thought there was more to a situation than what he could immediately discern. "She came in on the train with Willem back in September. What a godsend she has been!"

Tom stared at the priest, a confused expression on his face.

"I was so surprised to see you in town, it clean slipped my mind," the priest explained. "You passed her clinic. Dr. Joanna Cooper. You do know her? . . . Tom?"

The sheriff's office was a solid structure built of fieldstone and roofed with thick sheets of tin that had worn to a dusty brown. The outer office was furnished with a filing cabinet, a cot in one corner, a wallful of wanted posters, a gun rack and several belts of ammunition, a pair of kerosene lamps, another suspended from a wall mount. A desk dominated the rear wall and was set off to the side to allow passage to the jail cells at the rear of the building. Four cells, two to either side, faced one another across a dimly lit passageway that led to a bolted rear door.

Clay Benedict, sitting at his desk, had been forced to stand when his father had sat on the corner and crowded him out. From this perch Allyn Benedict had dismissed his son's two deputies and sent them home to their wives.

Allyn could have taken a seat in any of the three empty chairs, but he chose the corner of the desk. The founder and president of Benedict Exploration and Development was too proud and too powerful to sit dutifully before his own offspring like some errant child at his parent's knee, awaiting punishment.

Clay walked over to the Franklin stove that heated the office and lifted a blue enameled tin coffeepot off the iron plate, cracked the top, peered inside, and sniffed the soggy grounds while silently debating whether he ought to chance the remains of Abram Fielder's coffee. The gruff old deputy liked to brag that his coffee could float a horseshoe, and Clay was inclined to believe him. He added a dipper of springwater and sloshed the contents around.

Benje Lassiter, Clay's other deputy, often complained that frequent visits to the coffeepot had left him with a permanently soured stomach. Lassiter was tough but rail thin. Eggs, griddle cakes, and canned peaches made up the bulk of his diet. Clay had begun to suspect the man had a more serious problem than a "soured stomach" and suggested the deputy pay a call on the town's new doctor, but Lassiter said he couldn't see how some "pretend physician in skirts" could possibly be of help. The idea of a woman poking around at some stranger's innards left a pious soul like Benje Lassiter positively appalled.

On the other hand, a lecherous old bastard like Abram Fielder had warmed to the idea; after all, Doctor Cooper was a real looker. On more than one occasion Fielder had faked an infirmity just for an excuse to pay a call on the lady from New Orleans.

Tonight, however, the two men had been summarily dispatched without explanation. Clay regretted the abrupt way his father had sent the deputies from the office. Once again Allyn Benedict had usurped his son's authority. Sure, it was a matter of pride. Clay Benedict had grown accustomed to being treated and spoken to with a certain amount of deference for his office as upholder of the law. In this case the badge had indeed begun to make the man.

The trouble was that Allyn liked to snap his fingers and watch his underlings jump; he expected no less from his son. Clay could not help but resent his father's attitude. Recently their relationship had become even more strained—indeed, the tension in the room was thick enough to slice.

"You know, Father, it doesn't look right for you to go ordering off my deputies or treating me like just another of your hirelings," Clay said.

"I simply wanted to expedite matters so we could talk in private," Allyn replied. "You needn't raise a snit. I saw the light in the window while on my way back from the bank. Any luck?"

"Whoever saw Willem down south of here lied. Or they're blind. We didn't even come across a set of tracks."

"Well, there may be more trouble in the horizon, and I thought you ought to know," Allyn said.

"You mean Tom Sandcrane? I heard about him at dinner. Emmiline told me, since you weren't around to fill in the details."

Allyn shifted uncomfortably. "I heard your mother tell Consuela to serve up those goddamn stewed tomatoes again. They remind me of something a cat coughed up after being stepped on by a horse." He shuddered. "I had coffee and pie at Yaquereno's. But I didn't come here to discuss my habits at home."

"Maybe we should," Clay remarked, "the way you and mother have been acting. Just how much does she know?"

"Nothing!" Allyn snapped. "What passes between your mother and me does not concern you. Dammit, Clay, I'm here to talk about Tom Sandcrane. We don't need him around, stirring up the coals just when the fire's nearly out."

"I don't see what I can do about it."

"Run him out of the territory."

"He hasn't broken any laws. I have no reason to . . ."

"You are my son. That ought to be reason enough. Set the blasted law aside and listen to your father."

"I have done that already."

"Then it ought to be easier the second time," Allyn replied. He sighed and stood, thrust his hands into his coat pockets, searching in silence for an acceptable solution. The change in Clay was beginning to bother him. He walked to the window and peered out at the town just in time to see a carriage roll up and halt in front of the sheriff's office. He recognized the two women behind the harnessed gelding. "Look, son, you might be right. Perhaps Tom Sandcrane ought to stay. His presence might just draw Willem Tangle Hair out into the open. After all, they were friends. And when Willem makes his move, you can be there to cut him down."

Clay started to speak, but the front door opened, allowing

a briskly cold gust of wind to enter the office. The warmth generated by the Franklin stove seemed to be sucked out into the darkness as Olivia Flannery, the red-haired schoolmarm, swept through the doorway with Emmiline only a step behind. Both women were laughing at some private amusement that Clay suspected was at his expense. The wanted posters on the wall rustled as if stirred by some invisible hand.

The women seemed eminently pleased with themselves, as if they had intruded for the sole purpose of interrupting Allyn's meeting with his son.

"We were on our way back from Holy King Triumphant," Olivia said, "when we saw the light in the window and Clay's horse in the corral."

"What were Reverend Peltier and Mildred up to?" Clay asked, shifting uncomfortably as the schoolteacher stood at his side and took his hand in hers.

"Once I told her you were back in town, Olivia lost interest in planning the spring social," Emmiline laughed, chiding her friend. Her gaiety seemed a trifle forced in the presence of her father.

"I must be leaving," Allyn said. "If you will excuse me . . ." He nodded to his daughter and tipped his hat to Olivia Flannery. Glancing over his shoulder, he paused before the door and said to his son, "Be thinking about what I said. And don't forget all we've built here. And how it used to be. No man has so much that he cannot still lose it all." He bowed— "Ladies"—and departed.

"Well," Emmiline sighed. "I don't feel much like going on to the Peltiers' alone. I'd better go on home. Mother's had a bit too much sherry. Maybe I can put her to bed before she and father have another row."

"At least she stands up to him," Clay muttered, thinking of his own poor performance in that regard.

Emmiline appeared not to notice his reply as she watched from the window and gave her father ample time to climb into his buggy and head off down the road toward the center of town.

"I suppose he wanted to talk about Tom," Emmiline said, probing for information. "And me."

"The topic came up," Clay lied. It was easier than telling
her the truth.

"What I do is my own business."

"Tom Sandcrane is trouble. You'd do well to stay clear of
him. But you didn't listen to me before, and I doubt you will
this time." Clay chanced a swallow of coffee and grimaced.
The damn stuff would take the rust off yard iron. He emptied
the contents of the cup back into the pot and took it off the
burner plate.

"Before was father's idea. He called the tune and we all
danced and the song made us rich . . . ," Emmiline said. "But
not happy." She noticed Olivia standing quietly alongside
Clay, their hands still entwined. Emmiline pulled her coat
tightly around her shoulders, smiled at the couple, and vanished through the door. A gust of wind tugged at the hem of
her dress and nipped her cheeks and nose, but Emmiline had
no quit in her. She reached the carriage, climbed aboard, and
soon had the gelding headed for home.

"Well, now," Olivia Flannery said at last. The schoolmarm
had been a silent observer of this family's dissolution for several months now, but for the life of her she could not fathom
the cause of such unrest. The teacher was smart enough to
keep her distance from so much pain and anger. Her role was
that of listener, and once in a while, in the peace of night in
the hours when she lay alongside Clay, sweaty from lovemak-
ing, warm and satiated in the feather bed they shared, she offered counsel and encouragement.

"Escort a lady home?"

"Be my pleasure. Of course, I smell a mite trail-worn."

"Nothing a hot bath won't cure. I'll scrub your back and
you can scrub mine." She leaned against him and kissed his
stubbled jaw. "I feel safer with you in town. All the women
do. That awful half-breed Tangle Hair is capable of anything.
None of us is safe while he's loose. He murdered his own
kind, no telling what he's thinking. Anybody could be next."
She draped her arm across his shoulder. Clay Benedict was
just about the handsomest man in these parts with his soft
brown hair and slender build, and his features that could

seem rugged one moment and boyish the next; the school-marm wasn't about to let him get away.

"If you're that worried, maybe I ought to stay till morning," Clay suggested, anxious to avoid discussing his family or Willem Tangle Hair. Both topics had begun to wear on him.

"And cause a scandal . . . Mildred Peltier and the school board would fire me in an instant. No, thank you."

"You are quite a woman, Miss Flannery," Clay said. He extinguished the lamp and guided her toward the front door. The wind moaned beneath the doorsill, winter pawed at the panel. It would be a cold ride to the schoolmarm's house, but well worth the effort. He grabbed his coat off a wall peg by the door and ran his hand over the woolen material until he came to the star pinned to the chest. He reattached it to his vest.

Allyn Benedict's money may have insured his son's election to office, but somewhere along the way, with Olivia Flannery's urging, Clay Benedict had stepped out from beneath his father's roof and discovered sunlight. He liked the feel of it. For the first time in his life, Clay Benedict cast his own shadow, and he was loath to give it up.

Curtis Tall Bull followed the path from Panther Hall that led through a grove of white oaks and cedar trees. Jerel had left an easy trail to follow, with explicit orders that no one was to disturb him. But Curtis thought the news of Tom Sandcrane's return outweighed any such admonition. Besides, what was Jerel up to that Curtis shouldn't know about it? They were family, after all, and family should have no secrets.

Curtis walked his horse along the winding trail that cut across gullies and draws, and eventually he saw the glow of a fire filtering through the trees and heard an unearthly wail that made the hairs stand on the back of his neck. Chanting! He reached into the pocket of his frock coat and felt for the Colt revolver he kept there. Then, somewhat reassured by the smooth walnut grip, Curtis dismounted and, leading his horse, tracked the chanting to its source. A chilling breeze toyed with the black string tie he wore loosely knotted at his throat. He tugged his flat-crowned hat tight against his skull to keep the wind from snatching it away. Brittle twigs cracked underfoot. He tripped over a tangle of vines and cursed the frozen darkness.

Who the hell was out there? The Tall Bulls didn't tolerate intruders on their land. A thousand acres surrounding Panther Hall were their private domain, and Curtis welcomed the opportunity to show his brother he could be counted on to stand up for their interests. Where was Jerel, anyway? He had been acting peculiar for the past few weeks, taking off by himself, secretive and abrupt, even hostile, to anyone who called attention to his behavior. Perhaps Jerel was just ahead, stalking the unknown singer through the underbrush. The noise of these tired customs was out of place here. The Tall Bulls were entrepreneurs, businessmen; they had no use for the old ways.

Curtis cleared the trees at last and froze in his tracks as he emerged onto a small clearing in the heart of a thicket near a steep-sided creek that frequently flooded in the spring. The trickle of water between the steep banks was called Little Sister Creek by the locals. Every hard rain transformed it into a torrent that churned its way south to empty into the Washita, redistributing sediment and tree limbs along a wildly undulating course several miles in length.

The clearing was ringed with felled timber around an inner circle of fieldstones, at the center of which a roaring fire sent flames leaping upward taller than a man, and embers spiraling into the night sky. Jerel Tall Bull stood with his back to his younger brother, arms outstretched in the glare of the fire. He had discarded his hat, coat, and shirt. Despite the cold, his close-cropped hair was plastered to his skull, shiny with sweat from keeping so close to the flames.

Curtis could scarcely believe his eyes. How could this be? Jerel had learned well the white man's way, even to the point of securing the very fortunes of many of the southern Cheyenne. So this display of primitive ritual was the last thing Curtis expected and, in that instant, realized he did not know his older brother at all.

Jerel seemed to sense the presence of another, for he spun

around as Curtis started to approach. Jerel's upper torso was streaked with blood, the cause of which was plainly evident. He held the bloody talon of a hawk in his right hand, a cloth-wrapped bundle Curtis had never seen before in his left. Jerel's eyes were wide and, to Curtis's thinking, crazed. The muscles along his chest and shoulders and throat stood out in stark relief.

"What are you doing?" Curtis asked, stopping dead in his tracks, so frightened was he by his discovery.

"Taking back the power," said Jerel Tall Bull. "Each night I have come here, waiting, listening. Tonight the old ones spoke. Voices from my blood, our blood. Why have you come here?" He moved to conceal something on the blankets in front of him, tossing a deerskin pelt over what lay there.

"Tom Sandcrane has come home," Curtis stammered, frightened by his brother's appearance.

Jerel's eyes widened. "*Savaa-he!* Then it must be. He has come to stand against me. But he is weak. And I have the power!" Then, without warning, Jerel raised his hands and loosed a savage cry that seemed to be wrung from his heavy-set frame by unseen hands. The wail rose in pitch and, behind him, fire-gutted logs exploded and crashed in upon themselves, shooting a shower of lurid orange embers into the air, embers that fanned outward, like the wings of some terrible bird of prey.

Curtis fell backward, landing hard on his rump, then frantically crawled to his feet and dashed headlong toward the trees. Limbs tore at his clothing, ripped his coat, slashed his cheeks. He ignored the pain and fought his way through the thicket until he reached his horse. All he wanted now was to be safe within the walls of Panther Hall, with a bottle of strong whiskey in his hand and a whore to ease the confusion and dread that gripped his heart. Jerel's younger brother vaulted into the saddle and galloped off down the trail, risking a broken neck in his haste to distance himself from what he had seen, and from the brother who was a mystery to him now.

CHAPTER THIRTY-FOUR

THE EARLY HOURS OF MORNING WERE THE BEST TIME FOR shadow walking. Old, familiar faces like passing landmarks materialized out of the mists of memory: Seth Sandcrane offering the Medicine Pipe to his son . . . the ride from Cross Timbers, leaving the past and his own dishonor behind. A chance meeting with Philo and Tully surfaced, along with the faces of other soldiers striding onto the sunwashed Cuban shore. There were battles, and killing, a brief remembrance of a dark and bloody night. Now he was standing before Enos Stump Horn, who lay propped against a wall, crimson stained and dying from his wounds as he held out his tomahawk to Tom. Life for life, blood for blood. The dream shifted, like the surface of a pond suddenly stirred by an unseen hand.

He lay by a campfire, wounded, battered. Joanna was at his side, whispering. "No, Mr. Thomas Sandcrane, I will not let you die. There has been enough dying." Why should she concern herself over the fate of a ghost? The image dissolved, becoming Antonio Celestial standing in the overgrown, abandoned garden behind his house, his hand on Tom's shoulder.

"*Words do not seem enough. What can I offer but my thanks and friendship, Senor Tom.*" *His gaze lowered to the gloved left hand.* "*You too have paid a price for our freedom.*"

"Not as much as the others," Tom said.

"And what of Joanna—will you not wait for her?"

"Better that I leave," he replied.

He had believed at the time it was for the best.

Move on. The dreamer moved on. The rails carried him to the white man's cities, where he stood before the factories and took in the stench and noise of the industries that *vehoe* worshiped; in his dream he wandered once again the white man's world, which he thought held such promise, and relived the longing, then the realization that something was missing at the core of all this progress. And there was something missing within him as well. Tom Sandcrane had known it since Cuba, since the moment he'd begun to reclaim his life from the specter of his own mortality.

As if summoned by this last remembrance, the fire-winged wraith-hawk, with talons of living lightning, tore asunder the fabric of Tom's memory, shattering his dreams. Diving past his flailing arms, it tore at his chest. While Tom tried to fight off the hellish creature, he heard laughter and, behind the spectral image of the horridly familiar hawk, recognized the man who looked on, grinning. It was Jerel Tall Bull.

Tom Sandcrane's eyes opened; he stared at the ceiling for a moment and listened to the reassuring sound of his own breath, which told him he was still alive. He rolled out of bed, pulled on his trousers, boots, and a poncho made from a trade blanket, then walked out of the bedroom. He opened his saddlebags and removed the Medicine Pipe his father had given him, taking also the tomahawk, its blade dark with dried blood.

He stole across the front room, where Father Kenneth, wrapped in a couple of patchwork quilts, slumbered peacefully on the couch, then eased out the door into the gray gloom of early dawn. General Sheridan stirred and lifted his head but made no move to accompany the man. Curled before a warm hearth was the only position for a dog to be in at this hour.

The cold pressed against him as Tom made his way across

the front yard. The house faced the north bank of the creek, whose singing waters seemed to welcome the intruder on this frosty morning. A sheen of white blanketed the ground and dusted the tips of the wild fronds, weeds, and buffalo grass. The corral fence had not escaped a coating of ice crystals, either. The brittle grass crackled underfoot as he continued east and, skirting the willows on the creekbank, entered the gloom of a thicket of post oaks. He followed a path frequented by deer and bobcat, a trail he had often walked when he had come alone to this place and dreamed of the life he would begin to build, here where the waters flowed sweet and pure and the grass grew lush in the meadows. He kept alert for deadwood and soon had an armful of broken and decaying limbs and branches.

The ground rose to form a knoll, and by the time the trail played out, the trees had cleared and he stood on the crest of a small hill overlooking the land of the Cross Timbers, a place where the Southern Cheyenne had made their last stand against the unstoppable tide of progress. On this knoll he dug a small pit using a flat, jagged piece of stone for a crude spade. He arranged the limbs and branches, touched a match to kindling, and soon had a comforting blaze to combat the chill. That was easy; it was much more difficult to ward off the terrible vestiges of the dream. Some visions and dreams he experienced seemed to be leading him back to Oklahoma and the Southern Cheyenne. Some had been of Cuba and what had befallen him there. Granted, the images had been painful at times, especially the time when he had lain wounded and had warred with the spirit of the hawk. At the time, he'd thought his battles were over, and yet the hawk lingered on the periphery of his thoughts.

Why? And what did any of this have to do with Jerel Tall Bull? The master of Panther Hall meant nothing to Tom. And yet the Maiyun were warning Tom by linking the man to the vision of the hawk. "Well, the Old Ones have lured me here, and they will no doubt reveal the reasons for all that has happened," Tom muttered, warming the palm of his right hand. The wind tugged at his tangled black hair. But he couldn't lose the nagging, unsettling notion that all he had experienced—from betrayal and loss, to war and wounding and the journey of his tormented soul—was preparing him for something completely unforeseen, that which would take all his courage and all his strength to face. Zuloaga had not been an ending, after all, but possibly just a beginning.

A tall order for half a man, he ruefully observed with a glance at his gloved left fist. He tossed a fistful of dried sage into the flames, then took the Medicine Pipe and the tomahawk, crossed their shafts, and gripped them in his right hand. He stood and, passing the pipe and the tomahawk through the smoke of the fire, he sang:

> "Black lightning is in my body,
> Black water is here.
> White smoke carries my words.
> I carry the Pipe,
> Its Mystery is gray.
> I carry the tomahawk,
> Its Mystery is red.

Tom faltered. So much time had passed. The words came slowly. He hesitated, like a man stumbling in the dark over uneven ground. But he did not turn back.

> "My steps upon the Great Circle.
> To the Beautiful Place I walk,
> In the Company of Spirits.
> My steps upon the Path
> Have brought me here."

He repeated the chant, the words gradually becoming familiar until they flowed melodiously off his tongue. Time passed. The minutes were lost on him. There was only the song and the bleak dawn. Winter breathed upon him. But the fire held winter's worst at bay, and as his voice rang out, cranes rose from the wooded creekbank and took to flight.

While he sang, the world seemed to hesitate; the birds hung in midair, transfixed; the wind ceased; the barren branches grew suddenly still; the flames nearby might have been etched in stone. And then the moment passed, and the birds winged upward into the sky. The flames devoured another log. The world spun on. The dark clouds parted, and a shaft of sunlight like a hurled lance split the gloom and embedded itself in the meadow below. Gradually the sunlight spread and washed over the knoll, and the man continued to sing with his hand upraised, the crossed pipe and the tomahawk bathed in light.

And the world would not end that day.

Tom was aware of another presence behind him, and for a moment he feared to turn, half expecting to be confronted by one of Those Who Had Gone Before. Seth Sandcrane stood a few yards back, clad in his Levi's, red flannel shirt, hat, and boots, a blanket draped across his shoulder. His eyes were wide and filled with a mixture of wonder and astonishment.

"*Haa-hey!* Now I know," Seth exclaimed, shivering. His lips were drawn tight in a grimace from the cold, his breath clouded the air. "You have come for the Mahuts. You have returned for the Sacred Arrows!"

Tom did not need to answer. After all, truth was truth.

CHAPTER THIRTY-FIVE

TOM DROVE THE HAMMER DOWN WITH AN OVERHANDED BLOW and grazed the nail, shooting it off across the roof, where the projectile struck Seth a glancing blow to the cheek, raising a welt just below his eye.

"*Saa-vaa!* For one who talks with the Spirits, you can't hammer worth a damn," Seth said with a grin. "By the time you get the barn roofed, the horses will be nothing but bones in the dust."

"Well, why don't you come over and hold the nail for me, you old bastard?" Tom growled. He shoved another nail into the cedar shingle and managed to get it to stick upright, then picked up the hammer and tried again.

"Ha! Hold the nail? I want to keep both my hands," Seth chuckled.

Tom gave him a sharp look, then laughed despite himself. He had spent most of the morning perched on the roof hammering shingles into place and trying to figure out some errand that would take him to town. Throughout the morning he struggled to come up with a plan by which he could ride into Cross Timbers without arousing the suspicions of the priest or his own overly curious father. Joanna's presence in Oklahoma could hardly be called coincidental. But why was she there? The thought of seeing her filled him with a mixture of excitement and dread. After all, he had left Cuba without even saying good-bye. How could he explain such behavior? No matter—she had been on his mind more than once since returning to the States. It would be good to see her again, even if she spit in his face. The problem, of course, was coming up with an excuse to leave. Seth and the priest were bound to suspect the real reason for his departure.

Despite the cold, Tom's flannel shirt was patched with sweat. He had worked hard that morning, traversing the ladder single-handed, refusing to work below, where it was safe. He continued to push himself, as if striving to prove that his gloved left fist was nothing more than an inconvenience.

From the vantage point of the rafters he was able to appraise anew all that Seth had done in his absence. That his father was sober was astonishing enough, but that he had rescued the land along Coyote Creek, built upon the site, and done all that Tom had once planned for them both left the younger man with a feeling of renewed respect for his father.

A column of dust rising in the cold air, and General Sheridan's angry barking, signaled the arrival of visitors. Tom shaded his eyes and saw what appeared to be half-a-dozen men, their backs to the sun, riding out of the east from the direction of town. Seth grumbled a threat—anyone trying mischief with this barn was going to pay a hard price—and scrambled down the ladder. Tom followed his father over to the ladder and started to descend. Father Kenneth, who had been working below, put his weight on the bottom rung to keep the ladder from sliding. By the time Tom reached the ground, Seth was standing in the wagon bed, a Winchester cradled in the crook of his arm. General Sheridan trotted off to the side and peered through the wagon spokes; the dog's dark hackles rose, and a guttural snarl sounded deep in his throat.

"Now, Seth, it would be a fool troublemaker who comes to pay a call by daylight," said Father Kenneth, his fair features flushed, his cheeks cherry-red from exertion. He wanted to finish cutting and hanging the shutters over the two windows in the barn's lower level and didn't relish being caught in the middle of gunplay. Seth had been pretty edgy since the loss of his first barn, and rightly so. But Father Kenneth also figured his role there was as peacemaker.

"If they mean trouble, they'll find it today. This barn will stand," Seth said.

"Father Kenneth's right. Night riders have no use for daylight," Tom cautioned, placing himself between Seth and the approaching horsemen.

"Just the same, I'm ready. Now, get out of the way, son." Tom merely ignored the older man's request.

The barn builders did not have long to wait for the arrival of the visitors from Cross Timbers. Clay Benedict, riding a zebra dun, led seven hard-looking men into the yard of the Coyote Creek ranch. The posse for the most part was made up of townspeople, white men whom Tom failed to recognize. But two of the riders were Cheyenne—Pete Elk Head and John Iron Hail and they were another matter entirely. Elk Head and Iron Hail wore Levi's and leather chaps, dark flannel shirts, and plaid woolen coats and were armed with revolvers and rifles. The two Cheyenne walked their mounts up to Tom, who held his ground, even though he came near to being trampled. Pete Elk Head in particular seemed to take a kind of evil delight in crowding the one-armed man. John Iron Hail was not so reassured. Another shadow fell across Tom, and he looked up at the sheriff of Cross Timbers.

Clay Benedict touched the brim of his hat. "Good morning, hero. So you decided to pay your old home a visit, after all. Well and good. Lots of changes, though."

"Hello, Clay. Nice of you and your folks to take the time to give me a proper welcome."

"We rode out here for more than you, Sandcrane," Pete Elk Head snapped. Clay silenced the man with a frown, then addressed the man in the wagon.

"Seth . . . we're looking for Willem Tangle Hair. What with Tom being home, I thought it would be a good idea to check on you."

"I haven't seen him," Seth replied in a voice as cool as the north breeze.

"Maybe we better see for ourselves. Tom and Willem always sided with one another. Could be you're hiding him in the house," said Pete Elk Head as he started his horse past Tom, whose hand darted out and caught the man's reins.

"You hold up, Pete. I'm the sheriff here, and you'll follow my orders or clear the hell out," Clay snapped. "Now, get on back with Lassiter and the rest of the boys."

Elk Head scowled. It was obvious he had been anxious to provoke a confrontation with Tom Sandcrane. But Clay's words carried more weight than his own hunger for trouble. A year and a half was a long time to hold a grudge. Tom wondered if there was something more than wounded pride behind Pete Elk Head's open animosity.

"C'mon, Pete," John Iron Hail spoke up from alongside his companion. "Let's go."

"Nice to see you, young John. Appears you've grown some. Do the Tall Bulls still run you?" Tom asked, peering up at the young Cheyenne.

"They treat me good. I do all right. At least you don't see me slopping hogs, chasing chickens, and climbing around on some barn roof like a damn monkey." And with that reply John Iron Hail swung his mount about and walked the animal back to rejoin Benje Lassiter and the other members of the posse, all of whom appeared edgy and eyed Seth with suspicion.

"We ain't gonna check the old Injun's house?" Lassiter called out.

"I've never known Seth Sandcrane to lie. Not even when he was drinking," Clay remarked, much to Tom's surprise.

"Luthor's people are drifting into Cross Timbers," Pete said. "They aim to make certain your friend Willem pays for killing that girl." The Cheyenne pulled free of Tom's grasp and returned to the center of the yard.

Saddle leather creaked as Clay dismounted and stood in front of Tom Sandcrane. He fished in his pocket for makings and rolled himself a cigarette, then offered the tobacco to Tom, who declined.

"Walk with me a minute, Tom," Clay said, and led his horse away from the ranch house and out of earshot of the others. Tom fell in step alongside the son of Allyn Benedict, wary, suspicious of the younger man's motives. There had never been any love lost between them.

"What brings you back, Tom?"

"Not your sister, Clay, if that's your concern."

Clay frowned and pursed his lips, then nodded and blew a cloud of tobacco smoke. "Glad to hear it. Emmiline's special to me. I never cottoned to the way things were . . . before you left. I got nothing personal against you."

"You just didn't want her running with a buck from the reservation. Of course, your father had other ideas. He approved. Hell, he even encouraged. How far did he want her to go to keep me from finding out about his land deal with the oil company? Just what was she supposed to do? Would he have whored his daughter to keep me from discovering what he was up to?"

Clay stiffened and turned on the Cheyenne, his eyes mere slits beneath the brim of his hat. "You push hard, Tom Sandcrane. Don't expect me to keep backing away. Whatever my father did is better left in the past. Leave it lie."

Benedict's son had always appeared too handsome, almost foppish, until now. Time had trimmed the edges and hardened the exterior with age and experience. Perhaps it was true—he had stepped out of his father's shadow and been burned by the sun. It was a part of growing up and gaining wisdom.

Tom studied the sheriff for a long moment. Clay shifted uncomfortably beneath the Cheyenne's unwavering scrutiny.

"What the hell are you looking at?"

"I don't know," Tom said. "You've changed."

"We all have."

Tom nodded in agreement. He sensed a distinct feeling of torment and indecision in Benedict. These were emotions Sandcrane had learned only too well over the past months. Odd—the last thing he had ever expected was to feel a kind of kinship with Clay Benedict.

"If Willem comes around, you let me know," Clay said.

"So you can hang him?"

"Look. Most boom towns aren't fit places to live. But not Cross Timbers. I've kept the peace in this county and made it safe. Until this killing. Now I intend for Willem to receive a fair trial, which is more than he'll get from Luthor White Bear's clan. Pete spoke the truth. They are out for blood."

"I cannot believe Willem would have killed the girl. He loved Charlotte."

"He wouldn't be the first man to destroy what he loves," Clay replied, staring off at the creek, his tone distant and tinged with bitterness. He finished his cigarette, tossed the glowing white stub on the ground, and crushed it, leaving a sooty black smear underfoot. Sunlight glinted off the badge pinned to his coat. "Just remember I represent the law here."

"Which law? Allyn Benedict's? Did your father send you out here to speak for him and warn me off?"

The lawman scowled, his temper flaring. Tom's words were cutting close to home, made even more painful because they were the same questions Clay had been asking himself for the past week.

"I think you've returned and brought trouble, Tom Sandcrane," Clay gruffly answered.

"No," Tom said, and removed his hat, the cold breeze tugging at his shoulder-length hair, shadows and sunlight playing across his stern coppery features. What lay within this man had been forged by trial and blood. "Trouble was here long before I ever left." He reached out and tapped the sheriff's badge. "A man who wears that piece of tin has to be able to stand and shoot. Now, I know you can shoot; the question is, can you stand? And what will you stand for?"

Clay Benedict turned without replying, climbed into the saddle, and, tugging on the reins, backed away from Tom. The two men swiftly appraised one another in silence. Then Clay touched his heels to his mount, and the zebra dun trotted over toward the other men, who were watering their horses at a trough by the corral under the watchful eyes of Seth Sandcrane.

Clay barked an order and his posse assembled. General Sheridan left the wagon and began barking and nipping at the horses, causing the animals to buck and fight their riders' control. The dog chased the posse out of the yard and into the trees. They left the way they'd come, in a column of dust and drumming hooves, whose cadence could still be faintly heard after the riders were beyond the trees and the Blue Heeler had returned.

Seth climbed down from the wagon bed and with the rifle still resting in the crook of his arm sauntered over to his son, Father Kenneth following close behind. General Sheridan joined in the procession, loping along after the men, tongue lolling from between his jaws, sides heaving, and his breath clouding the cold air.

"What did Clay want? What were you two jabberin' about off by your lonesome?" Seth blurted out.

Tom rubbed his gloved left hand, a gesture of habit now, as he wrestled with his thoughts. He looked from his father to the priest, then shrugged. "Old times."

CHAPTER THIRTY-SIX

ON THAT SAME MORNING, AS THE DUST FROM THE POSSE WAS settling in the yard of the Sandcrane ranch, Red Cherries reined in and alighted from her horse before a hardscrabble farm about seven miles north of Panther Hall. She noticed the buggy first thing and knew she had found the woman doctor. Joanna Cooper had spent the night with Patrick and Kathleen Pretty on Top, helping Kathleen through a difficult birthing process. After more than ten hours of labor, just before dawn, Joanna had helped the exhausted woman deliver a little girl, the first child born to Patrick Pretty on Top and his wife. They named their daughter Hope. It was a good name, Joanna told them, and Hope had gurgled and squalled as if voicing her approval.

Sleep and a hot bath had been paramount in the doctor's mind until Red Cherries' arrival. The prostitute leaped down from her mare and, with her riding dress clinging to her legs, ran across the farmyard and entered the house unbidden, where she pleaded with Joanna to stop by Panther Hall on her return trip to Cross Timbers. One of the girls was sick, and no one seemed to be able to help her.

Joanna agreed to come only after she was assured all was well with the new mother and child. Then Red Cherries and the doctor departed the farm, covering the seven miles at a hurried pace and reaching Panther Hall by midday. The roadhouse was a notorious landmark along the well-traveled North Road to the oil fields. Joanna had heard stories of what went on there, tales of gambling and debauchery that were legendary. She had often ridden past the place, but it offered no attraction to her; after all, Joanna had seen enough of cruelly squandered lives in Cuba, during the war.

However, Panther Hall generated its share of patients for her. From time to time one of the Tall Bulls' wounded customers would wander into her office in town, bruised and bloody from a fistfight or knife wound incurred within the confines of the infamous roadhouse.

She had already met Jerel Tall Bull and his brother, Curtis, at a town meeting several months ago and was perceptive enough to realize the older brother was not a man to be taken lightly. So it was with some misgivings that Joanna followed Red Cherries around the roadhouse to a cabin nestled in a grove of post oaks behind the barn, which blocked a view of the hall.

"The respectable folks from Cross Timbers use this place when they want to be alone with one of my girls," Red Cherries explained, "and do not wish anybody to see them. Sometimes it is not even one of my girls they fancy, but another of their own choosing."

Red Cherries on horseback and Joanna in her carriage rode up to the cabin and tethered their horses at the hitching rail in front. The door of the cabin opened, and another of Panther Hall's "soiled doves," a dimpled, shy-looking brown-haired girl no more than fifteen years old, emerged from the cabin accompanied by both Tall Bull brothers.

Jerel was clearly surprised to see the doctor. He leaned over to the fifteen-year-old and whispered in the young girl's ear. She nodded and immediately scampered from the porch and hurried back to the roadhouse, without so much as a simple greeting to Red Cherries.

"This is no place for you," Jerel said, addressing the woman in the buggy. Joanna was bundled in a gray woolen dress with a hooded cape drawn about her shoulders and tied at the neck.

"Don't speak so fast, there, Jerel. Maybe it is," Curtis countered with a grin. He bowed and swept his hat across his chest. "Good day to you, Miss Cooper. Did you come out here for a dance or two? I'd be happy to oblige. You could be my personal guest."

Joanna recoiled at the notion, accurately judging the younger brother's intentions. She refused, however, to be cowed by the presence of the two men. She had seen their like before. Well, maybe not Jerel's. There was something different about him. . . .

Jerel stepped down from the porch, his large-boned, powerful physique moving with surprising grace, his manner gruff as he confronted the two women. He fixed his iron-eyed stare on Red Cherries. "I said we would handle this ourselves."

"Jerel . . . Mr. Tall Bull—Clarice needs tending. More than you or I can give her," Red Cherries replied, defending her actions.

"I might be able to help," Joanna said, speaking in a forceful tone of voice. "I'll know better when I see her." He glanced in her direction and she shuddered inwardly, then averted her gaze and stepped around the big man. Curtis made a move to block her, a smug expression on his face. Red Cherries hurried to stand at Joanna's side. She glanced over her shoulder and spoke to the older brother.

"Call off your dog." It was easier to speak if she didn't have to look him in the eye. Bull-necked and broad-shouldered, Jerel's sheer physical presence had always been intimidating, but there was something else about him now—a different quality that at times chilled her to the very core and made her spirit recoil when this dark mood came upon him. When he turned, she lowered her head and began to study the porch at her feet.

"Ain't no whore gonna talk to me that way," Curtis snarled, and started toward the women. A simple "no" from his brother stopped Curtis in his tracks. Jerel turned his smoldering gaze on Joanna, who flinched, though he never made a single motion in her direction.

"Go on, then, as long as you're here," he said in a voice like rumbling thunder. "You'll pay her fee," he added as an aside to Red Cherries. She nodded, and Jerel did an about-face and headed down the path that led to the rear of Panther Hall.

Curtis scowled, struggling to stem the tide of his anger. Jerel had not backed him up, and he felt humiliated. So he assumed an air of self-importance and took a step toward the porch and Joanna, who was standing with a hand on the door. "Red Cherries here thinks she's something special. But Jerel sees her for the whore she is—a whore through and through." He looked back at the Cheyenne woman. "Could be you're spreading your legs for the wrong brother."

"I like to watch Jerel tug your leash and make you jump," Red Cherries said, revealing nothing but her contempt for the younger man.

Curtis's expression became mottled. His hands clenched with barely suppressed rage, and for a moment Joanna wondered if he was going to attack the prostitute, but then he dug his fists into the pockets of his frock coat. "You've got a smart mouth. One of these days I'm gonna make you put it to better use." He looked up at the doctor on the porch and touched the brim of his hat as a gesture of farewell. He even bowed before starting off toward the roadhouse. This sudden gesture of civility was wasted on Joanna, who already knew too much about men like Curtis Tall Bull. It was Jerel, the elder brother, who was the enigma. Even in retrospect Joanna trembled at what she had glimpsed in the man's unflinching gaze—a most dangerous mixture of raw power . . . and madness.

"Doctor Cooper isn't here, mister. I guess that's who you must be lookin' for," the young girl said. She appeared to be about nine years old, a pretty child with long black hair that hung in thick ringlets past her shoulders and framed her olive features. One day she would be considered a sultry beauty, a heartbreaker, with every man at her mercy. But today she was simply a child, with the painful uncertainties of romance the furthest thing from her mind. Her days were filled with the excitement of pretty sunsets and fireflies and games of hide-and-seek and chase-the-sparrows, and picnics by the banks of the Washita River, whose waters once had run red with the blood of soldier and Southern Cheyenne in a none-too-distant past. Tom wished he could tell her all he had seen and learned, how the world was poised on the brink of change now, the age of the Wild West in its death throes, soon to be dust in the wake of the onrushing twentieth century.

Then, again, the child in all her innocence was part of that unstoppable juggernaut that had doomed his people's way of life. She was the future in which the Southern Cheyenne must learn to exist or perish. Where was the path, though? He'd begun to think it lay between the worlds of red man and white, drawing on the old to confront the new. Tom had returned to Cross Timbers with a heart full of questions, seeking answers from the truths of the past.

Oblivious to the stranger's inner turmoil, the girl arched her thick black brows, and her brown eyes turned lustrous in the afternoon light. She was bundled up against the cold in a brown woolen coat with dull-black buttons, trimmed with black stitchery about the wrists and along the hem.

"What's your name?" she asked, fidgeting nervously upon the porch. "My name's Anna Yaquereno. My papa owns the restaurant in town. What do you do? Are you an Indian? I kind of look like an Indian, don't I?"

Tom had to grin before the girl's onslaught of questions. He glanced sideways at his reflection in the clinic window. "Dr. Joanna Cooper, M.D.," had been painted on the glass pane and repeated on a wooden sign that hung above the porch—as if the owner had realized, as an afterthought, that the window could not be read from any great distance so long as the wooden shingle dangling in the breeze—INFIRMARY—was clearly visible from the center of town.

After the posse's departure Tom had saddled a blaze-faced roan and explained his actions to his father with a perfunctory, "I'm going to ride around and see if I can find Willem." He didn't linger to find out if Seth and the priest believed his explanation, but rode off in the opposite direction from town. Once out of sight, he had circled over to the Cross Timbers road. It was only early afternoon, and he was disappointed not to find Joanna in her office.

"It is a pleasure to meet you, Anna. My name is Tom Sandcrane."

"Then you *are* an Indian. I know, 'cause you have a funny name," the girl said with a smile, oblivious to the fact that someone might find a name like Yaquereno equally amusing.

"It is a pleasure to meet you, Anna." With her dark Italian complexion she might have passed for a Cheyenne child, though she wore a woolen dress, thick cotton stockings, and buttoned boots that most Cheyenne children would never have been able to afford. Business was obviously good for Mr. Yaquereno. "Shouldn't you be in school?"

Anna covered her mouth to stifle her laughter. "Jimmy Turner stuffed a great big old bullfrog in the stove chimney and plugged it up, and smoke filled the room, and it stunk something awful, so Miss Flannery told us all to go home until she could clean up." The girl burst out laughing. Then she pursed her lips a moment and pointed to the back of her parents' restaurant fronting Main. "Why don't you wait there for the doctor? My mama makes the best peach cobbler in all the world."

Tom hooked a thumb in his coat pocket and studied the town, then shrugged. Perhaps he wasn't dressed proper for a sit-down meal. Still, his fleece-lined denim coat was relatively clean, and he'd changed his shirt before entering town and even slicked his long hair back. "I've never been a man to turn my nose up at a plate of peach cobbler," he told the girl, and followed her off the porch. He caught up the reins of the roan gelding he had borrowed from Seth, then hoisted Anna into the saddle. She beamed with pleasure as he walked his mount toward Main. They reached Main Street in a matter of minutes, and Tom looped the reins around a hitching post in front of the narrow-looking saloon attached to the restaurant. Anna allowed him to help her down from the horse. A short, stout, broad-shouldered man emerged from the saloon. He wore an apron over his black woolen trousers and a long-sleeved checkered shirt rolled to the elbows. An immense black mustache covered his upper lip.

"Anna . . . what are you doing? Do not bother people."

"But, Papa . . ."

"Run inside. Your mama, she looks for you. Don't I tell you to come straight home from school? It is no safe for little girls until they catch that Indian." Mr. Yaquereno folded his arms and sternly appraised the man in the street as his daughter grudgingly obeyed.

"Your daughter told me her mother makes the best peach cobbler in all the world. Is that true?" Tom asked, meeting the man's stare.

"Anna tells no lies. Well, most of the time she tells no lies," Yaquereno gruffly said. Then he stepped back and motioned toward the front of the restaurant. "Maybe you better find out for yourself."

Tom climbed the steps to the walk and started past the girl's father, who reached out and caught the Cheyenne by the arm. Tom might have taken offense but for the circumstances. Mr. Yaquereno seemed more worried then belligerent.

"I'm a—how you say?—jumpy, like when you walk out at night and hear a rattler, but you don't know which way to go, eh? I love my little girl. And I don't want to wind up like Luthor White Bear." The Italian pointed up the street toward the mercantile with its black wreath upon the door. Tom recognized Rebecca White Bear's father and two brothers; Ned Scalp Shirt and his two sons, Matt and Little Ned; and several of Luthor's kin whose names he could not immediately recall—all hard men determined to avenge the death of one of their own. The irony wasn't lost on Tom that he had survived one war only to find another brewing at home. Clay Benedict had seemed surprisingly earnest about keeping the peace and seeing justice done. But how much weight did his words carry? Noble sentiments alone had never stopped a lynching.

The interior of Yaquereno's was divided into two brightly lit dining rooms, each heated by Franklin stoves, each with a homey feel. The walls were covered with pale-blue fabric and adorned with a variety of chromolithographs depicting the Italian countryside: white stone paths bordered with golden trees whose limbs rose like flames, whitewashed villas on hillsides overlooking quaint villages where everyone, even the most humble milkmaid, seemed cheerful. There were children frolicking in the shadows of aqueducts, oxcarts traversing roads built in the time of Caesar, and ruins of buildings, the origin of which Tom could not even guess.

A few patrons in the front room lingered over the last of their dinners, absorbed in their papers or books, yet they looked up as Tom entered, and their eyes followed the new customer until he found a table.

As it was midafternoon, Tom expected business to be a little slack. A chorus of women's laughter drifted in from the rear dining room, where several ladies were evidently indulging in some of Mrs. Yaquereno's desserts. Sandcrane chose to avoid intruding on the ladies and took a chair at a table by the front window. From this vantage point, if he leaned just right, Sandcrane could watch the mercantile.

A middle-aged Italian woman appeared at his table. The resemblance between mother and daughter was immediately noticeable, the same thick brows and dark eyes—it could only be Mrs. Yaquereno. The woman studied Tom warily. The recent killing had evidently left everyone suspicious of strangers, and Cheyenne in particular.

"Can I help you?"

"Your daughter told me her mother makes the best coffee and peach cobbler in all the world. Is that true?"

The woman blushed, pleased by the compliment, and thawing toward the stranger her own daughter had so recently described. "My Anna . . . she carries on so. But she is a good girl." The woman nodded. "I bring you coffee and a bowl of cobbler, and you tell me what you think, eh?"

Tom nodded. As Mrs. Yaquereno departed toward the rear of the restaurant, she paused in the second dining room, and Tom could hear her bidding farewell to the ladies within. A few moments later half-a-dozen women, ranging from their early twenties to a sprightly looking silver-haired woman on the threshold of sixty, emerged from the dining room. Tom would not have paid them any heed at all had he not spied Emmiline Benedict among their number. His eyes widened and numbness crept along his jawline. His pulse quickened.

Anger, hurt, and desire swept over him in a single instant. It was like being caught in a flash flood and struggling to keep from being torn apart by the unleashed fury. He willed his features into an impassive mask, a poker face, to guard the emotional hand that life had unexpectedly dealt him.

The Indian agent's daughter saw Tom at the same instant, and much to the murmured disbelief of her associates, she excused herself from their midst and crossed the room to sit down at the Cheyenne's table. Amazingly enough, she was all sunshine and gaiety, as if she had never betrayed him at all.

"The silver-haired woman is Mildred Peltier, the wife of the Presbyterian minister. I'll bet her mouth is wide-open." Emmiline spoke in the same voice, had the same flirtatious expression, as before. She shifted to the right, and Tom could see not only Mildred Peltier but the entire group of ladies staring at him. He stood and bowed slightly, a lascivious smile upon his weathered features. The women reacted as he knew they would. After all, he was a total stranger. The group crowded through the front door, gossiping among themselves about Emmiline's inexplicable and outrageous behavior.

Emmiline looked much the same. Her hair was coiffed and pinned atop her head in a lustrous dark wealth of curls. A narrow-brimmed hat was affixed to the side of her mounded hair. She wore a woolen riding dress and a thick cotton blouse covered by a short-waisted fur-trimmed coat, which was adorned with lace and stitchery. A faint, sweet scent of perfume tickled his nostrils.

As she spoke, Emmiline still had a habit of arching one eyebrow in a most provocative manner that had never failed to arouse his interest. Even now old emotions rushed through him; forgotten fires, long dormant, struggled to ignite, to be fanned into flames by her nearness. All that the embers of yesterday needed was a little coaxing to burst into life and consume him once again.

"Were you going to come see me, Tom?" she asked. That look again, but he was wise to her tricks. This time he kept his desire in check.

"No," he replied.

"Well, you should have. Nobody holds a grudge forever.

There is so much I wanted to tell you, to make you understand. . . ." She noticed his gloved left hand and realized he had not returned from war unscarred.

"What have you done to yourself?"

"Some blasted Cuban didn't want me to kill him." Tom rubbed the deadened limb. "But I did."

There, now, he thought. Remembering Cuba focused him. He allowed his mind to dwell on the carnage and bloodshed, the death of Zuloaga, the weary aftermath and painful recovery, the visions that had brought him back from the brink of death. He studied the woman seated across from him.

"Tom . . . please. What happened . . . my father made me. I never wanted to hurt you."

"But there was a fortune to be made and a people to be swindled out of their heritage."

"No. What would the tribe have done with the land? Sold it off to the first oil company that came along and made your people an offer. At least my family will keep the tribe employed and provide some stability."

"Yes. God bless Allyn Benedict . . . and his daughter."

Emmiline's features hardened. His words wounded her, left cracks in her flirtatious facade. She had assumed he had returned to Cross Timbers for love of her. Now she was no longer certain. "I don't think I like you now."

"Good. I'll be safer that way," Tom replied. A grin found its way through the jumble of emotions he was feeling. Memories of the passion he had once felt were ashes now, and the winds of time were blowing, scattering them at last, enabling him to see her in a different light. There was an aura of darkness surrounding her—he had seen this before. Yes. Around Clay Benedict, too, but he had not realized it until just this minute, with Emmiline seated before him. He shivered, despite the warm interior of the restaurant. Tom leaned forward on his elbows and spoke quietly and with authority. "I did not come here for any of the Benedicts or their damn businesses. No, not even for you, Emmiline." He eased back in his chair, and in that moment of freedom he almost felt sorry for her.

Mrs. Yaquereno arrived bearing a large stoneware mug of

coffee and a thick earthenware bowl full of peach cobbler. Steam rose from the split crust, and the aroma of the peaches mingled with the smell of fresh coffee would have set his mouth watering any other time. But not now. His appetite was gone. Tom slid the bowl of cobbler and coffee mug over to the young woman. "Here . . . you're looking thin." She stared at him in confused silence as Sandcrane stood and paid Mrs. Yaquereno for the food. Leaning over to Emmiline, he said, "*Heavohe netaxe eha-tova.*" Then he walked away and left her alone.

Emmiline frowned and clasped her hands in front of her, the blood draining from her knuckles. She had lived long enough among the Cheyenne to understand what he had said. Suddenly she lashed out at the earthenware bowl and sent it crashing to the floor. All eyes were upon her, startled by her destructive behavior, but she ignored the people in the restaurant and the Italian proprietress who arrived to clean up the young woman's mess.

What did he mean? she asked herself. And what did he know? His parting words reverberated in her mind.

"*Heavohe netaxe eha-tova.*" The devil is hanging over you.

The devil was hanging over a man as well, Tom thought as he entered the mercantile under the watchful eyes of Luthor White Bear's relations. Ned Scalp Shirt and his sons, Matt and Little Ned, had been joined by Pete Elk Head, who had just arrived in town with the posse. Acting under Jerel Tall Bull's orders, Pete had stopped by the general store to inform Luthor White Bear of the morning's progress and how they had checked the Sandcrane ranch at Coyote Creek. Pete could be seen muttering something to Luthor's relatives as Tom made his way across the street. Like Tom, Ned Scalp Shirt and his sons had only recently arrived in town, but they remembered him from past tribal gatherings. Little Ned, eighteen years old and half a foot shorter than his father, was nevertheless cut in the same image, with his square jaw and solid build. He stood with his thumb hooked in the beaded belt that he wore outside his coat, the palm of his other hand resting near the gun butt tucked in his waistband. Urged on by Pete Elk Head, who stood to one side with a malicious grin on his face, Little Ned stepped in front of Tom at the top of the steps leading to the entrance of the mercantile. Brother Matt and Ned Scalp Shirt, wrapped in their heavy woolen greatcoats, were seated off to the side, Winchester carbines resting across their knees, perusing the townsfolk as if sitting in judgment of all who passed by.

"Stop right there, Sandcrane!" Little Ned said, holding out his hand as he barked his order. "Any friend of that murderous bastard Willem Tangle Hair has no business . . ."

Tom caught the young man by the wrist and with a savage pull hauled Little Ned from the wooden walk and sent him sprawling in the dirt. Ned and his eldest son, Matt, stared at the one-armed man in disbelief. They were plainspoken, hardworking cowmen, dangerous if provoked, but slow to react. Pete Elk Head dropped a hand to the gun riding on his hip, but by the time he touched iron, Tom had already disappeared inside.

He froze inside the door at the sight of Allyn Benedict, standing by the counter at the rear of the store, one hand resting on a stack of folded blankets, the other thrust into the pocket of his frock coat. He was impeccably tailored, tall and lean. But his boyish features had aged, and silvery threads had managed to weave their inexorable course through his blond hair, once merely gray at the temples.

Luthor White Bear had trimmed off the twin braids that had once framed his features. His hair was close-cropped now, and he wore a stiff-collared shirt and string tie as befitting a prosperous storekeeper. Behind him the wall was filled with bolts of cloth, canned goods, and bottled elixirs from a variety of vendors. The interior of the store smelled of apples and spilled cinnamon, coffee warming on the Franklin stove, tobacco smoke, and the familiar aroma of leather goods: saddles and bridles and harnesses to Tom's left. And yet a pall hung over the room despite the sunlight streaming through the open windows, as if everything that entered the store were in some way filtered through the black wreath of mourning hung on the front door.

"Tom Sandcrane," Allyn said, and for a moment his eyebrows arched as he studied his erstwhile foe. The former Indian agent neither smiled nor frowned, but his lips were drawn in a thin, straight line. A muscle along the side of his neck began to twitch. "We're all proud of the way you conducted yourself in Cuba. I had even entertained the notion of having a statue built in your honor. But, then, most statues honor the dead . . . and here you are, alive and unharmed." Benedict lowered his gaze to Tom's gloved hand. "Uh . . . alive, anyway."

"I appreciate the thought," Tom coolly replied. His emotions were like a wild stallion he had to keep tightly reined. He removed his hat as Rebecca White Bear stepped through the hanging curtains separating the rear kitchen from the rest of the store. Luthor's wife glanced up in surprise as she recognized Tom. She did not wait for a greeting and made no move to extend any sort of welcome. She moved past the counter and started up the stairs, the dry wood creaking beneath her steps. Draped in a black shawl that covered a brown woolen dress and jacket, the grieving mother was bereft of words for any friend of Willem Tangle Hair. The men in the store watched her leave, and when she had disappeared upstairs, Allyn struck a match and relit his cigar.

"I will stand by you, Luthor," the oilman said, turning to the shopkeeper, placing a hand on Luthor's forearm.

"And Clay?"

"Badge or no, he is still my son," Allyn said, blowing a cloud of smoke that drifted past a jar of peppermint sticks. "I have no doubt but that we can count on him to do the right thing when the time comes." Benedict started across the store, making his way down the center aisle toward Tom. He slowed nearing the younger man. "There's been a lot of muddy water under the bridge, Tom. But I am willing to let bygones be bygones."

Tom glanced down at the man's gesture of friendship. He made no move to clasp the oilman's hand. "Reckon that bridge got plumb washed away, Allyn. Could be the water's still rising."

Benedict lowered his hand and nodded, his gaze narrowing, filled with questions as to Tom's motives and the meaning of his words. He continued on to the front door and vanished outside.

Luthor stepped around from behind the counter. He wore an apron whose hem was dusted with flour and torn at one corner. The shopkeeper opened a barrel and helped himself to one of the crackers inside. "Why'd you come here, Tom?" He slowly crossed to the makeshift table and chairs he kept near the stove. The chessboard and pieces were just as they had been on the night of Charlotte's murder, when Father Kenneth had staggered into the store and announced his grisly discovery.

"Just to pay my respects, Mr. White Bear," Tom said. Now was not the time or place to begin a discussion about the Sacred Arrows. Tom looked about him, wondering what was wrong. Of course the man's daughter was dead, but there was something else he sensed—a more profound emptiness that confused him. "I am sorry about Charlotte."

"That half-breed friend of yours killed her, choked the life out of her. My wife no longer sleeps. She hardly even speaks. She just waits, like me and the rest of us. The sheriff and his men will run Willem to ground. Mark my words." Luthor reached down and with trembling hands poured himself a cup of coffee. He did not offer any to his uninvited guest.

"What makes you so certain Willem is guilty?"

Luthor stared at the contents of the enameled tin cup in his hands. Tendrils of steam curled over the brim. These days Luthor preferred his coffee dark and bitter. "Charlotte was bored here," he said, becoming quiet as he reflected once again upon the painful past. "She liked to sneak off to Panther Hall, to dance with the roustabouts when they came in to spend their money. Willem wanted to marry her. But she never could settle on just one man." Luthor gazed off toward the far wall, his expression distant. "It was all a party to her, laughing and flirting and having a good time. A couple of weeks ago Willem confronted her. They argued and she left for home and he followed her. There were witnesses, plenty of them. Later that same night Father Kenneth found her in his barn. Willem probably forced her to join him there, and when she refused to have anything more to do with him, he killed her." Luthor absently gulped the coffee. A few droplets of liquid sloshed down his chin and stained the front of his apron. "In the shadow of the church . . . the white man's God failed her. I failed her. I should have known . . ." Luthor caught himself, grew suddenly aware of his audience, and fell silent.

Tom studied the shopkeeper for a moment, searching the man's grief-filled countenance. White Bear's sorrow was understandable—who could blame the man for desiring revenge—and yet Tom believed there was more there than met the eye. It was just something he felt . . . or perhaps did not feel.

Before he could press the matter, the front door opened and Luthor's relatives entered the store. The shopkeeper seemed relieved at their intrusion. And for Tom Sandcrane it was time to go. He hoped he could do so without violence—but he refused to leave without one parting remark.

"There is one way to be certain that she was killed by a Cheyenne," Tom said.

Luthor looked quizzically at the man.

"Call a council. Bring forth the Sacred Arrows. It is known that if one Cheyenne takes the life of another, there will be blood upon the Mahuts. This I learned from my father."

A fleeting look of horror flashed across the shopkeeper's face; then he glowered at the younger man and drew himself up, summoning all his dignity as he spoke. "Who are you to speak to me of such things? When the bundle was taken from your father's keeping at the Great Council, you turned your back on the Mahuts. Have you forgotten?"

"No. The Maiyun will not allow me to forget," Tom said.

Luthor White Bear was momentarily taken aback by Sandcrane's admission, his mouth framing silent words of protest and disbelief. He was no fool, and the implication of Tom's reply was not lost on him. But he shook his head and waved the younger man away. "Leave me alone. *Enanotse!*" The shopkeeper retreated toward the stairs before he heard any more troubling remarks from Sandcrane.

Tom considered pressing the matter, then changed his

mind. Luthor was deaf to him for the moment, perhaps until after his daughter's murderer was brought to justice. The shopkeeper followed his wife upstairs, leaving Tom to the less than tender care of Ned Scalp Shirt and sons. *Willem could not have done such a thing. He loved the girl. She meant too much to him.* Tom inwardly wrestled with what little he knew of the incident. It just seemed impossible his friend would have murdered Charlotte. "Time you left Uncle Luthor alone," said Little Ned, interrupting Sandcrane's speculations.

"Let it be," another voice counseled.

"Keep out of this, Matt," said the younger brother. His clothes were dirty from his tumble in the street, but he was otherwise unharmed . . . save for the most grievous hurt of all in a young man's mind—his wounded pride. Tom faced the chunky youth who stood in the middle of the center aisle, his hands near his belt where he kept both revolver and knife. Little Ned was flanked by his father and older brother, who remained a few paces back. In the shadows by the wall stood Pete Elk Head, fresh from the posse and ready for new mischief.

Sandcrane advanced until he stood toe to toe with Ned Scalp Shirt's quarrelsome son, who held his ground, watchful for any sudden moves like that which had landed him facedown in the dusty street.

"You hardly know me," Tom said. "Why?"

"Because you're Tangle Hair's friend. Pete here thinks you might even know where he's hid out," said Ned, his muscled arms folded across his chest, studying the one-armed man confronting his son. He was beginning to have misgivings about all this—despite Pete's words to the contrary, Tom was clearly a match for any of them.

Tom's dark eyes, like ice-glazed chips of obsidian, continued to bore into Little Ned. And when Sandcrane spoke, his voice was quiet and chillingly effective.

"Tell your son to back off, Mr. Scalp Shirt. You are letting Pete talk him into trouble. Now, Elk Head's all gut wind, nothing more. He will not stand. I say Little Ned here is man enough to see this through." As Tom spoke, Pete edged toward the front door, a premonition flashing through his mind that he might die this day and so had better escape while he still had the chance. "Listen to me," Tom went on. "I have . . . done things. I have stood knee-deep in bones and brains. I have washed my hands in the blood of my enemies. So I say: Tell your boy to back off." Now the voice became almost a whisper. "Or I will hurt him."

Little Ned tried to remain impassive, but his knees began to tremble and his throat constricted as if totally devoid of moisture. His arms had suddenly become leaded weights that lowered to his side, depriving the former soldier of the slightest excuse to act. Fortunately, his father came to his rescue. "Stand aside, son." The young man managed to keep himself from openly sighing with relief as he stepped out of harm's way, allowing Tom Sandcrane to pass. The bell over the front entrance rang as the door opened and shut.

"You should have backed me, Pa. You and Matt," Little Ned peevishly snapped, attempting to salvage a few tattered remnants of his pride.

"Now was not the time or place," the cowman replied.

"When, then?"

Ned Scalp Shirt shrugged and shook his head. What had he glimpsed in Sandcrane's features? "Never. I hope."

Upstairs in the hall Luthor paused and glanced toward his daughter's bedroom, then closed his eyes, squeezing back tears of loss and recrimination. He averted his gaze and entered his own bedroom. Rebecca sat in a rocking chair by the window overlooking the street. The room was comfortably furnished. Indeed, after having almost lost the store through his own poor investments in a dry hole that was supposed to make him a rich oil baron like Allyn Benedict, Luthor White Bear had recovered his losses, for business had been good. He was accepted by the white community, and by anyone's standards he lived well—unlike so many of the Southern Cheyenne who labored as roughnecks and lived out in Rabbit Town. Luthor had prospered. The four-poster bed came all the way from Baltimore, not to mention the china, and the porcelain lamps, and the polished mahogany tables and cushioned seats in the sitting room at the rear of the house. And yet none of it gave either of them any pleasure—not anymore. The price had been too high.

Rebecca continued to stare out the window, gnawing at her lower lip. One hand was constantly rubbing the palm of the other, then toying with a silk kerchief, then digging at her palm again. Luthor crossed the room, his footsteps muffled by the throw rug. He reached out to drape an arm over her shoulder. Rebecca drew back. "No!" she whispered.

"Wife . . . please."

"No! Bring me my daughter. I want my Charlotte back. You bring her to me!" she said, her cheeks flushed as she spoke, her voice a hushed rasping sound.

"By the Spirits of Those Who Have Gone Before, I wish I could," Luthor said.

"You killed her. Sure as Willem."

"Woman, what are you saying?"

"You know what I mean," Rebecca replied, the rungs of the chair creaking as she began to rock back and forth, moving from sunlight into shadow, darkness into light, then darkness again. "You know what I mean."

CHAPTER THIRTY-SEVEN

Joanna Cooper made her way by moonlight to the back door of the infirmary. A kitchen and adjoining bedroom at the rear of the building served as her private quarters. She had used the rest of the space for her practice. An outer office (with its book-lined walls, ceiling-high medicine cabinet, rolltop desk, and reading lamp) dominated the front of the clinic. From the office a set of double doors opened onto two examining rooms that served both as scenes of operation and as bedrooms for those patients requiring supervised care.

It had been a morning and a night of extremes. She had begun the day by helping to bring a new life into the world and ended it by holding the hand of a prostitute while the poor girl drew her last breath. Smoke and drink and too many sordid liaisons had driven Clarice to an early grave.

Joanna was no stranger to death, but she had yet to don the physician's mantle of callousness that kept anguish and pity at bay. There were still times when she wrestled with the awesome matter of mortality. Throughout the drive to town, an innocent's first gurgling, cooing breath and a worn-out whore's death rattle played over and over in her mind. And so, preoccupied, Joanna took no notice of the figure approaching her from the shadows. Perhaps she was just tired. No . . . weary, to put it more honestly. Despite the knowledge she was needed in Cross Timbers and the satisfaction that came with that realization, deep in her heart Joanna had another reason for being here. And on nights like this, with gloom draped around her like the cloak she wore, Joanna began to think of herself as a fool. Her heart had led her there, flying in the face of wisdom as the heart's errands are wont to do. A will-o'-the-wisp fantasy had brought her to Cross Timbers—a fantasy, the track of a "ghost," and the illusory sound of drums heard what seemed a lifetime ago on distant shores.

She shook her head, tried to clear her mind, and spied a few sparse snowflakes drifting down. *Fire's bound to have burned itself out by now,* she thought, unlocking the back door. Steeling herself, she stepped into the cold, cheerless kitchen.

The woman rubbed her hands together to get the circulation going, headed straight for the stove, and began to vigorously stoke the blackened chunks of wood in the chamber. She added tinder from the wood box, tore a few pages from a mail-order catalog kept on the nearby counter for just such an occasion, struck a match, and lit the pages. As the flames began to feed, she used a burning twig to light the ceiling lamp. Soon the interior of the room was awash with amber light, revealing a countertop crowded with jars labeled "flour," "sugar," "rice," "salt," and the like, cupboards for the earthenware, a row of pans suspended from hooks in the wall, a table and four ladder-back chairs, which dominated the center of the room. More cabinets lined the walls.

When she had patients stay over, the doctor often hired Rebecca White Bear to cook for them. Luthor's wife was good company and could always be counted on as a source of local gossip. However, since the death of Charlotte the woman had not ventured out of the store except to attend the funeral, and Joanna had begun to miss the woman's visits.

She shivered as a chill gust of wind tickled the back of her neck. *I shut that door,* she thought, and turned to find Tom Sandcrane standing in the doorway. They faced one another across a gulf of silence. He had appeared like a specter, and for a moment Joanna couldn't believe her own eyes. Then he stepped into the kitchen and closed the door after him. He was bundled against the chilled night air, gloved hand at his side and the other dug into the pocket of his fleece-lined denim coat. He removed his hat and tossed it onto the table, where it landed with a soft thud. His long black hair framed his coppery features, his expression uncertain and somewhat embarrassed.

Suddenly Cuba came flooding back to her: arriving at Celestial's hacienda to find Tom Sandcrane gone from her life without so much as a good-bye, the "ghost" she had nursed back to health, the Southern Cheyenne whose sad courage had won her sympathies and awakened even deeper emotions she had come to admit at last . . .

Bless him. Curse him!

"I don't know whether to slap your face or take you to bed," Joanna said.

"Perhaps I can help you make up your mind," Tom replied, a hint of a smile toying at the corners of his mouth.

"I think I've already made my decision," Joanna said, shedding her cloak, a hungry expression on her face. She unpinned her auburn hair, allowing it to cascade down across her bodice. In a silence broken only by the crackling flames bursting into life, Tom eagerly shrugged off his coat and tossed it onto the table as the woman drew close, her moist lips parting, her eyes twin pools of passion and desire.

"Tom," Joanna purred. And then she slapped him right across the jaw with enough force to raise a welt and cause him to stumble backward against the door. He looked stunned, she triumphant. Then she turned on her heels, set a couple of glasses on the table, and produced a bottle of Irish whiskey she kept handy for cold winter nights when the chill of mortality bit deeper than north wind. She motioned for him to take a seat.

"I guess I deserved that," he said, ruefully rubbing his jaw.

"You most certainly did. And more. The nerve, just disappearing like that, after what we went through together. You weren't hurt so bad you had to jump on the first hospital ship headed for the States." Joanna poured a couple of fingers of whiskey into her glass.

"I thought it would be easiest."

"The coward's way generally is," she remarked, tossing back

the first round like a veteran and gasping as the warmth spread from her throat to her chest. "Well, what brings you to town, Tom Sandcrane?"

He sat and poured a drink for himself, grinning now, glad she was in Cross Timbers; it was worth a stinging jaw. Indeed her presence merely added credence to the dreams and visions that had steered him home. There was more at work there than mere coincidence, he thought, resting his gloved hand on the table, his gaze clear and steady. "*E-peva-e.* Funny. I was going to ask you the same thing."

Consuela, the Benedicts' housekeeper and cook, cleared away the plates from in front of her employer and his family, moving swiftly around the great, long table which could seat up to ten guests, four to a side and one at each end. But, of course, there were three at supper this night. Allyn and Margaret sat at either end of the table, distant from each other, separated by several feet of polished walnut-and-silver settings, candelabras, and a soup tureen crafted to resemble some enormous seashell.

The housekeeper was anxious to be out of the dining room and away from this moody family, who took their meals in silence these days. Emmiline, seated midway between her two parents had tried to initiate a conversation and involve both Allyn and Margaret until it became evident the two had quarreled again. Despite the apparent trappings of success that had brought them their elegant surroundings, the two had grown irrevocably apart, almost in direct proportion to their financial gains. Allyn Benedict was a driven man, determined that his meteoric rise in prestige and his increasing wealth should not subside and sputter out. Ambition was one thing, and the prospect of wealth appealed to Margaret. But their relationship had become forced over the past couple of years; his infidelities mocked their marriage vows. The rumors concerning her husband and his dalliances with younger women shamed her. At first she blamed Jerel Tall Bull's corrupting influence, from the very first day she had counseled against becoming involved with the proprietor of Panther Hall. The innuendos festered like open sores, poisoning her mind and heart. The only time she had broached the subject with her husband, Allyn had ranted and roared and protested his innocence with such fervor that she was left believing the worst. And, wounded, she had withdrawn her affections from the man.

Emmiline had observed her parents grow apart. They kept to their separate bedrooms and maintained an icy truce for the benefit of the public and the smooth, orderly running of the household. Appearances had to be kept up; after all, there were Allyn's political ambitions to be considered. But the family was falling apart, like a garment unraveling at the seams. Emmiline couldn't remember when they were last whole and happy, but she thought it must have been years ago, perhaps when they'd been a poor Indian agent's family and the prospects of black gold had yet to be discovered on the tribal lands.

Margaret muttered a word of thanks as Consuela cleared the plates and then, with a smile in her daughter's direction, suggested Emmiline pay her a visit later.

"You can help me choose some things to pack in my trunk," Mrs. Benedict added.

"Your trunk?" Allyn spoke up, his interest piqued by this latest revelation. "Are you leaving?"

"It has been a while since I've seen my sister in New Haven. Oh come now, Allyn, don't look so shocked. It isn't as if you'll miss me. No doubt you'll find someone ... uh ... some way to pass the time and keep yourself occupied. "Margaret kept a friendly expression but her eyes were hard and impenetrable. Her dark-blue dressing gown rustled as she stood. Lamplight shown upon a cameo pendant, where it lay against her bodice, resting between the twin mounds of her breasts. The pendant had been a wedding gift from Allyn, the one treasure he had to offer, having received it from his grandmother. She wore the object more for spite than sentiment, knowing it caused her husband discomfort, reminding him of vows he had failed to honor. She turned and left the room.

Allyn was in no mood to call her back. Emmiline slid her

chair back and started to rise, intending to follow her mother upstairs.

"Just a moment, young lady," Allyn said.

"Yes?" Emmiline settled back, cautious, and folded her hands in her lap.

"What was the purpose of that little show today? And don't feign innocence with me. You abandon your friends and hurry to be with Tom Sandcrane. My God, what were you thinking of?"

"I was thinking how handsome he still is. Maybe I was thinking of what we did to him, and I wanted to . . . make amends."

Benedict shook his head in disbelief. "He's come here to destroy us. And you welcome him home."

"He cannot do us any harm. Anyway, I'm not so sure we're the reason he has returned." Emmiline toyed with the table-cloth's lacy fringe as she spoke. "You know, I think he still likes me a little."

"Dammit, girl, we have a place, our position to maintain." Allyn rose and leaned over the table, propping himself on his hands. "Once all the wells are in and producing, we can move to Tulsa and leave Cross Timbers behind forever. With a sound financial footing I might even run for territorial governor. Any indiscretion on your part could doom those chances."

"Isn't it a bit late for you to be worrying about indiscretions?" the young woman asked.

"What is that supposed to mean?" Allyn drew himself upright, his cheeks red, his backbone arrow straight, indignant that his daughter should even hint of impropriety on his part. "You will stay away from Tom Sandcrane—is that clear? You will do as I say."

Allyn sensed something standing to his left by the mahogany sideboard and china cabinet, whose cut-glass doors reflected the light and distorted the reflected images of father and daughter. Benedict whirled around only to find Consuela, who retreated a step before his scathing glare.

"Pardon me, senor, a man to see you. He waits in the kitchen. He says you sent for him."

"Damn!" Allyn muttered beneath his breath. He looked up as Emmiline rounded the table. The oilman hurried toward her and caught her by the hand. His tone and temperament changed dramatically, growing instantly conciliatory. "Sweetheart . . . wait. Listen. I'm saying all this for your own good. We have come so far. We have money and power and prestige . . . who knows what we can accomplish? Granted, each of us has made some mistakes . . . some errors in judgment along the way. But that's to be expected."

Allyn placed his hands on her shoulders and gazed into her eyes, wondering where the time had gone and how his daughter had so swiftly matured into such a beautiful woman. "I cannot seem to make your mother understand. But we are alike, you and I. Bear with me a little while longer. I will make it up to you and your mother. I promise."

Emmiline relaxed beneath his touch and, with a toss of her head, nodded. He was right. They *were* alike. And for that reason she had long ago resolved to learn everything possible about the oil business and how to make her way in a world of men. "Very well, Papa. I would never do anything to embarrass you."

"That's my girl," Allyn said, hugging her. "I'm only thinking of you and your mother and brother."

Emmiline smiled and hugged him, and because father and daughter were indeed so much alike, she did not believe him for an instant.

"I told you never to come here," Allyn said, appearing in the kitchen doorway. It was a broad, well-lit room with one wall dominated by a cast-iron stove that featured an assortment of hot plates and two ovens, and even a compartment for smoking a slab of beef brisket. The heavyset man helping himself to coffee was none other than Jerel Tall Bull.

"I heard you wanted to speak to me."

"For heaven's sake, in the law office next door. Not here in my house."

"Ah . . . in one place it's business, the other makes us friends." Jerel's black woolen coat was spattered with moisture where the snowflakes had melted on his shoulders. He gulped the coffee, seemingly immune to its burning effect. "Don't worry, Allyn, no one saw me. It's late, and everyone but a fool like me is home in bed." He set the mug aside and sauntered over to a pie that Consuela had recently baked and left to cool on a cabinet. Jerel sniffed the pie, then claimed it for his own, digging his hand through the crust and licking the sweet filling from his fingertips, relishing the taste of cinnamon and apple. He offered Allyn a sample. When Benedict made no movement toward him, the Cheyenne shrugged and continued to eat.

"When you are finished trying to intimidate me, we'll have our say and then you can be on your way," Allyn told him.

Jerel grinned. His boots left a pattern of wet prints on the floor as he began to prowl the confines of the kitchen like a caged beast. "You know, I've never seen the rest of your house. Is it as fancy as it looks from the outside?"

"Yes," Allyn replied, blocking the door into the dining room.

"Maybe I ought to see for myself."

"Take my word for it."

"Very well, Allyn." Jerel chuckled. He scooped out another morsel of pie and ladled it into his mouth with his hand. He returned to the center of the kitchen. "Speak, then. Make me a pretty speech, partner."

"No doubt you have heard Tom Sandcrane is back."

"Apparently from the dead," Jerel added.

"He has no proof of anything concerning how my company ended up with the oil fields. Indeed, my actions were legal and aboveboard—nothing more American than getting the jump on the competition. But some might say I misused my position as Indian agent. As least a man like him could make it seem so, if he was to talk long enough and loud enough."

"Which is where I come in," Jerel said, tossing the remains of the pie aside and wiping his hands on a towel "First I was a sooner, helping to insure your company had claim to the oil land before the rush. Then you want me to send my men out looking for Willem Tangle Hair. And now you want me to do your killing for you. But I'm not good enough to walk through your door."

"Spare me your platitudes," Allyn said, refusing to be cowed. "You've been well paid for your services. The percentage I pay you has made you a rich man. Why, you don't even need that damn Panther Hall to live comfortably and well."

"Every man needs his kingdom," Jerel said. "And my door is open to anyone. As you well know."

Color crept to Allyn's cheeks but his expression remained firm. "I'm waiting for your answer."

Jerel shrugged and walked around the table until he came face-to-face with Benedict. When he spoke, his breath fanned the oilman's cheek.

"I'll kill Sandcrane. But not for you, *ve-ho-e*. Not for you. What lies between Tom Sandcrane and me is more than you will ever understand."

Allyn was somewhat taken aback by the man's words and more than a little confused. "Just so long . . . uh . . . as he is dead," he stammered.

"Oh, he will be," Jerel Tall Bull replied. "And then maybe you will see what real power is." The man retraced his path to the door and vanished into the night. Allyn maintained his composure until his uninvited guest had departed; then he sagged into the nearest chair. *What the hell was that about?* he asked himself. Then again, maybe he didn't want to know.

After several minutes the man bestirred himself and left the kitchen, made his way through the house, and climbed the wide stairway until he reached the spacious hall. He noticed that the door to Margaret's bedroom was slightly ajar and could see her shadow as she moved about the room. The door opened at his touch and he entered the room. Margarite was busy arranging a layer of clothes in her trunk and did not notice her husband's intrusion until he spoke.

"Then your mind is really made up. There is no way I can talk you out of this. Uncle Maynard could wait another couple of months. Then perhaps we could all pay him a visit." He took his time crossing to her, reaching out to put a hand on her arm.

"No. Don't touch me."

"I'm your husband."

"Oh . . . how could I have forgotten?" Margaret said, drawing away. Her eyes were red-rimmed, her cheeks moist. She rubbed the tears away with the back of her hand.

"I know I have made some mistakes, but all that is in the past. Oklahoma will be a state one day. I could be someone important here; I want you at my side." He caught her by the arm and brought her toward him. "Stay here. I need you, Margaret."

She studied his finely chiseled features. How handsome he was, standing close to her, so earnest—why, he even sounded desperate. How utterly convincing. Indeed, there was no limit to how bright his star would shine. How unfortunate the luster was lost upon her.

"Then you will need me even more when I return," she flatly replied. "If . . . I return."

His gaze hardened, the room grew chill. The veins in his temples throbbed as he sought to control his anger. His fingers dug into her arms.

"You're hurting me," Margaret said. Her protest seemed to have no effect. "Allyn . . ." His lips were pale now, his breathing heavy. "Allyn!"

He blinked, then focused on her, suddenly aware of what he was doing, of her pain; then the rage left him and he released his hold. She slumped to the bed, rubbing her arms, fighting back her tears.

"I'm . . . sorry," Allyn stammered, and turned away from her. He hurried from the room, recoiling from that awful moment and from all that he had become.

He descended the stairs two at a time, threw open the doors to the house, and rushed outside into the cold and the darkness. His breath came in gasps until his lungs hurt from the freezing air. He stared at his hands, then brought them to his face. "No, no, no," he groaned. Margaret's wide-eyed, frightened expression mingled with another in his mind. Charlotte White Bear, comely and willing at first, attracted to his wealth, eager to satisfy his carnal needs, then accusing him of abandoning her, threatening, then frightened, and at last pleading for him to stop. He stumbled forward and leaned against one of the stone lions flanking the porch steps. Gradually he regained his composure. The images faded from his mind. Slowly exhaling, he admired the formidable-looking house and the trappings of wealth and prestige it represented. The house beckoned, the amber glow seductive and inviting, reminding him of his purpose and his need for courage. Allyn roused himself, and, shedding his guilt, the man gathered his thoughts and turned toward the house, drawn irrevocably by the siren song of his own greed.

"Talking with you is like watching snow fall," Tom said, standing inside the house, his features framed by the back-door window. Large white flakes drifted out of the stygian sky. It was a halfhearted snowfall, a pronounced precipitation trailing off after a few minutes, becoming a few scattered flakes, abandoned to a sudden gust of wind.

He had just finished recounting the vision he had experienced in Cuba, when he'd hung poised between life and death and at last, with the help of the Sacred Arrows, vanquished the wraith-hawk. "It was then I knew . . . the Maiyun had chosen me. I was the Keeper and must one day return to Cross Timbers. Sometimes a destiny can be written." He turned and leaned against the doorsill. "First I had to wander a bit, sort of retrace my steps, I had to see the white man's world with my new eyes."

"Our world isn't all bad," Joanna remarked.

"No. But we must walk the new world as Cheyenne. Without our heritage, without the voices and the songs and the mystery, we are lost, we are nothing more than one of those ice crystals, lost in the dark, vanishing with the sun." He ambled forward and stood near her. Lamplight added a reddish luster to her auburn hair. Her eyes were like dream catchers, able to hold a man's soul. "So tell me, Doctor, do you think me mad?" He continued on toward the front of the infirmary, checking the empty rooms, following the hall into the library.

"If you are, then I share the illness," Joanna called after him. The whiskey had done its work, leaching the chill from her bones and loosening her tongue. The door to her bedroom was open, and she could see the corner of her brass-frame bed and an inviting glimpse of her turned-down quilt. She shoved the bottle aside before the potent drink affected her will. She liked Tom Sandcrane, maybe even more than "liked"; she felt drawn to him by some force she could not put a name to. The emotions she was experiencing made her all the more determined to keep her senses clear.

"I thought my ideals, however naive, led me to Cuba. Perhaps your 'spirits' guided my steps as well," Joanna added, rising from the table and following him down the hall. She found him in the library, standing by a mahogany bookcase, running his hands over the bound books whose titles he could not read in the gloom.

"So many books, so much knowledge. You could have been anywhere. When my father told me you were here, I was surprised."

"Seth is a dear. We have had many visits. We've even talked about you," Joanna said, smiling impishly.

"Ah, I feared as much," Tom said.

"Yes. He told me everything, how the tribe trusted you and followed your lead and willingly ended their protected status. How Allyn and Emmiline Benedict misled you and betrayed your trust." Joanna moved toward him in the dark, her words like hurled spears, striking home. "He described the day you left, and how he used his own sorrow and guilt to overcome his drunkenness and give him the resolve to build something for you to come back to."

"I turned my back on the Sacred Arrows. That cannot be. I am the Arrow Keeper. I did not want to believe it and even tried to run from them." Tom crossed to the front window and peered through the letters of her name painted on the glass. The street was deserted looking save for an occasional coat-muffled figure that dashed past the front windows of the Lavender Hotel and disappeared inside.

"In Cuba one night you spoke of this frontier and told me how few doctors there were, and so it was easy to fool myself into thinking that's why I came to Cross Timbers." Joanna dropped a hand to the deeply padded armchair by the rolltop desk. The leather was cool to the touch. There was a small cast-iron woodstove in the corner, but she never lit it except on nights when she was caring for overnight patients. "But it was something else, really, that drew me to this place." Her voice grew faint with introspection. "But the dead do not speak to me," she added bitterly, the memory of a dying whore still fresh on her mind. The sad culmination of a broken, bitter life.

Lamplights gleamed in the windows of the houses, in the shops and false-front stores and offices. Cross Timbers was growing, becoming everything Tom had ever envisioned. But where were the Southern Cheyenne? His own people no longer belonged where once they were lords of the plains. They were becoming aimless, faceless even to one another, scattered across the lower range or clinging to a shadowy existence in the settlement called Rabbit Town. How could Luthor White Bear have allowed this to happen? Why had he not brought his lost people together? Had his own success made him blind? It was time for *ma-heonesto-nestotse*, the Sacred Ceremony of Renewal. The council fires must be lit and the tribe gathered so that the Maiyun could ride the Arrow Keeper's song into the hearts of the people, renewing one and all. The bond between Maheo the Mysterious One and the Southern Cheyenne must be restored and made whole again.

Joanna drew close to him, and in the faint illumination seeping through the unshuttered window, she could see moisture on his cheek. She reached out to touch his tears and found them warm on her fingertips.

"My fault . . . I broke the Circle," he said. "Sometimes I see Philo and Tully, sometimes even Captain Zuloaga, bloodied and dying beneath me. Other times it is a warrior I do not know, or I smell burning sage when there is no fire, or I hear the ceremonial drums. All these things are visions I can no longer deny. And all of them have brought me here." He turned to face the woman at his side and lowered his lips to hers, covering her mouth in a hungry, yearning kiss. She leaned against him, molding her lithe frame to his. Then he drew back. "You once told me you would not be laid hand on unless you wished it." His right hand reached down to brush a strand of hair away from the corner of her mouth.

"That's right," she replied. And then, taking the initiative, kissed him again. When she stepped back, both of them were a little breathless. "Now I think you had better leave, Tom Sandcrane. For I am tired and perhaps a little drunk, and I just might take you to my bed were you to stay any longer."

"Oh . . ." His interest was indeed heightened.

"But we will not share my blanket, my dear friend, until you are a whole man." She reached down and took his gloved left hand, lifting it to her lips. "And I do not mean this wound."

"I could stay with Coby Starving Elk," Sandcrane forlornly said. "But he snores loud as a bellowing bull."

"Good. It will serve you right." Joanna was wise to his tricks and not about to let him off the hook too easily, no matter what desires he had awakened.

Tom allowed himself another moment of shared warmth and then nodded. She was right. When he came to her, it ought to be as a whole man, not split apart by the mistakes of the past. There was much to be done. He must restrain his longing and his own needs. How could he find solace for his own pain while his people perished?

A great darkness had descended upon the Southern Cheyenne. Alone he must enter its center, alone he must find them and bring his people out into the great light. One-armed or two, the task was his.

CHAPTER THIRTY-EIGHT

WE ARE HERE. *WAITING . . . WAITING . . .*

For the better part of an hour Tom had paced the confines of the stable, his shadow gliding past the stalls and flitting over the carriage and surrey that were Allyn Benedict's personal conveyances. Sandcrane, lost in his own introspection, paid no heed to wagon or horse as he covered the straw-littered aisle from one end of the building to the other, while the north wind prowled the perimeter of the walls, plastered the moist flakes against the windowpanes, and, finding a loosened plank up near the roof line, slipped through with a keening wail like some lost soul in anguish.

Coby Starving Elk emerged from his quarters at the rear of the stable, holding in his right hand a couple of thick slabs of crusty bread surrounding half-a-dozen strips of bacon. The fat, still sizzled, its juices seeping into the thirsty bread.

"Want another one?" Coby asked, offering the sandwich in hand.

"No. I'm set," Tom answered. "But do not let me stop you."

Coby shook his head and, liking his bacon half cooked, took a bite. Grease dribbled down his chin and onto the bib of his overalls as he ambled down the center aisle. He wiped his mouth on his shirtsleeve and joined Tom at the window near the front door. Across the street the columns of Benedict's ostentatious dwelling rose like pillars of ice against the wintry backdrop of night.

"Yessir, Allyn Benedict did all right for himself," Coby muttered, his breath clouding the glass. He shivered and glanced sideways as a cold gust of wind swept through the open door, and saw Tom Sandcrane step outside. The iron hinges creaked in protest.

"*Saaa-vaaa!* What are you doing?" the stablekeeper said. He caught the door and followed Tom into the night. It was no longer snowing. The precipitation had tapered off, leaving only a patchwork accumulation on the wheel-rutted earth. Now and then an occasional flake fluttered out of the sky. One crystal struck Coby Starving Elk in the eyelid. The older man cursed, grabbed a checkered bandanna from his hip pocket, and dabbed at his face. The wind gust continued up the hill, rattling the branches of the oaks and cedars as it followed the well-worn path to the dark and silent ceremonial lodge some 250 feet up the slope.

Tom studied the hillside, turned the sheepskin collar of his denim coat up around his ears, then dug his right hand into his coat pocket for warmth.

"How long has it been since Luthor called a council and lit the ceremonial fire?" he asked.

Coby shrugged. "I cannot remember. A long time. After the land rush, maybe just once. Our people were selling and trading the land deeded them, everyone trying to be rich like Allyn Benedict. Including me." The stableman glanced over at the office and house of his employer. "See? I made it. I live right across the street from the richest man in the territory." He lifted the sandwich in salute, as if it were a drink, then brought it to his mouth, paused, scowled, and tossed the remaining bread and meat aside. "Now, see what you have done. I've lost my appetite." Coby snorted in disgust and tucked his hands into his armpits, resting his muscled forearms on his paunch. "Oh, some of us fared well. I heard Luthor paid off his debts a few weeks ago, though for a while there I thought he might lose the store. Little good it does him with Charlotte's getting herself killed. That fool Willem."

"You have him tried and convicted too," Tom said, continuing to scrutinize the hillside.

Come. We are here. We wait for you. The voice again. Coby could not hear it. But the words reverberated inside Tom's skull like an echo heard from afar.

"That's what everybody says."

"You open your mouth, but I hear Allyn Benedict's voice," Tom replied. He started up the overgrown path that led to the ceremonial lodge.

"Where are you going? It's too damn cold for such nonsense, Tom," Coby called out, his words falling on deaf ears. He turned and, muttering to himself about the foolishness of the young, retreated to the warmth of the barn and the back room he called home.

Tom stood outside the walls of the ceremonial lodge, his breath streaming on the cold breeze as he studied the building's bleak facade. Weeds crowded the doorway. Low-hanging branches scraped the rough hewn weathered exterior like talons clawing at the log walls.

Now that Tom had reached the entrance to the lodge, the voice in his head had ceased its demand. Sandcrane glanced over his shoulder at the sprawling settlement below and remembered how Cross Timbers had once been a cluster of a few buildings on a single street surrounded by a motley collection of huts and cabins. The amber glare from so many windows illuminated the darkness, the formless array of lights resembled the moon-dappled surface of a stream, sparkling in the wintry night. All that bright life offered a sharp contrast to the silent lodge lying in such a sad state of disrepair.

A shadow detached itself from the periphery of darkness. Tom froze and sucked in his breath as the spectral form glided out of the underbrush, the dry straw crackling beneath its footfall. This was no ghost. Tom's muscles coiled as the shape loomed over him and for a brief moment took on the form of some terrible bird of prey, until the "wings" became a black woolen cape draped across the muscled, sloping shoulders of Jerel Tall Bull.

"I knew you'd come," his voice rumbled. The moon poked through a veil of clouds and bathed both men in its boneyard glare. Tall Bull chuckled softly and tucked his large hands into the pockets of his frock coat.

Tom heard a horse neigh and paw the earth from somewhere behind the lodge. That explained how Jerel had arrived but had nothing to do with the reason for his being at the ceremonial lodge. Sandcrane held his ground as the man lumbered toward him. An inner voice cautioned him against retreating from the master of Panther Hall. First Jerel Tall Bull had invaded his dreams, now the man had intruded in person upon Tom Sandcrane's personal odyssey. Why?

"I saw you at Coby's. I knew with the lodge being so close you would have to climb the hill, to confront once more the scene of your disgrace."

Tom bristled. "None of this is any of your concern, Jerel."

"It has always been my concern." Jerel studied the younger man and, to his dismay, sensed the power in him, a force Sandcrane himself was only just discovering. Now was not the time or the place for a confrontation. "You think you know me. To you I am a gambler, a whore runner. But you know only my shadow."

Jerel glanced up at the moon, his features seemingly bloodless and solemn as he watched the clouds pass by, black bartentines sailing on some forbidden sea. "My grandfather's grandfather was Blood Hawk, the Arrow Keeper in the olden days when the Kiowa raided and stole the Mahuts. Blood Hawk pursued the Kiowa along with others of the tribe. Many battles were fought until the Sacred Arrows were at last recovered." Jerel's brows furrowed and his eyes hardened. "But the elders called a council and refused to allow Blood Hawk to receive the Mahuts into his care. By losing the Arrows he had broken the trust. Blood Hawk rode from his people and was never seen again. For many moons my family endured the shame until at last memories dimmed and the name of Blood Hawk was spoken no more." Jerel turned and stared at Sandcrane. "But I speak it, here and now."

"The past is a burden each of us must bear," Tom said.

"You have come home to your death, Tom Sandcrane. Most men run from their fate. But you seek it."

"Did Allyn Benedict send you to threaten me?" Tom asked, his voice hard.

"Benedict . . ." Jerel contemptuously repeated. "This has nothing to do with him. What lies between us is more than white man's gold. Or white man's oil."

"I do not understand you, Jerel," Tom said, wondering if the man had taken leave of his senses.

"I will tell you something. Listen. You will find it important one day. Behind Panther Hall is a trail through the woods that leads to Little Sister Creek. I have cleared a circle and lit a fire. I will be waiting for you there, holding your death in my hands."

"What new madness is this? Whiskey talk?"

"Do not worry. You will know the time." Jerel grinned. "The Maiyun will tell you. Or perhaps the hawk." He turned and with swiftness surprising for a man his size disappeared behind the ceremonial lodge. Tom remained still as a statue, puzzled by Tall Bull's remarks and shaken by their threatening tone and his reference to the hawk. He listened and heard the creak of saddle leather and then the sound of a horse picking its way upslope and brushing against ice-laden branches, showering the narrow path with broken twigs.

Memories assailed Tom Sandcrane, flooding back to the renewal ceremony when he had refused the Sacred Arrows and allowed them to pass from his father into Luthor White Bear's keeping. A mistake . . . perhaps . . . and yet he acknowledged the possibility even then that his actions might have been guided by the Maiyun, whose presence he had long denied. Steeling himself against the guilt, Tom walked to the entrance, hesitated, then ducked inside. The walls acted as a break from the biting wind. Tom cautiously approached the center of the circle. His legs felt numb from the cold seeping through his trouser leg, and he knew he ought to light a fire—but not here, not in this hallowed place, where a man must walk alone and face his troubled past. The images of yesterday danced in his mind as they had once upon the firelit walls. He had been so certain of the way of things, determined to bring about change without realizing the cost or the consequences.

I remember the firelight, the shadows on the walls, the drums beating like the heart of Maheo, the faces painted white for morning, red for thunder, yellow the color of sunset, and black, the killing storm, the stayed hand of death. . . .

The wraith-hawk came diving for him out of the deepest recesses of his mind, sweeping aside the other memories, its red eyes gleaming hatred, its talons once more eager to tear him limb from limb, to rip his heart out. Or his soul. The image blurred as Tom slammed facedown into the earth. The impact broke his concentration, loosed the hold of this horrid hallucination. Tom spat dirt and dust, then rose to his knees and sat on his haunches, gingerly rubbing his bruised cheekbone, still uncertain what exactly had happened.

Old terrors threatened to loose themselves once more upon his already damaged soul. When would it end? There was no doubting that the wraith's hellish resurrection was directly related to Tom Sandcrane's homecoming. Tom crawled unsteadily to his feet, shook the dirt from his frame, and gulped in several bitterly cold lungfuls of air until his head cleared.

"I am here," he whispered to the stillness, looking around at the circle of darkness. If the Maiyun were listening, let them hear. And if they chose not to reveal themselves, so be it. The time had come to find a bed and a fire to warm himself by. Summoning his courage, he turned his back on the gloomy interior and headed into the night.

A few moments later, and he was standing outside in the waning moonlight. As night's black cloak draped itself across the hillside, Tom Sandcrane made the best use of the fading moonlight to retrace his footsteps over a patch of snow. He crossed the clearing and picked up the overgrown path as it wound through the barren trees.

Tom had found no answers on the hillside. Indeed, the confrontation with Jerel Tall Bull had been the last thing he'd expected and left him utterly confounded, yet the effort had been worthwhile just the same. After all, he had learned at least two things.

One, the apparition that haunted his heart and mind had name. *Blood Hawk.*

And two, it was time to start carrying a gun.

CHAPTER THIRTY-NINE

A KNOCKING AT THE BACK DOOR ROUSED JOANNA FROM HER sleep. She sighed, a deep, sibilant exhalation that aptly expressed her very deep regret at being awakened and dragged from a rather sensual dream. She propped her head up and reached for the gold watch and fob she'd left on the dark-stained mahogany end table next to her bed. She opened the engraved cover and stared at the watch face.

Seven twenty-seven . . . oh my!

Could it be Tom at this hour? The dream had been of him. She blushed with the memory and laughed softly. Now, that was one dream whose contents he would never learn. Well, then again, maybe he just might, depending on how things worked out. She was worried for him; the visions, some of which he described, had chilled her blood. He had revealed enough of his intentions for her to know that Tom Sandcrane could be tempting trouble.

Visions . . . in another time or place he could be taken for a madman with such talk, but here in Oklahoma Territory things were different. This raw, primal frontier was evolving into a whole new world. But the gods of those who once had ruled this land died hard. It was enough to boggle her own sense of Christianity. However, as Father Kenneth often liked to quote from Shakespeare, "There are more things in heaven and earth than are dreamt of in all your philosophies." Joanna couldn't swear the priest's quote was entirely accurate—she had not read *Hamlet* in years—but the words sounded right, and she had come to accept their basic truth.

For the past three days Tom Sandcrane had ridden into town to keep a standing dinner engagement with her. Every night since his first visit, they had either prepared the evening meal in her kitchen or taken dinner at Yaquereno's. Of course, the relationship had not gone unnoticed. He was a Cheyenne and she was white, which offended the sensibilities of some of the locals.

And yet, as she was the only physician in the area, much of her conduct was overlooked or taken with the proverbial grain of salt. Joanna Cooper had also earned the respect of many of her neighbors, who would not tolerate any malicious gossip. In time those townspeople who worried about such matters would no longer care and move on to other scandals.

The knocking resumed. Whoever was at the back door was determined to see her. *Bang bang bang* . . . the glass pane rattled and the frame shook; the doorknob gave a furious turn.

"All right . . . I'm coming!" she called out, and swung her legs over the side of the bed, pulling on her dressing gown as she padded to the door. She released the latch, opened the door, and stepped back, surprised at the identity of her visitor. Red Cherries stood in the shadow of the house, a few feet from the door. The prostitute had wrapped her slender frame in a woolen shawl. Her features were hidden behind a smear of rouge and face powder. She wore a dress of indigo satin with silk ruffles across the low-cut bodice and torn pale silk trimming at the hem. Her long black hair was partly unpinned, and several strands fell across her shoulders and along her neck.

"Oh, it's you," Joanna said. She stared at the Cheyenne woman for a moment, then came to her senses and invited the woman into the kitchen. "Pardon me. Please come in."

Red Cherries hesitated.

"Please. I'm freezing," Joanna said, shivering. She was barefoot, and the cold morning air was pouring into the kitchen. Red Cherries nodded and then accepted the woman's offer.

"I left my horse around front. I looked through the window

and didn't see anybody, so I figured you might still be asleep."
Red Cherries glanced around at the kitchen, then ran her
hand along the table and took a seat. "Out at Panther Hall me
and the girls would just be getting to bed. To sleep, that is."
She lowered her eyes, for her meaning wasn't lost on the physician. Joanna Cooper nodded.

"Yes, then ... uh, well. If you'll excuse me for a moment,
I will just find my slippers. Make yourself comfortable."
Joanna retreated to her bedroom and closed the door. "Amazing," she muttered to herself. "What on earth ... ?" She
slipped out of her sleeping gown and into a chemise, cotton
hose, a dark-blue woolen dress, and a cotton blouse with a
row of tiny pearllike buttons down the ruffled front. She
tugged on a pair of half boots and tied back her auburn hair
with a leather string. By the time Joanna had finished dressing, she could smell the aroma of coffee. She arrived in the
kitchen to find that Red Cherries had built a fire in the stove,
filled a pot with water and coffee, and set it on to boil.

Red Cherries checked the pot and shook her head. "Coffee
isn't ready yet." She glanced in the direction of the skillet. "I
could fry you up some ham. Maybe make some fry bread."

"No ... just coffee when it's ready." Joanna sat at the table
and folded her hands on the dark, wine-colored surface. "But
help yourself," she added, finding this a most peculiar visit.

"No. I'll take some coffee, though. It's not as cold as it's
been, but I still took a chill." She chuckled ruefully. "Didn't
think to bring my coat. But I've always done things the hard
way." She glanced at the pot as if willing the coffee to be
ready to drink.

"It's probably strong enough," Joanna said. The prostitute
nodded and filled two cups, sliding one across the table to
the physician. Joanna nodded her thanks. "Red Cherries ...
this is an unexpected visit. Are you ill? Another of the girls?"

The Cheyenne woman shook her head no and gulped the
hot liquid. "I couldn't bury Clarice. The ground was too hard,
froze hard as rock out there. I tried but couldn't get much
dug, not enough to cover her proper." She kept her head lowered, staring at her reflection floating on the surface of the
contents of her cup. "Jerel gave orders to have her dragged off

and burned. Like some empty crate, or trash from the road-house. She didn't have anyone, no one to say words for her. And maybe she was a whore, but she was a fair and honest whore, and no man ever paid her that he didn't get his poke's worth." Red Cherries sniffed and wiped her shawl across her features, smearing the rouge and dabbing the moisture from her eyes. She swallowed, exhaled, and managed to regain her composure. It had been a long time since she'd cried.

"My God, he burned her?"

"Pete Elk Head hauled her off in an old blanket, soaked it in coal oil, and set her afire." Red Cherries' expression hard-ened. "I stayed by her side until the fire died out and all there was left was ashes and bone. I made up my mind right then and there I'd had my fill. There was a time I thought Jerel Tall Bull liked me. I even let him take me when it suited him. But none of it mattered to him—I was just another whore, that's all. Like poor Clarice. Damn men!" Red Cherries slammed the empty coffee cup down on the table. "I don't want to go back. And end up like Clarice—consumptive, coughing my lungs out, then dead and burned like yesterday's garbage. Miss Joanna, let me stay here. I can work, I can help you, you'll see. Blood doesn't scare me, and I've sewn up my share of wounds."

"Oh, I don't know . . ." Joanna said, somewhat alarmed, and taken aback by the woman's suggestion.

"I've seen your extra beds."

"Those are for patients."

"I can sleep on the floor in the front when there's folks staying over. I can cook. And when it comes to caring for a man, who knows better than one of us doves how to ease a boy's ailments?"

"Your treatment is not exactly what I would consider proper practice."

"You'd never want for customers."

"No, I can see that," Joanna laughed.

"Then I can stay? I'll be a help."

"But, Red Cherries . . . well . . ."

"I'll not go back to the Tall Bulls. Of course, they could

make trouble for you. I wouldn't blame you for being afraid of them."

Red Cherries stood and took a step toward the door.

"No!" Joanna spoke right on cue, galvanized into action by the prostitute's last remark, one that the Southern Cheyenne woman knew would elicit a response from the proud doctor. "No . . . you can stay. For a little while. Until we figure out what to do."

Red Cherries brightened. "I'll be a big help. You'll see."

Joanna closed her eyes a moment, envisioning the infirmary as the settlement's only bordello. *I must be mad*, she thought. "Please, Red Cherries. Not too big a help."

The navy-issue thirty-eight-caliber Colt spat flame three times in rapid succession, and the log in the gunsight jetted splinters of bark and wood slivers. Three slugs dead center. Powder smoke curled upward in the wintry sunlight.

The air was chilly, but not uncomfortably so. And with the barn completed Tom had taken a few moments for himself, strolling off from the ranch house with his gunbelt slung across his shoulder. He'd followed the tree-lined creek for a couple of hundred feet until an appropriate target presented itself, a cottonwood log abandoned in the mud by the last flash flood to turn the lazy creek into a raging torrent.

Then again, maybe it was the solitude he sought. Ever since Tom had told his father of the encounter with Jerel Tall Bull, Seth had been as protective as a mother hen, constantly on the lookout for his son, following him about the ranch and worrying into the night over what he considered Tom's casual response to Jerel's threats. Seth was all too familiar with Tall Bull's history and his family's connection with the Sacred Arrows. Blood Hawk, according to Tom's father, was a name to be reckoned with and nothing to take lightly.

Tom's description of his own dreams and the presence of the wraith-hawk when he lay wounded in Cuba and now here in Oklahoma only heightened Seth's concern. The elder Sandcrane had begun to fear for the safety of his son and the night before, on the porch, had even hinted that Tom ought to curtail his visit. But the choice was no longer Tom's alone, for he had set his feet upon the path the Maiyun had revealed, and he would follow it to the end, no matter the cost. That way, dead or alive, he would at last know peace.

He aimed and squeezed off the other three rounds, the checkered grip scraping the palm of his hand—*blam blam blam*—in rapid succession. Wood chips scattered over the opposite bank or floated down the gold-splashed surface of the creek. Tom lowered the revolver, and the swing-out cylinder allowed him to eject the shells easily. He tucked the barrel under his left arm and reloaded. The waters of Coyote Creek gurgled merrily underfoot.

"Not bad shooting," Philo Underhill laconically observed.

"Huh, better than you could ever do," said Tully, squatting on a nearby log.

"Don't you go giving me a hard time, you Creek bastard. Anyway, what would a plowboy like you know about anything? You couldn't hit the broad side of a barn from the inside."

"Now, see here, you sidewinding no-account half-breed . . . !" Nobody could muster up a good case of indignation better than Tully Crow.

"Both of you pipe down," Tom said, closing the revolver with a flip of his wrist. Tully always looked as if he could use a meal, and Philo, broad and sleepy-eyed, was a devil with the ladies, which drove his companion mad with jealousy. How could such a big, ugly lout attract the women? It was more than Tully could fathom. And both men had taken credit for Tom's success in the brigade as if he had reached the rank of sergeant solely through their intercession on his behalf.

"You'll spoil my aim," Tom added.

His arm shot out, the revolver an extension of that arm, his finger curled around the trigger, the gunsight centering on the log. Only this time there was a red-haired man standing by the target, his arms upraised, holding a Winchester carbine over his head, his freckled features split by a care-worn grin.

"Don't shoot, *na-vesene*," said Willem Tangle Hair. He was dressed in grubby Levi's and down-at-heel boots. His short-waisted wool coat was frayed at the cuffs, and his faded brown shirt was grease stained, but a broad, colorful bandanna circled his throat, and a sombrero hung down his back, caught by a leather string around his neck. He wore a Colt single-action revolver high on his waist in a battered holster. A saddle dangled from his left hand. The stirrups trailed in the water as he slogged his way across the creek, following a natural bridge of fallen timber until he could leap to the opposite bank and continue on along its sandy length until he stood face-to-face with Tom. Willem glanced down at the man he had called *na-vesene*—friend.

"You are still holding a gun," Willem observed. The barrel was pointed at his chest. Tom slowly lowered the weapon and tucked it into its holster. He wore the gun high on his left side, the butt forward, to facilitate a cross draw.

"Where have you been?" Tom asked. He put his arm around Willem's neck and hugged him. Willem reciprocated the embrace, then stepped back, studying Tom.

"Back in the timber. I still have family who will not believe the lies that are being said. They hid me." Willem waved his rifle in the direction he'd come. "It cost me a horse to get here. My old sorrel went lame back in the woods yonder."

"I figured you'd be gone to Texas."

"No, sir." Willem shook his head. "At least not until I find Charlotte's killer."

"What do you know of it?"

"Nothing much." Willem shrugged. "I found her at Panther Hall and tried to talk some sense into her. We quarreled and she left. I tried to catch up to her. Sure, I know she'd taken up with someone else. But I figured she'd come to her senses and see I was the one to build a life with. I never saw her again. The next morning my cousin brought word she'd been killed and everyone was blaming me." Willem shook his head. "I loved her, Tom. But things were never the same when I came back from Cuba."

He picked up a smooth oval stone and sent it skimming over the surface of the creek. "Then I heard you had returned and figured it was worth the risk seeing you."

"You risk a lot for friendship."

"No. I didn't just come to see a friend. I'm here to see the Arrow Keeper, for that's who you are. I knew that in Cuba, when you should have died but didn't, when you spoke your fevered dreams . . . I think the Maiyun brought you home to set things right. See, I too have come to believe there is value in the old ways."

"Come on to the house," Tom said. "We will seek my father's counsel in this as well." He turned and climbed the bank, carefully choosing his steps in the soft earth. Willem followed him, the saddle slung over his shoulder. Together the two men walked abreast, out of the woods and across the pasture. Sunlight bathed the ranch house nestled in its grove of barren trees. The two men hurried out of the pasture and into the yard. So much open ground made both feel uneasy and anxious for the safety of the cabin's interior.

A pair of gray mockingbirds alighted on the roof of the newly completed barn. Just the night before, Tom and his father had moved the horses into the stalls. The sturdy structure still needed finishing on the inside—the stalls were makeshift at best, and the tack room had yet to be walled in—but at least it provided shelter from the elements.

"I heard Seth's barn was burned," Willem said.

"We built it again. Father Kenneth helped a lot." Tom quickened his steps. The back of his neck had begun to tingle. Something was wrong, but he wasn't sure what. The best thing was to get under cover fast just in case any of Clay's deputies were lurking about. At least there was no one in the yard.

They hurried past the garden and the corral, where Seth saddlebroke his horses. Nothing seemed amiss, but of course Tom had spent most of the morning down by the creekbank. Perhaps he was being overly cautious. Seth might be in the kitchen fixing fry bread and beans, although it wasn't like him to spend much time indoors when the sun was shining and the wind was out of the southwest.

He heard a dog bark from the inside the house. General Sheridan announcing their arrival? He sure sounded angry at something . . . or someone. The dog abruptly changed its tone and began to howl as if kicked. Suddenly Tom grabbed his friend by the arm.

"Wait!" Before he could issue another command, the front

door opened and Abram Fielder, brandishing a long-barreled twelve-gauge, shotgun stepped out on the porch. Willem spun around, dropping his saddle, stumbling and issuing a sharp yelp of pain. Limping now, he made an awkward dash for the barn. Ahead of him, the big double doors swayed open, and a tall, lanky man, standing half in shadow, drew a bead on him. Benje Lassiter wasn't about to miss at this range. Tom could see the deputies had made good use of the barn, concealing their horses and enabling them to trap Willem in a cross fire.

Seth emerged from the house and stood alongside Abram. He held up his hands in a gesture of helplessness. General Sheridan came slinking out behind Seth, tail between his legs and looking somewhat embarrassed about the whole matter.

Willem halted in his tracks and, realizing he was trapped, raised his hands. Benje Lassiter stepped past the doors, his rifle steady. One false move and he'd drill Willem through the heart.

"Nice barn, Sandcrane," Lassiter said. It had certainly suited their purposes.

"Yeah," Tom scowled. "I may burn the damn thing down myself."

CHAPTER FORTY

B Y NIGHTFALL EVERYONE IN CROSS TIMBERS HAD HEARD OF THE capture of Willem Tangle Hair. One could only guess he was the subject of discussion behind every shuttered door, by home hearth and in restaurants and saloons. There were cries to see justice done from the men. And of course the women would sleep safe now that the cold-blooded killer was behind bars.

Cheyenne began drifting in from Rabbit Town, some gathering at Luthor White Bear's mercantile. Others clung to the shadowy alleyways or made rough camp at the base of Council Hill. They came with the thunderheads that had begun to billow to the north and west. Storms were coming. People could smell it in the air. Storms were coming soon.

In Allyn Benedict's house the storms had already arrived.

"You brought him in alive!" Allyn Benedict paced his study like a caged beast. He glared at his son slumped in the corner in a wing-back leather chair.

"Benje and Abram caught him. But if I had been there, I would have allowed him to surrender all the same."

"Are you mad?" Allyn paused in front of a liquor cabinet, opened the cut-glass doors, and poured himself a tumbler of Scotch. "I'd have expected such foolish behavior from your mother, trundling off back east at a moment's notice. But not you. I raised you smarter."

Allyn gulped the drink, closed his eyes, and allowed the alcohol to soothe his rattled nerves. All right, he had an alternate plan. There were always Luthor White Bear and his relatives. He imagined they'd already begun to pass the bottle. Give them another day to get their courage up, to let the fires of rage smolder and burn, to become a wildfire, out of control. Well, not out of his control.

"I'll send for the circuit judge in the morning," Clay said. "He could be here before the week's out. Then again, I might have to bring the half-breed to Tulsa."

"No, you won't."

"What's that supposed to mean?"

"Never you mind. I'm reporting a rash of thefts out at the oil fields. Leave tomorrow. Take a couple of days to investigate."

Clay rose from the chair and stalked across the room. "Do you know what you're asking me to do?"

"I do not recall asking. I'm your father. And I am *telling* you to do this." Allyn tapped the tin star pinned to Clay's vest. "I put that there and I can take it away. Maybe I ought to, since its luster seems to have blinded you to your own family."

Clay shook his head. "I'm like some piece of a puzzle. All my life you've been trying to fit me into the picture of your own ambitions. For the first time in my life I've been somebody, all on my own. And people have looked up to me. When I walk the streets, they say, 'Good morning, Sheriff' and 'Howdy, Mr. Benedict' and 'Thanks for your help.' I know you railroaded my appointment through the county officials. You probably bought a portion of the votes. But I've done the job. And been proud."

"Then all the more reason you should head out to the oil fields. This way you save your blasted pride and I do what needs to be done and no one is the wiser."

Clay turned away from his father and ambled toward the door. He placed his hand on the dark brass knob, then glanced back at Allyn.

"Maybe mother was smarter than any of us. She got as far from you as she possibly could." He opened the door and stepped into the foyer. He could hear his father's muffled footsteps on the carpet but did not wait to hear what the man might add.

Allyn called to his son but reached the foyer as the front door swung shut. Benedict stiffened. The lad's parting remark had hurt. *Ungrateful*, Allyn fumed. The boy was ungrateful. He turned and spied Emmiline standing behind him in the hall. She wore a pale-green dressing gown fronted with lace bows. In her right hand she held a book, in the left a teacup and saucer.

"How long have you been there?"

"Long enough," she replied.

"Forget what you heard," he said. "This does not concern you, my dear." He grabbed a coat and hat from a peg by the door. "I'll be back in a few hours." It was time for another ride to Panther Hall. Jerel Tall Bull could be a troublesome brigand at times, but he had his uses. And tomorrow Allyn would have need of the man's special talents. He walked over and kissed Emmiline on the cheek. She recoiled slightly, but he was too preoccupied to notice.

CHAPTER FORTY-ONE

I T ISN'T BROKEN," JOANNA SAID, KNEELING ALONGSIDE THE COT and cradling Willem's foot. He winced as she probed his ankle first, then began to massage the damaged foot gently. Tom watched from outside the cell. Benje Lassiter stood alongside him, munching on a griddle cake he ate rolled up like a tortilla.

"I could have told you that," the dour old bird sniffed. Abram Fielder poked his graying head around the doorway, and when he saw the tender treatment Willem was getting, the deputy's eyes lit up with envy.

"After you get done with 'red hair' maybe you could sort of take a look at my neck, Doc," Abram called out. "It's been powerful painsome of late." He gingerly touched his neck and turned his head from side to side with a great show of discomfort.

Joanna emerged from the cell and ordered Benje to heat some water so that the prisoner could soak his injured ankle.

"Ma'am, I can't see where we need to worry about his ankle. It don't make no never mind if he limps up the scaffold or takes them final steps two at a time."

"Heat some water," she said, staring him down. "I want that foot to soak. And see it keeps warm back here. He won't be able to wear a boot with all that swelling. I'll be back to wrap the ankle with strips of buckskin."

"Uh, yes, ma'am." Benje retreated to the outer office and set a kettle on the Franklin stove. Joanna followed him out of the cell area. Abram, with a ring of black iron keys in hand, sauntered down the aisle to Willem's cell and locked the barred door.

"He can't even walk, much less run," Tom ruefully observed.

"Just a formality," Abram said. "Like excusin' yourself when you break wind in church." He returned to the front room where he continued to complain of neck pain.

"Are you really hurting?"

"Oh, yes, ma'am." The grizzled old deputy made a pitiful face.

"Well, I need to treat it the same way as I did the prisoner's," Joanna said,

"Mighty kind of you, Doc," Abram replied, leaning forward so that she might massage his neck.

"As soon as that water's hot, fill a bucket for Mr. Fielder. I want him to go soak his head."

Lassiter chuckled. "My pleasure, ma'am."

Abram looked up, positively dismayed. The front door opened and Clay Benedict entered, glancing around the room to make a quick assessment of the people within. He saw Tom standing back by the cells, and the physician replacing the tools of her trade in her medical bag.

"Sure you didn't leave him a saw or stone chisel, Doctor Cooper?"

"Just some dynamite," she replied.

He brushed past her, showing no reaction, and continued into the back hall, where he stopped before Willem's cell. He glanced at Tom, then turned his attention on Willem.

"You've done it this time, Willem."

"I didn't kill Charlotte White Bear," the breed retorted. "No matter how many folks like Luthor and your father say I did."

"You should have kept running. It would have saved us all some grief. You most especially."

"Maybe you should be more concerned with seeing justice done than saving yourself *grief*, Sheriff," Tom interjected.

Clay spun around as if he'd been physically struck, his eyes wide and glaring. "And maybe I ought to lock you up for hid-ing out a fugitive."

"You'd have to build a case on lies," Tom said. "So, tell me, Clay, does that badge stand for something, or is it just another toy from your father's hand?"

"Get out of my jail. Get out before I lock you up and throw away the key!"

Tom Sandcrane waved in the direction of his friend, then slowly ambled up the passage between the cells. Joanna was waiting for him in the outer office, a black woolen cloak draped around her shoulders. Tom paused and glanced from Abram to Benje, assessing their strengths and weaknesses from what little he had gleaned during the ride from Coyote Creek. The deputies seemed decent enough, with no particu-lar prejudices. They had merely been doing their job that morning. They had come across a fresh set of tracks, discov-ered Willem's horse, then ridden on ahead to the Sandcrane ranch to set a trap.

But it was asking a lot of such men to make a stand against their own neighbors if a mob came against the jail. Fortu-nately, the fieldstone walls were built thick and strong. That was some security. Of course, once the door was breached . . .

As for Clay Benedict, Tom sensed the man's turmoil, the di-visions in his soul that were warring with one another. And why was the sheriff so dismayed that Willem had remained in the area instead of running off to Texas or the Far West? Clay was anything but overjoyed to have apprehended Willem Tangle Hair. Again, why?

Perhaps Clay was merely hoping to avoid a confrontation with Luthor White Bear and his mob of relatives and support-ers. On the other hand, the sheriff might know more than he was letting on about Willem's guilt . . . or innocence.

Tom opened the door for Joanna, then joined her outside on the raised porch that ran the length of the sheriff's office and jail. It was no more than a fifteen-minute walk from Luthor's mercantile uphill to the porch steps of the jail.

"What is it, Tom?" Joanna asked. She glanced up as blue lightning shimmered to the north, followed by the rumble of thunder like distant drums.

"It won't take them long to get here."

"Who?"

"Friends . . . neighbors, for the most part . . . but they'll be a mob, with the mind and heart and soul of a mob, coming for Willem and ready to go through anyone who stands in their way." Tom started down from the porch, his collar turned up around his neck, his black hair streaming past his cheek. He realized she wasn't with him and looked around for her.

"You'll be standing in their way, won't you, Tom?" she said, more as a statement of fact than a question.

"My dreams have told me this should be done, for *this* I am here, to make my people live again." From any lips but his, the words of madness. "The power of the Mahuts no longer protects and nourishes the Southern Cheyenne. We must be renewed if we are to walk the Great Circle again. Tomorrow may be the first step." He walked up to her and held out his hand. "Will you walk with me, Doctor Cooper?"

Ignoring his hand, she descended the few shallow steps without any assistance. He knew she would—predictability was one of her charms. The woman was strong and refused to be coddled. Even on the way back to the infirmary, though she enjoyed his company, Joanna couldn't help inching ahead.

The three lanterns lit the area around the woodpile, providing Seth enough light by which to chop wood. He had noticed Joanna was getting low on fuel for the stoves and thought he could put his time there to good use while Tom and the doctor were off to check on Willem. Also, this provided him the perfect opportunity to stay outside and avoid Red Cherries, whose presence at the clinic had him completely baffled. The woman had literally taken over the responsibility of cleaning and cooking for the doctor, which was a real improvement. He had never met a better or kinder person than Joanna—but intelligence and wit and compassion had nothing to do with boiling coffee, or making beans or stew, or frying chicken or rabbit, all talents that had eluded the doctor. So Red Cherries was a welcome addition, and at

least Joanna wouldn't accidentally poison some cowpoke after
setting his leg and then inviting him to dinner.

Seth was pleased to see Red Cherries away from Panther
Hall and the influence of Jerel Tall Bull. It shamed him to
think he had contributed to her downfall long ago. The notion of being alone with her made him weak at the knees and
reawakened in him the desire for drink, an ever-present demon he continually had to tame. So instead of raiding the
doctor's liquor cabinet he remained outside after brushing
down the horses and seeing them fed, and satiated his crav-
ings with a shot of hard physical labor.

Seth found his rhythm by the third log, the ax flashing in
the lantern light, biting into the wood, splitting it in two,
again and again. The pile of logs began to shrink. After the
better part of an hour Seth laid the ax aside, gathered an
armful of kindling, and carried it over to the wood box near
the back door. He had just completed his second trip when
Red Cherries opened the back door and caught him at the
steps.

Her clothes were simple now, a beige woolen skirt, a home-
spun apron, and a cream-colored cotton blouse buttoned at
the throat. None of the clothes from her former profession
would have suited the infirmary.

"Hard work can make a man thirsty. Come sit a spell.
You've earned your coffee and bread."

"Just coffee, *Kanee-estse*," Seth replied, closing the firebox.
It made a good bench seat for him to rest upon. He dusted
his hands on his trouser legs and gratefully accepted the mug
of coffee the woman handed him. She sat on the steps and
looked out across the backyard and the houses beyond,
whose windows glowed amber. "You surprised to find me
here?"

"I about fell off my horse."

Red Cherries softly chuckled. "Yeah. Me too. I reckon if it
wasn't for Willem's capture, my being here would be the talk
of the town."

"It'll take a while for some, but they'll come around. There's
no law I know of says you owe Tall Bull a damn thing. You

did right by leaving. That kind of life is a rough cut down a short road."

"You didn't think so when your hair was dark," Red Cherries pointedly observed.

"Hell, I didn't *think* at all—that was my trouble. And I brought misfortune to myself . . . and to you. I do regret that, *Kanee-estse*."

Red Cherries studied Seth's features. They had been lovers once, witless, foolish, deliriously passionate lovers whose union had sowed the seeds of dishonor and pain. But that was behind them.

"Ha. The sun has already set on those days. It is the morning we must face."

"Yes," Seth agreed, and drained the mug. When he handed it back to the woman on the steps, their fingertips brushed, a fleeting press of flesh, a moment come and gone. "We have room out at the ranch. That is, if things don't work out for you here in town. You could stay with us."

Red Cherries shot him a suspicious glance.

"No, I mean . . ." Seth struggled to rephrase his offer. "You could have my room, and I'd bunk in with Tom or in the front room. At least until we built you a place of your own. And you could help out with running things . . . or just do whatever you like."

The woman smiled and shook her head. "I think I'll try my own way for a while," she said, standing and smoothing her apron with her hands.

"Can't say I blame you," said Seth as he started back toward the woodpile.

"Seth . . . maybe on a warm spring day I might take a ride out your way and see what you've done," Red Cherries called out to him.

The man glanced around at her. "Be my honor to show you." Then he continued along the well-worn path to the pile of logs with which one farmer had paid his medical bill. On the plains in winter, firewood was always a welcome currency. Seth heard the rumble of thunder as the wind began to gust. Suddenly he heard the rush of wings and looked up as a horned owl swooped past on its nocturnal quest for food. But

to Seth this was more than a natural occurrence, no mere coincidence. The town was on the brink of an outbreak of violence. Some night soon Luthor's friends and family would
become a mob in search of vengeance. Blood was going to
flow like rain. The owl had warned him in its passing. And
owls don't lie.

CHAPTER FORTY-TWO

TROUBLE CAME FROM THE NORTH, LIKE THE STORMS THAT SPAT fire and scoured the plains, the wooded flanks of Council Hill, and the town below with a weeping wind. There were songs for days like this, mournful songs hinting at the violence and the death that men are often blind to and, in their ignorance, unleash.

A fine, misting rain began to fall before sunrise and brought a gray dawn, beginning the kind of day no man or woman cares to trade for a warm feather bed and a willing partner. But Olivia Flannery had children to teach, and to her that was more of a vocation than a job. And though she hated to quit Clay's side, she crawled out of bed, paid a visit to the privy, and returned complaining of the cold rain and miserable mud. A rumble of thunder underscored her sentiments. However, the storm never quite broke, and the rain tapered off before she had finished dressing. When she emerged from behind her dressing screen, all prim and proper and ready to stare down the older boys who continually attempted to disrupt class, she found Clay still in bed, propped against a pillow, a bottle of whiskey balanced on his hairy chest, a glass tumbler in his hand. He poured a drink and downed it in a single motion.

All night a dark mood had hovered over him like some harpy circling on black wings of misery and pain. But he refused to share his torment, keeping his revelations for the "friend" in the bottle.

"Rotgut liquid always has an answer," Olivia remarked. "Trouble is, it's always the wrong one. I know. We Irish have been looking in the same place for years. My father and brothers, lump them all together and you'd still not have enough to make one sober man."

"Don't lecture me." Clay poured another drink and continued to stare at the foot of the bed. "I'm not one of your students."

"No. But if you were, I swear we'd have a proper row." The schoolmarm crossed to the bed and sat on the corner, placing a hand on his ankle. "Are you still leaving for the oil fields? You will be careful, won't you? Those roustabouts are a hard crew, and even a thief could be dangerous if you corner him."

"There hasn't been any theft," Clay muttered.

"But last night you said . . ."

"What my father told me to say!" Clay drained the contents of his glass. The whiskey was burning a hole in his gut. Now, if it would only deaden his thoughts. "But I might as well stay here. It's as good a place as any. Just so long as I'm out of the way when Luthor's mob comes for Tangle Hair." He met the teacher's stare. "Don't worry . . . Abram and Benje will take off at the first sign of trouble. Those two aren't about to put themselves in harm's way for Willem."

"Oh, my God, a lynching . . . no, Clay, no. You cannot be a party to such a thing. Why it's . . . it's . . ."

"Murder. Of course it is. Oh, some will call it justice served. But I'll know—more than anyone except Charlotte's killer—that tonight an innocent man will die."

Olivia heard the clock in the outer room strike seven times. It was time to start for the schoolhouse, but she could not tear herself away from the man she loved, not after what he had revealed.

Clay held up the bottle and sloshed its contents. He still had plenty, but then again, the day was young. The minutes would fly and the night of shame would begin. His gaze settled on the star pinned to the vest he had tossed onto the bed the night before. That silly piece of metal had meant a lot to him over the past months. The badge had provided him something his life had lacked. It was impossible to pinpoint the moment he had begun to take the responsibility seriously—things just sort of evolved. A store was robbed, he caught the thieves. A horse was stolen, he tracked it down. In short, he did the job and handled it well; when he stood for the law, it meant something. Maybe this sense of honor had always been in him, though buried beneath the weight of his father's expectations. After tonight Clay could never wear the badge again. The life he had begun to dream of for himself would end as the lynch mob's noose tightened around Willem's throat.

"Innocent?" Olivia's hand gripped the blanket. "What do you mean?"

"Just that I know who really killed Charlotte White Bear."

"But how?"

"Simple. The killer told me."

Olivia wasn't sure she wanted to hear, yet she felt compelled to ask. "Who?"

Clay chuckled mirthlessly and poured another drink and, in a wavering voice, heavy with loss, spoke the name.

Two men walked side by side along the boardwalk fronting the buildings on Main Street. The rain had ended, at least for the time being, though the clouds threatened more precipitation later in the day. The advancing cold front had not gathered enough momentum to push it way south and so remained stationary over the territory while a second front hurled down from Canada.

Tom Sandcrane glanced aside at Father Kenneth. "You certain you don't want me to accompany you into the mercantile?"

"I see no purpose in it," said the priest. "Besides, I have nothing to fear from Luthor. We are old friends."

"He may not see it that way."

"I will take my chances. Good luck with Allyn. And be wary of those four who rode into town this morning."

Trouble from the north, Tom thought, where Panther Hall

stood silent and shuttered against the elements. The Tall Bull brothers, Pete Elk Head, and John Iron Hail . . . what where they up to, why were they there? Tom had spied them from the window of Yaquereno's restaurant, where he was having a cup of coffee and a bowl of cobbler, engaged in a congenial conversation with the owner. James Yaquereno, like many of the merchants, hoped to avoid trouble and wanted nothing to do with the hard lot congregating in front of the mercantile.

"Are you listening to me?" asked the priest. "I have a feeling Jerel and his brother are on the prod."

"Yeah," Tom glumly replied, and his tone of voice revealed how hopeless he felt the situation really was. Joanna had returned from the jail that morning with news that Clay had supposedly left town to investigate a rash of thefts up at the oil fields. Tom did not believe this excuse for a minute. He was certain Allyn had ordered the sheriff out of Cross Timbers, practically inviting the mob to storm the jail. Tom was determined to find out the reason for Benedict's actions and to save his friend whatever the cost. He was disappointed in Benedict's son, though. Tom had sensed a change in Clay and expected more backbone from the sheriff.

Father Kenneth started across the street toward the mercantile. Tom Sandcrane tensed as Little Ned Scalp Shirt moved forward out of a cluster of twenty or so hard-looking roughnecks to intercept the priest, who kept up an animated conversation with the young man all the way to the front door. Then he vanished inside, having talked his way past Little Ned before the Cheyenne could get in a word. Tom breathed a sigh of relief and pressed on to the offices of Benedict Exploration and Development, where an officious clerk assured his visitor that Allyn Benedict had not come in that day, but if Tom would care to leave a message, he would personally deliver it to the president of the company.

Tom excused himself and continued on to Benedict's house. The Tall Bull brothers were seated on the front porch, cups of coffee in their hands. Pete Elk Head lounged against one of the marble lions. John Iron Hail was just returning from the livery stable across the road. All four men wore rain slickers and carried Winchester rifles. No doubt they had revolvers hidden beneath their coats, but Tom started up onto the porch just the same. Curtis rose and placed himself in front of the mahogany double doors. Jerel stood, uncoiled his powerful physique, and plodded past the pillars, descending the steps until he came face-to-face with Tom.

"Mr. Benedict is a mite under the weather. He won't be seeing anyone today."

"I thought you and Benedict ran together only at night. People might start wondering what you two have in common." Tom stepped back and called out, "You hear me, Allyn? Can you afford to be seen with the likes of the Tall Bulls by the light of day?"

"Shut your damn mouth," Curtis exclaimed, starting forward. His finger curled around the trigger of the Winchester. "We don't need to listen to this."

Pete Elk Head, expecting trouble, began to crouch by the lion, bringing his own carbine to bear on Sandcrane. One quick shot and Tom would be lying facedown in the mud.

Jerel waved his brother back, then, shifting his focus, fixed Pete in an icy stare. The man by the lion relaxed and lowered his carbine.

"Yes, keep a tight rein on them," Tom said. "Just as Allyn keeps one on you."

"Perhaps it is the other way around," Jerel said.

"Why did Allyn bring you to town?" Tom stepped back and looked up at the window overlooking the street. He could imagine Allyn behind the curtains, watching and waiting and plotting. "Why are you afraid of a trial, Allyn? Are you worried Red Cherries might tell what she knows about how you entertained Charlotte in the cabin behind the roadhouse?"

A few moments later the great doors were flung open, and Benedict, nattily dressed in his frock coat, shirt and vest, and tailored trousers, appeared in the doorway, his features flushed with anger. He was full of bluster and protest, a man caught in the web of his own lust.

"Damn you, Sandcrane, hold your tongue."

"A scandalous affair with a Cheyenne girl might be just the sort of conduct that would kill a political career."

"I will not permit this slander to continue," Allyn snarled, becoming increasingly bellicose the longer Tom remained in front of his house. "Nothing of the kind ever happened. It will be my word against that of a whore's."

"I think enough folks will believe her, Allyn. But, of course, if there is no trial, that information might not see the light of day. So you brought in Jerel and the rest to make certain Willem dies without ever standing before a judge."

"You misjudge us, Tom. Mr. Benedict fears some kind of mob action could damage his property," Jerel explained. "We are here to keep that from happening."

John Iron Hail arrived and took up his place over by the second stone lion. He nodded to Allyn Benedict but reported to Jerel.

"Horses have been looked after," he said. The Cheyenne touched the brim of his hat as he faced the man in the street. "Howdy, Tom."

"John . . ." Tom nodded. He glanced up at Benedict, secure in his wealth, believing himself above the reach of lesser men, then looked back at John. "You're walking the wrong side. But there's still time to cross over."

"Kind of muddy looking where you stand," John laconically replied, rolling a cigarette. He found a match in his coat pocket, struck it on his rifle stock, lit the cigarette, and soon exhaled a cloud of tobacco smoke—all, possibly, a show for the benefit of the men with whom he rode.

"And hard going," Tom added. "But it is the right path."

"Maybe you better worry about yourself, Sandcrane. From where I'm standing, you're the one who's got a long walk up an empty street," Allyn called down. "Now, get away from my house or I'll have you shot for trespassing." He retreated inside and slammed the doors, as if to punctuate his threat.

Tom glanced toward town. Indeed, Cross Timbers seemed deserted. There was little traffic on Main Street or on the walkways. Everyone seemed to be waiting for the worst to happen, for an outbreak of violence. No one wanted to be caught outdoors when they could watch and wait from the safety of home or shop.

The only sign of life was the crowd in front of the mercantile, a gathering of angry, quarrelsome men, fueling their outrage and bracing their courage with copious amounts of whiskey. Come nightfall they'd have talked themselves into a lynching.

"Look at them," Jerel said, drawing close. "Things are going to get ugly by sundown."

"With your help, no doubt," Tom said without facing the man.

"Maybe so. But none of it matters. We have more important business, you and I," said Jerel. "When this is ended, remember, we will be waiting for you. In the clearing beyond Panther Hall."

" 'We'?"

"Yes. Blood Hawk and I." Jerel softly laughed. "The Maiyun have brought you home to die. I, who have walked in your soul, know this."

Tom's blood ran cold at Jerel's words. Nightmares of old filled him with doubts. Yet he refused to buckle before Jerel's steel-eyed stare. And when he spoke, it was in a voice so quiet that Jerel had to strain to hear. Yet that was power, to make a man lean forward, off balance, and listen.

"I am a singer. I too can walk on moonlight. Remember, the Old Ones are tricksters. Honor them, but do not trust them. We will see who the Maiyun have called by name."

Tom stepped back and indicated the others with a wave of his hand. "Tell the white man who runs you I will be waiting at the jail. There will be no hanging tonight." As if casually dismissing the threats he had heard, Sandcrane turned on his heels and started back into town, sensing his barbed words had struck home.

Jerel's features bunched and became ugly, his eyes narrowed into slits. Curtis left his position by the door and ambled forward to stand alongside his brother.

"What'd he say?"

"Nothing," Jerel growled. He glanced over his shoulder at the stained-glass windows in the double doors. Jerel Tall Bull didn't care why Benedict wanted the half-breed dead. Allyn had paid him in gold to see that Luthor's mob didn't back down at the last minute, and that was all that mattered.

Lynching Willem Tangle Hair was a business matter, simple as that. But Tom Sandcrane was something else entirely. The man had to die. Of that there was no doubt; Jerel's own ghosts demanded it.

And killing him was going to be a pleasure.

CHAPTER FORTY-THREE

NIGHT FELL AND THE WINDS OF CHANGE WERE RISING. THE sky shimmered with electric light, blue lightning that coruscated among the ugly thunderheads, and still the rain held while the town waited in fear of the coming storm.

Earlier that afternoon Tom and Seth had pushed a freight wagon in front of the jail to use as a makeshift barricade at the first muzzle flash. It wasn't much, but afforded a better field of fire than the jail itself. Despite the thick stone walls, the sheriff's office had too many blind sides; once trapped inside, the defenders could always be burned out. To the surprise of both father and son, Benje Lassiter and Abram Fielder had remained at their posts, though neither deputy looked thrilled with the prospect of facing down a lynch mob. Joanna had arrived at sundown, and for the past hour Tom had been trying to talk her into returning to the infirmary.

"What can I say to make you see how foolish it is for you to stay?" Tom was exasperated by her stubborn resolve to place herself in danger.

"Nothing that you haven't already said," Joanna told him, pouring a cup of coffee for herself. The interior of the sheriff's office was filled with tension that arguing failed to alleviate. Abram and Benje had excused themselves and wandered outside with Seth, leaving the couple to hammer out their differences.

"Look, Joanna, there might be shooting. All it takes is one

drunk to pull a gun, and we could have a real war on our hands."

"I have been shot at before, or have you forgotten?" the woman firmly replied. "And if war breaks out, then all the more reason for me to stay."

"Both of you are crazy," Willem called from his cell. "I don't want your blood on my hands."

Tom stood in the doorway to the cell block and saw his friend slumped forward, arms dangling through the bars. "You've got no say in this."

"Both of you are stubborn. You're going to get yourselves killed, dammit," Willem protested. It was clear the prisoner did not expect to see the sunrise.

"Not if I can help it," Tom said, closing the door. Then, turning, he confronted Joanna for the last time. "You aren't going to leave, are you?"

"No."

"At least stay inside."

"I'll go where I am needed."

Tom smiled despite himself and, realizing they were alone, reached out and pulled her to him and kissed her. Joanna was a willing recipient, her eyes gleaming in the lamplight and warm with affection for this man. It had been a long afternoon—the waiting had taken its toll, leaving him drawn and solemn looking. And yet that one kiss seemed to revive him, restoring the fire to his soul, renewing his determination.

He might have spoken what was in his heart at that moment but for Clay Benedict, who unexpectedly appeared in the doorway.

"Savaa-he!" Tom exclaimed in his native tongue.

"Yeah, I'm a little shocked to be here myself," Clay said.

He entered the office, followed by Seth Sandcrane and Benje Lassiter, the latter making no attempt to hide his relief at the sheriff's return. Abram remained on watch, standing upon the wagon bed and staring off toward the center of town. Clay headed for the gun rack and helped himself to a twelve-gauge shotgun, then crossed to his desk to search the side drawer for a box of shells.

"I heard you'd left for the oil fields," Tom said.

"I hid out at Olivia Flannery's house," the lawman replied. "Tried to crawl inside a bottle but couldn't find one big enough." A couple days' growth of stubble, and eyes red-rimmed from lack of sleep, added to Clay's disheveled appearance. Neither Tom nor Seth looked any too rested, for that matter.

"I tried that myself," Seth added. "Took me a hell of a long time to find out it couldn't be done."

Clay glanced in the man's direction, then nodded and shoved a handful of shotgun shells into his coat pocket. He found a couple of extra tin stars in the top drawer.

"I don't suppose either of you intend to leave." His answer was plainly visible in the expression of the two Cheyenne men in the office. "Might as well make your being here offi-cial." Clay added, handing the stars to Tom and Seth.

Tom picked up the deputy's badge and pinned it to his coat. His father quickly followed suit. Clay tossed a set of keys to Benje.

"Release the prisoner," the lawman said.

"Huh?"

"You heard me."

"We gonna let him go just like that?"

"Why not? He's an innocent man."

Lassiter's eyes widened. Tom did not seem as surprised by the sheriff's announcement. He filled a tin cup with black cof-fee and placed it on the lawman's desk. Clay muttered his thanks, took the coffee in his trembling hands, and gulped the steaming liquid.

"And you know who did murder Charlotte White Bear," Tom said.

Clay nodded and took another swallow of the bitter brew. "My father had just left a meeting at the bank when he saw Charlotte riding down Commerce. He followed her to the church and confronted her in the barn. Charlotte was furious. They had been together several times out at Panther Hall, in the guest house Jerel keeps there for those who require pri-acy. Father had been trying to end the matter . . . but Char-otte wouldn't hear of it. She wanted to confess to Father Kenneth all that had happened and how she was carrying my father's child." Clay stared at the contents of his cup, unable to face the people in the room. "My father must have gone crazy. They argued and then his hands were around her throat. And she was dead. He came to me that night, desperate. That's the only time I can remember him so frightened. I told him to wait, to see what happened when her body was discovered. How could I arrest my own father? And then word spread round about Willem's quarrel with Charlotte at Panther Hall, and everyone just assumed he had killed her. As long as he was free, I had time to wait. I could put on a show of looking for Willem and bide my time." He finished the coffee and looked up at Tom.

"He *is* my father. . . ."

Willem emerged from the cell looking utterly confused by the turn of events Tom motioned toward the gun rack.

"Better grab a rifle. You might have to convince Luthor's people at gunpoint that you had nothing to do with Charlotte's death."

"Will somebody please tell me what's going on?" the red-haired breed grumbled, but did as he was told.

"Appears you're a free man, just like I said," Benje Lassiter told him. "Lucky, ain't you?"

"Hey!" Abram called out from the wagon. "They're coming! A whole dad-blamed army of 'em!"

Tom started toward the door. "Willem, you better stay put. And keep Joanna with you."

"Now, wait a second," Joanna exclaimed. But Tom had already vanished through the doorway, followed by Seth and Benje Lassiter. Tom, however, reappeared, his wiry physique filling the doorway as he addressed the man behind the desk.

"You've come this far, Clay. Are you going all the way?"

Allyn Benedict's son glanced aside at the Cheyenne. He set the cup down, slid back his chair, and slowly stood. Cradling the twelve-gauge scattergun in the crook of his arm, he stepped around the desk and started out of the room. "All the way," he said.

There was law in Cross Timbers after all.

*   *   *

Father Kenneth kept up a steady stream of entreaty, hurrying to keep abreast of the volatile group of men who had left the mercantile armed with guns, torches, and a lynch rope and were marching a straight path among the cabins and houses on the south side of town. Frightened residents hurried to close and fasten their shutters and bolt their doors so as not to have a part in what was about to transpire. This was justice meted out frontier-style, as harsh and cruel as the crime that had been committed.

"Luthor, stop them!" the priest cried out, attempting to shoulder his way past Ned Scalp Shirt and his sons. Matt held the lynch rope, a rough hemp cord with a proper noose at the end. Little Ned, bathed in torchlight, had already drawn his gun and was ready and anxious for trouble. Liquor burned in his gut, giving him the raw, senseless courage fools are made of.

"Eye for an eye, Kenneth," Luthor called out. His vision had narrowed until all he could see was the act of vengeance he hoped would heal his tortured soul. Willem had to die, and maybe then Luthor might be able to expiate himself of the blame he felt, the responsibility he bore for all the misfortune that had befallen him. "Blood for blood and life for life!" he shouted. "I read that in your books, priest."

"You cannot take the law into your own hands. Do so and you will forfeit your almighty soul. In God's name I demand you turn aside." Father Kenneth glanced around at the men, many of whom he recognized, for he had baptized their children and nursed their sick in the days before Joanna Cooper. Joshua Mule Ride . . . Andrew Sharp Horn . . . and you, Dolph Landers . . . I know you to be good men. It's whiskey that's clouded your thoughts. I know you . . . every man here. And so help me . . . oooohh!"

Curtis felled the priest with a sharp, quick blow to the back of the head. Luthor heard the man cry out and altered his course to work his way over to the priest's side. Father Kenneth lay sprawled in the street, a trickle of blood oozing from a lump on his scalp. Curtis grinned and holstered the revolver he had used to club the priest. "That put an end to his chattering."

Luthor slapped Curtis across the face hard enough to

knock the man on his backside. Jerel rode up on is gelding
and put the horse between Luthor and Curtis. Pete Elk Head
and John Iron Hail rushed to help Curtis to his feet.

"Let me alone," he snapped, pulling free of their hands.
"You crazy old bastard."

"He was only trying to help, Luthor. We all are." Jerel had
to fight to keep his horse under control as lightning crackled
and thunder rode the sky.

"Go to hell! I curse the day your path ever crossed mine,"
Luthor snarled. His voice quivered as he spoke; his hands
whitened where he gripped the Winchester rifle in his hands.

Jerel leaned over. "If it wasn't for me and my money, you'd
be just another shiftless red nigger from Rabbit Town, and
don't you forget it."

"C'mon, Luthor!" one of the men carrying a torch called out.

"Ain't no time to fight among ourselves, Luthor," said Ned
Scalp Shirt. "Any man wants to see justice done is welcome."
He tilted a bottle to his lips and rained the last drop of whiskey. "And any man tries to stop us . . ." He tossed the bottle
in the air and then drew, but Little Ned was the first to snap
off a shot, followed by a half-dozen guns in a ragged volley.
The bottle exploded in midair, and a cheer rose from the
mob. The men started forward again, sweeping Luthor along
at the forefront, in a tide of bloodlust and righteous anger. An
innocent girl had been cruelly murdered. The killer had no
right to live, to see another dawn while she lay cold and lifeless in her grave.

Like a vengeful beast with a single mind the mob surged
forward, crossing the final stretch of open ground between
the last few houses and the jail itself, the solitary fortresslike
structure now besieged.

From horseback Jerel recognized Clay in front of the wagon,
with Tom Sandcrane at his side. Now, that was unexpected.
What kind of game was Benedict's son playing? No matter.
There was Tom, defiant, a sitting target. And the lynch mob was
heavily armed and as easy to ignite as a powder keg. Jerel nodded to Pete Elk Head and Curtis, who began to fan out through
the crowd. John Iron Hail appeared to balk at Jerel's unspoken
command, as if at the last minute he was rethinking his options.

and had become uncertain of his own loyalties. Jerel mentally noted he would deal with the man at some later date; he slowly drew his revolver from his belt and thumbed the hammer back, all the while keeping the Colt out of sight.

Tom glanced over his shoulder at Seth, who was standing behind the wagon, a rifle balanced on the wooden siding. Abram and Benje were standing on the porch. Lanterns hung from every post, their glare mingling with that of the oncoming torches.

"Keep your head down, old one," Tom called to his father.

Seth frowned. "Ha. Old. You be wary. The Maiyun come and may call your name this night."

"And I will answer," Tom replied.

Clay studied the man at his side. The irony of the situation was not lost on him. "I never thought we'd be standing together for anything," the lawman said to Tom. "Hell, I don't even know you. Not really." The sky shimmered with a lurid bone-white glare. A moist wind, thick with the smell of rain, moaned as it gusted through the alleys. Heaven was poised to unleash its torrent. A single heavy drop spattered off the iron-rimmed wagon wheel behind the two men. Others followed, increasing in number as the clouds dissolved into a downpour. Lightning forked down and struck a tree on Council Hill, limbs burst into flame, the trunk split and twisted with a terrible crash.

"There have been steep gullies between us, yet our shadows crossed over. Now we walk the way of the Great Circle together." Tom stared down at his gloved hand. Rainwater funneled off the brim of his hat as images of Cuba flooded his thoughts, of the friends he had led to their deaths, of the horror and the dark and bloody ground. He drew his revolver, the long-barreled Colt thirty-eight, a double-action weapon that fired as fast as he could pull the trigger. A second gun, also a thirty-eight, with a shorter barrel, bulged in his right coat pocket.

"If you say it's a good day to die, I may shoot you myself," Clay grumbled. Yet he had begun to understand some of Tom's remarks. Indeed, confession was good for the soul. It was as if he had unburdened himself of a terrible weight. Bitter times might lie ahead, but he would meet them head-on.

"No problem, Sheriff," Tom said. "That's one of the old ways I can do without."

The lynch mob massed before them, the hostile faces taking in the fact that there were several well-armed men blocking the path to the jail.

"Stand aside!" a voice called out. "We aim to have Willem Tangle Hair and will not be denied."

"Go on home, men. Disperse, I say. Cross this road and it will go badly for you."

"We've no quarrel with you, Sheriff," a figure in the rain bellowed.

"There be some of your friends and neighbors here, Clay. Would you shoot us down?"

"I have no friends in a lynch mob."

"And is that Tom Sandcrane with you? Trust him to turn on his own kind!" another voice cried. Tom thought it sounded suspiciously like Curtis Tall Bull, but he could not locate the man among the torchlit crowd.

"You've come to do harm to an innocent man," Tom shouted, striving to be heard above the downpour. The road separating the mob from Willem Tangle Hair's defenders was swiftly being transformed into a quagmire. Tension was as thick as the electricity in the air. Luthor's men, already rattled by the storm's violent display, were primed and skittish as a herd of cattle.

"Willem is an innocent man," Tom added.

Lightning flashed. Squinting through the rainy curtain, Tom saw Jerel Tall Bull on horseback behind the throng, raising a long-barreled pistol. "The time for talk is over, boys. Get the murderin' bastard you came for!"

"No!" Tom yelled as Jerel took aim. A tongue of flame spat from the gun barrel, and Clay winced and jerked to the right, his fingers inadvertently tightening on the shotgun's trigger. With a roar the weapon discharged low, crippling a couple of men with its load of buckshot. Deadly blossoms of orange fire flowered in the night; the mob opened up with their guns as

Tom dropped beside the wounded lawman. Clay cursed and clawed at the bloodstain spreading across his right sleeve.

"Dammit to hell!" the sheriff groaned. Both men ducked as bullets fanned the air overhead. The jail's defenders replied in kind. Seth levered shot after shot. Abram and Benje, each with a carbine, and Willem, standing in the doorway, joined in the furious exchange that lasted no more than half a minute. Separated by a dirt road, the men fired point-blank at one another; lead slugs flew thick as hail through the soaking rain. And men began to die.

The crack and bellow of gunfire cut with unmistakable authority through the storm. Fathers and husbands paced their rooms, mothers hurried to calm their children. The drenching rain failed to wash the stench of death from the sodden air.

Seated at his desk in the library, Allyn Benedict heard the gunfire drifting through the window he had left open for the purpose of hearing what transpired. Emmiline appeared in the doorway of the study, her features pale. She was dressed in solemn tones of gray and black, her hair pinned high off her neck.

"You should be in bed on a night like this," Allyn said.

"Do you hear?" she asked.

"Yes."

"It is your doing," she said.

"Yes," came his tired reply. He had no patience for a scolding.

"Why? Father . . . why?"

"You wouldn't understand," Allyn said. Suddenly he was standing in the priest's stable with Charlotte White Bear limp in his arms. *What have I done? What have I done?*

The horrid image faded and allowed him to return to the study, book-lined walls shimmering into focus. He saw his daughter staring at him as color slowly crept back into his features.

"Leave me now, there's a good girl." He forced the guilt and the enormity of his crime from his mind. Money would buy him a new conscience. There was no better salve than gold. He eased back in his chair and waited, confident of the outcome of his plans.

*   *   *

Tom rose in front of the wagon as slugs whined past him, thudding into the wagon bed, glancing off the iron-rimmed wheels.

"Stay down!" Seth shouted to his right, blasting away with his rifle.

But the son as deaf to his father now, for an old bloodlust was upon him, the same soul-numbing fury Tom had known once before. If the mob had come for a killer, so be it. Damn them for fools, for *they* had unleashed this dog of war. Now let him slake his thirst. Tom loosed a shrill war cry as the Colt bucked in his hand. A figure on the other side of the rain yelped and sank to his knees. Someone charged him through the storm. Tom fired. Pete Elk Head flew backward, his face a mask of crimson, a hole where once an eye had been. He was dead before he hit the ground. Tom fired again and again. Another man stumbled and sank to his knees in the mud, hands clutching his belly. A blur of motion off to his side, too late to turn. Then Seth's rifle cracked twice, and Curtis Tall Bull screamed his brother's name—"Jerel!"—spun in a slow arc, and emptied his revolver into the muddy furrows until a second blast from Clay's shotgun flung him aside like a discarded rag doll. Tom squeezed off the last two rounds, tucked the pistol into his holster, and drew his second gun from his coat pocket. At close range and blinded by the rain, he methodically fired every time he glimpsed movement. Torches fizzled, landing in the puddles. Rifles and carbines thudded in the dirt.

Willem was busy shoving shells into his carbine when Joanna brushed past him. He tried to catch her but she tore free.

"No," she snapped. "Not again!" She carried her black bag and darted out onto the porch. A bullet smacked the wall a few inches from her head. Abram leaned against the wall, firing his pistol with one hand and trying to stanch the flow of blood from a painful wound in the fleshy part of his thigh. He started to protest, but Joanna told him to shut up and went to work.

Whiskey courage ran shallow that night. The men at the rear of the lunch mob had taken off at the first gunshot. The others in the forefront held long enough to empty their weapons, but as their friends and neighbors began to drop, and Tom Sandcrane, seemingly impervious to harm, advanced through the downpour, his gun blazing, the unruly mob lost its collective stomach for the confrontation. They broke and ran, disappearing into the night as quickly as they had materialized, leaving behind seven of their number either wounded or dead.

Tom pressed on through the rain, his gun centered on a silhouette in the storm. John Iron Hail tossed his rifle aside.

"I never fired a shot. Jerel started it, on Allyn Benedict's orders. Then he took off with the others." John indicated his weapon in the mud. "The chamber's full and the barrel's cold, Tom. You gotta believe me."

"If I didn't, you'd be dead," Tom snarled. "The killing isn't over yet. Make yourself scarce."

John did not need to be told twice.

Tom heard another moan of agony and spied Little Ned Scalp Shirt cradling Luthor White Bear's head in his lap.

"I'm sorry. I'm sorry, so help me I am." The youth looked up at Sandcrane standing over him. "I shot him in the back. It was an accident. Everyone just started blasting away, and I joined in. I couldn't see a damn thing. He must have stepped in front of me. Papa! I never meant to."

Ned Scalp Shirt sat close by, his left knee shot through. He crawled through the mud toward his son, who was unhurt save for his stricken soul. "You young fool, what is this? Oh, no. God, no!"

Tom knelt by Luthor, removed his hat, and shielded the older man's face. Luthor opened his eyes, and a look of recognition lit his pained expression. He motioned for Tom to lean forward, and the younger man complied.

"My fault . . . all mine . . . Charlotte's death . . . this evil . . ." He coughed pink spittle as he struggled to speak. "I sold the Arrows!" The enormity of his guilt tore at his soul. The words struck Tom with the force of a thunderclap.

"I lost all . . . money . . . store . . . and Jerel . . . gave me gold . . . for the Sacred Arrows . . ." Luthor sucked in his breath, made a hideous sound, and coughed blood. "Forgive me." He reached up with a feeble hand and caught the front of Tom's coat. "You . . . you . . . !" And then he was gone—his expression went slack, his body grew limp, and his chin dropped to his chest. Little Ned continued to weep.

Tom stood, somewhat dazed, his heart pounding against his rib cage. It took a few moments for him to realize that his father and Clay Benedict were standing close at hand and with them Joanna and Father Kenneth, who had just staggered into the street. Joanna was already wrapping a crude bandage around the priest's scalp.

As Father Kenneth knelt and began to administer the last rites to his old friend, Joanna stepped to Tom's side and laid a hand on his arm.

"Are you all right?"

"Yes," Tom replied, "but I have to go."

"I know. Just make sure you come back." She reached out and gave his hand a gentle squeeze, then returned her attention to the wounded.

"Did you hear?" Tom asked his father.

Seth nodded. "That explains much. A man makes mistakes. But to sell the Sacred Arrows . . ." He shook his head in disbelief. "I knew he had sunk most of his money on a dry well to the south. But I never thought he'd be so desperate."

"If you're going after Tall Bull, I'll ride with you," said Clay. "Just give me a minute."

"No," Tom said. "This is for me to do."

"Now, see here . . ."

"There is more at stake here than your law," Tom firmly replied.

Clay met the man's dark gaze a moment and acquiesced. "Reckon I have business in town to tend to." One more duty to perform before he could pay a call on a certain schoolmarm and show her he was alive.

Seth fell into step alongside his son. He would walk with Tom to his horse but go no farther. This hour had been a long time coming; it had been whispered in the dreams of both father and son. What had begun long ago at the gathering of the elders would end tonight. The path ahead was for Tom to walk—alone.

CHAPTER FORTY-FOUR

A LOOSE SHUTTER UPSTAIRS SWUNG TO AND FRO IN THE RAIN, slamming against the outer wall, sounding for all the world like some unseen visitor trying to gain entrance. *Should have latched the damn thing,* thought Allyn Benedict, laboring over a reply to a rival oil company whose president had suggested they reach some sort of a mutual agreement on the price of the crude that companies were transporting to eastern refineries. But it was difficult to concentrate on such matters. The former Indian agent's thoughts were all a blur. He felt as if his life were unraveling despite all his efforts to gather the loose threads back into a constructive whole.

The whore, Red Cherries, was a problem. Allyn cursed himself for a fool. Like all the painted harlots at Panther Hall, she had been invisible to him. It had never entered Benedict's mind to exercise discretion around such a woman. The cabin at the roadhouse had seemed the perfect place for a dalliance with Luthor's hot-blooded daughter. Why worry if the whores noticed his coming and going? They were the property of Jerel Tall Bull and knew better than to cause trouble. Unfortunately, Red Cherries was proving the exception to the rule. Damn Tall Bull for not keeping his soiled dove in her coop. Now she'd have to be dealt with, before she blabbed about his indiscretions to the entire town. Red Cherries might have to suffer the same fate as Charlotte White Bear unless she learned to curb her tongue.

The pen snapped in Allyn's grasp, and on reflex he jerked back his hand and inadvertently tipped the inkwell over on its side, ruining the first draft of the letter he had just completed. The former Indian agent struggled to regain his composure and cursed the doubts and misgivings that plagued his resolve.

"Damn!" He slid the chair back and searched the desk for a scrap of cloth to stop the rivulet of ink he had unleashed among his ledgers and books. In an act of desperation he grabbed a silk kerchief from the pocket of his waistcoat and used it to sop up the black ink. He tossed the cloth into the wastepaper basket near the corner of the desk.

A drink was in order to steady his nerves, for the storm had him on edge. It should be finished. Willem had to be swinging from a barn beam or an upturned wagon hitch by now. Charlotte's "killer" had been punished, case closed. Now things could get back to normal. He'd have to patch things up with Margaret; buy Red Cherries' silence, it wouldn't do to have her spreading gossip. Down the road he would sever his alliance with the Tall Bulls in such a way as to keep the depth of his relationship with them a secret. *Well, all good things come to those who wait,* Benedict told himself. And with that he filled a deep crystal glass with a measure of French brandy.

The front door opened and closed with a bang, and voices drifted in from the front entrance. Emmiline must have intercepted their guest, for Consuela had been sent home for the night. Allyn was expecting Jerel Tall Bull to report on all that had transpired at the jail. The last thing he wanted was for this gambler and ne'er-do-well to have anything to do with Emmiline.

"I'll see to it, my dear," Allyn called out, and started across the room, but Emmiline appeared suddenly outside the door. She looked pale, her features betraying her alarm. She entered the room, and another figure loomed behind her in the shadowy hallway.

"Now see here, Jerel, I . . ." Allyn's voice trailed off as he recognized his son. Clay was spattered with mud; a red-stained bandage circled his right arm. His clothes were rain soaked and plastered to his skin, and his coat left a trail of muddy water down the hall and into the study. His features were grimed and powder burned. "What are you doing here, son? You are supposed to be up north, dammit all, that was the plan. Well, never mind now. Is it over? Have you been to the jail? Is it ended?"

"Ended . . . no, sir," Clay said, glancing aside at his sister and then directing himself to the man near the desk. His father. "It has only begun." His left hand held the scattergun he had reloaded along the way. He thumbed both hammers back, an ominous sound in the sudden stillness that filled the room. "You are under arrest for the murder of Charlotte White Bear."

CHAPTER FORTY-FIVE

THE RIDER IN THE RAIN SKIRTED THE BLACKENED FACADE OF Panther Hall; rounded the ominously silent, tomblike structure; passed the fighting pit whose mudslick walls in the flash of stormlight were the color of dried blood; passed the silent, shuttered cabin where Allyn Benedict, corrupted by his lust of wealth and the desires of the flesh, had sown the seeds of his own demise; passed the barn and the clearing where the ashes of a dead whore's makeshift pyre leached into the soil, leaving a blackened skull to watch with sightless eyes.

"This way," moaned the wind through the bones of the rain. "He passed this way. The Mahuts await."

The horse shied and fought its rider. Tom tightened his grip on the reins as the animal reared and pawed the air. And there in the graveyard glare he saw the warrior who had haunted him down the labyrinth of his days. The specter lowered his spear, indicating a dimly visible path through the woods. Then, shrouded by the rain, it vanished. Or had it ever been? Tom understood and slid from horseback. He tethered the gelding to a nearby oak, checked the loads in his Colt, and started down the path. The rain began to lessen in intensity, and though the branches of the white oaks and cedars overhead afforded some protection, the knotted trunks and the weedy overgrowth had a disturbing way of closing round him like the jaws of a trap.

The flames of the fire leaped upward toward the roof of the arbor overhead. Twisted limbs and dried thatch would ignite if Jerel Tall Bull wasn't careful. The man kneeling in the lurid light paid no attention to the danger at hand. He added another couple of logs to the fire, then sat back on his haunches and passed his hands over the Sacred Arrows. The obsidian points gleamed black in the firelight. The long shafts, banded with white, red, black, and yellow paint, seemed to glow with a life of their own, as if drawing on the flames. The wind tugged at the gray and white eagle feathers adorning the Mahuts. Jerel closed the deerskin and mallard-skin folds of the pouch, secured it, then held the bundle before him, his voice rising and falling with the familiar tones of the cadence. He no longer thought of the debacle at the jail; the death of his brother left him unmoved. These things paled to insignificance when compared with what was at hand. It had been revealed to Jerel in a dream that he would never be the Keeper, never know or possess all the power of the Mahuts while Tom Sandcrane lived.

Let him come now and be destroyed by the very relics he sought to recapture. Jerel Tall Bull held the bundle over his head, then lowered it to the blanket. With one hand on the pouch he raised the other and pointed at the trail.

> "The power is with me. I am the Keeper,
> the blood of the Hawk is in me. Who can
> stand before me? No one. I am not seen.
> I cannot die. My enemies tremble and
> fall upon their knives."

Tom Sandcrane stumbled and dropped to his knees, a searing pain in his chest. He dug his hands into the mud and gasped. He rolled over onto his side as a winged shape dislodged from the branches and plunged toward him. It was a hawk, old and powerful, with cruel talons like curved sword blades. Tom held up his hand to ward off the attack—he screamed and flailed at the predator, but to no avail. The hawk raked his forearm until the flesh hung in tatters.

No. You are not real. The one who sent you walks in my soul. But this I will not allow. Return to him. Be gone!

Tom's vision cleared. Raindrops splashed off his cheeks and eyelids. His right arm was unmarked. He crawled to his knees and came face-to-face with Captain Diego Zuloaga, arrogant, handsome, absently tugging at his goatee. The man pulled a revolver from his belt and fired it point-blank at Tom, who instinctively ducked. He drew his Colt and squeezed off a shot, but Zuloaga was gone and the bullet thudded into the trunk of a nearby oak.

Stop this. Get out of my head. Get out of my mind! Tom holstered the gun and closed his eyes, rubbing them with his knuckles, doubled over. When he looked again, he was kneeling in blood, in a rain of crimson, and there were his dead comrades, Philo and Tully, bloated and dead, their flesh wasted away, food for the worms, and they were waving him onward, inviting Tom to join them in the arms of death. And behind them the shadows lengthened, the blackness swept toward him, spreading its wings. . . .

Jerel Tall Bull lost all grasp of time. Minutes were as indistinguishable as hours. He only knew his song had outlasted the rain. The fire had outlasted the storm. There was a feeling of exultation in his heart. His very being soared. He felt stronger than ever before, and his eyes blazed with triumph as he lifted the bundle in his hands and stood. Behind him the flood-swollen waters of Little Sister Creek raged with a fury all their own. Winds gusted around him, wrapping him with the tendrils of the ceremonial fire. Flood and flame were a part of him now, as were all the savage elements of creation.

"The storms shall do my bidding.
I will walk unseen among my enemies,
I am the healer and the destroyer.
The power of the Ones Who Have

Gone Before is mine. They call
me by name. I am the Keeper!"

And a voice answered, a quiet voice, weary, but from one
unbroken. "Not tonight, Jerel Tall Bull. Not ever."

The world came crashing in on the man by the fire. One
second he felt airborne, the next anchored fast to the mud
and the clay and the wreckage of his dreams and ambitions.
Jerel's jaw dropped as Tom Sandcrane emerged from the
woods and walked toward him, his gun drawn and aimed at
Jerel's heart.

"No," said Jerel.

Tom entered the clearing and circled the fire. "Put the Arrows down."

"No!" Jerel snicked, and, whirling on his heels, threw the
bundle over the edge of the creekbank. The Sacred Arrows
hung poised in the air for a fraction of a second, then
dropped toward the savagely racing waters below.

"Savaa!" Tom shouted, and brushed Jerel aside as he dived
in vain for the bundle. He lost his footing and plummeted toward the floodwaters, slipping and sliding, rolling down the
embankment toward the raging torrent. Tom managed to
twist and dig to gain footing, stopping himself just at the water's edge. Something loomed out of the dark. The shattered
remains of a tree trunk careened past, bristling with roots like
spears that missed him by inches. He flattened against the riverbank. Something white-hot grazed his cheek, clipping the
flesh away and leaving a streak of blood. Where was the bundle? It was too dark and he was blinded by the mud. Had it
been carried off by the flood? Destroyed when he was so
close?

Jerel prowled the top of the riverbank, a carbine in hand,
determined that a bullet should succeed where his magic had
failed. He cursed and called Tom by name and fired again. A
geyser of mud erupted inches from Tom's leg, but the human
target did not react.

Rushing water, mud and fear and pain, all memories rushing back. His fevered dreams, the wraith-hawk—yes, he remembered. Only Jerel was the hawk now, and yet as the

dreams foretold, everything else was the same. Then, as he
had in the dream, Tom reached out, stretching, slipped and
caught himself as the floodwaters lapped at his boot heels,
reaching, clawing in the mud, inching along. His muscles
protested. He jammed his left arm into the bank, propping
himself as best he could with the near-useless limb. Reach out
. . . nothing . . . nothing . . . and then his fingers closed round
a leather string and then another. His heart soared and he
drew the bundle to his breast.

But the next flash of lightning would make him an easy target for Jerel's carbine. There were stories of the Sacred Arrows, how the tribe had been protected from pursuing
enemies through the power of the Mahuts. Clutching the
bundle to his chest, Tom began to chant; though the deafen-
ing roar of the rain-swollen creek obscured his voice, he
mouthed the words all the same, hearing them in his mind:

> "Power is in me, birth and death,
> Sacred is the way of my truth.
> Swift as the eagle, strong as the eagle,
> from the four skies I am coming.
> I will shelter my people."

At that moment shimmering fire lit the sky, bathing the
creek in its lurid glow. Not twenty feet away Jerel Tall Bull
stood on the edge of the riverbank, staring right at Tom, who
tensed, bracing himself for the bullet, and continued his
chant. Jerel held his fire and then, apparently confused, began
searching the bank a few yards upstream.

Tom dug in his heels and started to crawl, working his way
up the bank. He held the bundle with his teeth to free his
right arm, and the going became easier. Slowly, taking his
time, he worked his way up the treacherous wall of clay and
mudslick stones, distancing himself from the deadly torrent.
Near the top of the bank he checked his holster. The long-
barreled Colt was gone. But his sore ribs reminded Tom of
the second revolver he had tucked away in his coat pocket.
Unfortunately, he could not remember reloading the weapon
after the fight at the jail. He glanced in Jerel's direction. The

man was several yards away but walking toward him, carbine held waist-high.

Tom dragged out the Colt thirty-eight, for a heart-stopping moment nearly lost it in his muddy grip, flipped open the cylinder, emptied the shells, and began pulling cartridges from his belt loops and sliding them into the cylinder. One-two-three.

"You!" Jerel shouted. The carbine cracked, a bullet whined overhead.

Tom swung the cylinder shut and climbed onto solid ground, rising to one knee, the Sacred Bundle on the ground before him. It was stained with mud and water and blood. Jerel was firing, he could see the muzzle flash, but all Tom heard were the voices of warriors surrounding him, voices chanting, crying down the corridors of time and calling him by name.

Years later, as an old man, revered by his people and surrounded by his friends and the children of his friends, Tom Sandcrane would tell the story of the way it was that night, kneeling in the mud, his gun firing though he had not consciously squeezed the trigger, the Colt thirty-eight recoiling in his grasp. His arm was not his own, his hand belonged to the "others," they centered him, held him up, and aimed the weapon.

The story might grow, but the kernel of truth would remain the same. Tom would recount how Jerel had stopped in his tracks before the first bullet ever struck him, how Jerel Tall Bull, in those final few seconds of his life, must have been given the Vision, the Truth. Still as a statue, a look of awe and terror on his face, the man at last beheld the heart of the mystery he had struggled to command and that, in the end, had destroyed him. Jerel was dead long before the bullets struck him—one-two-three—in the chest, pushed him over the creekbank, and flung his lifeless body into the flash flood's crushing embrace.

EPILOGUE

CHAPTER FORTY-SIX

IN THE MORNING THE PEOPLE OF CROSS TIMERS AND THE SOUTHern Cheyenne on both sides of Council Hill woke to the sign of prayer smoke drifting above the treetops, a lazy spiral against a limitless expanse of azure sky. The storms had played themselves out, in their wake the clear, cool air carried the scent of an early spring, a rebirth for the land and for the People who dwelled upon the land. A voice rode the trail of prayer smoke, weaving a song that echoed over the lonely land and stirred the hearts of a people asleep. Men turned their eyes to the hillside, to the Council House at the summit; women and children alike were caught up in the spell and listened in respectful silence. Elders stumbled forward, drawn by the magic in the voice.

Joanna heard and, standing in her backyard, saw Seth, his eyes pouchy from lack of sleep, stumble from the barn where he had been tending the horses. An expression of such peace washed over his features that Joanna nearly wept at the sight of it. Tom was alive and whole again. And Red Cherries, she who was lost, appeared at the back door of the infirmary and, looking out upon the sunrise of her own new life, began to laugh, a girlish laugh, almost innocent. Seth glanced at Joanna, who smiled with understanding and watched him leave the yard as he began walking toward the hillside. Joanna listened. A familiar sound caught her attention, faint on the breeze, the tap-tap-tapping of a distant drum, recalling the vision that had brought her home to the wilds of an untamed land.

The voice called out and sang so that the world would not end and so that the Southern Cheyenne would never die, but live the old ways and the new, setting their feet upon the white road and the red.

The hand of Maheo, the All Father, appeared in the center of the Sacred Fire; Tom Sandcrane's features were etched in stark relief by the brightness of the apparition. The heartbeat of Maheo filled the air and caused the earth to tremble. The Maiyun, Those Who Have Gone Before, leaped soundlessly one moment, gyrated madly the next, as if to distract the singer from his ritual.

Once Tom might have seen merely flames and shadows cast by sunlight, or heard no more than the tapping drum he held. But no longer. He had walked the Great Circle and learned to see what lies beyond sight. He was alone now, but he knew in his heart it would not be so for long. Setting the drum aside, he gathered the Sacred Arrows in his hand and sang:

> "Maheo. All-Father.
> To the four winds I cast my
> prayers. Upon the four winds
> my voice drifts like smoke.
> I hold my People as I hold the Arrows in my
>   hand.
> What am I? What am I?
> Fire in the blood of *nako-he*, the Bear;
> The crack of ice on frozen rivers,
> The call of the wild geese.
> I ride upon *hotama haa-ese*, the North wind.
> Call me Spirit Catcher, Sweet Medicine,
> By many names men have called me.
> I am the Arrow Keeper's song.
> I walk here."

ABOUT THE AUTHOR

If you loved Kerry Newcomb's
THE ARROW-KEEPER'S SONG

you'll love # SCORPION

Now on sale

*Across a land ablaze with war, a man
with no name embarks on a perilous quest
for survival—and honor.*

South of the border, U.S. and Mexican forces prepare
for a showdown. Joined by a defiant ex-slave, Ben
McQueen will confront an army of brutal killers—
only to come face to face with his own bitter past . . .
of cowardice, betrayal, and savage death.

___29447-4 $4.99/$5.99 in Canada